continued . . .

"Griffin's lyrical and moving debut marks her as a most talented newcomer to the romance genre."

"Another appealing romance full of gentle humor, small-town charm, and enormous heart."

Also by Patience Griffin

The Accidental Scot
Some Like It Scottish
Meet Me in Scotland
To Scotland with Love
The Trouble with Scotland

It Happened in Scotland

A Kilts and Quilts Novel

Patience Griffin

BERKLEY SENSATION
New York

BERKLEY SENSATION
Published by Berkley
An imprint of Penguin Random House LLC
375 Hudson Street, New York, New York 10014

Copyright © 2017 by Patience Jackson

Excerpt from *The Trouble with Scotland* copyright © 2017 by Patience Jackson
Penguin Random House supports copyright. Copyright fuels creativity, encourages diverse
voices, promotes free speech, and creates a vibrant culture. Thank you for buying an
authorized edition of this book and for complying with copyright laws by not
reproducing, scanning, or distributing any part of it in any form without permission.
You are supporting writers and allowing Penguin Random House to continue to
publish books for every reader.

BERKLEY and BERKLEY SENSATION are registered trademarks and the B colophon
is a trademark of Penguin Random House LLC.

ISBN: 9780451476401

First Edition: January 2017

Printed in the United States of America
1 3 5 7 9 10 8 6 4 2

Cover art by Deborah Chabrian
Cover design by Steve Meditz

*For my daughter, Cagney,
who changed everything.*

Acknowledgments

Thank you, Tracy Bernstein. I couldn't have asked for a better editor to guide me through the beginning of my career. There are days where I'm sure it's you, my friend, who is whispering edits as I put words on the page. I'm beyond grateful for all you have done.

Here's a big shout-out to the whole team at Berkley. It's so amazing to hand over a story, and like magic, my novels show up in bookstores! I appreciate everyone's hard work. You've helped to make this writer's dream come true. Thank you!

PRONUNCIATION GUIDE

Aileen (AY-leen)
Ailsa (AIL-sa)
Bethia (BEE-thee-a)
Buchanan (byoo-KAN-uhn)
Cait (KATE)
céilidh (KAY-lee)—a party/dance
Deydie (DI-dee)
Lochie (LAW kee)
mo ghràidh (mo GRAAG)—my dear
Moira (MOY-ra)
shite (shite)—expletive

DEFINITIONS

braw—fine, grand
Drambuie (dram'booē)—a sweet Scotch whisky liqueur
Gandiegow—squall
Hogmanay—the Scottish celebration of the New Year
Irn Bru—Scotland's most popular soft drink
ken—understanding
Royal Edinburgh Military Tattoo—musical performance at Edinburgh Castle of military teams, consisting of bagpipes and drums
postie—postman
reiving—stealing (something)
trainers—sneakers, tennis shoes
wynd (wīnd)—a very narrow street

Quilters of Gandiegow

Rule #5
Quilting is about second chances . . .
for the fabric and the quilter.

Chapter One

Holding her daughter's hand, Rachel Granger stood at the baggage claim alongside the woman with whom they'd sat on the flight from Chicago to Glasgow. Rachel's new friend, Cait Buchanan, was flying home, whereas Rachel was bringing her daughter to Scotland for the first time.

Rachel had been to Gandiegow, the small town on the northeast coast of Scotland, twice before. Once to marry her husband. And again to bury him. She glanced down at five-year-old Hannah, who looked so much like her father, Joe. Rachel had been avoiding this trip for the past three years, but it was time for Hannah to meet her great-grandfather whether the village of Gandiegow despised Rachel or not. Her spunky daughter was growing and changing so quickly that Rachel knew this year she had to pull herself together for Hannah's sake. No more using work as her scapegoat to get out of going to Scotland, especially during the holidays. This year Rachel was going to give her daughter a Christmas. A Christmas with a real tree, gingerbread cookies, and a family gathering.

Cait stepped up to the luggage carousel. "There's mine."

"It's huge. Let me help." Rachel turned to her daughter. "Can you stay here and watch my things?"

"Sure, Mommy."

She didn't have to worry; Hannah would guard Rachel's tote along with her own *Frozen* backpack like a loyal and headstrong soldier if anyone got near.

As the large suitcase approached, Cait laughed. "I always pack too much. I was only gone a week, but I brought three times what I needed." She reached for the handle, Rachel for the wheels. Together they tugged it to the floor with a *whoompf.*

"I'm glad ye're taking me up on my offer," Cait said. "Especially since I'm heading to Gandiegow, too. What are the odds?" A green tinge came over her face and she grimaced. "Do you mind, um, watching . . ."

"Go," Rachel urged. "We've got your luggage."

Cait raced for the toilet sign while Rachel rolled the humongous bag over to Hannah. The few steps provided just enough time and space for apprehension to once again seep into Rachel. She wasn't looking forward to staying in Gandiegow, but she'd come a long way from the twenty-four-year-old bride who'd walked down the aisle in the village's church and then the young widow who'd laid a rose on her husband's grave. The village hadn't known when she'd been back for the funeral that she and Joe had separated and were heading for a divorce, but they'd spurned her just the same for bringing one of their own home in an urn.

Rachel rested Cait's bag beside Hannah and sighed heavily, feeling much older than thirty. Death, responsibility, and parenthood could do that to a person.

"Mommy?" Hannah said. "Is Cait going to be okay?"

Rachel wrapped her arm around her daughter's shoulders. "Yes. Cait will be fine." Nothing seven or so months wouldn't cure.

The way Cait had been downing saltines all through the flight, especially during the turbulence, made her pregnancy obvious. Rachel had experienced the same joy and anxiousness which showed on her new friend's face.

Right when Rachel was beginning to worry, Cait reappeared—white, wrung-out, but with a small smile on her face.

"Sorry about that," she said when she'd rejoined them. She studied Rachel. "So ye've guessed."

"That depends on whether you want anyone to know or not."

"The morning sickness is much worse this time. The doctor says it's a good thing. But I haven't told anyone. Not even my husband."

Automatically, Rachel's eyebrows shot up, but she got her reaction under control quickly. She wouldn't judge. Cait's relationship with her husband was her own business.

Her new friend bit her lip. "I don't want to get his hopes up. I've miscarried twice before. It's been hard on him because he travels a lot and he worries about me so." She glanced at Rachel, hopeful. "So ye'll keep my secret?"

"Mum's the word." She gave her a reassuring smile. Rachel knew a lot about secrets and keeping them hidden. She looked over at her daughter, who was singing the song "Let It Go" quietly to her doll.

Rachel shivered as the words of the chorus rang out, "*The cold never bothered me anyway.*" Yes, it was winter in Scotland, but it wasn't the cold which *bothered* Rachel. It was what lay ahead in Gandiegow which haunted her.

Her luggage came around the conveyor, much smaller than Cait's as they were only going to be in Scotland for a short while. Just long enough for Hannah to spend some time with her grandfather, Abraham Clacher, sing a few Christmas carols, and go back to the States at the beginning of the New Year. In and out without a worry or a fuss.

Rachel pulled their bags off the carousel as Cait's cell phone chimed.

"Our ride is here," she said. "I'll wait for you on the other side of customs."

The line for them was surprisingly fast and it didn't take long to meet back up with her. As the little group wheeled their things through the doors, three people rushed toward Cait, and she tugged Rachel over to meet her friends.

"This is Ross Armstrong. His wife, Sadie. And Ross's mother, Grace." Cait smiled at them fondly.

Rachel remembered Ross and his mother—when she'd been to Gandiegow before—but had had little interaction with them. At least this visit was under better circumstances. Sadie, a brown-haired pixie from the United States, was a new addition and welcomed her warmly.

"Thank you for letting us hitch a ride." Rachel had canceled her rental car when the plane landed. She only needed transportation to and from the small coastal town, as it was a closed community—no cars, no roads, only walking paths along the ocean and between the buildings.

"I'm glad it worked out," Ross said. "We got a break in the weather. But a winter storm is coming in later tonight."

"We were closing down the house here in Glasgow," Grace explained. "My sister passed last month and I'm moving back to Gandiegow."

Rachel already knew the particulars through Cait. Grace's sister had died from complications of pneumonia, though she'd been dealing with MS for years. "I'm so sorry for your loss," Rachel said, but cringed inwardly as the words came out. She'd been the recipient of that phrase too often.

Grace smiled at her kindly as one who accepted things easily. "Thank you. Glynnis is in a better place."

Sadie took Grace's arm lovingly, giving her a sad, understanding smile. They seemed closer than most mothers and daughters-in-law.

"Let's get on the road. I'm anxious to get home," Ross said.

As they drove to Gandiegow, Ross and Sadie filled Cait in on the gossip from the last two weeks.

When there was a break in the conversation, Rachel inquired after Abraham. "How is he doing?" She knew of his illness, only because when she'd called, he had a coughing fit while they were on the phone. She had no idea how long he'd been sick and how bad it was.

Ross glanced at her in the rearview mirror. "He's the same ole Abraham. But if ye're speaking of his health, he's not well. He quit fishing about six months ago, which told the rest of us how serious it really is."

"Oh." More guilt. Rachel should've brought her daughter sooner to get to know the only grandfather she had.

An awkward silence came over the van for a few moments, but then Ross jumped in and filled it. "Mum, are ye going to be okay staying at the family cottage?"

Grace turned to Rachel, explaining. "I moved to Glasgow to help my sister a few years ago, leaving my lads to care for the cottage in Gandiegow. My eldest son, John, and his family live there now, and it's time for me to come home." She patted Ross on the shoulder as if to assure him. "I'll be fine. So, Rachel, where will ye and Hannah be staying this time? Thistle Glen Lodge?"

"The quilting dorm," Cait clarified to Rachel.

Cait had explained all about her venture, the Kilts and Quilts retreat, which had turned the sleepy fishing village of Gandiegow into a go-to quilting destination.

"I'm not sure," Rachel answered sheepishly. Though she'd talked to Abraham two weeks ago, and he'd asked her to come and bring Hannah, she'd made no promises. She'd booked the flight and a hotel room in Glasgow to get her bearings. Yes, she wanted a family Christmas for her daughter, but had given herself an out. If she had second thoughts about going to Gandiegow, she and Hannah would have had their own special Christmas vacation at the Jury's Inn in the big city.

But Providence had stepped in when Rachel had taken her seat next to Cait. Rachel had innocently told her of Gandiegow, having no idea Cait hailed from the village of only sixty-three houses.

"You can stay with me and my son, Mattie, in the big house," Cait offered.

"That's so kind." But Rachel wouldn't impose. "I think Hannah and I would like to stay at Thistle Glen Lodge. The way you described it, it sounds perfect." She kissed her daughter's head. "That is, if it's okay. Do you have a quilt retreat going on right now?"

"One's starting tomorrow, which is why I couldn't stay longer in the US. But there's plenty of room. Deydie, my gran, said we had to keep the retreat small as we're so close to Christmas."

"Sounds fantastic."

"When will Graham be done shooting?" Ross asked.

"Graham?" Rachel said, more in disbelief than a question.

Suddenly, all the pieces clicked together. From the first moment, Cait had looked familiar. *That's where I've seen her.* On the cover of *People* magazine, along with her famous movie star husband.

Rachel remembered bits and pieces of the article, the headlines announcing that the most eligible bachelor on the planet was no longer available—that he, in his mid-forties and sexy as ever, had married the thirtysome-thing Cait. Hearts had been broken everywhere. But that wasn't the biggest shock. Graham had a grown son who had recently passed away, and he and Cait were raising his grandson.

How could Rachel have missed it . . . to have read the article and for it to have *not* registered that Graham was from Gandiegow? Her only excuse was that she'd just been trying to make it through day by day back then. "So Graham still lives in the village?"

Cait gave her an impish shrug. "When he's not work-ing on a movie."

Rachel understood why her seatmate hadn't shared about who her husband was. It must be hard being in her shoes. From the day Graham Buchanan's biography was released, Cait's life must've been turned upside down with the paparazzi, and the knowledge that women ev-erywhere lusted after her husband. Rachel suspected it had been nice for Cait to have made a friend who didn't know her husband was a BBC star.

"*Yeah. Graham*," Sadie said, kind of dreamily. "My reaction exactly."

"Hey, now, lass," Ross said with mock hurt. "Yere husband's in the vehicle with ye."

Sadie patted him. "You've nothing to worry about. Graham only has eyes for Cait."

Cait reached over and laid a hand on Rachel's arm. "Sorry I didn't say anything sooner."

"I completely understand."

Cait nodded and spoke to Ross. "Graham'll be home Christmas Eve. He has a break between movies, though. It'll be great for Mattie and me to have him back."

Rachel wondered if Cait would tell him then about the pregnancy. Surely she wouldn't keep it hidden from him for too long.

The conversation switched to Christmas, and Rachel turned inward, thinking more on her own turmoil than the joyous occasion they were describing. Hannah leaned against her and fell asleep. Rachel dozed, too.

She came awake as the van pulled down the hill toward the parking lot. Ross was talking on the phone.

"Good. We could use your help getting my mum's stuff to the cottage." He hung up.

Rachel gently woke Hannah. "We're here, sweetie." She glanced around at the familiar site of the bluffs looming out of the earth at the back of the village, and how the small houses sat precariously at the edge of the ocean—a quaint row of dwellings daring the sea to engulf them.

Ross parked the van and jumped out to help his mother.

Rachel felt stiff from the flight and then the long drive to Gandiegow. She slowly climbed out and then helped Hannah.

As she reached in to grab her tote, something on the walkway caught her eye.

No. *Someone* caught her eye. *It can't be!* Strolling toward the parking lot, he looked so much like Joe. Tall, broad, with dark hair. But where Joe's hair had been kept short, the better to peddle pharmaceuticals, his cousin's long hair blew in the wind off the ocean. Six years had changed him. His features were chiseled, and where an easy smile for her had once existed, a stony frown had taken its place.

But he was as beautiful as ever and Rachel stopped breathing. Maybe he was a manifestation. But he kept walking toward them, while the voice in her head shouted loud and clear, *What is he doing here?*

"Mommy, are you all right?"

For the life of her, Rachel couldn't stop staring at the man she never thought she'd see again. They all turned to look at her.

When he got close enough, he nodded in her direction. "Ye're back."

How could he have no emotion on his face? She was dying here.

"Hey, Brodie," Ross said. "Grab a bag from the boot."

What in the blazes is she doing here? Brodie Wallace couldn't believe his eyes. It felt as if Ross had sucker punched him in the stomach because he'd said nothing when they'd spoken on the phone. Yet here Rachel Granger was standing in Gandiegow's parking lot. The woman who had ripped his heart out. The only woman he'd ever allowed himself to love.

He reached into the back of the van and pulled out a suitcase.

Six years ago, when she'd arrived in Gandiegow, he wasn't the only one toppled by the instant attraction between them. He knew she had felt it, too.

He grabbed another bag.

His cousin Joe had brought her home to Gandiegow two weeks before their scheduled wedding. Brodie was taken with Rachel from the start, which was no surprise. He and Joe had always gone for the same type of lass. Funny, smart. Even as lads, they'd competed, and Joe had always won. Whenever Brodie found a girl, Joe would swoop in and steal her away. Brodie understood. Joe was a charmer with the gift of gab, and women couldn't help falling under his spell.

Day in and out, Brodie tried to keep his distance from Joe's future bride, but they had been constantly thrown together at Abraham's house. In spite of this, they successfully danced around and avoided their feelings. But on the day of the wedding, he'd climbed up the bluff to hide out in the ruins of Monadail Castle while he cleared his head. When he arrived, though, Rachel was there, as if it was meant to be. She turned at his approach but didn't budge from the stone ledge under the archway. He noted her tearstained cheeks and knew she'd been crying.

Cautiously, he'd gone to her and carefully lifted her chin so she would look at him. "What's wrong?" But the question would prove fatal.

"Why didn't I meet you first?" she cried, and threw herself into his arms, kissing him, and knocking him from his moorings. A tidal wave picked up his heart and slammed it against the rocks, changing his life forever.

That kiss and the way she'd looked at him had meant everything! For an hour they held on to each other, Brodie confessing to her that he'd never felt that way before. He knew it was love, but couldn't voice it aloud until she called off the wedding. Which he was certain she would do. More certain of it than the snow on the ground, the tide in the ocean, and the blood in his veins. Rachel loved him as he loved her. But an hour later, she walked down the aisle, repeated her vows, and effectively tossed Brodie away as if he were nothing more than spoiled bait.

Grandda's incessant warning coursed through Brodie again—*Women can't be trusted.* Every man in their family had firsthand knowledge of the unfaithfulness of women—whether she was a wife, a mother, or a grandmother. Their male lineage could lay testament to the coldhearted dealings of the opposite sex.

Ross nudged him, pulling him back to reality.

"What?" Brodie's voice sounded harsh to his own

ears. He stared down at the luggage dangling from his arms.

Cait eyed him curiously as if he'd cast his line into a crosswind. "You and Rachel know each other?"

"Aye." Brodie's eyes fell on the little girl holding Rachel's hand. The child gaped up at him. *God, the girl has Joe's eyes. Brown. Rich as the soil on Here Again Farm.* It was the place Brodie had run off to when Rachel had betrayed him so he could suffer alone. He snapped his gaze away from hers.

"Brodie was best man," Rachel said quietly, her voice cracking, "at my wedding." She paused for a second, then added, "To Joe." As if she was clarifying which wedding.

Had she married again? Brodie's gaze dropped to her hand, and he hated himself for looking, because he sure as hell didn't care. He didn't care if she was married. He didn't care if she was in town. He didn't care if she disappeared altogether.

But there was no ring, and idiotic relief spread through his chest. He shouldn't give a shit if she was taken or not.

When he glanced back at her face, her frown was matching his.

Good. Let her frown. He didn't give a damn. She was nothing to him. *Nothing.* Just another heartless female.

He stalked away with the bags, not certain where he was supposed to drop them off.

As if Ross had read his mind, he hollered after him, "The quilting dorm. Thistle Glen Lodge."

Thoughts pummeled Brodie like someone's fists.

Aye. A heads-up would've been helpful. Why hadn't Abraham, his own grandda, told him she was coming? Brodie didn't need this monumental headache right now. He had his hands full with taking over Abraham's fishing business, plus trying to nurse the old man back to good health.

Brodie wondered if he dropped the bags in the sea whether Rachel would leave. *And take the kid with her.* Maybe he should call Ewan and hightail it back to Here Again Farm. Or maybe Ewan's cousin Hugh could use help at the wool factory in Whussendale. Anything to get out of town and away from *her.*

He took the bags to the quilting dorm, dropped them in the entryway, and didn't return to the vehicle for a second load. Instead he headed home to have it out with Grandda.

As he opened the door to the cottage, he heard Abraham coughing, and Brodie's fury disintegrated. He couldn't roar at the old man. He owed his grandfather nothing but gratitude for first taking him and his mother in when Da died, and then for letting Brodie stay on when his mother remarried shortly afterward.

He found his grandfather nearly hacking up a lung in the kitchen while trying to pull down a mug.

"Here," Brodie said. "Let me get the tea. You sit."

Abraham nodded and coughed some more.

Brodie retrieved two cups, laid them on the counter, and stared out the kitchen window. Having Rachel in town was ripping open all his closed wounds—losing Rachel, Joe dying, and the guilt he tried to keep buried. Grandda never questioned Brodie as to why he hadn't come back for Joe's funeral. But just having Rachel over at Thistle Glen Lodge made Brodie want to give his grandfather that explanation now: *I wanted to pay my respects to Joe, but I couldn't bear to see Rachel again.*

The kettle whistled, stopping the painful train of thought. Brodie poured water into the teapot and put the lid on.

He turned to Abraham. "She's here."

His grandfather spun around, searching the kitchen with rheumy eyes. "Who's here? Deydie?"

Brodie looked around, too, in case the old head quilter had miraculously appeared. But it was just the two of them. He settled in next to Abraham. "Joe's widow has arrived."

"What?" His grandfather looked truly confused. Then a smile stretched across his face, one Brodie hadn't seen in quite a while. "So she came. Did she bring the babe?"

The girl was hardly a baby. "Aye." Brodie stared hard at his grandda. "So ye really didn't know she was coming?"

The old man rose, ignoring him. "If Rachel's in the village, why isn't she here right now?"

"She's settling into Thistle Glen Lodge."

Abraham's eyebrows pulled together. "Nay. Ye know she has to stay here."

"She wants to stay at the quilting dorm." *And I can't have her here.*

"Git over there now and tell her she's staying with us." Abraham might be a sick old codger, but when he wasn't coughing, he could bark out a command as if he were the admiral of the fleet.

Brodie stared back at him for a long moment, but finally caved. If his grandfather hadn't done so much for him his whole life, he would've argued.

"Fine. I'll fetch them after you have yere tea." Brodie poured the steaming liquid into their cups.

"Go now. I want to see the lassie." Abraham started coughing, and for a moment, Brodie wondered if he did it to get his own way.

To stall, Brodie pulled out the to-go mug he took with him on the boat and filled it for himself. "I'll bring her back," Brodie said out of duty. Aye, that's all it was . . . duty.

Once outside, he sipped his tea while making his way to the back of the bluffs where the quilt dorms sat— Thistle Glen Lodge and Duncan's Den. Often the dorms were used as a place for visitors to stay, but sometimes it was full to capacity when a quilt retreat was going on. In those cases, a visitor was forced to stay in the room over the pub or with one of the villagers.

Brodie paused at the doorway of the dorm, steeling himself against seeing Rachel. There would be no repeat of the crazy attraction he'd felt before. He was over her. *Completely.* He had to be.

Automatically, Brodie's hand covered his heart, the place where the tattoo artist had inked the blasted partridge into his chest the night after Joe had married Rachel. As the tattoo artist worked on him, Brodie had basked in his pain, remembering every detail of Rachel's deceit, lest he ever forget how the American lass had broken his heart. While the needle dug into his skin, he tortured himself with how they'd kissed. How they'd clung to each other. How time had stood still, while a partridge had lingered nearby in the snow at the ruins of Monadail Castle. This was the reason he'd permanently marked himself. To remember the lesson he'd learned. One minute the partridge was there, and in the next it had flown away. *Like Rachel.* The problem with the *bluidy* tattoo, though, was every time he looked in the mirror, instead of remembering the lesson . . . he remembered the woman. The symbol of Rachel was embedded on his chest forever—a rash decision he wished he could take back—but even worse was that she was ever present in his thoughts and weighed heavy on his wary heart. As if it were yesterday and not six years ago.

He dropped his hand and knocked on the door to Thistle Glen Lodge. Running could be heard on the other side. The door flew open and the little girl stood there.

She cranked her head around toward the hallway. "Mommy, the man that looks like Daddy is at the door."

Brodie nearly dropped his cup. He stabilized his hand, then shoved his free one in his pocket.

She gazed up at him, studying every inch of his face. "I have a picture of my daddy. Do you want to see?"

He didn't get to answer. She grabbed his hand and tugged. He was too surprised to stop her from pulling him over the threshold. She towed him down the hallway to the living room. When Rachel saw him, she looked stunned, as if the little girl had dragged in a ghost.

"He wants to see Daddy's picture," the girl said.

"I never said—" Brodie started.

"Don't worry about it." Rachel gazed down at her daughter with a mixture of exasperation and love. "I never know what she's going to do or say next."

"What's her name?" Brodie asked, for lack of anything else to say.

"Hannah," the two females said together.

Hannah dropped his hand and leaned over her roller bag, unzipping it. "I wrapped my guzzy around Daddy's picture."

"Guzzy?" he said.

"The quilt I made for her," Rachel answered.

"She made it from Daddy's soft shirts." The kid pulled out the *guzzy*, which was a patchwork quilt of different plaid flannels. She unwrapped the small frame and held it up to Brodie. "See."

It was Joe. Not in jeans and a T-shirt as he had worn here in Gandiegow as a lad, but in a suit, standing next to a Volvo.

"Mommy says Daddy was handsome."

The cold finger of betrayal pierced the tattoo on Brodie's chest.

Hannah turned to Rachel, but thrust a thumb at him. "That makes him handsome, too. Right, Mommy?"

Rachel's mouth dropped open as her cheeks tinged to a bright shade of red.

"Abraham wants you over at the house," Brodie said abruptly.

At another time and in another place, he might've found the kid cute or funny. But she was Rachel and Joe's kid, and there was nothing cute or funny about what was going on here. He was holding the picture of his dead cousin, and he was standing in the same room with the woman who had ruined him for all others. From the first moment of meeting Rachel, he'd known she was his soul mate. Aye . . . loving her as he had, and continuing to feel the effects of that love after so many years, was foolish. And inconceivable. How could a reasonable man such as himself be taken in so completely? But he had been . . . hook, line, and sinker. None of the lasses he'd dated before her or the few he'd forced himself to date afterward had ever captivated his heart like she had. Even seeing her now made him feel as if a winch strap had been tightened around his chest.

If Brodie had never met Rachel, he might be happily settled in this village. Gandiegow was filled with dozens of contented families; the village seemed to sprout them as easily as the summer vegetables in Deydie's kitchen garden. But the second Joe married Rachel, Brodie could never see himself settling down and having a family of his own.

"About Abraham . . ." Rachel took the picture from Brodie and held it at her side, not looking at it. "I want to see your grandfather. Hannah does, too. We're just going to settle in first. Maybe take a nap. It was a long flight."

"Nay." God, he didn't want to do this. "Ye've got it all wrong. My grandfather wants ye to stay at the cottage. With him."

Not me. Brodie needed to make that perfectly clear. He wanted her and her kid to return to Glasgow, Chicago, or Timbuktu. It didn't matter. Everything about her made his blood pump faster, ruining the semblance of peace he'd had since returning to Gandiegow.

She stared from one of his shoulders to the other, as if he was too broad to fit in the cottage with them. "We'll be much more comfortable here."

As would I. "But old Abraham insists. He's not well."

Rachel chewed on the inside of her cheek. He'd forgotten she did that when she was worried. Six years ago, he'd caught her looking at him many times, gazing at him with yearning, and worrying the inside of her cheek. He'd known back then she wanted him, too. He would've bet the boat on it.

"I can't stay there," she admitted.

"Why?" he asked as if the question wasn't filleting him, too.

"It would be too . . . hard." She looked away. "Too difficult."

Tough shite. She didn't know the half of it. She couldn't possibly know the fresh hell she was putting him through.

He wouldn't tell her either, or give her the satisfaction of knowing the pain she'd caused him when she'd walked down the aisle and pledged herself to Joe.

"Ye'll do as Abraham bids." He took the picture from her and handed it back to the little girl. "Put that away. Ye're going to go see yere great-grandda."

Chapter Two

Rachel studied the bookcase behind Brodie, focusing on the holiday garland instead of the man, and it took every bit of her concentration. The quilting dorm had been decorated with lights and a few Christmasy knickknacks, but no tree. Being in the hotel business, Rachel understood why ... lack of space. A sizable lobby could accommodate a Christmas tree—actually several were at her hotel, the luxurious Winderly Towers in the heart of Chicago—but Thistle Glen Lodge was a converted cottage where floor space was at a premium.

Like her mother, Rachel had been raised in the Sunnydale Hotel, their small family-run business. Rachel had grown up cleaning rooms, delivering towels, and working on her homework while manning the front desk. Everyone expected her to take over one day. Yes, Rachel went to college for hospitality management, but with bigger dreams than running a mom-and-pop establishment like the Sunnydale. The first thing she did after registering for classes was to get a job at the Winderly, only a short train ride from the university. She loved the different climate—fast-paced with high-powered guests—and was promoted several times while working on her degree. When the Sunnydale burned down at the end of her final semester, Rachel felt guilty for being relieved.

Faulty wiring had saved her from confronting her mother and telling her she had no intention of becoming the next proprietor of their hotel. That was . . . if she really could have gone against her mother's wishes.

"Mommy!" Hannah exclaimed. The clothes from her suitcase was strewn about the floor, but Joe's guzzy-wrapped picture was tucked safely back inside.

Rachel bent down, gathering her things. "I'll help."

She felt Brodie's eyes boring into her and she couldn't ignore him any longer. She had trouble believing he was actually standing four feet away. She'd been so certain he wouldn't be here in Gandiegow.

From the moment she took her wedding vows, she'd been punishing herself for forsaking Brodie, and for not loving her husband like she should've. When it came to tormenting herself, Rachel had incredible tenacity. When Joe died, she refused to seek out Brodie. She didn't deserve to be happy after what she'd done. She told herself Brodie was dead, too, just like her husband. She'd convinced herself, so much so, that she was still in shock that Brodie was alive and well. And looking better than ever.

All the memories of being here before engulfed her. The moment she met Brodie six years ago, she'd been drawn to him. He was Joe's opposite, though they looked so much alike. Where Joe was outgoing, loud, and gregarious, Brodie was quiet, strong, and peaceful. A man comfortable in his own skin. His calm demeanor had pulled her in and hooked her from the start, making the earth under her feet shift, knocking her off balance. The longer they were thrown together in Gandiegow and the more time she had to compare her husband-to-be with his cousin, the more glaring their differences became. Joe's need to always be the center of attention and on the go outweighed Abraham's clear desire to spend time with his living-abroad grandson. Brodie, on the other hand, stuck close to Abraham, doing as the old man wished. Joe was always searching for the next thrill while Brodie was content to be at home. She'd fallen so suddenly and resoundingly for Brodie that she had a hard time believing what she was feeling was real. Every time Rachel thought she really could call off the wedding, her mother's voice would chime in her head: *But what will people think?*

As Rachel glanced across the room now and saw Brodie scowling at her, a shiver ran down her spine. She couldn't stay at Abraham's . . . she just couldn't. Not with Brodie there. She still cared for him, and his loathing of her would be too much.

"Do you live with Grandfather?" Hannah asked, though Rachel already knew the answer.

"Aye," Brodie replied gruffly. By the way he gripped the mantle, he clearly wasn't happy Rachel would be staying under the same roof as him.

She was thrown off balance, too. Part of her—the part filled with guilt and regret—wanted to flee, head back to the airport, and take the first flight out of Scotland for the pain she'd caused Brodie. At the same time, being near him jolted her to her very core. Life suddenly surged in her veins again. Feelings she'd tried to bury long ago were resurrecting themselves at record speed. For the last six years, she'd been going through the motions of living . . . except where Hannah was concerned. Her daughter had been the one thing that mattered, the sunshine in her every day.

A strange thought lingered in the outer reaches of Rachel's mind, waiting, as if it were a finger tapping patiently on her shoulder. She finally gave it her full attention. *You and Brodie can have a do-over, now that you're back.*

But his eyes held such animosity for her. Maybe even

hate. But hadn't her psychology teacher said love and hate were only different sides of the same coin, so very close to being the exact same thing?

Rachel's eyes met his scowl, and the strangest thing happened; she felt *hope*.

But she was rational enough and mature enough not to completely believe that morsel of possibility.

A delayed thought stabbed her. A lot of time had passed. What if Brodie already belonged to someone else?

Hannah stopped suddenly and peered up at him. "Are you married?" It wasn't the first time her child sensed Rachel's emotions. It happened so often she wondered if her daughter could truly read her mind.

Brodie didn't answer right away, and Rachel's stomach fell. Hit the floor. She could've kicked it around like a soccer ball.

He glowered at Hannah, and Rachel's mother bear instincts came to life.

She opened her mouth to give him hell, and as she did, he turned his cold blue eyes on her. He pinned her to the wall with calm, steady hatred before answering, "Nay. I'm not married." His look wrapped it up into a nice neat package. It was an accusation. A declaration. A promise. What he was feeling was *final*.

She recoiled. She really should grab her things and get out of town. But deep down, that crazy ember of hope still burned.

Wildly, she wondered if Hannah would ask the next question weighing on Rachel's mind. *Does Brodie still have feelings for me, buried so deep he can't see them?* By the scowl he was giving her . . . it seemed rather unlikely. But six years ago she'd been sure he loved her.

Hannah tugged her hand, and Rachel looked down.

"I want to see Grandfather." Then her daughter tilted

her head back to gaze up at the large Scot. "Mommy packed our Christmas tree. Can we put it up at Grandfather's house?"

Brodie glanced around as if expecting a Douglas fir to have materialized itself in the corner.

"It's in her suitcase," Hannah said.

Brodie bristled and raised an eyebrow, conveying clearly that fibbing, especially to adults, wouldn't be tolerated here in Scotland. But instead, he said, "Yere great-grandda is waiting."

Rachel would make him eat that look he was giving her daughter. Hannah didn't lie. Rachel did bring their seven-foot-plus tree, packed neatly away in her 28-inch roller bag.

Brodie cleared his throat. "I'll be waiting outside for ye and the bairn." He slammed the door behind him.

"Come on, sweetie," she said. "Get your coat on." That was one thing that would have to be fixed—Brodie's dislike of Hannah. He had to love her; she was his blood relation. They would always be a part of each other's lives. *Because of Joe.*

Rachel lifted the handle on her spinner and gave her daughter a fortifying smile. She wheeled her bag to the door. "Be careful with your backpack, honey. I put the iPad in there."

Hannah smiled up at her, always the confident little girl. "Don't worry, Mommy." She wheeled her small case outside.

Rachel took a deep breath, squared her shoulders, and followed her. Once through the threshold, her eyes landed on Brodie's back as he gazed out at the ocean. He didn't look as if he needed a fortifying breath. He stood rod-straight, stoic, as if heading into battle.

None of this was a picnic for her either. She'd screwed up her life, and being back in Gandiegow only dredged up more of the past, all laid out for her to analyze, whether she wanted to or not.

She met Joe at the Winderly, when he'd sauntered up to the counter on the first day of a pharmaceutical conference. He flirted and seemed almost confused when she wasn't falling all over herself to flirt back. Over the next week, he upped his game and wooed her relentlessly with his never-ending supply of charm. Finally, she acquiesced and went out with him. Everyone loved Joe and said she was the luckiest woman in the world. He was four years older, so sure of himself. Handsome, well built, and Scottish—a dangerous combination for a young woman who had dreams of a happily-ever-after for herself, and a staff who swooned every time he came by to visit. It had been a whirlwind romance. They were engaged with her mother's blessing after only three months of dating. But following the engagement party, red flags started to appear that maybe Joe wasn't the perfect guy for her. He began frequently changing plans at the last moment, claiming something had come up with work. She'd brushed it off, wanting to believe what others said—that theirs was a match made in heaven.

But deep down, she had more bothering her than a few missed dates. What really troubled her was the animosity he held toward his mother. The woman who'd given birth to him abandoned him and his father. Rachel was appalled. *To grow up without a mother's love?* Unfathomable! Joe made light of her commiseration, saying all the men in their family had been bamboozled by women. *No man should have to sacrifice his heart to a woman, not even to his mother.* That should've had her returning his engagement ring, or at the very least, discussing how his offhand comment had hurt. But she'd glossed over it and ignored her gut feeling that she shouldn't marry a man who didn't love his mother.

Hannah smiled up at her. "I'm going to catch up to him." Before Rachel could say anything, her daughter was running after Brodie.

This only gave Rachel a clear path to remembering it all.

Brodie had every right to be angry with her. Hell, she was angry with herself. When she kissed him at the ruins of Monadail Castle, she was determined to call off the wedding. But when she'd told her mother, Vivienne . . .

Rachel pushed from her mind the horrible conversation when she'd told her mother she'd fallen in love with Brodie. It had taken every ounce of courage and backbone she had.

At the same time, she'd been so weak. So sure if she didn't do as others expected, they might stop loving her.

Bits from her mother's argument that day trickled into her consciousness. *Joe is a catch.* Which implied Brodie wasn't. *Joe can support you with a real job, not a fishing boat. He owns his own home, not some cottage he shares with his grandfather.* Her mother was relentless. *You made a promise to Joe when you took his engagement ring.* And, *What will people think?* But her mother's reasons weren't the basis for why Rachel had gone through with the ceremony. It was her mother's heartfelt declaration: *I only want what's best for you.*

Her mother had always been there for her—both mother and father. And Rachel was the dutiful daughter, who aimed only to please. Looking back, it wasn't the soundest excuse to ignore her heart, which was crying out for Brodie.

But as it turned out, what was *right* in her mother's mind hadn't been *right* for Rachel. She'd walked down the aisle with red puffy eyes, knowing she was making a terrible mistake. When she'd moved into Joe's house, owning a home had lost its appeal. She hadn't known what to do with the full-size appliances, and the house only seemed big, empty, and cold with Joe gone more than he was home.

Rachel gazed at her daughter, who walked beside Brodie, feeling bad for her baby. If only she'd tried harder, she, Joe, and Hannah could've been a real family. But from the day they tied the knot, no amount of sheer determination on Rachel's part had made her marriage work. She needed to quit beating herself up over it, picking apart every detail. Joe seemed to have lost interest in her after the initial hunt, when the thrill was gone. Rachel tried the age-old remedy of attempting to fix things by getting pregnant, certain a baby would settle them into a loving family. But having a newborn only pushed Joe away farther. He was gone all the time to pharmaceutical conventions, parties, and drinks with colleagues. When he didn't want to stay home with her and their infant, Rachel threw herself into work. Guilt ate at her for the amount of time Hannah had to spend in daycare. The guilt for having failed at wedded bliss was wearisome. But the call she received after her six-week postpartum checkup proved her disastrous marriage wasn't completely her fault. Joe had not been a saint. The next morning when she'd set their his-and-hers antibiotics next to his coffee mug, she only had one thing to say.

"Thanks for the STD."

Of course, he'd denied it, but the lab report didn't lie. Two days later, when three staff members at the Winderly quit unexpectedly, Rachel used their leaving as the excuse to pack Hannah's diapers and bassinet and move them to the hotel. They never moved back home, repeating her mother's life by raising her daughter in a twelve-by-twelve room with a hotplate and Mr. Coffee as their only means of making a home-cooked meal.

At that moment, Hannah reached up and took Brodie's hand.

He stopped short and looked down at where they were linked. Rachel's heart melted when he didn't let go, but started walking again, his stride not quite as long with Hannah in tow.

Suddenly, Rachel could see it. It was as if everything had lined up, like the stones in the cottages, each one stacking against the other to build a house. From the time she'd gotten on the plane and sat next to Cait, until this very moment . . . everything had been a *sign*.

This really was Rachel's chance to reclaim what she lost.

Her second chance. *Their second chance!*

The three of them could be a family. Brodie, Hannah, and herself.

Rachel hadn't dated since Joe's death, too busy with work and raising Hannah. But the truth was . . . no one ever measured up to the Scot now holding her daughter's hand.

Instead of a patient finger tapping on Rachel's shoulder this time, a fervent hand was clutched around her heart, compressing it, and urging it back to life. Hope surged through her. Then her brain got on board, *I'm not going to let Brodie slip through my fingers again!*

She glanced heavenward, thankful for the opportunity, feeling certain the *what-ifs* that had plagued her since marrying Joe would evaporate.

Though this was her chance to make up for the past, Rachel wasn't sure what she was going to do next. She could hear Hannah chattering away at Brodie, but couldn't identify what she was saying over the waves crashing against the walkway. She wanted to rush ahead to see how it was going between them, but held back, letting them get to know each other.

For the first time since arriving, Rachel took in the salty smell of the North Sea and soaked in her surroundings. Gandiegow was the same as she remembered, still perched on the edge of the ocean, but there were some improvements. Fresh coats of paint, signs pointing out the businesses, and a couple of cottages which she didn't remember from before. Overall, the village's essence was unchanged—a time capsule of a nineteenth- century fishing village with lobster pots, dinghies, and life preservers positioned strategically, proclaiming its heritage, its viability, and its future.

The sea was churning, the waves foaming more than when they'd arrived. Ross had mentioned an incoming winter storm, and Rachel was glad she and Hannah were prepared for the cold weather. They were, after all, residents of Chicago, where winter had been invented. Before they left home, Hannah demanded she wear her new star-covered rain boots. Rachel only agreed after she'd put in the warm inserts and made Hannah don thick socks, too. A wave splattered Brodie's feet, but Hannah's remained dry as if he'd positioned her far enough away to keep her safe.

When they arrived at the cottage, Rachel did hurry to catch up then. She reached out and touched Brodie's arm.

He flinched as if burned and gave her a *what-the-hell* look.

"Thank you," she said, glancing at Hannah to let him know what she was talking about.

His stare conveyed he hadn't done it out of kindness, and that he hadn't done it for her. "The girl needs to be watched while she's here. It's dangerous in Gandiegow." He opened the door—*at least that was a consideration*— and let them walk in.

Nothing had changed in Abraham's cottage. The entry

was all wood, from the oak floors to the wood paneling. No bright, pretty curtains hung in the front window, only strong, masculine brown drapes for this fisherman's house. Rachel slipped off her coat and peered at the two pictures on the wall, the fishing boat pictures. One of Abraham with his son Richard. One of a much older Abraham with his grandsons, Brodie and Joe. On their first meeting, Abraham had said these photos were his prized possessions. But no photos of Robena—Abraham's daughter and Brodie's mother—were displayed of her as a girl or as a woman though she lived nearby.

Brodie guided Hannah to the small bench where she was to sit and remove her boots. He then pointed out the rubber mat for her snowy foot gear. He took her coat and placed it on a hook, all the while ignoring Rachel, who was on her own when it came to boot mats, coat hooks, and attentiveness.

"Yere great grandda should be in the parlor. Through there." He pointed down the hall.

Hannah skipped away, humming a nondescript tune.

They were alone. *Perfect.* Rachel could start a dialogue between them. "Brodie?"

"Not now." He gestured to where Hannah waited.

Rachel stepped past him, went to her daughter, and stood behind her in the doorway. The parlor, too, was the same as it had been, except there was a Christmas tree decorated with antique ornaments with a length of burlap as a tree skirt. Magazines and books were on the coffee table, and Abraham was sitting in his old wingback chair across from the fireplace.

Hannah looked up at her. "Is that him?"

"Aye," Brodie said from behind Rachel, making her breath catch. "Go on in and say *hallo* properly."

Hannah smiled at Brodie then went into the room, coming within a few feet of the old man.

"Hello, Grandfather," Hannah said.

Abraham looked up from his magazine. He stared at her for a long second and then broke into a smile. "Oh, lass, come here an' let me see ye."

Hannah took a step closer and stared at her great-grandfather while he stared back.

Abraham shifted his gaze to Brodie. "Doesn't she remind ye of Joe?"

"Aye," Brodie muttered.

Hannah glanced at Rachel. "Can I give Grandfather a hug?"

Rachel nodded and Hannah threw her arms around the old man.

"You're my very own grandfather," Hannah whispered with an air of awe.

Abraham patted her back. "Aye." He reached in his pocket, not letting go of her, and pulled out a handkerchief.

Either the woodstove was making the old man's eyes leak, or the little slip of a lass was making his grandfather mist up as if the ocean spray had set his eyes to burning. But Brodie had never seen his grandda tear up. A salty fisherman and tough Scot like himself wouldn't allow it. Certainly he'd never seen his mother—who lived just outside of town on a small farm—incite soft emotions in his grandfather. As Abraham dabbed at his eyes, Brodie turned away to let him have his moment, but not before he saw the girl, Hannah, patting her great-grandda also.

She broke away from him and tugged Rachel over. "This is my grandda." She'd said it just like Brodie, burr and all.

Abraham beamed at Rachel as they exchanged pleasantries. It was strange his grandfather seemed so fond of Joe's widow. But why wouldn't he? Brodie had never told his grandda how she'd kissed him one moment, and then stabbed him in the back the next.

The child hopped from foot to foot. "Can we show Grandda our Christmas tree now? Can we? Can we?"

Brodie could've argued they didn't need Rachel's tree; they already had one in the corner. He'd cut it down himself at Colin's farm. The decorations weren't much, but he'd put them on himself as Abraham had been resting at the time. The star at the top had been his mother's—the one she'd left here for him, Abraham, and Joe, when he and Joe had been boys. One of only a few things she'd given him that he'd kept.

At the same time, Brodie was curious to see this tree Rachel had packed in her bag. "I'll roll yere luggage in here."

Rachel nodded, smiling at him as if he'd offer to bring her roses. He had no intention of starting up with her again, but he could still be civil. He strode into the hallway, retrieved her bag, and brought it back to the room.

"Thanks," she said, taking it and laying it down on the floor. As she unzipped the bag, several personal items fell out.

Of course, with his terrible luck, the pieces couldn't be wool socks and long underwear, but a lacy blue bra and flowery panties. While she quickly shoved her undergarments in the outside pocket of her luggage, Brodie heated up.

He should've looked away, but instead kept his eyes glued on her suitcase, in case anything else interesting tumbled out. At this moment, her lingerie was making it hard for him to be indifferent about her being here.

One thing he didn't see in her luggage were the plastic branches he'd expected to catch sight of, shoved around her jeans and sweaters, evidence of an artificial Christmas tree. He'd decided that's what the girl had meant when she'd said her mother had packed one. It had to be small to fit in there.

However, it was a rolled-up quilt which Rachel retrieved.

"There it is, Grandda," Hannah said, pulling at the end. "Our Christmas tree!" She extended it all the way out and was halfway across the room before he could blink.

Brodie had never seen anything like it . . . a Christmas Tree quilt. It was in the shape of a truncated triangle, indeed as high as the ceiling, made from green and red fabrics, and it had a quilted star crowning the top. He glanced over at Rachel, but she was already staring at him, seeming to be waiting for an apology.

Well, he might owe one to the little girl. "Hannah," he said, "ye spoke true. 'Tis indeed a fine Christmas tree."

"Bring it over so I can see," Abraham said.

But a hard knocking came at the front door.

"Brodie, see who it is," Grandda ordered.

Brodie went down the hallway and opened the door. Deydie, the town matriarch, barreled her way in, wearing potholders and carrying a covered dish. "I've brought Abraham his meal."

By the way she was looking past Brodie, her real errand was to have a good look at Rachel.

"She's in the parlor with Grandda. The girl's with her, too."

"I'll see my way in," Deydie said.

Most of the time, Brodie didn't mind Deydie and the other quilting ladies. They kept him and Grandda fed and didn't interfere with them as they did with the others in town. Brodie counted himself blessed. But something about how Deydie was acting made him think the tides were turning and his good fortune had run out.

Deydie moved past him into the parlor. He followed. But Deydie halted in the doorway, staring at the quilt. "Where'd ye get that?"

Rachel glanced up. "I made it."

Brodie heard himself saying, "Ye remember Deydie, don't you?" Like he was in charge of the hospitality brigade or something.

"Yes," she replied.

But Deydie wasn't interested in pleasantries, especially where quilting was concerned. "Tell me how ye come to make it." The old woman seemed to be enthralled, unusual for her, since Deydie and the other townsfolk were none too happy with Rachel the first time she came to Gandiegow; Deydie blamed Rachel for Joe not moving home to raise his family there when they got married.

Hannah pulled her end of the quilt over to Deydie. "Mommy says our hotel room is too small for a real tree. She hangs it up and we put our presents under it. Even though we don't have a fireplace and chimney, Santa comes anyway, because we have a tree. Right, Mommy?"

Deydie stared at the girl as if cataloging her features, appearing pained by what she saw.

Aye. The girl looks like Joe.

Finally, Deydie set the covered dish on the bookshelf, slipped off the potholders, and took the quilt by the corner, peering closely at the stitches.

"That sure smells good," Abraham said.

But Deydie wasn't listening. She held the fabric under the light. "Who did the quilting?"

"I did. On my machine," Rachel said.

"Hmmm," Deydie answered. "Ye did a nice job. Where'd ye get the pattern? I think this is something we should make at the quilt retreat that's starting tomorrow."

"It's my own quilt design." Rachel was acting a little

defensive and for good reason. Deydie had a way of putting everyone on edge. Even when she was trying to be halfway nice.

Deydie dropped her end of the quilt and stared directly at Rachel. "Get settled and then ye need to come by Quilting Central. We have to talk. Bring along that Christmas Tree quilt, too."

With great effort, Abraham pushed himself to his feet. "Stay and eat with us, Deydie." Lately Brodie had been surprised how much his grandfather acted as if he liked the old woman. Grandda could definitely tolerate her better than most.

Deydie shook her head, the white bun at the back of her neck coming loose. "Nay. I have to get back. Caitie looks like she ate something that doesn't agree with her." She fussed with the pins, positioning her hair back into place. "There's so much to get done. Now I need to scrounge up some red and green scraps for the group that's coming so we can make the Christmas Tree quilt." She motioned to Brodie and the covered dish. "Put that in the oven and heat it up for twenty minutes." Deydie shoved her potholders on like they were mittens and nodded in Rachel's direction. "Do what ye have to do quickly, and then hurry on over to Quilting Central." She jabbed a potholdered finger at Brodie. "Ye'll show her the way."

He didn't have time to argue with her as she hustled from the room and was gone with a slam of the front door.

"That woman is always up to something," Abraham mumbled. Then he turned to Brodie. "After ye get the pan in the oven, take Rachel upstairs so she can put her things away. The lass and I will wait here. I want to show her the photo album of Joe that the quilting ladies made for us." He pointed to a shelf. "'Tis over there. Are ye strong enough, little lady, to get it?"

"Aye, Granddda," the girl said, once again copying the brogue.

Brodie wondered if she was playing at being Scottish, or if her little heart was telling her she really belonged here.

He used his flannel shirt to hold the warm dish and left the room to put the casserole in the oven. When he returned, Rachel was draping the folded quilt over the sofa. They'd have to find a place to hang it. *For the girl's sake.*

Abraham pointed at him. "Git yere camera. I need all of us in a family picture."

"I left my mobile on the boat," Brodie lied.

Rachel pulled her phone from her pocket. "I came prepared." She stood back while Hannah climbed on Abraham's lap.

Reluctantly, Brodie stood beside them.

"Rachel, come and get in the picture," Abraham commanded. "I want all of us together. The whole family."

She frowned as if she might argue. Brodie didn't necessarily want her in the photo, but his grandfather would be obeyed.

Rachel brought him the phone. "Brodie, your arms are longer than mine. Do you mind taking the picture?"

Hell yes, he minded! Because she stood next to him, making him feel uncomfortable.

"Take a couple," Abraham ordered. "I want to hang it on the wall with the other family photos."

Brodie held up the phone and did as he was told. It was hard to smile with Rachel being so close, making him feel things he didn't want to feel. When they were done, he returned the phone to Rachel without meeting her eyes. "I'll show you where ye'll be sleeping." To prove he wasn't completely bad-mannered, he zipped her suitcase and toted it from the room, speaking to her over his shoulder, "Come."

She followed him out and then up the stairs. He had no choice but to put the two of them in the room he and Joe had shared as children. Seven months ago, when Brodie had returned to Abraham's, the thought of staying in their old bedroom had been a sad reminder of the cousin he'd lost. Not just when he'd died, but also when he'd married. Perhaps it had even been before then, when Joe had turned his back on all of them, leaving Scotland, declaring he would have a better life somewhere else. Brodie inhabited his mother's old room, decorated in faded green and pink florals.

He opened the door of his childhood bedroom and set Rachel's suitcase inside. "Feel free to use the bureau. 'Tis empty. If we'd known ye were coming, the bed would've been made up." He pulled the sheet from the mattress, which the quilting ladies had put there to keep the dust off. "I'll get the linens." He didn't look into Rachel's face as he passed by her. He didn't have to. He knew her features. His whole being inhaled her, dredging up old images, old memories, things he'd rather remained buried.

That day at Monadail Castle, she'd smelled the same way, something so enticing it took his breath away.

Six years ago when Rachel arrived, Brodie had been so taken with her that he'd begun carrying around his mother's locket. The locket was special, given to his mum as a keepsake from his da and something his mother wore every day when Da was alive. On the day Mum married another, she passed the locket on to Brodie. *I guess she couldn't keep such a thing and be wed to another man.*

Aye, he loved his mother, but her betrayal against his father's memory remained fresh in Brodie's heart. Da hadn't been gone but a month when his mother had stood at the altar and pledged herself to another man.

Brodie had never used the term *stepfather* when he referred to Keith. He was just the man who had married his mother.

But that day at the ruins of Monadail Castle where he and Rachel had shared their first kiss, Brodie had presented the locket to her, pressing the black velvet pouch into her hand. Now he stood at the linen closet, wondering if she still had the necklace or if, like his mother, she'd disposed of it because she couldn't be married to another man and have it near?

With an exasperated sigh, he pulled the sheets and blankets from their shelves. He couldn't stay here with Rachel in the cottage. Maybe he should take a bedroll and camp out on the boat until she took her bairn and left Gandiegow.

At that moment, the wind outside howled as if to remind him a winter storm was moving in. He shook his head at his bad luck. But then another feeling stole over him.

But this is my home. He'd be damned if he'd let Rachel run him off and keep him from a good night's sleep in his warm bed . . . across the hall from her.

He returned to her room, dropped the linens on her bed, and went to the door, still not meeting her eyes. "Hurry up. Abraham will want to eat with you. Then Deydie expects ye at Quilting Central."

Chapter Three

Rachel sighed with relief as Brodie shut the bedroom door behind him. Not thirty minutes ago, she was anxious to be alone with him to talk, but now she needed a minute to herself. Brodie was not in the mood for a heart-to-heart so she couldn't tell him outright how she was feeling. She'd have to get creative to get her point across.

Quickly she unzipped the front pocket of her roller bag and pulled out the items she'd crammed in there. Thank goodness her bra and underwear had fallen out along with the black velvet pouch which held Brodie's locket. And thank the heavens above, Brodie was your typical man who'd only noticed the lingerie scattered on the floor. For years, she'd kept the locket hidden within her socks. While packing for this trip, she felt compelled to bring it along. She opened the dresser drawer, carefully laid the locket inside, and set her blue bra on top of it.

From downstairs a giggle drifted up through the vent. Well, at least one thing was going as she'd hoped. Abraham and Hannah were hitting it off. She and Brodie . . . not so much. He wouldn't even make eye contact with her. She finished unpacking, brushed her

hair, applied another round of lip gloss, and then returned downstairs.

She was disappointed when Brodie was no longer in
the parlor. Hannah was standing next to Abraham, snuggled up against him, the two of them acting as if they'd
known each other forever.

"Mommy, come see the pictures of Daddy. Look how
different he looks from my pictures of him."

Rachel crossed the room and leaned over. Sure
enough, there was Joe . . . on the beach, on the boat,
climbing the bluff, wearing blue jeans, T-shirts, and with
his wavy hair touching his collar. Not the polished Joe
she knew. Also, in every picture, Brodie was there beside him.

Hannah looked up at her with a puzzled expression.
"If Daddy and Brodie are cousins, does that mean
Brodie's my uncle?"

"Nay," the man-in-question said from the doorway.
"Ye and I are cousins as well. First cousins, once removed."

"Once removed?" Hannah looked at him as if she
didn't understand. She hopped away from Abraham and
went to him. "I'm going to call ye *Brodie.*"

The way he looked at Hannah stabbed at Rachel's
heart, because he looked as pained as she felt. If she had
married Brodie instead of Joe, Hannah could've been
his. But then again, maybe she wouldn't—and Rachel
wouldn't change a thing about her daughter.

Brodie cleared his throat. "Grandda, you and yere
guests need to come to the table. The food is laid out and
ready to eat." But he had his coat on.

"Aren't you going to stay and eat with us, too?" Rachel
said, before she could keep herself from asking.

"I've things to do."

"Aye," Abraham said as he pushed himself out of his chair. "Things to do, like taking Rachel to Quilting Central after we've eaten. Ye've not forgotten, have ye, that Deydie expects ye to bring Rachel to her?" He started coughing.

Brodie's face hardened, as if he was preparing to tell Rachel to go to Hades to avoid taking her anywhere. Instead he schooled his features. "I've not forgotten. I'll be back in a short while to fetch . . . *her.*" He wouldn't even say her name and he still refused to look at her. He'd kept himself in check for Abraham, and certainly not for her.

"Nay," Abraham said. "Ye'll sit with us and we'll enjoy our first family meal together." He reached over and patted Hannah's hand.

Brodie glared at Rachel as if she were the one who'd ordered him to stay.

She deserved his disdain, but she'd never meant to hurt him. She just didn't know how to let Brodie know how sorry she was for the pain she'd caused him. She looked up at the face of the man who had once adored her. How could she tell him she wanted a second chance with him? Especially since he didn't seem receptive.

The clouds in her head cleared. "Oh, good grief," she said aloud. She'd just buried the one thing that would send a message to Brodie. She'd totally missed it as another sign when it had fallen out of her luggage onto Abraham's parlor floor.

A moment later, she caught on that they were all staring at her. "Ummm. Excuse me for a minute. I forgot something very important."

As she left the table and ran upstairs, she bolstered herself up. Putting on Brodie's locket would be the bravest thing she'd ever done. It would make a clear statement, one she hadn't been able to make on her own. When Brodie saw her wearing the locket, he would know unequivocally that she meant business.

With more patience than he knew he had, Brodie waited with Abraham and Hannah for Rachel to return. He could get through the ordeal of her in Gandiegow if he focused on the fact she wouldn't be here long. As soon as this meal was over and he dropped Rachel at Quilting Central, he'd be one step closer to her leaving, and that much closer to the return of his normal life.

Rachel strutted into the room, taking the chair next to Hannah's, which was positioned directly across from him. She toyed with the necklace at her neck with a secretive smile on her face that hadn't been there before.

Grandda put his hand out for Hannah to take. Automatically, Brodie took his grandfather's hand as well.

Abraham nodded. "Lad, it's yere turn to lead the grace."

But Brodie was staring at Rachel's outstretched hand. He didn't want to complete the circle. If he touched her, then what? He brought his eyes up to meet hers.

But the pendant around her neck caught his attention first. It wasn't polite, but he couldn't stop looking at her chest . . . and the locket he'd given her so long ago.

"Holy hell." He scooted his chair back and jumped to his feet, with the scraping sound on the floor accentuating his irritation.

Rachel glared at him. "Little ears." She nodded in Hannah's direction.

Right now, he didn't care what language he used. Nothing made sense. Why would she have the locket with her? She seemed as shocked to see him as he was to see her in Gandiegow. Then why?

Was she wearing the locket to rub in her rejection and

betrayal of him? Was she on a mission to inflict more pain? Why would she want to bring up the past? He'd vowed to never speak of it. Especially with her.

"Sit down, Brodie," Abraham said.

"I'm not hungry." He felt as petulant as when he was a ten-year-old boy and refused to move in with his mother and her new husband. "I'm going to check on the boat," he said as an afterthought. "I'll be back to take *her* to Quilting Central." He stomped from the kitchen and down the hallway, not waiting to hear what either of them had to say about it.

He was out the front door and halfway to the boat when he realized the storm had arrived, making the North Sea churn. Father Andrew MacBride and his brother, Tuck, were walking toward him. Tuck was a year older than Andrew, a good-looking bloke, blond like his brother, but had a laughing glint of mischief always playing in his eyes.

"We were looking for you," Andrew said. "Tuck heard from Ross that ye need a hand on yere boat."

When Brodie first arrived, everyone referred to the boat as Abraham's, but as the months wore on, they'd slowly started speaking of the boat as if it was his.

"Aye. An extra hand would be welcome with the fishing," Brodie said.

Tuck's stay in Gandiegow had been awkward, to say the least. He'd gotten off on the wrong foot with everyone by showing up two months late for Andrew and Moira's wedding. Gandiegow viewed such an offense as unforgivable as family was the lifeblood of the community. The gossip was that Tuck was useless, but Brodie had seen him helping out on various boats and doing odd jobs around town. The man appeared to work hard. Others complained about Tuck not being considerate because he was horning his way in on the newlyweds' time. But

Moira and Andrew were hardly the typical newlyweds as they had her cousin Glenna to raise. Andrew seemed to take his brother in stride, and so Brodie did, too.

"Good," Tuck said. "I like to stay busy." He winked at Brodie. "I hear there's a new bird in town. What's up with her? She's staying at Thistle Glen Lodge?"

Keep your hands off Rachel! Fire burned through Brodie's chest and his fists clenched. Of course, he didn't want Joe's widow, but that didn't mean Tuck should have her. Brodie considered himself even-tempered. But since Rachel arrived in town today, she'd turned his world upside down and him into a hothead. *Just like she did before*.

He wanted to yank Tuck to a stop and tell him Rachel was off-limits.

Andrew gave his brother a warning glance. "Do me a favor and leave her alone? From what I understand, she and Abraham's great-granddaughter are only here for a short time. Moira says she's had a rough go of it."

If the playful determination in Tuck's eye was any indication, the warning his brother gave him would be ignored. "What's her name? Rhonda?"

"No, Rachel," Brodie hissed, maybe a little too quickly, because Andrew and Tuck both looked at him strangely. "She was my cousin's wife," he supplied as a lame excuse. "Family," he added, which sounded even lamer.

"Weren't ye headed for yere boat?" Tuck asked.

Brodie realized he'd come to a halt and was staring out at the sea. It was cold out here. "Nay. I have someplace to be." He should build the fire up for Abraham. And the little girl. He wouldn't be doing it for Rachel.

Brodie turned in the opposite direction and left Andrew and Tuck as he hurried back to the cottage. His urgency made perfect sense. He had a duty to perform.

He needed to get Rachel to Quilting Central . . . and then get her off his mind.

At the house, Brodie slung open the door and advanced down the hall. He found the three of them in the kitchen, where he'd left them.

"Let's go." He wasn't in the mood for niceties.

Rachel glanced up, but he turned away, not wanting to see the locket around her neck. Instead he busied himself by clearing the table while he waited for her to be ready to leave.

"I'll take care of the dishes when I get back, Grandda," Brodie said, calming his emotions for his grandfather's sake.

"Nay. Little lass and I will work on them."

Hannah bobbed her head up and down excitely. "I can stand on the chair and wash. Sometimes at the hotel, Chef lets me help when the restaurant's closed."

"It's now or never," Brodie said impatiently.

Rachel didn't acknowledge his statement, but kissed the top of Hannah's head. "I'll be back soon. Be good." As soon as she turned away, her mood changed. She flounced by Brodie without as much as a glance.

Maybe his tone with her had been a bit gruff. But considering he was the one who'd been blindsided by her being here and then put out because he had to escort her all over God's creation, he was justified. He followed, trying not to inhale her, but he caught a little whiff . . . and wanted more. *Pathetic.* Hadn't he gotten enough heartache from her before?

She walked by the parlor without stopping.

"Weren't ye supposed to bring yere tree?" he reminded her.

She gave him a puzzled look, and when she did, the light caught the damn locket and its reflection twinkled at him.

"Oh," she finally said.

He wouldn't offer to get it for her either. This was between her and Deydie. Rachel was just lucky he remembered the quilt, or she would've been traipsing back in the cold to retrieve it.

She moved past him into the parlor and came back a second later with it cradled in her arms. He couldn't help cataloging the changes since he'd seen her six years ago. Her coffee-colored hair was longer, fuller, cascading down her shoulders to the middle of her back. Her brown eyes, once filled with wonder of the sights of Gandiegow, were now overflowing with worldly wisdom.

And God, he hated himself for noticing, but she'd gone from a skinny young adult to a full-fledged woman who had filled out in all the right places.

She laid the quilt on the bench where Hannah had sat earlier as she shrugged into her coat. Brodie picked up the mail lying on the hall table and busied himself, flipping through each piece until she marched out the door with the hood of her parka bouncing like a bobber. He hesitated a couple of seconds, swallowed the attraction he felt for her, and then followed her out, feeling more than a little used. Why should he have to babysit her to the door of Quilting Central?

The storm was getting right angry with the wind kicking up all around them. And damn him, he wanted to wrap his arm around Rachel's shoulders to protect her from the sea lapping at the walkway. But she had on proper boots and he'd seen her pick her steps carefully before. He did, however, close the distance between them, in case he needed to fish her out of the ocean. Not out of any sentiment for the woman, but it'd be hard to explain to Deydie why he hadn't brought her to Quilting Central as promised.

Rachel stopped and turned on him, wrapping her

arms around her waist. "I don't appreciate the way you spoke to me in front of my daughter."

Before he could answer, he saw the breaking wave. He grabbed her by the shoulders and snatched her away from the edge, saving them both from a good drenching.

Rachel's big rounded eyes shifted from the wrathful water back to him. She was terrified and he was ashamed. If it had been any other woman new to town, he would've guided her toward the safer route behind the buildings instead along the ocean's edge, where it was dangerous.

He gently shook her shoulders. "I'll not let anything happen to ye." He wanted to pull her close to prove his body could protect her. But he fought the urge, letting his hands fall away.

Gads! His emotions were fluctuating from one extreme to another, as unpredictable as the crashing waves. But wasn't this what had happened to him six years ago when Rachel had been here?

She napalmed him with her *blasted grateful eyes.* Even worse, she seemed comforted that he was near. Or maybe the wind had clouded his vision. He wished the streetlamp wasn't burning so bright. The look she gave him comforted him, too, filling in all the places she'd left empty in him long ago.

Dammit. Brodie's insides were tangled-up, a mess, just like the fishing line after a storm. All it took was one glance from her, and he was sucked right back in.

But he couldn't let that happen. Not this time.

A minute later, they arrived at Quilting Central.

"Ye're here," he said, ready to walk away.

She touched his arm. "Come in with me."

"No."

But the door opened and Deydie was there with her broom. "Git in here. You, too, Brodie. I've got Abraham's shirt that I mended. I need ye to take it back to him."

Begrudgingly he followed Rachel in and waited by the door. But he would've rather stubbornly faced the freezing cold while the older woman retrieved the shirt. He noticed Rachel acting like a codfish out of water, inching closer to him as if he could help her breathe easier. He stepped farther away while she glanced around uncomfortably. *The quilting ladies won't bite.* But the second he thought it, he corrected himself. Aye, Deydie *verra* well could, but not the rest . . . as long as ye didn't cross them.

Deydie pointed a gnarled finger at Rachel and lit into her. "It's about time ye brought the girl around to see Abraham. With that cough lingering the way it does, 'tis clear his time is drawing near."

Whereas Deydie is too ornery to let death take her, Brodie thought. He hated when Deydie spoke as if Grandda was going to kick off any minute. Brodie had a moment of sympathy for Rachel because Deydie had perfected the art of being untactful. Also, the old woman was famous for her persistent badgering.

The next thing he knew, the ill-tempered *badger* glowered at him as if he'd broadcasted his opinions of her to the room. Then Deydie spun and waddled away.

Bethia, Deydie's closest friend, and Moira approached him and Rachel. Bethia was tall and slim, and had the demeanor of a friendly, welcoming housecat. Moira gave Rachel a shy smile. Glenna, her young cousin, stood behind her.

Bethia held out a vial to him. "Can ye give this essential oil to Abraham? It's my latest concoction." While Brodie had been away, Bethia had become a certified herbalist. She pulled a small sheet of paper from her pocket. "Here are the instructions. He can either hold the vial a few inches from his nose, or put a few drops on his pillow before bed. It will help soothe his cough."

Moira guided Glenna to stand in front of her, as if it was her turn. The little girl stepped up to Rachel and handed her a homemade rag doll that wore a plaid dress matching her own.

"For yere daughter," Glenna said. She was older than Hannah, maybe six.

Moira nodded. "We wanted to welcome Hannah to town. Glenna thought to give her the doll we were making."

Brodie was sure Rachel's girl had plenty of store-bought toys and wouldn't want a homespun doll, but Rachel took it with a sincere smile.

"Thank you," she said to Glenna. "You'll have to stop by and meet her." Rachel looked as if she'd like to have her daughter with her right now.

Deydie came rushing back over with Abraham's shirt. She thrust it at Brodie. "Here. Now off with ye." She glanced at Moira. "Aren't ye supposed to be meeting Kirsty at the school?"

Moira smiled kindly. "We're on our way right now to help put up the Christmas decorations."

"Good. Be careful out there or the storm'll carry ye away." Deydie turned to Rachel and took her arm. "Git to the front now and show them the quilt ye brought."

Rachel's smile fell away and she turned pleading eyes on him.

Brodie had no sympathy. "Ye're on your own." Without a backward glance, he turned and walked out into the cold.

At first Rachel couldn't believe Brodie would abandon her like this. But honestly, what else could she expect? She'd abandoned him long ago. What stung more was that she didn't get the reaction she'd expected from him when he saw her wearing his locket. He should've been happy, but he'd only seemed angry. Not the best way to start off their do-over.

"Git up there," Deydie barked again. "Hold up the Christmas Tree quilt really high. Some of the ladies have poor vision."

As Rachel made her way to the front, she glanced about. Quilting Central resided in a huge open room with tables everywhere and sewing machines on each one. Two longarm quilting machines sat at the back. Several design walls were covered with quilt blocks. There was a kitchen area, several spots with comfy sofas and chairs, and what looked like a library in the corner.

The room was quiet with all eyes on Rachel. Was everyone remembering her last appearance and the urn that held Joe's ashes? How they'd barely spoken to her? The only one who'd been kind had been Abraham, but he had little to say as he'd been torn with grief. She'd never forget how he'd gone from a commanding patriarch to silent tears pouring down his face at the funeral. Or the slump of his shoulders as he took the shovel to scoop the first dirt into Joe's grave. Or the shuffle in his walk as he made his way down the bluff, a man nearly broken.

"Wait a minute." Deydie hustled up beside her and took her place on the stage, speaking to the crowd. "Before the retreat-goers get here, there's something I need to say. I know we'd agreed to clean out our cupboards and work on our UFOs—" The old woman turned to Rachel as if she was clueless. "UFOs are quilt projects that seem to never get finished." Deydie huffed and pointed to her desk piled with what were clearly several bundles of uncompleted projects. "But the retreat-goers will have the option to work on the Christmas Tree quilt from Rachel Clacher as well. Ye know I always want to give a little something extra to our customers."

"Rachel *Granger*," Rachel corrected in a whisper. "I never took Joe's last name."

"Of course ye didn't," Deydie said on a frown. "Headstrong, ye are."

Bethia stood and spoke to the room. "But don't forget, we're collecting any UFO blocks ye may not need for our charity quilts. We're going to make two quilts to auction off this time: one for Kidney Research UK and one for the National Kidney Foundation in America. All, of course, in honor of Sadie."

Sadie raised her hand and smiled. "I really appreciate everyone's support."

Rachel was glad the focus was off her, and at the same time, she wondered what that was all about.

Deydie bobbed her head as Bethia sat. "We'd like to have those blocks before the end of the year."

Rachel's relief was short-lived.

Deydie shot her another glare and pointed to her desk. "Now for our retreat-goers who are interested, I pulled out a stack of red and green scraps for what *Rachel's* brought us. Hold up yere Christmas Tree quilt again and let us have a good look at it."

Next to the scraps of green and red on Deydie's desk was another stack of remnants—*plaid remnants*.

Rachel couldn't look away from the tartan scraps. She could visualize a quilt made of the clans' colors for Hannah. Something whimsical, to remind her little girl of her heritage, a lovely memory quilt that would commemorate her father's people. Rachel smiled at the vision as the pieces fell into place. A child's quilt with plaid fish. With maybe a boat at the top like the one Joe used to work on with his grandfather. *Brodie's boat now.*

Deydie spoke to the group as all the past arguments Rachel had had with her mother about Joe filled her mind. Vivienne, her mother, loved Joe from the start. Her mother and husband were more alike than Rachel was to either. They were outgoing and easily talked with others, while Rachel had spent her life becoming comfortable with people. Vivienne had been sorely disappointed in Rachel when she'd left Joe. Embarrassment kept her from telling her mother the reason why she'd moved back to the hotel. Then Joe had died, which devastated her mother. Ironically, Vivienne didn't understand why Rachel kept Joe's memory alive for Hannah, always questioning her at every turn—*if you didn't care enough to live with the man, why make such an effort to make him part of your life now?* For Rachel, it was easy: She loved her daughter. Joe was a part of Hannah and she deserved to know him. Rachel didn't have a relationship with her own father. It still hurt that her mother had cut ties with him. He'd remarried, started a new family, and Rachel had both grown up without a father, and felt forgotten. She would do anything to spare Hannah that fate. Hannah would grow up with her father in spirit, if nothing else.

Rachel glanced again at Deydie's desk. Would the old stick-in-the-mud quilter be willing to give up the tartan scraps to her? By how Rachel was being treated now, and the shunning she'd received before, the answer was *no*. Pigs would have to fly first. Unless . . .

Rachel touched the locket. She'd been strong enough to take a stand on a second chance with Brodie. This next bit should be a piece of cake. She clutched the Christmas Tree quilt close to her chest.

"I said to hold up the tree so we can all see it," Deydie snapped.

"Not so fast." Braver words had never been uttered. "Make a deal with me first."

The room gasped, then whispered exclamations

spread from sewing machine to sewing machine. Rachel knew she was messing with the proverbial fire by not jumping-to when Deydie ordered, but she could be as stubborn as any Scot, couldn't she? At least she felt that way since she'd arrived in town. Besides, she hadn't survived this long in the hotel business to not have developed at least a semi-strong backbone.

"I'll happily share my tree with you, even give you the template and teach everyone how to make it." Rachel paused to take a breath, or to fortify herself. "But only if you'll let me have that stack of tartans on the desk."

Deydie glowered at her. "What would a Yank like ye want with a stack of old tartans from the folks here in Gandiegow?"

"I just do," Rachel said boldly, which produced a second gasp from the captivated audience.

Bethia picked up the stack. "These? They aren't very good pieces. I could find ye some better ones."

Deydie put her hand up. "Nay. Those'll do just fine for *her*. Ye give us yere pattern and teach us how to make the tree, and afterward, I'll give that pile of *crap*, I mean scraps, to you."

The room reverberated with nervous laughter.

"No. I want them now."

Deydie squinted over at her broom, leaning against the wall. Did she mean to whack Rachel with it?

"Fine," the old woman finally agreed.

Rachel nodded as if they'd shaken hands. "Thank you." Without waiting for Deydie to tell her again, Rachel let the Christmas Tree unroll as she held it high in front of her. The room *oohed* and *ahhed*, and for Rachel, this was nearly the best part about quilting, second only to designing her own patterns.

Deydie took one end of the Christmas Tree and held it out for the room to see. It struck Rachel that she and

Deydie had hit upon some common ground, which was something she'd never expected. Not in a million years.

Brodie crept back in her thoughts. Now if only she could convince Brodie that they should work together, too. Rachel wondered what bargaining tool she could use with him. It would take more than a Christmas Tree quilt. It would take luck and some serious persuasion on her part . . . and a miracle.

Deydie was talking to her.

"Excuse me?" Rachel said.

The old woman sighed exasperatedly. "I said ye'll start first thing in the morn."

"That doesn't give me much time."

"Then I suggest ye get busy figuring out yere lesson plan."

Rachel hadn't come to Scotland to teach quilting, though she'd taught quite a few people at the hotel how to sew. People she'd worked with, even a couple of men who wanted to learn to hem their own pants. But mostly, she'd taught a small group of her staff how to quilt so they could make gifts for the ones they loved. She also hadn't come to Scotland to be bossed around. Or to see Brodie. Or for a second chance. But it looked like she was getting more than she imagined when she'd left Chicago.

She folded up the quilt as best she could and snatched the stack of tartans from the desk before Deydie could change her mind. But she didn't get to rush out the door. Bethia and Sadie waylaid her at the exit. Not exactly waylaying, but giving her a notebook, a ruler, and plenty of encouragement that she would do fine when she began her quilt class in the morning. Deydie stood on the other side of the room.

"Don't worry about her," Sadie said. "Her bark is worse than her bite. She just doesn't take to outsiders very easily."

"Don't I know it," Rachel scoffed, remembering her last two visits to this town.

Bethia tilted her head toward Deydie. "She's had a rough go. I think she's remembering others who've left Gandiegow and never returned."

The subtext was there . . . *who left Gandiegow and never returned—alive.* For a moment, Rachel relived walking up the bluff to the cemetery. The cold urn in her arms hadn't been able to compete with the frosty treatment the villagers had shown her.

Bethia patted her hand, her touch seeming to coax Rachel to understand Deydie's point of view. *All their points of view.* Rachel got it, and a sliver of comprehension seeped in to soothe her bruised feelings. Perhaps there was more to Deydie than glares and being crotchety. Perhaps there was a loving soul underneath all her thorny barbs.

Chapter Four

Brodie wasn't the type to escape into the whisky, but the call to get stinking drunk was powerful right now. He stood at a crossroads—go to the pub and knock back a few so he could survive the night with Rachel in his house, or go home and help Grandda survive the evening with a little girl running about. A third option—disappearing again—was the most compelling, but Brodie wasn't one to shirk his responsibilities, especially when it came to his grandfather. He headed home.

When he walked in, he heard Abraham coughing. He hurried into the parlor. Hannah was covering up the old man with a quilt Deydie had made for him. Brodie thought the quilt made up of boat blocks had been insensitive of the old quilter since Grandda could no longer fish, but Abraham always seemed comforted to have it near.

"I'll get ye a cup of honey lemon tea," Brodie said from the doorway.

The girl looked up and gave him a concerned nod, as if she were the old man's matronly nurse. "That would be grand." She climbed up next to Abraham and patted his arm.

The cough calmed. "Thank ye, lass."

She leaned up against her grandda, and something in

Brodie's chest tugged uncomfortably. He shifted his gaze and left for the kitchen.

Once the kettle was on, he stared out the window. He'd have to talk to Doc MacGregor about what could be done for his grandfather, though he already knew the answer. He'd been under the care of the doctor for months. It didn't help it was winter now, which was making his cough worse.

When the tea was ready, he fixed a tray and returned to the parlor. Abraham had dozed off. Quietly, Brodie set the tray on the side table beside the old man, remembering to leave the vial there from Bethia as well. He didn't make eye contact with the little girl, but took the wing chair across from them.

Hannah slipped off the couch, grabbed her *guzzy* from the coffee table, and boldly came across the room to him. Without his permission, she scrambled into his lap and stuck a thumb in her mouth. Brodie didn't know what to do. He sat there like a wooden chair. She snuggled in deeper. He glanced down at her face and saw she'd closed her eyes. Finally he wrapped one arm around her . . . to make sure she didn't fall off his lap.

A million thoughts zoomed through his mind. Why was this little girl acting this way with him? And was she always so trusting of strangers? He'd have to talk to Rachel about this, but the prospect of talking to her about anything seemed unlikely. He didn't trust himself when it came to her—Rachel set his blood to boiling for what she'd done to him in the past, and at the same time, he wanted to know why she was wearing his locket. Frankly, he was afraid of what the answer might be. He had to remain strong. Fight off this urge to be near her and find out the inner workings of the woman she'd become.

He looked over at his grandda, wondering if Abraham would sleep long. He glanced down again at the little girl . . . Hannah. She was a gentle little thing. Rachel must've babied her and someone should toughen her up. Maybe Brodie should take her fishing in the summer. His chest felt tight, more uncomfortable than before at the realization Hannah wouldn't be here long. Besides, he shouldn't be the one to teach her how to fish. That was a father's job. It should be Joe here holding his daughter, not him.

The front door opened.

"I'm back," Rachel said, and the child stirred awake.

Instinctively, he slipped the girl from his lap, nearly dumping the lass on the floor. He couldn't let Rachel find him holding her daughter.

"Mommy?" She found her feet and ran for the doorway the minute Rachel appeared. "Guzzy took a nap." She peered back at Brodie, smiling. "Only a *wee* one."

The child was quick; he'd have to hand it to her. She'd picked up on the word from Abraham and said it with just the right lilt.

"It's good ye're back," Brodie said quietly, but firmly. He got to his feet. Rachel watched his every move, her eyes traveling up the length of him. He tried to ignore her, and at the same time, he needed to deliver his message concisely and clearly. "I've things to do. *Babysitting isn't one of them.*" He moved toward the doorway.

"Thank you for watching Hannah," Rachel said, just as quietly.

"And guzzy," the child added.

Rachel stepped in his path. "From now on, I'll make sure to take her wherever I go."

"Nay," Abraham said with a scratchy voice, his eyes still closed. "The *wee* bit is no trouble."

Brodie was a little taken aback. Had his grandfather been awake the whole time?

"Go on now, lad, and check the boat," Grandda ordered, pinning him with rheumy eyes. "The lasses and I have things to discuss."

The words stopped Brodie in his tracks. But he left the house anyway, wondering, *What is the old man up to?*

Thirty minutes later, sitting across from Abraham, Rachel still clutched Deydie's plaid scraps, frustrated with Hannah's great-grandfather. No amount of argument would dissuade him from his tack. But she had to convince him that what he proposed was wrong. *Very wrong.* She moved over to where he sat while Hannah wrapped her guzzy around the doll Glenna had gifted her. Rachel laid a hand on the old man's arm. "I promise we're fine. Better than fine." She lowered her voice. "The life insurance was substantial." Though she hadn't touched it in the three years since Joe's death.

"It's the right thing to do," Abraham said. "When I leave this mortal coil, half the fishing business will go to Hannah. End of story."

Rachel shook her head. Not only because she disapproved of what he was trying to do, but she could only imagine how Brodie would take the news. "If you're going to be stubborn"—she could be hard-nosed, too—"then you'll just have to live forever."

The old man laughed heartily, but then she regretted her jab when his merriment turned into a coughing fit. She grabbed Bethia's vial from the side table, opened it, and put it into his hand. "Here. Sniff this. It should help."

After a while, he calmed down. Hannah retrieved his water cup, spilling only a little in the process as she handed it to her great-grandfather. As Rachel wiped the dribble from the hardwood floor, she thought about Brodie and how she would broach the subject of the fishing business with him. If anyone could convince Abraham to rethink his asinine plan, Brodie could. Hannah owning half the fishing business while Brodie did all the work was wrong.

Speaking with Brodie about picking up where the two of them had left off six years ago would have to wait. Abraham's bombshell took precedence. *Best to clear that up first.*

In the past, Rachel would do anything to avoid confrontation and difficult conversations, but there was something about Scotland that had her feeling more capable and confident. As soon as she could get Hannah into bed, she'd find Brodie, and at least this one thing, they'd get settled between them.

And maybe while they did, she could further her cause and let him know she still cared for him.

The front door opened and slammed shut. Brodie appeared in the parlor doorway. He took in the scene.

"What's wrong?" he asked her.

"I'm off to bed," Abraham said, coughing as if emphasizing his sudden need to lie down.

Rachel didn't believe it for a second because it didn't sound like the genuine fit of earlier. "Are you afraid he'll talk some sense into you?" she said to the old man as he passed.

He kept walking, but he did respond, firmly, but not unkindly. "Mind yere elders. Ye're in Scotland now and ye can't sass whenever ye like." He disappeared.

Rachel was left alone with Brodie and Hannah.

"Can I have a snack?" Her daughter had great timing. Hiding out in the kitchen would be good, for Brodie was sure to yell the cottage roof off when he learned what his grandfather intended for the business.

"Biscuits are on the table," Brodie said.

Hannah frowned at him.

"Cookies," Rachel provided.

Hannah took her doll and headed from the room.

Rachel placed her tartan scraps on the side table and then moved closer to Brodie, gathering her thoughts—possibly courage—and not meeting his eyes.

"Out with it," he said. "What's troubling ye?"

She turned around slowly, choosing her words one at a time. "Has your grandfather spoken with you about the future? What he has in mind?"

Brodie frowned. "Concerning?"

Rachel was getting used to that frown. "Concerning the fishing business. After he's gone."

"What about it?" His mouth transformed into a hard straight line, as if bracing himself to hear a bad weather report.

Rachel sat, crossed her legs, trying to look relaxed. "He thinks Hannah, being Joe's daughter, should get half the fishing business when he passes on." There. She'd spit it out.

Brodie's body expanded, or at least that's what it felt like. He was red in the face, too. Scots were known for their tempers, and she wished he would remember there was a little girl in the other room before he exploded. He turned, giving her his back, and was silent for a long moment. Finally, he spoke. "Aye. It's only right the lass gets half."

"What?" Rachel shouted. "You agree with him?"

"It's her birthright," Brodie said.

"You Scots are all nuts. Hannah needs half of a fishing business as much as she needs a Ferrari and an e-cigarette factory."

"What?"

"Never mind. Well, I'm Hannah's mother, and I say she can't have it."

Brodie raised an eyebrow as if she was the one who was cracked instead of him and Abraham.

"We don't need your money," she said. "I do fine on my own."

"This has nothing to do with money," he said. "Weren't ye listening? It's what is right to do. Joe is gone. Hannah will get his half."

"But it's wrong." Rachel looked Brodie over, from one bulging muscle to the other. "You're the one doing all the work." She didn't need to say it; it was glaringly apparent.

Hannah wandered back into the room with a cookie in each hand and crumbs around her mouth.

"How many did you have?" Rachel asked.

Hannah shoved another cookie in her full mouth as if to get rid of the evidence.

"Where's your doll?"

Hannah smiled and more cookie crumbs fell out. "Left her in the kitchen. She likes these cookies."

"You need a bath," Rachel said.

He cleared his throat. "Towels are in the linen closet."

Rachel scooped up Hannah and glanced back at him. "We're not done talking."

He gave her that eyebrow-raising thing again, which said, *I think we are.*

"Not by a long shot." She took Hannah up the stairs with every intent of picking up where she left off when her daughter was in bed. But after a good scrubbing, retrieving dolly from downstairs, and reading a story, Brodie was gone. Either he'd left the house or was hiding behind his closed bedroom door.

Chicken. She wanted to tell him why she was wearing the locket. But actually, she felt a little relieved not to have to do it yet. It was one thing for her to be hell-bent on having a future with Brodie, but it was quite another to blurt it out and take him off guard. He might reject her outright just from the shock of it. Wearing his locket was the perfect subtle hint that they belonged together.

It was best if he had time to adjust to the idea first before they had their heart-to-heart talk.

She went to the whisky cabinet and made herself at home by taking down a tumbler and pulling out the Glenfiddich. She wasn't tired in the least—jet lag—but knew if she didn't get some sleep that teaching at Quilting Central in the morning was going to be tough. Also, she'd need all her strength to deal with Deydie, who was sure to critique her every move.

"Want to make me one, too?"

She jumped at the rumble of Brodie's baritone.

"It's not polite to sneak up on people."

He gave her a look that said he wanted to remind her of the impolite things she'd done to him. "How long are ye staying?" It sounded more like, *When are ye leaving?*

Rachel wasn't one for taking a vacation. She'd accrued an enormous amount of time off. Before leaving Winderly Towers, she'd handed over the reins to the capable assistant manager, and had left her return date open-ended. She'd guessed she'd stay a week or two. But now, standing here with Brodie in front of her, she wanted to answer him with, *I'm staying for as long as it takes.*

"I don't know," she said honestly.

His eyes dropped to her chest, where subconsciously she had been rubbing the locket between her fingers.

It would've been the perfect time to bring up how she hated the way she'd left things between them six years ago. But she needed that drink first. More air in her lungs, too.

She took down another tumbler, poured in a bit of whisky in both, and a splash of water. She quit biting her lip before she turned and gave him his glass.

"What should we drink to?" she asked bravely.

He gave her a hard stare. "How about to winding up

yere business here quickly and to ye going home?" He didn't wait to clink glasses, but knocked his drink back as he walked from the room.

Brodie set his glass in the sink, turned on the faucet, and didn't realize he'd let the water run so long until his fingers were nearly scalded. How was he going to survive Rachel's visit in Gandiegow? Hell, how was he going to survive the night?

He washed the tumbler and set it in the drainer to dry. He wanted to go to the pub and knock back a few more, but he had an early morning ahead and Tuck on the boat to contend with as well. As long as Tuck did his job and didn't want to talk about Rachel, they would get along fine.

Brodie had to pass the parlor on his way to the stairs. He wouldn't let himself look in to see if Rachel was still drinking alone or if she'd gone up already. He was grateful the little girl was in the cottage. Having Joe's daughter here was a great deterrent, keeping Brodie from checking in on Rachel and tucking her into her bed. *Or tucking her into mine.*

Brodie trudged up the steps, thinking it might be a long sleepless night. At the top, he didn't expect the bathroom door to open and for Rachel to run into him.

"Oh!" She pushed away from his chest, but he caught her arms to keep her from stumbling.

Oh hell. She smelled great. *Woman and soap.* Her scrubbed face had been washed of the makeup she wore. She looked young. Enticing. All it would take was one pull on the tie of her robe to reveal what she had on underneath. In her hand, she held a small case. On her feet she wore fuzzy slippers, and he could see the bottom hem of her flannel pajamas—sheep lining the cuffs. The pajamas shouldn't have looked sexy to his crazy eyes, but they were.

She stared at him, searching his face. He wondered what she saw there. Could she see he was at war with himself? He should let her go. But as he wrestled with the decision, she reached up and gently pushed his hair away from his face, then left her hand resting on his cheek.

"Brodie?" Her voice was filled with earnestness.

Her hand was warm and it was as if six years had slipped away . . . to when they'd kissed. A torturous time warp. But six years ago, she hadn't been wearing his locket.

"No." He stepped back, being the one who stumbled. He couldn't do this to himself. Not again. He held his head high and stomped to his door, slamming it behind him. Immediately he regretted it. He might've woken Grandda, and the little girl.

He stood fuming in his room for a long moment, wanting to go back in the hallway, wanting her to implore him with her eyes again. Wanting her to touch him as she had. She was putting him through hell. But it was the call of nature that had him venturing from his room. He entered the loo and flipped on the light switch and stopped cold. God help him, her black bra was looped over the towel rack, displayed like some peepshow advertisement. He nearly roared. Had she done it to torment him further? Like she'd done by wearing his locket?

He couldn't leave her sexy contraption here. He pulled the hand towel from the rack, and without touching the offending bit of lingerie, he used the towel like oven mitts to pick up the bra. He didn't know what to do next. He couldn't very well knock on Rachel's door and give it to her right now. He'd wake the girl. Instead, he hid the garment within the towel, shoved it under his arm, and walked across the hall. He hooked it on her doorknob, not caring one damn bit if she was embarrassed about it hanging there when she discovered it in the morning.

He still needed to take a piss. He stomped back to the bathroom, thinking about how life had become a lot more complicated since the two females had arrived. What the hell would tomorrow bring?

Indeed, Brodie had a sleepless night. Mornings come early to fishermen, but with little to no sleep, it made getting up for the boat more of a chore than what it was normally—a blessing. In the hallway, outside Rachel's room, the bra still hung on her doorknob. Not touching it, Brodie laid his ear against the door, wondering if she'd slept like a babe while he'd been tied in knots all night. He heard nothing from the other side and forced himself to get on with his morning.

Soon Brodie stood on the dock, waiting for Tuck. "Screw it." He stepped onto his boat, ready to cast off.

"Hold up." Tuck was waving his arms and running toward the boat. He hopped aboard just in time.

Brodie walked to the wheelhouse, talking over his shoulder. "Do I need to remind ye the catch waits for no man?"

Tuck laughed, but got right to work. Once underway, the bloke was such good help that Brodie nearly forgot about him being late.

As they made their way to the next fishing spot, a storm unfortunately blew in, cutting the morning run short. Unfortunate for both Brodie's bank account and his peace of mind.

When they pulled back into Gandiegow, Tuck jumped off and secured the lines as well as any seasoned fisherman. But no sooner did Brodie have that thought than his day worker went and ruined it.

"How's about I come back to yere house and have a cup of coffee. Or tea." He shot Brodie a cocky grin. "I hear the bird and her daughter are at *yere* cottage. I'm feeling thirsty."

"No," Brodie said with force.

"I see." Tuck laughed. "Want to keep her all for yereself?"

That wasn't it at all. Brodie wanted to wipe the deck with Tuck's grin. Instead he ignored the bastard and stepped off the boat, marching toward home.

His mood didn't improve once he opened the front door either. The scene hit him like gale force winds. The cottage had been transformed from good old-fashioned male starkness to *bluidy* female warmth.

Hannah's pink backpack hung over the newel post and her *guzzy* was draped over the banister. Her new ragdoll was sitting on the bottom step like it was resting there before making the climb upstairs. Her cute pink puffy coat hung on the hook. His eyes fell on her black boots with the multicolored stars, sitting right where he'd told her to leave them yesterday. But they irritated the hell out of him. It all irritated him. Why? Because it looked like Hannah had *bluidy* well moved in. But it wasn't only Hannah's things. Evidence of Rachel was everywhere. Her coat hung next to her daughter's. Some sort of woman's novel was resting on the side table, which should only have the day's mail and an extra set of the keys for the boat on it. And the smell! God help him. Rachel's scent had taken up residence in his nostrils and he hadn't walked two steps indoors yet. It was enough to make a man want to run for the hills . . . and become a monk.

Laughter drifted to his ears in the entryway—wee laughter, followed by adult female laughter. Could he take much more?

He sat on the bench, removed his boots, and chucked them onto the mat. He stalked into the kitchen and found the blasted females entertaining his grandda around the small table loaded with the most delicious-looking breakfast. Made more delicious because he hadn't been the one to cook it. Scrambled eggs topped with cheese. Toast. Mugs of coffee. The girl's must have been cocoa. They all smiled up at him as he blew into the room.

But it was Rachel's smile that affected him strangely. The partridge on his chest warmed as if she was a bit of sunshine on this gloomy winter day.

He poured a cup of coffee for himself and stood at the counter, farthest away from her.

Abraham pointed at the slatted basket. "When ye walk the lasses to Quilting Central, take that along for Deydie. It was my mother's, ye know. Her prized possession. Deydie's had her eye on it for some time. I think she wants to stack fabric in it. I might as well pass it along now, as I won't get a chance to do it later."

His grandda had changed, turned maudlin while Brodie had been hiding out at Here Again Farm. The moment Brodie got wind that Grandda was ill, he moved home to take care of him and the fishing business. The congestion in his chest seemed to never get better and Brodie suspected that being ill for so long had done a number on his grandfather's mental state, too. One by one, Grandda had been giving away the possessions he thought others might want. At first, Brodie tried to ignore the final orders his grandda gave him, about what to do with this bit and that. But over time, Brodie had started to accept the truth. Maybe the old man's time was nearing. But what the Almighty didn't understand was that Brodie couldn't let his grandfather go; he just couldn't do without him.

Begrudgingly, Brodie went to the basket. "Are ye ready then?" he said to the females.

"Aye," Hannah said, hopping up.

"Aye?" Rachel said to her daughter, shaking her head and smiling. She stood and faced his grandfather with concern on her face. "Will you be all right?"

It was shite like this that really inflamed Brodie. She shouldn't give a whit about his grandda. *She hadn't given a whit about me back in the day.* Also, Abraham had drilled it into Brodie's head from the time he was a wee lad that women cared only about themselves—always leaving, never sticking, never standing by their men. Rachel was behaving as if a leopard could change her spots.

"I'll be fine. Doc said he'll be by to check in on me."

Brodie didn't like it either that Grandda had stopped walking to the surgery. The exercise was good for him, but at the same time he understood how the frigid weather wasn't always kind to weak lungs.

With basket in hand, Brodie stalked to the front door. Rachel and Hannah could find their own way to Quilting Central, but he found himself waiting anyway.

The girl chatted all the way to where the quilters gathered on a daily basis. Brodie only half listened. When they walked in the door, Deydie frowned in their direction.

"What's up with her?" Rachel asked. "She told me to come to teach."

Deydie waddled over to them. "Young One, go get a scone over there at the table. Amy will pour ye some hot tea to go with it."

Hannah skipped away with her ragdoll held tightly to her chest. When she was out of earshot, Deydie turned on Rachel. "*She* wasn't part of the deal."

What the hell. "What do you have against the girl?" Brodie blurted.

Rachel appeared muted with bewilderment. Two seconds later, her face reddened as the old woman's meaning sank in. Rachel spun on her as if she wasn't scared of Deydie's notorious broom in the least. "Why can't Hannah stay?"

"Because she can't." Deydie seemed unwavering. "Before ye go off in a huff, we have a deal. Ye're the one who made it."

"Forget the deal," Rachel said on a growl.

"What deal?" Brodie said, before he remembered this had nothing to do with him. It was as if some twisted sense of gallantry had charged forth and taken over.

"What's it to ye?" Deydie said, eyeing him. She jabbed her thumb in Rachel's direction. "*She* said she'd teach a class for a stack of tartan scraps." The matriarch quilter glowered at Rachel. "A deal's a deal, dammit."

Rachel glared, not backing down. "My daughter stays with me."

Brodie admired the lass for standing up to the quilting harridan. He couldn't think of another person who was fool enough to do it.

But then the old she-badger swung on him. "Brodie, take the girl to Abraham's."

"Why me?" But he knew the answer.

"Because ye're family," Deydie said.

Why the hell had he come in with them? He looked down at his grandfather's basket still in his hand. "Here." He thrust it at Deydie. "Grandda wanted ye to have it."

The old woman took it, nodding.

Brodie looked from Rachel to Hannah, then back to Rachel. He felt like the only levelheaded one in the room, but he wouldn't do anything without her permission. Rachel was, after all, Hannah's mother. "Ye know Grandda would love to spend the day with the lass."

Rachel was silent. He could tell she hated giving in to Deydie, and at the same time, he was making a lot of sense. "I give my word no harm will come to yere bairn." As soon as he said it, he wanted to kick himself. He owed Rachel nothing. *Nothing.*

But at his words, Rachel's shoulders relaxed. Her eyes

went all soft on him and it was too *effing* late to renege. He guessed he could get Amy or Moira to look in on Abraham and the girl to make sure they were okay while Rachel was busy.

She chewed her lip, looking from him to Deydie. "All right. But tell Abraham to call if he needs me . . . for any reason. Any reason at all."

Brodie thought about Doc coming to check on Grandda, a piece of information that Rachel must've forgotten during the quarrel. Hell, he could watch the kid for a few minutes while Gabe took Abraham's temperature and blood pressure, and listened to his chest. "I'll let the lass know she's to leave with me." Anything to get away from Rachel while she gazed upon him as if he was her champion . . . her knight in shining armor. He wasn't; he was just going to walk her daughter down a few houses and leave her with Abraham.

He stalked over to the small café table. The little bit was stuffing a big chunk of blueberry scone in her mouth when he sidled up to her.

"Slow down there. Ye don't want to choke."

She gave him a smile filled with crumbs that spilled into her lap.

"Ye're to come away with me, back to sit with yere great-grandda for the day. Do ye ken?"

She crinkled up her nose. "Ken?"

"It means, *do ye understand.* Come now."

She hopped out of her chair and planted her hand in his as if he'd offered. Which he hadn't. She acted like she'd known him forever. Which was so far off the mark. He might be family, but didn't she know a stranger? Was she always this trusting of everyone?

He wanted to shake her grip loose—perhaps shake Rachel, too, for getting him in this mess—but he supposed he was stuck.

On the way to the door, Hannah stopped in front of her mother. "I'm going back home to sit with Grandda. Do ye ken?"

Brodie sighed exasperatedly as Rachel stared at *him*. As if he had anything to do with what the lass said. He put his hands up. "Don't blame me." The lass was a gifted parrot, he'd give her that. She'd said it perfectly with the same inflection he'd used.

Hannah grinned at her mother. "See you later, alligator."

"All right, you. I'll let you go, but be good for your grandfather. Please." Rachel might have a smile for her daughter, but she gave Brodie a meaningful glance as the wind howled outside. He interpreted it with ease . . . *take care of my girl.*

Outside, he kept a grip on Hannah's hand, hyperaware that she could blow away as strong as the wind was and with her as little as a mite. He wasn't strong enough for this kind of worry. Once Doc was done with Abraham, Brodie would hand the girl off and be free. He had no big plans. Maybe he could make himself useful and wait tables at the restaurant. Or drive just outside of town, up to the North Sea Valve Company, and take on extra chores there.

But back at home, he found Doc helping Abraham on with his coat. "What's going on here?" Maybe they were headed over to the surgery. "Gabe, did ye forget one of yere instruments?" Brodie glanced outside; Abraham shouldn't be exposed to this weather.

Gabe shot Brodie a serious expression, like the engine on the boat needed a complete overhaul and not just a couple of spark plugs replaced. "I'm taking yere grandfather to Inverness for an X-ray."

"X-ray? Why?" It was a dumb question, but panic made Brodie ask nonetheless.

"As a precaution," Gabriel said. "I want to make sure he hasn't developed pneumonia."

"I'll take him," Brodie said. Grandda was his responsibility.

"Nay," Gabe said firmly. "I have to be there. I'll want to read it myself."

Now Brodie was really worried.

Hannah tugged on his hand. He'd forgotten about her. "Grandda is going to be fine. Right, Doc?"

What was it with this kid that she had to copy him at every turn?

"Listen to the child," Doc said. He knelt down beside her and stuck out his hand as if she were an adult instead of a bit. "I'm Gabe."

"I'm Hannah. Brodie's cousin." She grinned at him with her irresistible smile that could charm a hungry polar bear.

"I heard ye'd come to town, Hannah," Gabe said. "I promise to take good care of yere great-grandda."

"I know ye will," Hannah said, her brogue perfect.

Gabe patted her head and stood. He addressed Brodie. "Maybe Hannah would like to play with Glenna over at the parsonage?"

"Ye're a genius." Brodie breathed a sigh of relief. "Thank you." He could dump her there, then catch up with Gabriel and head to the hospital with them.

Hannah hugged Grandda and then took Brodie's hand again as they walked to Father Andrew and Moira's house. But when they got there, Andrew was pulling his front door shut with him on the outside. "What can I do for you, Brodie? I was heading out to make a call."

Brodie glanced down at the child beside him. "I was wondering if Glenna was home."

Andrew gave him a confused look. "Nay. She's at school."

"Oh," Brodie said, feeling stupid. "Of course she's in school. Thanks."

As Andrew walked away, Brodie frowned down at the girl. "So . . . what do ye want to do?"

She screwed up her little face as if she was thinking hard. Finally, she answered, "Have a tea party."

"Tea party?" He wasn't quite sure what that entailed. He guessed he could make her some tea.

The girl seemed to read his mind. "We'll have one like Mommy and I have." Hannah hopped up and down. "We'll have so much fun. But ye'll have to do what Mommy does."

"What does yere mother do?" he asked, circumspect.

"We both put on our pretty dresses, sit on the floor, and drink tea with our pinkies up." The kid demonstrated how she sipped tea . . . as if she were the blasted Queen!

"Ye expect me to put on a dress?" he asked, horrified.

"Aye," the girl said. "Why shouldn't ye?"

"Because I'm a *bluidy* man."

Hannah raised an eyebrow at him as the wind nearly picked her up and blew her away. He clutched her hand tighter. He shouldn't have raised his voice and he shouldn't have sworn.

"Let's get home," he groused, worried about her, even though she wasn't his. He felt sorry for the girl also. Did her mother abandon her often to strangers? Brodie suspected she did. He was stirred up and indignant for the little girl and decided he would tell Rachel how she was doing things all wrong.

All the way back to the cottage, Hannah chattered away as if she didn't have a clue he was stewing. When they were safe inside, she slipped off her boots and gazed up at him.

"I'll put my party dress on, then we'll have our tea." She paused as if looking for the right word. "And biscuits?"

"Aye, biscuits." Her cuteness was starting to grate on him because he felt himself being sucked in. He hung up his coat and then frowned at her. "I'll be down in a minute."

She grinned at him. "Ye make the tea, and I'll set up the parlor."

He rolled his eyes and stomped up the stairs. What had Deydie gotten him into?

Brodie went into his room and changed for the girl. But not into a damned dress. He returned downstairs to the kitchen without her seeing him. He made the tea, carried the tray to the parlor, hoping the child would tire of this game quickly.

But as he set the tray on the coffee table, his heart went into his throat. Aye . . . she'd set up their tea by spreading out her *guzzy* on the floor. Her new ragdoll was propped up into a sitting position with the help of a few books from the shelf. Hannah sat on a pillow and had laid out a pillow for him as well. But it was the other person attending the tea that really had Brodie speechless.

Joe.

His cousin's picture took the fourth spot at their make-believe table, the picture resting on its kickstand with clean-cut Joe overseeing the proceedings.

"Ye did dress up," Hannah said, surprising him.

Brodie glanced down at his kilt. "It's not a party dress like yereself, but it's the best I could do." He took his place like a proper gentleman.

"I like it. It's a pretty skirt," Hannah said innocently.

Brodie *tsked* her harshly. "Nay. 'Tis a kilt. Warrior's attire." He pounded his chest with one hand, right where the partridge was, but he softened his tone with an in-kling of a grin, and added a wink so as not to scare the child.

Hannah nodded approvingly, but then turned her gaze to Joe's picture. "Was my daddy a warrior, too?"

"Aye." At one time when they were lads. "When we played clan wars, he would insist on being the Chieftain."

"What's a chieftain?"

"He's the head of the clan."

"And what part did ye play?" she asked.

"Whatever yere father told me to be. He was the older one." By nineteen days. Joe had a way of always taking control, which had been fine as kids, but became a problem as they grew into men. Not just for Brodie. Others saw it, too. Joe always wanting his way, never having compassion toward others as he should've. Or empathy. It could've been what happened to him, or it could've been who he really was. As an adult, Joe had a smooth, hard outer shell. One of the reasons Brodie knew from the start that Rachel wasn't right for his cousin. Joe needed someone who wanted the same things . . . wealth, status, shallow dreams. Rachel seemed to only want . . . love. The thought made Brodie's chest hurt. Or maybe it was the truth.

In the end, Brodie found out he'd been wrong about her.

He motioned to the picture of Joe. "Do ye take the picture with ye wherever ye go?"

Hannah shrugged. "I've never been anywhere but here. Daddy sits right beside my bed in our hotel room. Mommy and I say a prayer for him every night that he's happy in heaven."

Brodie wasn't exactly sure that was where Joe had gone. Which wasn't the Christian thought he should have toward the dead, and his cousin *ta boot*. But Brodie knew more things about Joe than others did. On his stag night, Joe seemed pretty sober when he'd led *the entertainment* upstairs to the room over the pub and didn't return for some time. Brodie wondered if infidelity kept you out of heaven or not.

"So yere mother," Brodie broached carefully, "she loved ye da very much?"

Hannah took a sip of her tea. "Nay."

Nay? Her Scottish burr was cute as hell, but Brodie was reeling from her answer.

"Mommy said she and Daddy didn't live together."

"Didn't live together?" Brodie said incredulously. Was that an American thing?

"I was little and don't remember, but Mommy says we lived at the hotel where we live now, and Daddy lived in his house."

What a strange arrangement. But then again, Yanks did have their odd thinking.

"Mommy and Daddy were getting a divorce."

An anchor fell on Brodie's chest.

The girl reached over and laid a hand on his cheek. "It's okay. Mommy said they both loved me very much. She talks about it all the time." And then as if reciting, *"Just because two parents can't be married, doesn't mean you weren't loved. Even now in heaven, your daddy loves you very much."*

Brodie felt both strange relief and a little choked up. Rachel had kept Joe alive for their little girl. It was the most heroic thing he'd ever heard of—for Rachel to put aside any animosity she felt for Hannah's sake. Brodie knew Joe and was sure there had been animosity. Plus, he'd seen what others had gone through. When the Mac-Murrays separated, they fought and put their kids in the middle. When they finally moved away with the two of them divorced, their family and their children had been ripped to shreds. Rachel, from Hannah's account, was a saint compared to the dysfunctional MacMurrays, and Brodie's opinion of her rose a little from the muck and mire he'd buried her in the last six years.

"Can ye pour Daddy a cup of tea? He looks thirsty."

Brodie frowned at the lass, but did as she asked. Next, dolly needed a cup of tea and two biscuits, because *she is extra hungry*. He noticed the girl was helping Dolly knock off her snacks. For a moment, he worried he was letting the lass spoil her lunch, but what did he care. It was Rachel's problem, and Deydie should take the blame.

Hannah corrected him repeatedly about how to hold his pinky, and regaled him with the adventures from the hotel. He started to relax and enjoy himself.

Brodie decided the girl wasn't so bad after all. She was his cousin and he could like one of his relations without betraying himself. He could separate mother and daughter in his mind . . . because at the end of the day, he still didn't give a rat's ass about Hannah's mother. But his resolve didn't bring any comfort and he felt all alone in his turmoil. Surely no one else was as miserable as he was in his unforgiving heart.

Chapter Five

Grace Armstrong was miserable as she pushed a loaded wheelbarrow through Gandiegow, heading to Quilting Central. She couldn't help glancing this way and that, hating herself for looking about like some lovesick seal, searching for her mate. She'd been in town a day, but had yet to see retired Reverend Casper MacGregor. She needed to stop being such a ninny. So they'd spent time together after Andrew and Moira's wedding—talking and laughing—into the wee hours of the morning. That had been five months ago and she still couldn't get him out of her mind. The fact that Casper had moved to Gandiegow to help with his grandchildren—Gabriel's boy, Angus, and Dominic's daughter, Nessa—had nothing to do with her deciding to move home. Without Glynnis to care for, Grace had no reason to stay in Glasgow. She was needed here to help with her own grandchildren, even though John and Maggie, her daughter-in-law, seemed to have things well in hand with Dand and baby Irene. Grace looked up at the steeple of the kirk. It was only coincidence that her decision to move home happened after Casper was already settled here.

She sighed. Really, she was too old and too wise to believe the time she'd spent with Casper had been magical.

The wedding had played a trick on them, like weddings had a tendency to do. Besides, she was the fifty-eight-year-old widowed mother of three grown men—John, Ross, and Ramsay—all married, and settled.

She let her eyes fall on the things in the wheelbarrow—her sewing machine, her projects-in-progress, and a container of sewing notions. These things were enough. These things and her family. Her grandchildren and working at the Kilts and Quilts retreat would occupy her time. She had plenty to do without losing sleep and wasting precious hours worrying over a man.

This feeling will pass. She said these words so often to herself that they had become her mantra.

The door opened to the General Store. Adrenaline rushed through her system and she spun around fast enough to make a top dizzy. But it was only Dougal, the postie, coming out with his mailbag over his shoulder.

She felt utterly stupid for letting her feelings run rampant like some hormonal teenager. Rome wasn't built in a day. A complicated quilt couldn't be pieced together overnight either.

She put Quilting Central in her sights and steamed ahead without looking this way and that anymore. It would take time, but her little crush on Casper Mac-Gregor would fade. He was just a novelty to her. A crazy fantasy playing tricks with her heart. She was a strong Scottish woman, and she would get over Casper if it was the last thing she did.

Rachel nodded at Grace as she came through the door, but then turned back to Deydie, who was onstage welcoming the out-of-town quilters to the retreat.

She still couldn't believe she'd let the old woman make her get rid of Hannah like that. She had enough guilt about her daughter growing up in daycare, and now, the first vacation she'd had since Hannah was born, and her poor daughter was once again thrust upon strangers.

But Abraham isn't a stranger; he's family. Rachel only wished she'd told Brodie to call when he dropped Hannah off.

Bethia joined Rachel. "The lass'll be fine. Just fine."

"Why wouldn't Deydie let Hannah be here with me?" It seemed such a small thing.

Bethia patted her hand. "If I had to guess, it's because yere daughter reminds her too much of Joe. Deydie didn't take Joe's death well. It was hard on her . . . still is. Did ye know she cared for him as an infant when his mother ran off? And she helped out with him as a lad, too. She was attached to that boy. We all were."

Yes, it was a reason, but it stung that Hannah was not included but instead cast out.

"Give Deydie some time." Bethia glanced across the room to where Moira gave her a half wave. "Excuse me. I have to speak with her for a moment."

As she hurried off, two gray-headed twins, dressed in matching red and green plaid dresses, rushed over to Rachel, each with a brown sack in their arms. They kept glancing over their shoulder nervously in Deydie's direction.

"I'm Ailsa," the green plaid lady said.

"And I'm Aileen."

Ailsa leaned in conspiratorially. "Sister and I have brought you a gift."

"They're extras. But ye can't let Deydie know we gave them to you," the red plaid twin said.

They shoved their sacks at her. Rachel started to peer inside, but Ailsa stilled her hand.

"Not here."

Aileen shook her head, glancing around, more nervous than before. "Later. Look at them later."

Ailsa grabbed her sister's arm and they scurried off.

Rachel was more than curious, but she didn't get a chance to take a peek.

"Rachel!" Deydie hollered from the stage. "Stop yabbering. Do ye need to use the copy machine to make the templates for that tree?"

"Yes," she answered.

"Hurry it up then. Be sure to make a test copy. Ye never know with copiers if the size will be correct. It's always better to measure twice," Deydie said to the room. All the women nodded.

Rachel retrieved the template for her Christmas Tree quilt, the one she'd traced last night. When she saw the color copier, she was struck with an idea of what to get Abraham for Christmas. She'd print out the family picture they'd taken together and have it framed. He would love it. But Rachel might have to make another deal with the devil . . . or his closest relative in Gandiegow— Deydie. The old woman was scowling at her from the front.

Moira joined her, sheepishly handing over a list. "Fourteen quilters would like to work on the Christmas Tree quilt. You might make twenty templates, though. Once the Christmas Tree blocks go up on the design walls, others are bound to want to make one, too."

Rachel printed out the first template. Moira handed her a ruler to make sure it measured correctly.

"I've got a question." Christmas was only a few days away. "Who should I ask if I want to use the copier to make a photo for Abraham?"

Moira smiled. "Help yereself. Cait said we should all consider the equipment as our own. Deydie is certainly putting ye to work for it."

"Thanks."

Rachel ran off the next nineteen. *Just in time, too.* Deydie was ready for her to take the stage.

Rachel spent the morning showing the quilters how to make the star at the top of the tree, using half-square triangles. She also admired the UFOs the others had brought with them. Most were complicated patterns from kits, though many of the Gandiegow women were designing and sewing their own quilts, too.

At one point, Deydie ordered Rachel off the stage so she could make announcements about the rest of the day. Rachel took the opportunity to grab her coat, the two sacks from the matronly twins, and slip out the door. She needed to check on her daughter, no matter what Deydie said.

Outside, the storm had kicked into high gear. She held the bags close, hoping whatever was in the sacks could withstand getting wet. To be safe from the crashing waves, she took the path behind the houses instead of the more direct walkway.

When she arrived at the cottage, she quietly let herself indoors, and slipped out of her wet overcoat. She peeked inside the first bag and was shocked to see tartan scraps neatly arranged in a stack. She looked in the other bag and found more plaid fabric. The gift was thoughtful. But what was Rachel going to do with these scraps?

She snuck down the hall to spy on Hannah and Abraham; the two of them had already formed a special bond. But when she peered into the parlor, she didn't see the elderly man in his chair or on the sofa. What she did find was so unexpected and surreal that she stopped breathing.

Hannah was chattering away about her daddy and her dolly. Brodie sat on the floor next to her little girl, a full participant in the crazy tea party. He was listening intently with a smile on his face while sipping from a very feminine teacup with his pinky raised in the air. But there was nothing feminine about him, quite the opposite. The scene only accentuated his masculinity to the point of making Rachel's heart turn gooey. God help her, she was a mess over him. What woman wouldn't fall for a man who was being so good to her daughter?

She started to step away, go back down the hall to let her presence be known, but her eyes fell on the barrette clipped in Brodie's long hair. Her heart squeezed and twisted and she must've sighed or done something to draw his attention, because he spun around and saw her.

He set his cup down and pulled the clip from his hair. "Party's over. Yere mum's home."

Hannah jumped up and ran to her, hugging her, and talking a mile a minute.

"Dolly and Daddy had tea with us, too. Brodie tried to be a warrior, but I told him only gentlemen can come to tea parties. He let me fix his hair and I taught him how to drink tea *properly*."

Brodie stood, giving Rachel a full view of his outfit. His tight T-shirt. His kilt. His muscular legs. The sight of him set off a series of hot sensations pulsing throughout some very personal places on her body. She thought about stepping back outside to cool off in the winter storm.

"I'll be going." He walked from the room, but stopped in the doorway, his expression serious. "But you and I need to talk."

"Wait a minute," Rachel said. "Where's Abraham?"

"Hospital."

"What? Is he all right?"

"Aye. Just an X-ray." But a worried expression crossed his hard face.

Rachel chewed her lip, worried, too. "When will he be back?" And she couldn't leave Hannah with Abraham if he was so sick as to have to go to the hospital.

"I don't know."

She couldn't take Hannah with her to Quilting Central either. Not that she was worried about Deydie lecturing her. But Rachel wouldn't put her daughter in a situation where she would feel unwanted.

"What do you have going on right now?" Rachel ventured.

Brodie's eyes narrowed. "Why are ye asking?"

"Well . . ." Rachel paused, reaching for the right words. "My time at Quilting Central isn't quite done."

"And that's my problem, how?" His eyes fell on Hannah, and he did seem truly perplexed.

"I need someone to watch her."

"We could make a fort," Hannah said, taking Brodie's hand, while still hanging on to Rachel's.

With the three of them physically linked together, Rachel couldn't help seeing the vision more vividly than before—she, Hannah, and Brodie could be a family.

"It will only be awhile longer, until Deydie lets me go."

Hannah tugged on his hand. "We could use Grandda's quilts over there in the corner. I'm sure he won't mind. When he comes back, he and Doc can sit in it with us." She batted her eyelashes at him.

Rachel wondered where she'd learned that. And her baby girl was picking up the Scots accent as if she'd been born to it. She stood back and let her daughter's magic do its work.

"I have some books ye could read to me." Hannah yawned. "I'm not tired at all." She yawned again.

Rachel turned to Brodie. "I'll put her down for a nap."

"Mommy, I said I'm not tired," Hannah whined.

"But Brodie is. We've talked about the importance of beauty sleep."

Hannah scrutinized Brodie. "He doesn't need beauty sleep. He's already pretty."

"Handsome," he growled, and then playfully added, "ruggedly."

Ruggedly handsome was the perfect way to describe him, but Rachel kept the sentiment to herself. "Do as I ask, then you and Brodie will make your fort after he gets some rest. He looks all tuckered out," she added for fun.

Even though he hadn't quite agreed to it, and he was frowning at her for good measure, she knew she wasn't putting him out too much. "I'll owe you." Several not so innocent ways of how to repay him crossed her mind and her cheeks heated up.

Brodie was watching her as if reading an open book . . . *one with large print*. But he didn't look as happy about the private thoughts playing out in her mind as she would've liked. The kisses they'd shared six years ago still burned in her memory. Their time at the ruins of Monadail Castle had been magical.

Hannah raised her arms to him. "Up."

He didn't hesitate but lifted her baby girl. For the third time today, Rachel was waylaid. Nothing in the world was sexier than a warrior gently holding a child. Especially when the child was her own.

Hannah laid her head on his shoulder. "I'll lie down. But Brodie has to come get me when he wakes up. I want to make my fort for Grandda."

"Aye, lass. I'll wake ye. I won't rest long either. Promise." But his next words were for Rachel. "You and I still need to talk about the bairn."

She was pretty sure he was going to let her have it for getting stuck babysitting, and that he didn't want a repeat of it tomorrow. Maybe if she talked extra fast, and nagged the quilters, she could make them finish their Christmas Tree quilts today. But the way the quilters were lingering over their sewing—gabbing about family, Christmas, and all sorts of things—they wouldn't be done until *next* Christmas.

"Here." Rachel put her arms out. "I'll take her up and get her settled."

"Nay," Hannah said. "I want Brodie." She squeezed him extra tight.

This time, though, Rachel felt a pang of something else. The way her daughter latched on to this man had Rachel wondering if she'd deprived Hannah of a father figure for too long. For a second, Rachel regretted not dating the last few years, but the thought passed just as quickly. She'd seen enough divorced moms at work to know what they went through—the stress of dating and raising kids at the same time. Sometimes the kids lost out.

The other something that niggled was jealousy. Rachel had been everything to Hannah, but now she seemed to have Brodie, too. The thought of sharing Hannah with someone else played uncomfortably against her wanting a second chance with the only man who had ever truly captured her heart.

Be careful what you wish for sang through her memories, something her mother used to say to Rachel when she was growing up. Her decision to talk to Brodie about starting over was feeling more complicated by the minute.

"I'll take her," he said. "But stay put. We will talk."

As he walked away with her daughter, she reached up and toyed with the necklace. Maybe she'd jumped the gun. She wasn't in her early twenties anymore, when love and romance were her greatest desire . . . to secure at all costs. She was older, wiser, and had Hannah to consider. Was she really ready to bring a man into the Girls Only Club she'd formed with her daughter?

Her inner voice barged in, *Do not second-guess yourself now. You're just scared of getting everything you ever wanted.*

Maybe that little voice was right. Maybe Rachel was letting her doubts sabotage her one chance with Brodie. Her only chance at true love.

Brodie is worth the sacrifice, the voice said. *Besides, this is it. He'll be down in a minute. He wants to talk about us.*

"Perhaps," Rachel said aloud. Right now, though, she wasn't quite sure of anything.

It took more than a minute for Brodie to get the little mite down. She insisted he sing her a song, but he refused resolutely. It wasn't that he was scared to sing to her or anyone else. Hell, every time Gandiegow gathered, they were making him stand up to sing.

It was just the ductwork in the cottage. Voices carried. Songs carried. *Other things* carried as well . . . but that was an awful memory Brodie kept locked away. He also refused to think about the heartache he'd felt when he'd heard through the vent that his mum was marrying again . . . before the snow was even melted on his da's grave.

Regardless, if he sang to Hannah now, Rachel would be able to hear and he didn't want her to get the wrong idea about things. Well, any more wrong than whatever she thought already. By the way she was looking at him with cow eyes and wearing his mum's locket, he wasn't sure what she was up to.

"Now be good and I'll be up to get ye before ye know it," he said to Hannah as he went to the door.

"Okay." By the way the little girl's eyes were drooping, she'd be asleep before he crossed the threshold.

Outside on the upstairs landing, he took a minute to figure out what he was going to say to Rachel. He was steaming mad at how trusting Hannah was, and Rachel had to know she was in the wrong of it.

He didn't stomp down the stairs, though his mood called for it. He found Rachel in the parlor, waiting, as he'd told her to do. Her fingers still clutched his mother's locket and he watched as his mood registered on her face. *Good, she has a clue.* She dropped her hand to her side.

"What's wrong?" She seemed worried and concerned. "Is it Hannah?"

"Not here." He wouldn't let the girl be subjected to their argument, through the vent or otherwise. "Step outside. I've something to say."

She glanced upward, as if seeing through the floorboards to the bedroom where her daughter napped.

"We'll stay on the porch. The bairn will be all right for a couple of minutes."

She headed for the door, and from the hook, she grabbed her jacket. He didn't, as the cold would do his ire good.

As soon as they were outside, she jumped in again. "Tell me. What's going on?"

He raised an eyebrow. "Yere daughter."

"I'm sorry you had to babysit." She seemed to be thinking about her words. "And sorry you'll have to babysit some more this afternoon. But you understand, don't you, I can't have Deydie making Hannah feel like she's unwanted at Quilting Central?"

He sighed, exasperated. "That's not it. It's you and how ye're raising that girl." The lass took to people too easily.

"What?" Rachel's pitch rose. "You don't have any right—"

He put his hand up. "First off, she doesn't know a stranger. She's too naïve. She went away with me and she doesn't know me from Adam."

Rachel shook her head adamantly. "You're family. And you're a dead ringer for Joe." Immediately her eyebrows pinched together as if her choice of words pained her. She looked away.

"Exactly. What happens when the next person who looks like Joe comes along? Is Hannah going to let him carry her off, too?"

"It's sweet you're worried about her." Rachel reached out, but he pulled away before she could touch him.

He stepped back to put distance between them. "Ye've got it all wrong."

"It's okay." She stared at him intently. "You don't know this about Hannah, but she's special."

"I know she's special." *And precious*. Though the thought made him feel weak. He was acting way too protective. Hannah wasn't *his* bairn.

"My mother and I agree on this one thing; Hannah has an excellent crap detector. I've seen her radar work a thousand times. She can sense who the bad ones are and pick out the good ones. You ought to see her at the hotel. She knows who she can trust." Rachel paused for a moment as if she was gauging whether to say more. Finally, she boldly stared into his eyes. "And she trusts you."

"That's ridiculous," he hissed. "Ye need to tell her to be more cautious of people. Which takes me to my second point: Living in a hotel, the way that ye do, how often do ye abandon yere child?" The words felt wrong the second he said them. Of course she was a good mother. That was as evident as the water in the ocean and the clouds in the sky. "I didn't—"

But Rachel had already slammed her hands on her hips. "Don't judge my parenting skills. You don't know anything about it. About me." But once again her words seemed to pain her.

But from the moment he met Rachel, he did *know* her. *Really know her.* Soul-mate-level stuff.

"You can't let anything happen to her." Brodie felt like he was pleading. Bad things could change people irrevocably, especially children. He'd seen it happen to Joe.

Rachel wasn't looking at him compassionately now. She was incensed, glaring at him like he'd accused her of neglect. Which he had, and didn't mean to.

She had more fillet knives to throw at him. "Just because my daughter is a good judge of people doesn't mean I don't watch her like a hawk. I worry over her like any other mother."

He didn't get to open his mouth to tell her she was a great mum because Rachel was on a tirade.

"Scratch that. I worry *more* than other mothers. Because I'm *both mother and father* to her. I've talked with her about the danger of strangers. I need to make this really clear . . . raising Hannah is my business." But then her features stilled as if she was weighing her words and her thoughts. She looked down like she was rethinking everything. Perhaps even her decision to come to Scotland. And she seemed lost.

He didn't like her looking like she missed her chance at the lifeboat. He wanted to pull her into his arms and assure her everything was going to all right. But he couldn't.

Dammit! He absolutely couldn't allow her to bewitch

him again. He couldn't withstand another one of her blows to his heart. He needed her gone from Gandiegow, and he knew just the thing to say to send her packing.

"Aye. Right. None of my business," he said sardonically. "Now who was it that got stuck babysitting yere daughter this morning?" The truth was he'd really enjoyed the tea party with Hannah and wouldn't take back one moment of his time with the wee lass.

Rachel huffed as well as Deydie ever did, and didn't back down when she went in for what she thought was the kill. "I never meant for you to end up at tea with your pinky in the air." As if it was an afterthought, she added the rest. "I'll make sure to pay you for your time."

She could've said anything. She could've made fun of him for the barrette Hannah insisted he wear. She could've called him Nanny McPhee. But Rachel Granger had to drive home the point and remind him of the one reason she'd married Joe six years ago instead of him. Joe was slick, smooth, successful. Brodie was nothing more than a fisherman, working on his grandda's boat. Not good enough for the likes of her then. Not good enough for her now.

Rachel walked away angry at Brodie for illuminating the hole in her plan for them to live happily ever after as a family. Why couldn't life be simpler? Why couldn't she have the man she wanted without the hassle of real life interfering? Maybe her second chance with him was nothing but a fantasy cooked up in her wishful-thinking heart.

Since Hannah's birth, Rachel had been the be-all-end-all in the household, the adult, the queen mama, the one who called the shots—the one luxury of being a single parent. The only one who ever questioned her choices was her mother, Vivienne. But Rachel had learned to become slightly deaf in that camp. Rachel liked not answering to anyone.

That little voice piped up again. *But don't couples argue about parenting?*

Yes. And money, sex, and everything else under the sun.

Then don't give up, encouraged the little voice.

Rachel would have to be more realistic going forward. They weren't a couple yet. She guessed if she and Brodie and Hannah were to be a family, she'd have to give up some of her control. Was the chance at true love worth that? *Hell, yes,* said her heart. But fairytale endings were easier to believe in when she didn't have to think about the compromises that successful marriages required.

She knew of some successful marriages—people she worked with—but the majority of her employees had failed at relationships.

Well, Rachel said to herself, *I'll just have to compromise and work with Brodie. Maybe listen to his ideas . . . and heed a few.*

She looked up to realize she'd made it back to Quilting Central.

She didn't want to go in just yet. But she couldn't stay out here either. At that moment her cell phone rang. For a second, she wondered if it wasn't Brodie calling her, wanting her to come back so he could apologize. *Just more wishful thinking.*

She pulled the phone from her coat pocket and saw it was her mother calling.

"Hi, Mom." Rachel tried to sound as sunny as the beach her mother was lying on. *With her latest beau.* Rachel didn't begrudge her mother's male companionship; her retirement had turned into an endless cycle of new men. After working all those years in hospitality and taking care of others, her mother had finally found a hobby.

Mom cleared her throat on the other end, which didn't bode well for Rachel. "A text message isn't exactly the same as hearing your voice to know you made it to Scotland safely."

No hello, just guilt.

"Sorry. We've been busy."

"Doing what? I thought you said Abraham was sick."

"It's a long story."

"I've got all day."

"What about Roberto?" Rachel said, redirecting.

"That's over."

No. "You're all alone in the Caribbean?"

"I came home to Chicago."

"You can't be alone for Christmas." More guilt piled onto Rachel. She worked all the holidays, but her mother always came to take up the slack, never missing a Christmas since Hannah was born. She'd come to the hotel and hang out with her granddaughter, then the three of them would have the special meal that Chef would cook just for them. This year, with her mother traipsing off to the island, seemed like the perfect opportunity for Rachel to bring Hannah to Scotland to visit Abraham. Vivienne was busy so Rachel didn't have to worry about her. But now she did.

"I'll be all right." But Vivienne's voice wasn't convincing.

"Come to Scotland," Rachel blurted. "We'll find some place for you to stay." When she'd gotten married in Gandiegow, her mother had stayed with one of the local quilters. Or maybe Deydie would let Vivienne have one of the vacant beds at the quilting dorms.

But just as quickly, Rachel wished she could rescind

the offer. Vivienne would be another added complication to the already complicated situation that Rachel was in.

"I believe I will," Vivienne said excitedly. "Christmas in Scotland might be just the thing to raise my spirits. I'll have to book right away. I'll text you and let you know when I'm going to arrive. I thought Gandiegow was charming when I was there before."

She must've forgotten all the sour looks she'd gotten from Deydie and the others.

Rachel thought about mentioning Brodie, but for only a millisecond. Vivienne would be all over the subject like flies on dead fish. That conversation could wait. Rachel shuddered, reliving her mother's long list of grievances when speaking of Brodie, but one stuck out above the others: *He's not good enough for you.*

Rachel sighed heavily. Christmas was turning into a disaster. "I'll tell Hannah you're coming." And maybe give Deydie and the rest of the village a heads-up. All Rachel wanted was to come to Gandiegow for Hannah to have a quiet visit with Abraham. Slip in, slip out, with no fuss.

But her idea of an easy visit had taken an off-the-map turn the moment she saw Brodie in town. Her heart still wanted that second chance, but as she said good-bye to her mother and hung up, she felt Brodie slipping through her fingers again.

She looked heavenward. "Help." It was the most straightforward and clear prayer she'd ever said.

"Are you okay?"

Rachel jumped at Cait's voice.

"Oh, hi," she said, feeling stupid for having spoken aloud. "How are you feeling? Better?"

Cait looked good, no green around her gills today.

"Aye. I'm well. Especially since I just spoke with Graham and he'll be home soon. Mattie is so excited." Cait looked excited, too.

Rachel wanted to ask whether she planned to tell Graham right away about the baby. "I'm anxious to meet Mattie. He sounds like a great kid."

Cait laughed. "He is." She paused for a second. "Since we have a moment, I wanted to let you know something about Mattie. He doesn't talk much." She looked as if she had more to say but didn't know how to go about it.

"Oh?"

"Aye. He was traumatized when he saw a boat go down over there." She pointed to the rocks at a distance from the shore. "All the fishermen drowned. Mattie had nightmares for a long time, but with therapy he seems to be getting better."

Rachel noticed Cait didn't bring up that Mattie's father had died as well. Poor kid.

"Thanks for letting me know," Rachel said.

"We better get inside before we freeze. But before we do, I have something for you." Cait gave her a Ziploc bag full of tartan scraps. "I thought you might need more for your collection."

"These are fantastic." The Buchanan plaid jumped out at Rachel as it had bright yellows in it. "Thank you so much." She smiled at Cait, but then remembered Deydie was waiting. "I better get inside. I've been gone quite a while and your grandmother might string me up if I don't get back to teaching." Rachel screwed up her face. "I kind of slipped out when she wasn't looking."

Cait laughed, looping her arm through Rachel's. "I'll grab her broom when we step in to save ye from a good whack, but I can't save you from one of Gran's famous tongue-lashings." She pulled the door open. "Good luck."

Thankfully, Deydie was busy balling out a young woman who was named Sinnie. Cait settled herself behind her sewing machine, but not before giving Rachel a wink while she safely stowed Deydie's broom under the table at her feet.

Rachel deposited her bag of plaid scraps next to her sewing machine, returned to the front, and started the next lesson. Deydie glanced up and glowered. *Uh-oh . . . busted.*

The rest of the day went well, everyone making progress on their Christmas Tree quilts. Several times, though, when Rachel returned to her sewing machine, she'd find more bags of plaid fabric scraps stashed with her things. Freda, Pippa, and Moira were brave enough to deliver their tartan scraps to Rachel in person. By the time it was late afternoon, she needed a good-sized container in which to store all her newly acquired fabric.

Deydie lumbered over and frowned at all the plaid pieces Rachel was organizing, but thankfully, said nothing about them. "Git on home to yere bairn. I expect ye back here first thing in the morn."

Rachel bit her lip, dreading the upcoming conversation. "We have to talk first."

Deydie harrumphed. "Not unless I have a cup of tea in my hand. I'm feeling a mite chilled."

"Are you coming down with something?" Rachel asked, concerned.

"I'm fine," Deydie barked. "I went outside a moment ago and the temperature's dropped. Now, what is it ye want to say?"

"I'd like a cuppa, too," Rachel said, stalling for a few more seconds. "Let's go to the kitchen area and I'll put on the kettle." Offering to help should soften up the old woman. Rachel led the way.

Once the tea was brewing in the pot, Rachel dove in. "My mother has had a change of plans and is all alone this Christmas."

"And?" Deydie acted as if she was anticipating the worst.

"She's coming here to Gandiegow and she'll need a place to stay," Rachel said. "Can she have one of the beds at the quilting dorm?"

Deydie eyed her shrewdly. "What do I get out of the deal? Do ye have any more quilts tucked away in yere luggage that we'd like to make?"

Rachel hesitated. Should she tell the old grouch about Hannah's plaid Gandiegow Fish quilt that she'd designed last night? "Can I think about it?"

"Nay. What is it ye have?"

"It's just a drawing, not a quilt yet, but it will be," Rachel said.

"Is it something us Scottish quilters would like?"

Rachel took the teapot and poured them both a cup. "It's over there."

"Well, what are ye waiting for? Go git it."

Rachel nodded and went to her purse, pulling out the drawing. She brought it back to Deydie, smoothing out the pages. "If I'd known anyone else was going to see it, I would've done a better job."

Deydie took it and examined the quilt drawing, making clucking noises as she nodded her head. Not negative sounds, which was surprising, but sounds of approval. "How quickly can ye put this together?" She shook her head. "Never mind that. Be back tonight after the evening meal. We'll help ye cut it out and ye can start the piecing."

"And my mother? She'll have a place to stay?"

Deydie tapped the drawing. "Aye."

"What about Hannah? Will you welcome her here at Quilting Central, too?"

Deydie looked as if her haggis had gone down the wrong way.

Before the old woman could shove the drawing into

her pocket, Rachel snatched it from her hand. "Hannah is part of the deal. Take it, or leave it."

"Fine. The lass can stay at Quilting Central. But shouldn't she be in school during the day?" Deydie seemed pleased to have figured out a way to pawn Hannah off on someone else.

"We're not going to be here very long." Just for Christmas. *Maybe a little longer for my second chance with Brodie.* But the school idea was interesting. "When does Gandiegow's school break for the holidays?"

"I don't know. The twenty-third? Ye'd have to ask Kirsty, our schoolteacher. Ye could ask her tonight when ye come back to sew."

Deydie might be right. Hannah would only be happy here at Quilting Central for maybe half a day, but then she would become bored. *And possibly get into something she wasn't supposed to.* Maybe someone could babysit her in town; certainly not Brodie as Rachel had already imposed too much on him today. Besides, he had a fishing boat to run.

But her daughter loved school. Maybe the teacher wouldn't mind if Hannah spent a little time there while Rachel taught here. Split her day three ways—school, Abraham, and Quilting Central since Deydie had agreed.

Even though Rachel still couldn't stand up to her mother, Gandiegow was making her feel braver and sassier than she'd ever felt in her life. Rachel took a sip of her tea and smiled at Deydie over the rim of her cup. "And be nice to my mother."

Deydie surprised her by giving her a frightening grin. "Don't go pressing yere luck, lassie."

Everything was coming together. Maybe this trip was going to work out after all.

"Oh, crud."

Deydie raised a questioning eyebrow at her.

But Rachel wasn't going to tell her that Vivienne was going to lose it when she saw Brodie was in town. Or explain how her mother would throw a royal fit when she realized Rachel wanted to be with him.

Rachel gulped her tea. It was Gandiegow's fault after all. Gandiegow was infusing courage into her, making her feel as if anything was possible. Even what she'd dreamed of and assumed she'd never get. A second chance with the one who had gotten away.

Chapter Six

Robena Aitken pretended to read the flyers hanging on the bulletin board near the door of Quilting Central, but really she was waiting for Rachel Granger. Deydie was sure taking a long time with Joe's widow at the back café table. Robena only needed one quick look. She stepped in front of the next flyer, flipped it up, and peeked over her shoulder. Finally, the American lass was headed toward the door. As Rachel got closer, Robena zeroed in on her target and got an eyeful.

Aye, it was her locket.

Robena glanced around the room to see if anyone else had noticed. Not a soul. But she guessed they hadn't remembered the locket she'd always worn until the day she married Keith.

Keith. It would be many years after becoming his wife before she would fully realize what she'd done—she'd married an amazing man, who was loyal, true. But by doing so, in some respects, she'd lost her son, Brodie.

He'd been too young when Niall died. Too young to understand the decisions she'd had to make for them. By the time Brodie was old enough to hear the truth, he wouldn't talk to her about it. Aye, he was cordial to her if they crossed paths after church or ran into each other at the General Store. But he'd never forgiven her for marrying so quickly. The pain was physical, even to this day. She loved Brodie so much, but he kept her at a distance.

But what about the locket? What had possessed her morally superior son to give her locket to another man's wife? Did this mean Brodie was vying for Rachel's attention? Or maybe that was the reason Rachel was back in town.

Robena knew one thing for sure—it was time to get to the bottom of this. Tonight she'd force herself to make an appearance at her father's house for supper. She'd leave Keith at home with leftover carrot and coriander soup, and the rolls she'd made this morning. His favorite meal. She didn't go to her father's cottage often as the memories of living with her da and his slanted views on women had left her feeling dejected when she was a young lass. But tonight, she'd step into her childhood home, because curiosity about the locket and whatever was going on over at Abraham's cottage, won out over her painful past.

Brodie stood at the front door, listening to Doc MacGregor's instructions.

"Make sure to keep the humidifier going in both the parlor and his bedroom," Gabriel said. "We're going to keep an eye on him."

Brodie nodded and let Doc out. The X-ray had shown a small spot of pneumonia, which they were treating aggressively with antibiotics. But it was up to Brodie to keep his grandfather hydrated.

Hannah came skipping into the hallway. "Should I get Grandda a cuppa?"

Brodie smiled. *Correction, it will be up to me and Hannah to keep the old man in tea.* "Aye. Help me in the kitchen." He was enjoying the lass, but they'd had very little time to work on their fort after she'd woken up from her nap and before their grandfather had gotten home. Only one quilt had been positioned in place, trapped by the books on the shelf. There was always tomorrow, though.

She took his hand and pulled him through the hallway. As they passed the parlor, she hollered in, "We'll be back with yere tea, Grandda."

Abraham laughed. "Thank ye, lass."

Brodie winked at her. "It's a shame ye're such a quiet little thing. You'll have to learn to speak louder."

Once in the kitchen he gave her the tea canister. "Put one scoop into the ball. While we're making the tea, tell me what kind of Italian food you like. I'm going to place an order at the restaurant for us. How does that sound?"

Before she could answer, the front door opened and closed. It would be Rachel. He didn't realize he'd been waiting for her until his pulse kicked up and eagerness spread through him.

"That's Mommy!" Hannah ran from the room.

Brodie hated himself, because he wanted to run and greet Rachel, too. But it was only his damned urges, out of control again, that made him so eager. He tamped down that particular craving and kept his arse in the kitchen. When she didn't appear, he figured she was in with Abraham, and possibly avoiding him, too. Though Brodie had initiated the talk they'd had earlier, he didn't like how things were left between them.

There were still more things that needed to be said. More things he needed to ask. He needed to know if Joe had ever raised a hand to her.

When the tea was ready, he loaded a tray, prepared to go in the parlor and take everyone's order for dinner. *And to see Rachel.* But as he walked down the hallway, there was a light tap at the door, and then it opened.

His mother smiled at him. "Hello, Brodie." She waited and watched, as if he were a dog who might bite.

"Mum," was all he said. Seeing her always dredged up the sticky feeling of unforgiveness. He took the tray into the parlor, aware he had more than Rachel to concern himself with now. *Why in the hell is my mother here?*

She followed in behind him, not coming completely in, but standing in the parlor doorway uncomfortably. "How are ye doing?" she said to Abraham. "I heard ye went to the doctor today?"

"Inverness. X-ray," Brodie heard himself saying.

Abraham coughed as evidence. "Just a precaution." He smiled over at Hannah. "This is my best girl."

At first his mother seemed elated, but then tensed and looked embarrassed when she realized it was Hannah he spoke of. Brodie felt embarrassed for her, too.

She recovered quickly, putting her hand out to the lass. "I'm Robena. Brodie's mother."

Hannah looked up at Brodie. "So she's my grandma?"

"No, little one." He almost said his mother was *no one to her*, but he rearranged his words before speaking. "She was yere da's aunt, so she's yere great-aunt."

"Just call me *Auntie,* if ye like," his mother said with a smile. His mother was always kind and thoughtful. But Brodie couldn't let it go that she'd married again so quickly, as if Da, who had been everything to him, had been nothing to her.

Hannah looked at Rachel with wonder, as if she'd been given a present. Rachel nodded and the girl ran to Robena, hugging her.

His mother was just as surprised as Brodie was. But he shouldn't have been. Hannah was constantly amazing him with the things she did. Also, being American, she showed her emotions when Scots didn't.

Still holding on to his mother's middle, Hannah stared back at Rachel. "I have an auntie."

"Yes, you do," Rachel said, smiling sadly, making him

wonder what that was all about. Just another thing to ask her when they were alone. That's when he noticed the notebook Rachel was sketching in. Was she drawing up another quilt?

Hannah let go and pulled Robena over to Abraham. "This is my auntie."

The old man chuckled. "So I hear. Did ye know, lass, that yere auntie is also my daughter?"

The girl spun around and stared at Robena with bugged eyes. "Really?"

"Yes." Mum walked all the way into the room and stood by the hearth.

She was always uncomfortable around her own father, and Brodie knew why. Abraham never watched what he said when it came to complaining about his wife who'd left him for the traveling grocer. Brodie had seen clearly the pain in his mother's eyes every time old Abraham said, *Women can't be trusted.* She didn't come by often to the cottage, so it must've been something important to make her come here tonight.

His mother glanced over at Rachel, her eyes flitting to the locket around her neck, and then back to her face as if she hadn't done it at all. Brodie was beginning to get a clue why she was here, which made his stomach queasy. Mum was just as curious as he was as to what Rachel was up to.

"Do ye mind if I join ye for dinner this evening?" Mum said nonchalantly.

Only if ye don't make assumptions and get the wrong idea.

"We can make room, can't we?" Rachel turned to Brodie. "Right?"

"I was just getting ready to call in an order at Pastas & Pastries, Dominic and Claire's restaurant. Ye probably haven't met them. Claire was raised here." He noticed his mother nodded solemnly as if remembering when Claire had left. "Dominic is her husband. They make fantastic food." Brodie should stop his rambling. But dammit, Rachel was making him act like a fool. *No, his mum.* Hell, all of them! He should've made other plans for this evening. *Anyplace but here.* He was beginning to feel constricted. "Is lasagna okay?"

"Aye," Abraham said. The others nodded.

"Do I like it, Mommy?"

Rachel squatted down. "Chef made it for us two Christmases ago. You loved it."

Once again, it hit Brodie that he and Rachel lived totally different lives. Her meals were catered to her. He had to catch his with his fishing pole, clean out the guts, and fry it up in a pan.

But that wasn't completely fair. More times than not, the village women made sure he and Grandda were fed. Dominic was constantly bringing over leftovers and popping them in Abraham's freezer, too.

"How long are ye in town?" his mother asked Rachel, bringing Brodie back to this reality, and the problem at hand.

"I'm not sure," Rachel said.

"Oh?" Robena's pitch had risen. Her eyes flitted down to the locket and back up again.

God. He was going to have to set his mother straight. He'd never told anyone about the kisses he and Rachel had shared at the ruins of Monadail Castle. Never planned to. But he would have to let Mum know that the locket didn't mean anything, that he'd given it to Rachel long ago, and that her having it wasn't a recent development. *Though her wearing it was.*

Brodie frowned at the group of them. "Instead of calling the order in, I'll run over there. It'll be quicker." More importantly, he could get out of the cottage and away from his mother's scrutiny.

Mum raised her eyebrows at him. "Do ye want some company? Rachel could go with you to help carry it back. It might be nice to have an extra set of hands."

"No." *Hell, no!* "I've got this." He stomped from the room, grabbed his coat, and was out the door before he could be pinned to the wall with one of his mother's meaningful stares.

He didn't know what Rachel was all about either—wearing the locket. He wasn't happy with the looks she gave him every now and then . . . as if she wanted something. Something he couldn't give. He'd given her his heart once before, but that was when he was young and naïve and certain his grandfather had been wrong. But the truth was, *women really couldn't be trusted.*

The storm had eased, which was good; he didn't want his mother to have a reason to stay longer than she already would be staying. Maybe he should've had Rachel come along. It would've given them a few moments to discuss the things on his mind. But agreeing would've raised his mother's eyebrows even higher, possibly to her hairline.

At the restaurant, he placed his order, and thankfully, he got in and out without much conversation. He wanted to get the food home and his mother gone.

Back at the cottage, Hannah was inquisitive, asking his mother all kinds of questions. Some about her father, some about Scotland, and some having to do with nothing at all. Mum watched him and Rachel like a sparrowhawk, ready to jump to conclusions at any moment. Brodie breathed a sigh of relief when the meal ended. He gathered his dishes and stood, hoping the others would take the hint.

Rachel snatched Hannah's plate and her own and transported them to the sink. "Okay, little miss, time for your bath and then bed."

"But Grandda needs me to read to him."

Brodie knew *verra* well the child was too young to read, but he kept his mouth shut and filled the sink with water.

"I better get home, too," Robena said.

"Aye." He didn't offer his mother the customary after-dinner tea. He also didn't ask about Keith, Mum's husband. It felt pretty glaring to him, but he couldn't bring himself to be amicable on this point. Right now, he just wanted his mother to leave.

Hannah threw her arms around his mum. "Night, Auntie."

Robena looked up at Brodie with love in her eyes. "Night, lass." And hugged her back.

Rachel and Hannah left the kitchen. Brodie turned to the stove and put the kettle on for Abraham, expecting his mother to follow them out. He stared at the kettle until the first sounds of it starting to boil. When he turned around, he was stunned his mother was still there.

But he should've expected it.

"The locket," his mother said, getting right to the point. "Do ye want to tell me what's going on?"

If only Keith would do him a favor and call up his mother right now, asking her to hurry home. Brodie stood there silent, wishing for her mobile to ring.

"Does this mean ye're courting Rachel?"

"Hell, no!" he said. "I want Joe's widow to go home to America!"

Rachel gasped, hearing the argument through the vent clearly, as if she were chopping vegetables in the kitchen beside them. Thank God, Hannah was splashing in the tub across the hall and couldn't hear. Brodie's words would've devastated her daughter.

His words devastated Rachel. Since seeing him again, all her hopes and dreams of them together were resting on the assumption that Brodie still cared for her. Even a little. Couldn't he give her a chance?

She sat down, pulled the quilt from the end of the bed, and wrapped it around her shoulders. She'd give herself one moment to feel bad.

"Mommy?"

Or not.

Rachel stood and let the quilt crumple on the comforter. She wouldn't fall apart. She couldn't. Mothers didn't have the luxury of indulging in pity parties. Mothers pulled themselves up by the bootstraps and soldiered on. She marched out of the room toward the bathroom.

Rachel also couldn't ignore she had a real problem. *Brodie's resentment.* If only he could get past it. But he wouldn't if she was here in the house, where he could sling her sins at her every chance he got.

Didn't absence make the heart grow fonder?

She looked in on Hannah and an idea came to her.

No, she wouldn't go home to Chicago, but she would go far enough to make Brodie miss her a little.

"Mommy? Do you think Auntie can come back tomorrow and work on the fort with me and Brodie?"

Probably not. Robena had been giving Rachel strange looks all evening. Not mean, but thorough looks, as if searching for something.

Rachel grabbed the shampoo from the side of the tub. "Let's get your hair washed."

Hannah handed her the plastic cup. "Don't get the soap in my eyes."

"I won't." As she wet her daughter's hair and lathered it up, she mentally listed all the things she'd tell Deydie she could bring to the table if she moved back to the quilting dorm. Rachel was, after all, an expert at hospitality, and who better to take care of the retreat-goers than the manager of a swanky hotel.

As she rinsed Hannah's hair, Rachel put aside her hurt feelings. She wasn't giving up hope yet. But she did have to wonder. Shouldn't it be easier than this?

Another complication came to mind, though it played well into her plan to make Brodie's *heart grow fonder.* Rachel's mother was coming to town. She could use that excuse with Abraham as to why they had to move back to the quilting dorm. Everything was falling into place.

"Hannah, I have a surprise for you," Rachel said.

She beamed up at her. "What is it? A new toy?"

"No, silly. Grandma Vivienne is coming here for Christmas."

"Yeah!"

For the rest of bath time, she and Hannah made up silly songs, singing about Scotland, her new doll, and the fort in the parlor. By the time Hannah was as pruney as an elephant, Rachel—certain the argument downstairs had ended—finally helped her daughter from the tub.

After getting Hannah settled into bed, Rachel found Abraham in the parlor watching a Christmas movie. "Hannah is down for the night. Deydie expects me back at Quilting Central. Is it all right to leave her here with you?"

He smiled at her. "Of course. Ye never have to ask. Having that girl here makes me feel better, like I was seventy again."

Rachel smiled. He really was a dear. "Thank you." She kissed the old man on the cheek. She had the urge to look for Brodie as she left the house, but she tamped it down.

She rushed off to Quilting Central, where Deydie and a skeleton crew of quilters were ready to help her make the Gandiegow Fish quilt meant for her daughter. Kirsty, the village's teacher, stopped by and Rachel took the opportunity to talk to her about Hannah.

"Sure," Kirsty said. "She can come for a visit at the school until we break for Christmas. She can sit with Glenna since they are close to the same age."

They chatted for a few more minutes about the particulars of the arrangement, but then Rachel got back to work because Deydie was giving her the eye. When nine o'clock came, everyone shut down for the night and left, except her and Deydie. Rachel marched toward the old woman.

"I need to revise the last deal I made. I've decided to move Hannah and me back to the quilting dorm . . . with my mother coming, and all."

Deydie scrutinized her. "Ye're a cheeky one, I'll give ye that. And brave."

The old woman's noncombativeness threw Rachel off guard, but she still felt on the defensive. "It'll be best for everyone."

"I'm sure it will."

"I'll be able to help with the retreat-goers while I'm there. I do run a hotel, you know."

Deydie handed her the recently sewed pieces of the plaid Gandiegow Fish quilt. "As long as ye're going to teach my group."

From where Rachel stood, suddenly Deydie didn't seem quite as overbearing as she had before.

Deydie pulled on her pea coat and began fastening the huge buttons. "Take yere time in the morning. I'm teaching a little class first. Ten o'clock will be soon enough for ye."

Rachel walked back to the house, feeling as if things couldn't have gone better with Deydie. In the morning, she'd speak with Abraham about switching her residence, but she didn't know what to do about Brodie. Should she discuss it with him or let him figure it out for himself?

Everything had shifted on her. She couldn't force Brodie to see what she saw—that they could be a couple. She'd given him enough hints. If Brodie wanted them to be together, he'd have to make the next move. The ball was in his court.

When she got to the cottage, Abraham wasn't in the parlor and Brodie wasn't either. She breathed a sigh of relief. But on its tail came worry. If Brodie wasn't here, was he out with someone else? He'd done nothing but twist her into knots since she arrived. She trudged upstairs and readied for bed.

She woke up early and packed their bags while Hannah still slept. While she showered and fixed her hair, she recited her argument in her head—the one she was going to give Abraham for why they were leaving.

Back in their room, Rachel gently shook Hannah awake.

"Hey, sleepyhead. Time to get up."

Hannah put guzzy over her head.

"I've got another surprise for you. Do you want to hear it?" Rachel cooed.

"Is it a present?"

Rachel laughed. "You've got a one-track mind. How would you like to attend a real Scottish school while you're here?"

Hannah popped up, wide awake now. "Really?"

"Yep. I spoke with the teacher."

Hannah jumped out of bed. "When do I go?"

"After breakfast."

"Can Dolly go?"

"Yes, Dolly can go. Now let's head downstairs and tell your grandfather what you're doing today." That they were moving out.

As Rachel put the last of their things into the suitcases, Hannah got dressed, jabbering about what they were going to learn at school. Rachel made sure to explain to Hannah the importance of being a good student, especially staying quiet. Hannah promised.

Rachel left their packed bags in the room and went downstairs to talk with Abraham. Once again she wondered how Brodie would react to them leaving.

But Brodie was already on the boat like yesterday. As soon as Rachel made tea for both her and Abraham, she carried their mugs to the parlor to break the news while Hannah ate her porridge in the kitchen.

"My mother is coming to Gandiegow," Rachel started.

"I remember yere mother. She's a handsome woman." Abraham nodded his head. "Like yereself."

"Thank you," Rachel replied, thinking more on her next words than what she was saying now. Better just pull off the Band-Aid. "With Mom coming in, she's going to need a place to stay. I've decided Hannah and I will be moving back to the quilting dorm this morning."

Abraham opened his mouth, but Rachel held up her hand, knowing she would have to be gentle with the old man. The opposite of what she was with Deydie. "But don't worry. We will be seeing you just as much." To make Brodie miss her, Rachel would have to schedule her time at the house when she was sure Brodie was gone—like first thing in the morning.

A snippet of doubt buzzed around her like an annoying fly. *What if Brodie doesn't miss me at all?*

Negative thinking was never productive. *Never.* She put her thoughts back on Abraham. "Hannah will be staying here with you quite a bit. I promise."

"All done!" Hannah ran in from the other room and laid her hand on Abraham's shoulder. "Mommy said I can go to school today. Then I get to spend time with you."

Abraham brightened as if hearing it from Hannah made it true.

Then the old man turned to Rachel. "But have ye told Brodie yet?"

"What the hell," Brodie muttered under his breath. Rachel was wheeling her suitcases through the wynd toward the houses at the back of the bluff. Two cottages sat there, the quilting dorms—Thistle Glen Lodge and Duncan's Den. He finished tying off the boat and started to chase after her.

No. If he did run after her, he'd look like some smitten pup. Which he wasn't. He hurried home instead.

He found Abraham in the kitchen writing on a sheet of paper. Brodie was too worried over Rachel to ask him what he was doing.

"Where is Rachel going with her luggage?"

"Her mother's coming for Christmas. She's gone to stay at the quilting dorm with her," his grandfather said.

"Is her mother already here?" *And when did this come about?* Why hadn't she told him?

Maybe Rachel might have told him, but he'd been too busy giving her a lecture on how to be a parent and then avoiding her afterward.

The lines between Abraham's eyebrows grew more pronounced. "I assumed her mother was here already."

"And Hannah?" Brodie asked.

"She's gone to school for a few hours, then she'll be back to stay with me this afternoon."

Brodie didn't like it. Rachel was settled in here one minute then gone the next. Was she just trying to yank him around? First, she'd dropped into Gandiegow un-announced, and now she'd gone to the other side of town without a word?

"I'll be back." Brodie walked away, determined to find Rachel and speak with her.

But outside, he stopped. Running after her would be stupid. He didn't care what she did.

Instead he headed up the bluff. The pathway had been cleared and salted. Before he realized what he was doing, he was standing at the edge of the ruins of Monadail Castle. He hadn't been here since that day six years ago. He half expected Rachel and a partridge to be waiting for him in the snow, but he was all alone. If he was being honest, he was disappointed.

Graham had built his mansion near the castle, making the ruins not nearly as secluded and private as they had been. Which wasn't a problem for Brodie. He had no one he wanted to bring here for a liaison. Not anymore.

To prove to himself he could, he went to the exact spot he and Rachel had kissed . . . under the archway. From that vantage point, he could see the North Sea rolling and the waves crashing. Only a crazy idiot like himself would be up here sightseeing on a nasty day like today. He turned and looked the other direction through the arch-way to where the partridge had been. He'd been ridicu-lously happy with Rachel in his arms . . . and delusional to think she was his. He was thoroughly disgusted with himself for being so naïve when it came to women. Abra-ham had warned both him and Joe about how duplicitous they could be.

Brodie turned back to the sea, which as a fisherman was his past, his present, and his future. He stopped short. He stopped breathing. Everything stopped, except his heart, which was beating too fast. His eyes lied.

Rachel stood five feet away, her hood pushed down,

and looking so vulnerable that she had to be some awful mirage come to haunt him. They both stared at each other, and then suddenly, she was rushing into his arms, kissing him. She'd knocked the breath from his lungs on impact, and it took a second for his body to respond, but then he made up for lost time, kissing her back.

The message started deep inside, a muffled warning— *you can't do this, not again*—and at first he ignored it. All that mattered was Rachel was here, they were together, and she was kissing him again. But the voice grew louder in his head, *Stop this!* His hands moved to her arms, gripping them, but still he kissed her. The pounding in his head and in his chest became dual war cries, the battle turning full-blown, yet he couldn't let her go. Finally reason tipped the scales, and without his heart's consent, he set her away.

"No!" he roared, his hands, even now, locked on her arms. He shook her a little.

But then, because he wasn't in his right mind, he pulled her back to him, crushing her against him, kissing her, brutalizing her lips, wanting to punish her. *Punish himself.* Wanting to make them both pay for what had been between them in the past. What was between them right now.

She took it. His bruising kisses, and she gave it back to him with tenderness by way of running her hands in his hair. Her mewing sounds. She was trying to crawl inside his skin, though he was being a beast.

Somehow his kisses turned tender, too. He remembered everything. Felt everything. The love he had for her. How right it was to be with her. How their future had seemed so clear. His brain stopped there and didn't remember the rest. Because there was nothing more in the world right now than the two of them. Together.

Cherishing her lips was amazing, but he wanted more. He pulled at her collar and moved to her neck, needing to love her there as well.

But the second his warm lips hit the cold metal of the chain—*the chain which holds my locket*—he jumped back.

"Son of a bitch!" He was breathing hard, his warm breath visible, clouding the space between them. "Why are ye here?" *Why are ye doing this to me?* He felt like a sunk man—his legs strapped to an anchor and thrown in the deepest waters of the North Sea. For all the strength he had to resist her, she might've well have been wearing his balls around her neck instead of his locket.

She stumbled backward as if his words had slapped her. "I—I came for a walk."

"Nay," he said, angrier than he'd ever been in his life. "Ye came to crush me." He pointed to the space between them violently. "What happened here doesn't mean a thing. Do ye ken?"

She pulled her hood up, shadowing her face. The wind howled. A dog barked. Suddenly, Brodie remembered that maybe they weren't completely alone. He turned to see Dingus barreling toward them, his Sheltie body bounding through the snow, his playful canter in vast contrast to the serious byplay that had happened under the arch. Brodie's gaze moved to the Big House, and sure enough, Cait stood near with the leash hanging from her hand. It might as well have been a noose . . . because someone, beside Rachel, could see he was nothing but a weak bastard.

Chapter Seven

Rachel was shaking, not from the cold, though it was bitter, but from the emotional upheaval of kissing Brodie. She kept her eyes forward, refusing to watch as he tramped off through the snow. Cait's dog, Dingus, was barking at her, trying to get her to play.

"Come here, boy," Cait called. But as she neared, she must've seen Rachel's face. "Oh, no. Are ye okay?" She hurried to her and put her arm around her shoulders. "Come to the house. We'll get you warmed up."

But Rachel felt rooted to the spot. Too stunned by what she'd done. Too affected by Brodie. Too over-whelmed. Too frazzled. Miserable. Shaken.

"To the house," Cait said, as firm as Deydie, but as soothing as coffee with Drambuie. Rachel let herself be led away with the dog at her side.

But when they got to the back door, Rachel dug her heels in. "I can't. Quilting Central."

Cait clucked at her gently. "Nay. I'll text Gran, tell her ye'll be a while. She'll understand."

"Not from what I know about her."

Cait opened the door and Dingus rushed in first as if showing them the way. She led Rachel through the kitchen and down a hall to a parlor with wood-paneled walls, comfy sofas, and the promised fire in the hearth.

Rachel's teeth chattered. "You saw." She didn't have to spell it out for her.

"Not if you didn't want me to." This sounded like what Rachel had said to Cait at the airport.

Rachel turned toward the fire and away from her new friend. "Can you keep it a secret?" Brodie would hate everyone knowing. Especially if the villagers started making assumptions and drawing conclusions about how long this had been going on. Plus the fact he was caught kissing Joe's widow. Once again Rachel would be raked through the coals for trying to corrupt another Gandie-gowan man with her Yankee ways.

Cait came over and squeezed her shoulder. "We'll keep each other's secrets."

So she hadn't told Graham yet. But her secret would become apparent with time whether Rachel told or not.

"Do ye want to talk about it?"

What could Rachel say? *I have this plan, you see. One where Brodie, Hannah, and I are going to be a family.* But the plan had fallen apart. "It's complicated."

"I know. It always is." As if Cait was reliving her own past, she looked over at a picture on the side table of her and Graham. "I'm going to put the kettle on and take care of that text to Deydie. Make yereself at home. I'll be right back."

Dingus looked up at Rachel, then climbed into the dog bed, collapsing as if being a pampered dog was a lot of work.

She didn't know how she was going to face Brodie again. She shouldn't have thrown herself at him. It was exactly as she'd done six years ago, but today's encounter hadn't been the loving experience they'd shared before. This time it had been a tornadic whirlwind of pent-up emotions, and she had experienced every bit of anguish she'd put Brodie through. She was only beginning to see the pain she'd caused. She'd been so caught up in her own hurt and disappointment, she hadn't realized how her betrayal might have crushed him. Changed him. Maybe to the point of not wanting her again at all.

A few minutes later, Cait returned with a tray containing two teacups. She laid her phone beside the picture she'd been staring at earlier and handed one steaming cup to Rachel. Cait's phone pinged, but she ignored it.

"Don't you want to see what Deydie has to say?"

Cait blew on her own teacup as she stood by the mantle. "She'll be fine. I promise. After we have these fortifying cups of tea, then I'll walk you down the bluff and make sure the old bird's ruffled feathers are put back in place. Don't worry. I have my ways with her." She scrutinized Rachel. "From what I hear, you have skills also when it comes to dealing with my gran." She took a sip. "I'm impressed."

Rachel took a sip, too. "Did you hear my mom is coming to Gandiegow for Christmas?" She still had mixed feelings about it. She took another sip, the tea warming her.

"I did hear about yere mother. Why the frown, though?"

"That's complicated, too. You know how it can be with mothers."

Cait's expression fell. She set her tea down on the coffee table and forced a brave smile. "I know how grandmothers can be. Mothers, not so much." She paused for a second. "I lost mine when I was thirteen."

"I'm so sorry," Rachel said. She couldn't imagine not having her mom.

Cait moved to the couch. "It's been especially rough, being pregnant and not having her. I know it's irrational, but I want my mama." Her voice cracked and instantly she looked embarrassed.

Rachel sat beside her. "I know what you mean. Mom and I don't see eye to eye on so many things, but while I was pregnant, I wanted her near. I had a ton of questions for her about when she was pregnant with me. Her answers helped me to not be so afraid."

Cait looked up, surprised. "That's it exactly. I would feel better if only I could talk to Mama about it." She looked down. "When I was pregnant before, every woman in the village shared their experiences with me, but it's not the same—"

"As hearing it from your own mother," Rachel finished for her, giving Cait a hug.

Cait laughed. "I didn't mean to put my burdens on you."

"You didn't. You brought me in to help me and it worked."

"I know you don't want to talk about what might've happened or didn't happen at the ruins, but just know I'll always be here for ye if you want to talk," Cait said.

"I appreciate that. The truth is I'm not quite sure yet what to think myself."

Both women looked at each other and said at the same time, "It's complicated." And they laughed.

Rachel stood. "I have to get back to Quilting Central, but you don't need to go."

Cait chuckled. "I wouldn't miss this for the world. I know you can hold yere own with Deydie, but I'd like to watch and see how ye do it this time. Maybe take notes for myself. There's very few who are brave enough to take on my gran, and though I don't think ye'll need it, I can be there for you as reinforcement."

After putting their cups in the sink, the two walked

down the bluff companionably. Rachel was so grateful for Cait's friendship. She'd helped to ease the earthquake in her soul.

As luck would have it, when Rachel walked into Quilting Central, the worst she received from the crotchety head quilter was a frightening glower as Deydie was on the stage demonstrating how to use selvages to make a quilt top. As soon as the old woman was done, she found Rachel with her eyes, and barreled in her direction. Cait, *God bless her*, did as she'd promised and came to the rescue, stepping in Deydie's path, and pulling her in the opposite direction. Rachel could hear snippets of her excuse, something about *needing help to the fix the tension on her sewing machine*. As Cait pulled her away, she looked back over her shoulder with a smile and a wink for Rachel. Yes, having a friend in Gandiegow was priceless.

Rachel took the stage and continued to the next step in making the Gandiegow Christmas Tree quilt—as she'd taken to calling it in her head. Before she knew it, Bethia was stopping everyone for a lunch break. Rachel slipped out, rushing to the school to pick up Hannah.

Her daughter chattered excitedly all the way to Abraham's cottage about making new friends besides Glenna. Apparently Dand and Mattie had made quite an impression on her, too.

"They're coming to Grandda's after school so we can play," Hannah said.

"We better check with your grandfather first to make sure it's okay with him. Don't you think?"

When they arrived at the cottage, Abraham had the checkerboard set up ready to teach Hannah how to play. But first, all three of them ate the sandwiches Amy had left in the refrigerator. Rachel said good-bye and hurried off to Thistle Glen Lodge, trying her best not to look for

Brodie along the way. She was both disappointed and relieved when she didn't see him.

She hurried inside the quilting dorm and made a quick run-through, as if she were one of the cleaning staff at the Winderly Towers back in Chicago. She wiped down the bathroom, straightened all the beds, and put a load of towels in the washer. The dorm was spotless before she headed back to Quilting Central.

Although no trouble broke out in the afternoon session—apparently Deydie had forgiven her for being late this morning—Rachel's insides were wound into knots from being thoroughly kissed by Brodie. Knots pulled tight with anxious frustrations. Frustrated that everything was unsettled in her life. Frustrated because Brodie wasn't seeing things her way. Frustrated because more than anything in the world, she wanted to be kissing him again.

When Rachel was done with her lesson in the afternoon, Deydie pulled her aside.

"Moira and Sinnie told me the quilting dorm needed no maintenance when they slipped over there a while ago. What did ye do?"

"It was nothing. I only tidied up a bit."

Deydie frowned at her. "It 'twasn't nothing to us." Then she looked extra pained. "Thank ye." She walked away.

Well, that was a shocker. Rachel took a moment to revel in it, but not too long. She rushed home, knowing she and Brodie needed to talk. She hoped to get him alone before dinner so they could discuss what happened at the ruins of Monadail Castle. But back at the cottage, he wasn't there. Just when she'd almost worked up the nerve to ask after her missing fisherman, Hannah looked up at Abraham.

"Grandda, why isn't Brodie eating dinner with us?"

Abraham smiled at her with tenderness, the wrinkles about his eyes crinkling up more. "Och, lass, I believe he went to Inverness to pick up a part for the boat." Abraham grinned, chuckling. "I could read between the lines. A young man needs more excitement than what Gandiegow can provide." He chuckled again.

Rachel could read between the lines, too. Brodie's intent was to pick up more than just boat parts. Jealousy barreled through her, wreaking havoc, banging around in her chest, and plummeting her stomach into the abyss. Was he really out looking for a woman . . . or women? Wasn't the *excitement* they'd shared at Monadail Castle today enough for him? But maybe Brodie ran off to Inverness to find another woman so he could forget how much she'd affected him.

Abraham continued on as if Rachel's mind wasn't racing. "'Tis the reason we lose so many of our young ones to the city. It's a real problem. We all worry what will happen to Gandiegow down the road. At least we have Quilting Central and the North Sea Valve Company to keep some of them here."

Hannah, the old soul that she was, patted his hand as if she understood perfectly.

When dinner was over and Hannah and Abraham had settled into yet another game of checkers, Rachel excused herself to do the one thing that had to be done—visit Joe's grave. For this first visit, she wanted to be alone. She had things to say to Joe that were too harsh for her daughter's innocent ears.

Joe shouldn't have screwed around on her. He should've sold his damn sports car before he got himself killed, driving too fast, always daring fate. He should be here for his daughter so she didn't have to grow up without a father. Rachel knew it was foolish to talk to the dead. But she had some final words, words she should've said to him before he passed on. When she was done with all the unspoken things that weighed on her heart, she would be able to bring Hannah up to the cemetery at the top of the bluff to visit her father.

It was a nice night, calmer than it had been, the stars out, the wind subdued. She trudged up the path behind the village, the one leading to where the Gandiegowans buried their dead. The cemetery was in a clearing which overlooked the North Sea. Seeing it brought back everything. Rachel would never forget her last visit to the gravesite. Her guilt for not being a good wife. The cold reception from the town. Joe's ashes being laid to rest. Strange, it was all a blur, yet her emotions were fresh, as if it'd happened this day.

A few more markers had been added to the collection with their headstones clearly standing out—white, not worn from time and the weather. Rachel took a moment to read their names and dates: Kenneth Campbell, Moira's father; and Duncan MacKinnon Buchanan, Mattie's father and Graham's son. At Quilting Central, she'd heard talk of both of them and how losing these loved ones had impacted the community. She said a little prayer for each, hoping they were whooping it up in heaven. A more earnest prayer she said for their loved ones still here on earth, knowing they'd need help to heal.

Finally, Rachel looked up, ready to make her way to Joe. But when she did, Brodie was there, stopped at the edge of the tombstones—as if he'd only just arrived at the perimeter of the cemetery—when he saw her, too.

Brodie was taken completely off guard, and disgusted with himself that the partridge, tattooed on his chest, flapped its wings wildly at the sight of Rachel. He should've anticipated she would come to pay her respects. But dammit, this was his time to spend with Joe.

Since returning to Gandiegow after his six-year absence, Brodie had spent a lot of time at Joe's graveside. For what? *Hell if I know.* He didn't talk to him. Mostly, he came to just be here. Sometimes, the good times the two of them had as lads would visit his thoughts, but mostly Brodie felt guilty.

The source of his guilt stood at Joe's grave. Brodie should leave her to it and get the hell out of there. But suddenly, he wanted to know. Needed to know what had happened with Joe. Did Joe turn bad, become like Joe's father, and hurt Rachel? With determined steps, Brodie headed toward her.

The way she stared at him as he drew near, she seemed stunned, shocked as if he were an apparition. That wasn't his intent; he had to have answers.

When he got close enough, he spoke. "We need to talk."

She cocked her head to the side as if to hear him better. "Okay."

The locket caught the light of the full moon and twinkled at him. This time, though, instead of it making his blood run cold, seeing her wear the locket warmed him. But immediately, he hated himself for this weird feeling of standing over Joe's grave while coveting his cousin's wife. Emotions battered him—anger, guilt—because he'd given himself to her when she'd belonged to Joe. He tamped down his feelings. The only thing he wanted from her now was an explanation of what had happened between her and his cousin.

He glanced around, making sure this time they didn't have an audience. What he had to say couldn't be repeated. "Did he hurt you?" he blurted, before he could get his emotions under control.

Her head snapped back. "Who?"

Brodie stared pointblank at Joe's grave. "Yere husband. Hannah told me you and Joe were separated when he died. I just wondered if it was because he hurt you."

"What do you mean?" The way her brows pulled together, she acted as if she had been wounded, but not necessarily in the physical sense.

Brodie would have to spell it out. He exhaled deeply. "What I mean is . . . did Joe *hit* you?"

"God, no!" Rachel said. "Why would you say such a thing?"

Suddenly, shame washed over Brodie for thinking the worst of his cousin, his best friend. "I was afraid . . ." Brodie trailed off. "Then what happened?"

"The truth?"

He nodded, not really sure if he could handle knowing any of it.

"I tried to make our marriage work, but my expectations were too high."

The partridge on Brodie's chest craved her, which made him a prick. Part of him wanted her to say her marriage hadn't worked because of what the two of them had shared. But that was only his ego's wishful thinking. It was obvious he'd cared more for her than she did for him. She'd turned around and gotten married and he'd become a virtual monk. She hadn't pined for him at all. She'd really loved Joe. Brodie's guilt should've lifted, but the fact that he'd carried an *effing* torch for her all of these years had been wasted time. *A bluidy waste of time.* He didn't want to hear any more. But he heard himself saying, "Yere expectations were too high?"

She gave him a weak smile, and her eyes were misting up. Brodie wished he hadn't seen them. This was too much.

She shook her head. "I thought the only way our marriage was going to work was if I was the only one in his life." She paused for a long second, staring out at the ocean. "But Joe loved women."

Relief hit Brodie. Maybe Joe hadn't been *everything* to her. Maybe she had cared for him just a little. Maybe Brodie hadn't been completely duped in his love for her. He cleared his throat. "You don't have to say anything more about Joe and women. I understand."

She turned to him, looking perplexed. "But I don't get it. Why would you think Joe would've hurt me?" A brittle laugh, which edged on being bitter, escaped her. "He was home so very little that he barely even talked to me or saw his newborn."

For a second, Brodie started to keep it to himself, cover it up like it had been covered up before, but Rachel deserved to know why Joe might have been who he was. That he wasn't always so shallow and polished. That at one time, he'd been a carefree lad.

She reached her hand out as if to touch him, encouraging him to go on, but he stepped away.

"I saw a program on the telly about . . ." He couldn't say the word *abusers.* The program had really been about the *children* of abusers. The show stilled haunted Brodie. He hadn't caught the documentary until after Joe had died and been buried. If Brodie had seen the program before Rachel married him, he would've stopped them from getting married, or at the very least warned her. Now she needed to know the truth.

Brodie took a deep breath. He'd start at an easier place. "As kids, Joe and I spent a lot of time together. Sometimes getting into mischief. Maybe doing things we shouldn't have. Some called us little terrors."

She looked at him strangely.

"Normal stuff. Things ye'd see today by any of the lads here in town."

"And?" she said.

"We may have borrowed ole man Martin's boat once—at night to go fishing—without his permission."

Aye. They'd been stupid kids. It was in the middle of winter. Anything could've happened to them. "The old man caught us bringing it back to town. Gave us a good lecture. Made us pay for the petrol. We had to clean the boat from top to bottom before we were allowed to head back to Abraham's and go to bed. We laughed when we got to Grandda's about getting away with it, and even talked about borrowing the boat again."

If only Brodie had gone home to his own cottage with his mother and father instead of Grandda's, he wouldn't have heard.

"Joe must've gotten up to get a drink. I don't know. I only know I woke up when it started."

"What started?" Rachel was looking worried.

Brodie hesitated, not knowing exactly how to tell her. Finally, he just said it. "The beating. I heard it all through the vent in our room. Uncle Richard was drunk and mad at Joe for embarrassing him with ole man Martin. He'd heard what we'd done at the pub. Abraham's never spoke of it, but I suspect Uncle Richard wanted to get on ole man Martin's crew; it's no secret Uncle Richard and Grandda didn't see eye to eye."

Rachel was biting her lip and shaking her head. "But . . . what happened to Joe?"

Brodie couldn't tell her everything he'd heard, though he remembered every lash of the belt. Every slap to Joe's body. *His cousin begging his da to stop.* Every time Joe cried out, Brodie cried, too, hidden under the bed, lest he'd get a beating if Uncle Richard knew he was in the house, too.

Brodie prayed and prayed for it to end. "Grandda came home and saved Joe. He and Uncle Richard had a terrible fight and then he threw Uncle Richard out." The vent relayed it all in great, horrible detail. "Grandda told Joe he was going to live with him from now on." Then

Grandda carried Joe upstairs and laid him in the bed. Brodie had worried Joe was half-dead, the bruises everywhere, his eyes swollen, his lip bloodied. Though they considered themselves grown at ten years old, Brodie held Joe that night while he cried himself to sleep. But the two cousins never spoke of what happened. *Never.* "Joe was different after that. He acted happy and outgoing as he always had, but he was different." Joe didn't go to school the rest of the week. No one ever spoke of the beating, though the townsfolk had to have known.

"Oh, God, poor Joe," Rachel cried.

The only person Brodie had talked to about the beating had been his own da, the day after it happened. The guilt had been too much; if only Brodie had been stronger and stopped Uncle Richard instead of cowering under the bed. Da listened to the story and had been angrier than Brodie had ever seen him. At first, Brodie thought it was because he'd let his da down. But Da held him fiercely and made it clear why he was angry. *Ye did the right thing to hide, son. For if Richard had laid a hand on ye, I would've killed him. Yere mum would've never forgiven me for murdering her brother.*

Da was Brodie's hero. He'd felt the loss of him every day since he'd died.

Rachel was staring at him intently, so he got to the point.

"I was worried when Hannah said ye weren't living together, that Joe might've turned into his father." There. Brodie had spit it out. The documentary on the television had shown case after case of people who abused others because they themselves had been abused. Joe had all the personality shifts the psychologist mentioned. Brodie had warred with this information for so long, going back and forth, trying to answer the question for himself. He just had to know.

"No. Never." Rachel held such sadness in her eyes. "He had a temper. But he never hurt me and he never hurt Hannah." She shuddered as if imagining it. "I left because he was cheating on me." She paused for a long second, then squared her shoulders. "When he gave me an STD, I moved out and took Hannah with me."

Brodie couldn't help himself. He reached over and took her hand, squeezing gently. "Ye did the right thing." She didn't need to hear his words, but he needed to reassure her anyway.

She nodded her head as if she agreed.

He didn't let go of her. Maybe he needed bolstering up while he told her the rest. "It was a week later, ye know, when the *Rose* went down." He glanced over to see if she took his meaning.

Her puzzled look said she didn't.

"The ship our fathers were on. Joe's, mine, Claire's, and many others in town. Fourteen in all. The *Rose* was lost in a storm on Valentine's Day. That accident changed Gandiegow and we lost more than the men. We lost whole families. Many of my friends had to leave town so their mothers could find work. Like Claire's mum had to do."

She squeezed his hand back. "I'm so sorry about your father. It must've been horrible for you and your mother, and the others in the village."

"It was." He and his mum moved in with Abraham. Until, of course, she remarried. "But in a weird way, it was especially hard on Joe. Though ye never would've known it for how he acted." Now that Brodie had maturity and perspective on his side, he couldn't imagine what his cousin must've gone through. "Joe never grieved for his da. At the time, it made sense—a week earlier, his father had nearly killed him. But he should've grieved. Even a little." And this was the reason Brodie would always love Joe. He grasped why his cousin had turned hard, calloused, and shallow . . . and smooth. His emotional growth had been stunted on the night his father had taken him to task. For Joe had been beaten when he'd done nothing more than do the things lads were known to do.

It also had to be the reason Brodie felt such a strong need to protect Joe's child. He felt it in his soul he'd do anything to safeguard Hannah so she would never have to know the pain her father had gone through.

Rachel, though, was still chewing her lip. "But Abraham . . ." She hesitated. "Did he ever . . . hit your uncle? Or you? Or Joe?"

Brodie understood what she was getting at. If abusers come from abusers, then that would mean Grandda must've taught Uncle Richard how to be the way he was. "Nay. Not once. Grandda runs a tight ship but never uses corporal punishment. He's a fair man." Brodie had given this a lot of thought and believed he knew why Uncle Richard was the way he was. "Uncle Richard drank too much. He was so bitter toward Joe's mum for leaving him. He never got over what she did. He never moved on." Abraham, in that respect, was responsible, because he had a habit of speaking disparagingly about women. Though, since Brodie had returned home from Here Again Farm, Grandda hadn't spoken ill of women once. Not a word about them being untrustworthy.

But Brodie's own thoughts became a snare and tightened around his chest. *Uncle Richard was so bitter toward Joe's mum . . . he never moved on.*

Brodie's temples throbbed. He couldn't find his breath. He dropped Rachel's hand suddenly, remembering how she'd hurt him. How bitter he still felt toward her. How he hadn't moved on. A terrible thought hit him, *In this, I'm exactly like my Uncle Richard.* Through his

whole life, Brodie had judged his uncle, never understanding how he could've been that *kind of man*.

Brodie stalked away, without a word to Rachel, suddenly needing to be alone more than he needed his next
breath of air.

Rachel stood at Joe's graveside, not quite sure what had
transpired. She was still processing what had happened
to her husband when he was only a boy. More perplexing,
and at the same time satisfying, was that she and Brodie
had connected, talked like they had six years ago . . .
before she'd hurt him. He'd even held her hand. But she
hadn't anticipated he would run away.

"It's all your fault," she said to Joe's tombstone. Immediately, she felt guilty. She hadn't known what her
husband had gone through. It explained a lot.

"Sorry," she said to Joe.

That was the problem when remembering someone
who was dead, especially when it came to her husband.
She had a tendency to either blame herself, or Joe for all
the ways he'd wronged her, or make him a saint for the
good things he'd done. Joe wasn't completely good or
bad . . . he had only been a flawed human being like everyone else in the world. From what Brodie told her,
there was a reason Joe might've been the person he was.
For the next hour, instead of venting to Joe about how
he'd let her down, she filled him in on Hannah and the
kind of person she was turning out to be. By the time
Rachel was done, she felt lighter, as if the weight of their
failed marriage had been lifted a little. She wiped away
the tears and headed back to the cottage to get Hannah.

She found her daughter in the parlor, next to Abraham, with her tablet in his lap.

Hannah looked up and grinned at Rachel. "I taught
Grandda how to use yere iPad. I told him to keep it and

play games while I'm at school in the morning. It'll give him something to do until I can get here. Is that okay, Mommy?"

"Sure. That's fine."

Abraham smiled up at her, too. "Ye look as if ye could use a nightcap."

So even to his worn-out eyes, her spent tears were visible.

"Mommy, are ye all right?"

"Yes. It's just the cold outside." Rachel remembered the last nightcap she'd made in this parlor and how it hadn't turned out well. It seemed nothing was turning out as she'd like it.

There was a knock at the door. For a brief moment, she hoped it would be Brodie, but he wouldn't be knocking. "I'll get it."

She left Hannah and Abraham and went to the front. When she opened the door, a tall, blond, very good-looking man stood there, smiling at her.

"Hallo," he said. He looked over his shoulder as if someone might be watching. "I'm Tuck MacBride. Father Andrew's brother."

Yes. Moira's brother-in-law. There'd been a lot of talk about him at Quilting Central among the natives. As it was, she wasn't the only one who wasn't in good favor with the people of Gandiegow. Tuck had wronged them in one way or another, but none of it seemed specific. The only thing Rachel knew for sure was he'd missed his brother's wedding. In Gandiegow, loyalty to family and community stood head and shoulders above everything else. According to the whispers in town, Tuck only cared about himself.

He leaned against the doorjamb, crossing his arms over his chest nonchalantly, seeming to assess her from head to toe. "I've seen ye from afar. Would ye like to go to the pub with me and have a drink?"

He was so overly confident that she laughed.

Tuck frowned, standing up straight, but then he donned another smile.

"I can't," she said, shaking her head. "I have to get my daughter to the quilting dorm." She could think of a hundred reasons why she shouldn't go to the pub with him. Number one on the list was Brodie.

"Can I walk ye and the lass back then?" Tuck was very charming.

"No. But thanks for the offer." She went to shut the door, but he put his hand out to stop it.

"Hold up," he said.

But from behind him, as if she had binoculars for eyes, she saw Brodie off in the distant. Brodie halted, taking in the scene. Then he stomped in her direction.

"I have to go." She pushed Tuck's hand out of the way and closed the door. She thought about locking it. Something in the way Brodie moved toward the cottage, like a stalking panther, made her think all hell was going to break loose any minute.

"Hannah, come get your coat," Rachel said, walking down the hall. The way Brodie looked at Tuck and at her, she could picture him busting through the door. Was she imagining it or was he really jealous?

Brodie had done nothing but surprise her since she'd set foot in this village.

When Rachel stepped into the parlor, Hannah hadn't budged.

"I said, let's go."

"I want to stay with Grandda. I want to show him Angry Birds next."

"Come away now, or you're going to have Angry

Mother to contend with," Rachel said, half-joking, half-not-so-much.

The front door opened and slammed shut. Brodie was to the parlor before Rachel could grab Hannah's hand and make a run for it.

"What did he want?" Brodie said quietly. It would've been better if he yelled.

"He was selling Girl Scout cookies," Rachel said sweetly. "Want some?"

"What?" Brodie raised his voice then.

Rachel walked over, laid a hand on his chest, and drove him backward into the hallway. He was all steel. If he'd wanted to stay put, no man on earth could've moved him.

"It was nothing," she said, almost in a whisper, so as not to upset her daughter or Abraham.

As if on cue, Abraham started coughing. Rachel wondered if the old man wasn't covering so she and Brodie could argue without bothering Hannah.

"Get in the kitchen." She grabbed his hand and pulled Brodie in that direction.

When they got there, Brodie stood in the doorway, blocking her from leaving. "Tell me the truth. What did he say?"

"He introduced himself," she said honestly.

"And what else?"

"Nothing else," she lied. But then she inserted *nothing else that mattered*, just to ease her conscience.

Brodie raised an eyebrow. "Ye have to watch out for him. Tuck," he said, as if he needed to qualify the *him*.

"He seems harmless," she said. "He's just a good-looking flirt." She shouldn't have added that last bit, but part of her wanted to push the boundaries to see if Brodie might feel something toward her.

Brodie grabbed her arm and got very close to her face.

She didn't need binoculars now. She had a front row seat to his irises, every emotion playing out in his eyes. He wanted to kiss her. As God as her witness, she wanted to kiss him, too.

She'd always been impatient. Some might call her impulsive. She grabbed his other arm and pulled him in until his lips met hers.

He growled against her mouth, "Dammit, Rachel."

She didn't know if it was because he was mad about Tuck or because she hadn't kissed him sooner. But she didn't care, because Brodie kissed her back.

She felt like they were all alone in the world, but they weren't. Her daughter was in the other room and Rachel didn't want to confuse her. She, herself, was baffled about what the future would hold, though the two of them kissing was a great place to start. But she couldn't allow Hannah to see them together until she had a commitment from Brodie. She pulled away, but held on to him, breathing hard.

"Mommy?"

Rachel spun around, horrified.

"Why are ye kissing cousin Brodie?"

Chapter Eight

"Ah, hell," Brodie hissed. He dropped Rachel's arm and grabbed a magazine off the counter, holding it in front of his jeans.

Rachel looked to him as if he should explain the birds and the bees to the lass. He'd do anything for this little girl, but he wouldn't tell her what kind of things could transpire between a man and a woman. He marched from the room. He shouldn't have come home until he knew the two females were gone.

A better idea came to him; he should find Tuck and kick his arse.

He didn't make it but a step out of the kitchen before he heard Rachel talking soothingly to the girl. He peeked back in.

Rachel was sitting with her back to him in one of the kitchen chairs with Hannah in her lap. Seeing the mother and child with their heads together was enough to make his heart melt. But then Rachel spoke. "Sometimes adults kiss like that."

"I know," Hannah said. "I've seen the people on TV, but I've never seen ye do it before."

Though it didn't mean anything, the revelation pleased him *verra* much.

"Is that how ye kissed Daddy?"

Rachel paused for a long second, but then answered, "Yes."

"Does that mean ye're going to marry Brodie?"

Brodie wanted to leave, but he couldn't. This scene was like an accident on the highway in which he couldn't look away.

Finally Rachel answered, "I kissed Brodie because I like him."

He found he could barely draw breath. The partridge on his chest stirred, warming him and nestling in for what seemed like the long haul.

"I like him, too. Does Brodie like ye back?" Hannah asked.

Rachel shook her head. "I don't know, sweetie."

He skulked away, because he didn't know either. If only Rachel hadn't stomped on his heart before, all this would be so easy. Would he ever be able to forgive her? He didn't even know where to start. He could ask her why she'd gone through with the wedding, but Brodie wasn't sure he could withstand the answer. *Because I loved Joe and I didn't love you.*

He went out the front door, walked to the General Store, and signed out one of the community cars. He needed out of this town. Now.

He drove to Lios and stopped at the pub on the corner. But when he took a seat at the bar, he couldn't bring himself to order a whisky, thinking it was what Uncle Richard had done on the night he beat Joe. Brodie ordered a soft drink instead, but only drank half before leaving and climbing back in the car.

Twenty minutes later, he found he was pulling down the lane to his mother's house. *No, Keith and Mum's house.* Brodie threw on the brakes, bringing the car to a screeching halt. Keith and his mother had bought a small farm a few miles from Gandiegow, raising sheep, chickens, and ducks. Brodie had never been to visit, and by God, he wasn't going to visit now. The house in front of him held another female he couldn't forgive. To let his mum off the hook would be like betraying his own father. Twenty-four years ago, his mother had no problem two-timing his father's memory, by marrying Keith within a month of his da dying.

The curtain in the front picture window stirred and then it was pulled open. Brodie could see his mother's face staring back. Neither one of them moved as if locked in a strange game of chess. He understood why she didn't come out to get him. She'd tried hard over the years. At first, she did everything within her power to get him to move in with her and Keith. Later, she had invited him to dinner. Or she'd ask him to Christmas at her house. But he'd stood his ground. *Someone in this family had to*. He and his mother had come to a cordial understanding, and over the years, he'd settled in for the long haul in his unforgiveness.

He put the car in reverse, turned it around, and headed back to Gandiegow, making a decision for how it was going to be. He'd survived over the years by putting the heartache aside. He could continue on the same route until Rachel was gone after Christmas. He would do everything in his power not to be around the cottage when she was there with Hannah visiting. He would be congenial to her at their Christmas gathering. But that was it.

No more kissing her.

No more pining.

Being a stubborn hard-ass had worked for him up to this point. It wouldn't fail him now.

Rachel and Hannah were both quiet as they left Abraham's. She worried about her daughter. Had witnessing the kiss traumatized her?

Hannah looked at her. "I'm okay, Mommy."

Rachel squeezed her hand. "I know you are." Hannah was an extraordinary child. She couldn't really read people's minds, but she was as sensitive as a Geiger counter when it came to picking up emotions.

Rachel sighed. Her second chance was much harder to bring about than she ever dreamed it would be. Now Hannah was involved.

Farther down the walkway, she spotted Grace Armstrong, looking this way and that, as if on the lookout for someone. Rachel guffawed, Grace's actions reminding her of her own when she'd been looking for Brodie.

Rachel pulled her daughter to a halt. "I need to stop in Quilting Central, sweetie. I left my notebook." She wanted to work a little more on her directions for the Gandiegow Fish quilt. If there was time, she'd like to cut out the pieces after Hannah went to bed.

"Can I see if they have any biscuits?" Hannah asked, grinning.

"Aren't you full from dinner?"

"Nay."

"We'll see. There may not be any." Quilting Central, though, was a mecca when it came to snacking. It was a wonder the town's quilters weren't three feet wide. But Gandiegow was a walking village and everyone received a lot of exercise with their feet as their only means of transportation.

Inside the building, the room was abuzz.

"What's up?" Rachel asked Amy as Hannah ran off to the counter where the cookies sat.

"We have a mystery going on here in the village. Things have gone missing. Now that everyone is comparing notes, they are finding out it's no coincidence."

"What kind of things?" Rachel asked.

"Maggie left a pie on the crate outside her door to

cool for a couple of minutes, and when she came back, it was gone. Also, Lochie swears his sandwich was taken from his lunch bucket. Aileen finished a quilt and left it by her sewing machine, but now it's gone." Amy leaned in close. "Everyone's saying it has to be Tuck."

"Why?"

"Because he's the only stranger in town," Amy said matter-of-factly.

Rachel frowned at the young woman. "But isn't he Father Andrew's brother?"

"Aye. But he missed the wedding, and he was supposed to be the best man. What kind of brother does that? No one trusts him." Amy chewed on her lip for a moment. "I wonder if I should start locking up the General Store. We've gone to the honor system since I had baby Wills. I leave the store unlocked in case anyone needs anything while I'm away. All ye have to do is write down what ye take and either leave yere money then or pay later. It's worked well for us all these months. But what if Tuck decides to rob that, too?"

"Surely, he wouldn't." Rachel was feeling sorrier by the minute for Tuck MacBride. Maybe she should've gone to the pub with him. She could sympathize with him, knowing how the villagers didn't take to outsiders.

But Brodie's angry face invaded her mind, chasing her innocent thought of Tuck away.

Rachel kept her sentiments to herself and plucked up her notebook from her sewing machine. She retrieved Hannah before she ate all the cookies and told the quilters good-bye. As they stepped into Thistle Glen Lodge, Rachel got a text from her mother.

She turned to Hannah. "Grandma is flying in tomorrow."

Her daughter's mood amped up another notch.

But Rachel wasn't feeling the same as Hannah. With

her mother in town, Rachel anticipated a whole new set of problems were about to come to life and there was no way to prepare for what could happen next. She just wished she could speak with Brodie about it. When Vivienne Granger made an appearance, things were bound to get a thousand times more complicated.

It took a while to get Hannah settled in for the night. Thank goodness Sadie had the foresight to drop off a selection of picture books. Sadie also left some novels for Rachel. Her stack included popular women's fiction, some quilting fiction, and a romance with a cottage on the front. Though Rachel had plenty to do for Quilting Central, she took the romance out to the sofa and escaped until the out-of-town quilters arrived back at the dorm. Rachel put her book down and hopped up to wait on them until they were settled in for the night, too. Rachel didn't mind helping. Hospitality and the hotel business were in her blood. Keeping busy also kept Brodie off her mind. *Really.*

The dorm was becoming quiet. Rachel picked up the novel, but couldn't concentrate, feeling too restless to settle in for the night just yet. With her mother coming tomorrow, she felt overwhelmed with what was left to do. Like work on Abraham's Christmas present. She checked to make sure Hannah was asleep and then she knocked on the bedroom door of the two sisters from Edinburgh.

"Do you mind if I leave Hannah? I want to head back to Quilting Central to get some more done." Abraham's present wasn't the only thing left on her list.

Bessie, the older sister, stood at the desk and smiled at her warmly, holding up her rotary cutter and fabric. "Ye go on. We were going to do some *fussy cuts* before we go to bed. We'll listen for the lass."

"Thank you." There were advantages to her daughter

being used to daycare and spending time alone in their hotel room. Hannah was resourceful. If she woke up, her daughter would simply wake the quilters for help. They'd all taken a shine to her, each one comparing her to their own granddaughters. Besides, Rachel wouldn't be gone too long.

She grabbed her coat and hurried to Quilting Central, learning from Amy that the building was being kept open as it was so close to Christmas.

When Rachel arrived, Cait was the only one there, sitting behind her sewing machine.

"Couldn't sleep?" her new friend asked.

"I need to work on Abraham's Christmas present. Do you mind if I use the copier to print a few pictures?"

"Help yereself. Photo paper is in the bottom drawer."

Rachel walked over to her. "What are you working on?"

Cait smiled, clipped a thread, and then held up a miniature Christmas stocking made up of baby blue, soft violet, and yellow blocks.

"Is that what I think it is?"

"Aye. It's how I'm going to surprise Graham. But I still want to keep it a secret after that." She paused and looked away sadly. "Just in case, ye know . . . if something happens." She looked up at Rachel. "So you see why I wanted to work on it late . . . after everyone else left."

"I understand completely. I'll leave you to it."

"I was just finishing up." Cait stood and stretched. She was looking a little pregnant around the middle.

"Is there anything I should do when I'm done here?" Rachel asked.

"Just turn out the lights to conserve electricity."

"And the door?"

"Leave it unlocked, in case someone else has insomnia and decides to stitch her worries away."

Rachel's predicament exactly. It was nice of Cait not to speculate or question her as to what was keeping her from sleeping. Cait was perceptive so she must've known it was Brodie.

They said good night, Cait left, and Rachel got down to business, transferring photos from her phone to the computer by the copier. Surely one of them, taken on their first day, would be good. But when the first picture came up, she gulped. She, Hannah, and Abraham were smiling at the lens, but Brodie . . . *was staring intently at her.* While hitting the zoom button, she leaned in closer to see if his gaze held love, hate, or if he felt complete indifference toward her. She sighed. That was longing on his face. Hope soared through her heart like a gull winging over the ocean, more hope than she'd let herself have since she'd arrived in Gandiegow.

But this picture would never do for a family portrait for Abraham. She clicked through the next three images. Brodie was staring straight ahead in these, no smile, his mouth set in a determined line as if bearing up against an untimely storm. Rachel chose one, enlarged it to fit the paper in Deydie's bottom desk drawer, and hit the print button.

From the copier, like a metaphor for rebuilding her relationship with Brodie, the picture came together a pixel at a time. When it was completely printed, she could see their life together more clearly. His obstinate behavior had been chipping away at her dream, but now she felt reenergized. Because no one else was at Quilting Central, Rachel selected the picture of Brodie staring at her and shrank the picture to the size of the locket which hung around her neck. She located Deydie's paper scissors, which were clearly marked with DO NOT REMOVE! Rachel carefully cut out the picture of him and her.

She looked around one more time to make sure she was alone and unclasped the necklace. She wouldn't be so bold as to cover up the picture of one of Brodie's parents, but she did pop out the picture of his mother to place the picture of them behind it. Now Rachel had what she truly desired close to her heart.

She borrowed an empty folder from Deydie's desk and slipped the large family picture inside. In the morning, she'd talk to the head quilter about locating a piece of MacFarlane tartan, Abraham's clan, for which to make the frame. She laid the folder by her sewing machine, satisfied to have made some headway on the Christmas present. Yawning, she let herself out of Quilting Central, turning off the lights on her way.

But when she stepped outside, her eye caught a figure ducking between the buildings as if he didn't want to be seen. She thought about Amy's report of the things which had gone missing. For a second longer, Rachel waited to see if the person would reemerge. For surely if it was one of the townsfolk, they would make themselves known. But when he didn't appear, she headed for the quilting dorm. She was more intrigued than afraid, but nonetheless, she was happy for the streetlamps and a well-lit path back to Thistle Glen Lodge.

Brodie stalked toward The Fisherman, Gandiegow's pub, feeling relieved to have made it back to town without doing something stupid . . . like confide in his mother about what had been going on with Rachel. He shivered. He hadn't answered his mother's questions before, and he wouldn't now as to how her locket had ended up with the Yank. He was just going to wait it out until Rachel left, then he'd get on with his life. What was a little more pain?

He'd waited six years before . . . hiding out at Here Again Farm where the memories of Joe's widow shouldn't have been able to find him. But he'd thought about Rachel every day. Hell, every hour. Even worse was what he did after Joe had died. Rachel was on his mind in ways he shouldn't have allowed, things he couldn't admit to anyone. He envisioned how the two of them could be together now that his cousin was gone. The guilt from those thoughts alone kept him from finding Rachel after Joe's death. Plus, his grandda's constant reminder that *women can't be trusted* had reinforced his stance over the years afterward. But Brodie never stopped fantasizing about her, and he hated himself for it.

He pulled open the door and stepped into the noise of the pub, pausing to take it all in. Lochie was playing guitar in the corner. Coll was delivering food. As usual, Bonnie was passing out drinks and zeroed in on him the second he walked in. She was always looking at him as if she was chocolate deprived and he was a Cadbury bar. Most of the tables were full, and for a moment, Brodie felt calmed. There was safety in numbers, and being around the townsfolk would help him not to think about Rachel. Also, being here was going to keep him from rushing to the quilting dorm to find her and kiss her again. And again. Though that's what he *effing* well wanted. The good news was there was no chance of Rachel showing up at the pub this late with Hannah in bed for the night.

God, he liked that little girl Hannah. She made him laugh. She seemed to have gotten the best of Joe and the best of Rachel.

Brodie's chest clenched. He hated that some small thought of Rachel could tear him up so easily. He couldn't have it both ways. He couldn't have Joe's widow and hold on to his principles. He'd gotten burned once and he'd learned his lesson. He wasn't stupid enough to have a go at her again.

Brodie made his way to the bar, but was stopped with a hand on his shoulder.

"Join us." Gabe pointed to an empty table nearby. Behind Gabe was his father, Casper, who had moved here after Moira and Andrew's wedding. The retired reverend relished in watching his grandchildren, but had quickly become active in the community, too. He helped Father Andrew at the kirk with everything from maintenance on the furnace to being a sounding board for next Sunday's service.

"Sure." Brodie took a seat and so did Gabe.

"I'll get our drinks," Casper said. "No sense in making Bonnie wait on us."

"I'll take a whisky," Gabe said.

"Irn Bru," Brodie added.

Gabe nodded. "Change mine to Irn Bru, also."

"Ye sure?" Casper said to his son.

"Aye. Early morning. I'm needed at the North Sea Valve Company to check a motor on one of the lines." It was interesting—and their good fortune—that the town's physician was also a damned good mechanic.

Casper nodded and left them.

Brodie pointed to the retired pastor. "He seems happy and settled here." It felt good to hang out with Gabe and not discuss Abraham's deteriorating health.

Gabriel laughed. "Da is happier than the Pope on Sunday; retirement agrees with him. It agrees with me and Emma, too. We're able to get out by ourselves some. Dominic and Claire are making use of his grandda babysitting services, also. I'm so glad he's here."

"When will his cottage be started?" Brodie knew

Casper had been sharing a room with his grandson Angus in the small doctor's quarters.

"Mr. Sinclair says he'll start construction in the early spring. A cozy two-bedroom will be just the thing to let Da rest between playing with the grandbairns."

"Gandiegow is certainly expanding." Brodie thought about all the new faces since he'd left six years ago, plus all those who were no longer here—either moved away or had passed on. Rhona, his old schoolteacher, moved to Dundee to help her daughter. There were a few deaths, too—Kenneth Campbell, Moira's da, who had recently died, and Joe. Life had a way of changing and moving forward whether you wanted it to or not.

Gabe was talking.

"What?" Brodie asked.

"I said, when I get a free moment tomorrow, I'll check the timing on yere boat's engine."

"I'd appreciate it. It sounds a bit off."

"Sure."

The door to the pub opened. Ross, Sadie, and Grace appeared. But whereas Ross and Sadie continued their conversation and walked in, Grace stopped suddenly, gazing across the room as if a rock star was in their midst. Brodie followed to where she looked and was surprised at who she mooned over—Gabe's da, Casper MacGregor.

Casper had stopped, too, about three feet from the table and stared at her, a grin starting in his eyes and expanding across his face. A look back at Grace said her temporary paralysis had lifted; she was glancing side to side as if going to make a run for it.

The retired reverend's eyes dropped to the drinks in his hands as if he only just remembered they were there. He set them on the table and walked toward Grace with determination, giving no explanation to them first. He caught up to her before she could flee.

"Did ye know about this?" Brodie asked Gabe.

"What?"

Brodie nodded toward Gabe's father, Grace, and the door. "Grace Armstrong and yere da."

Gabe looked in their direction. "No. I didn't. It's interesting, though. Growing up, the single women of the kirk always vying for my father's attention. My mum died when I was a baby, ye see. But he never dated, not once. He always seemed too busy with church business to worry about the women clucking around him. Of course, Dominic and I were always up to some trouble or another." Gabe laughed, but then seemed thoughtful for a moment. "It might be nice for him to have some companionship."

But Grace seemed torn. Casper looked back at their table a couple of times while he was talking. Brodie suspected he was trying to get Grace to join them. Finally she left him to sit with Ross and Sadie, who were laughing, their heads together in the back corner booth.

Casper returned and sat down, but not before he glanced one more time at Grace.

"When did that happen?" Gabe asked.

"What?" Casper said, more than a little distracted.

"Grace Armstrong."

"Oh, aye. Grace and I had a nice visit after Andrew and Moira's wedding." With his eyebrows pulled together, Casper sipped his drink, no smile on his face now.

"Ye couldn't get her to join us?" Gabe asked.

"She said she wants to sit with her son."

But Ross seemed totally engrossed in conversation with his wife, Sadie, while Grace looked miserable.

Casper pushed his drink back and stood. "I think I'll take a walk."

"Night, Da," Gabriel said.

Casper nodded to them. He didn't look again in the direction of where Grace sat, but Brodie was pretty sure he was thinking about her as he trudged out the door.

Not ten seconds later, Grace rose, weaved her way through the crowd, and slipped out the door, too. Brodie decided maybe he wasn't the only one in Gandiegow who was having problems.

Chapter Nine

Once outside, Grace skimmed the area to make sure no one saw her before running after Casper. He was heading between the buildings, probably back to the doctor's quarters. She had to explain why she couldn't sit with him in public. She caught up with him before he reached the other side of the wynd.

"Wait. Please."

He stopped and turned.

She was a little out of breath, not because of running but because of the adrenaline flooding her system. "I want to talk."

Casper raised an eyebrow. "Ye didn't want to a few minutes ago. Why wouldn't ye sit with me?"

She chewed her lip. "My son was in the pub."

"So? Mine was as well."

"It wouldn't be right," Grace said.

Casper reached for her, his large hand feeling warm in hers, making her feel safe, secure. "When I heard ye were moving here, I'd hoped we could see each other." He looked down at her hand and then brought his eyes up to meet hers. "I want to court ye, Grace."

Part of her wanted that, too. But she'd been over it a million times in her mind. She couldn't. She had to think of her sons. What of their feelings? Surely they would see her dating Casper as betraying their father, who'd died four years ago. She felt like she was betraying Alistair, too.

Casper squeezed her hand and gazed into her eyes, making her lose focus. He was such a kind and good man, a man any woman would want. For him to proclaim he wanted to court her? The thought made her breath hitch. He sealed the deal by leaning in and kissing her. Not the kiss on the cheek he'd given her when they'd parted after Andrew and Moira's wedding. But a real kiss. A proper kiss. A kiss that had her feeling all kinds of things she assumed she would never feel again. She felt like butter heated up and poured over fresh-from-the-oven bread. When her stomach began to ache and she wanted more of him, Casper pulled away.

He searched her eyes. "What do ye say?"

"All right," she heard herself whisper. But then her senses partially returned. "But I don't want anyone to know."

He frowned at her, but softened it by resting his hand on her back. "I don't like it, Grace."

She laid her hand on his cheek, but couldn't look him in the eyes. "Just give me some time." It was a plea, but also, it was a lie. Time wouldn't change anything.

He kissed her again, but seconds later, she pulled away.

"I have to get home." She wasn't a young lass anymore—not like when she married the boys' father and could do whatever she wanted.

"Okay." But Casper had a determined gleam in his eyes which said he wasn't giving up.

She left him standing between the buildings as she rushed back to the cottage with her brain spinning . . . *Casper MacGregor wants to court me!*

But in the next second, rational thinking returned. She had to set an example for her family.

She was too old to feel like this. What would her sons think about her pining for another man? Love, like she'd shared with her husband, didn't come around twice.

Nothing would change her mind. Nothing.

The next morning at Thistle Glen Lodge, Rachel helped the quilters get packed. The retreat-goers, after one more quilting session this morning, were heading home today. She located a lost phone, a missing hairbrush, and a pin cushion which was hiding. As the ladies zipped up their luggage and pulled them into the living room, Rachel went around straightening up as much as possible, while making mental notes of things to do this afternoon when the ladies were gone. Before she left for Quilting Central, she was able to get a load of towels in the washer, planning to start the sheets after lunch.

As they walked to Quilting Central in a group, Rachel wondered why Gandiegow didn't have a bed and breakfast. The lot next to Thistle Glen Lodge seemed to have plenty of space to build a fairly large house. Since arriving in town, the thought of owning a bed and breakfast kept crossing her mind. She laughed, the idea both funny and strange. When Rachel was growing up, she didn't want their family hotel—though everyone expected her to take over one day. The Sunnydale Hotel had been too small and quaint for Rachel's big dreams. For her to be thinking of owning her own place now felt so foreign, but something was happening to her. Suddenly she wanted more than a hotel room and a lobby to call home.

At Quilting Central as Rachel was ready to take the stage to deliver the final instructions on the Gandiegow Christmas Tree quilt, her phone blipped. She checked: a text from her mother.

I have arrived and checked into a hotel.

"What?" Rachel said aloud to her phone. Deydie and Bethia glanced over at her. Rachel read on.

Christmas shopping in Edinburgh. Will see you soon.

Her mother changing her plans wasn't completely un-expected. Besides, it made perfect sense to shop in Scot-land instead of bringing presents across the Pond. The news was good for Rachel in that it gave her more time—time to finish putting her mother's present together and time for the all-important mental prep she would need before Vivienne Granger invaded Gandiegow.

Rachel silenced her phone, stepped on the stage, and began her final instructions for finishing the top of the quilt. "The last thing to do is to trim the leftover triangle pieces from the side. Just hold your straightedge at an angle like this"—she demonstrated with the quilt she'd been making along with the group—"and cut off the ex-tra bits." Lastly, she shared how she'd hung her Christmas Tree quilt at her room in the Winderly. By eleven, when the retreat was over, everyone had pieced their quilt tops with some further along, who had already started pin-ning the three pieces together—the front, the batting, and the back.

Deydie told the retreat-goers to put their things away. Rachel was surprised when men—most of them wearing wellies—came filing in the door and leaned against the back wall. Her breath caught when a certain fisherman stalked in and took his place among the others.

Amy gently elbowed her. "They're here to help load the quilters on the bus. Our men have already taken their bags from the dorm to the coach." Amy raised her hand, waving at her husband, Coll. He worked at the pub, both bartending and cooking the occasional sandwich and soup.

Rachel wished she had the right to wave to Brodie, as if he were *her man*. But then he surprised her when he looked in her direction, staring straight at her. He wasn't frowning or anything, and hope surged in her heart.

"Okay, everyone, let's line up." The Gandiegowans went to the stage, forming three lines, the men included. But Deydie pulled Brodie to the front. "Use yere God-given talent and lead the group."

Brodie did frown then . . . at Deydie. Resigned, he turned to the makeshift choir. "Comfort and Joy," he announced and then started singing. "God rest ye merry gentlemen . . ."

His voice was deep, rich, and his pitch perfect. The rest of the choir didn't join in right away as they were as mesmerized as Rachel was. When they did start singing, she only had ears for Brodie, hearing him above the others, his voice resonating with every cell in her body, from her heart to her soul.

An old memory came back to her. Six years ago, Brodie was scheduled to sing at her wedding, but when the time came, he hadn't. She'd been relieved.

"Oh, tidings of comfort and joy," rolled over Rachel as Brodie's beautiful voice complimented the voices around him.

She knew now that not hearing Brodie sing before had been her loss . . . only one of the many losses Rachel had experienced on her wedding day and beyond.

When the song ended, Deydie bade the quilters farewell and shooed them toward the door. The Gandiegow men gathered sewing machines and bags and followed them out.

Brodie was near the back of the line, watching her. Rachel gave him a smile with a shrug.

His eyebrows pinched together and he looked away.

She wanted to run to him and tell him how well he'd sung. How much she loved his voice. How much she still *loved him*. How sorry she was for not listening to her heart, but relying on the counsel of others.

If only he'd walk by her sewing machine, he would see his Christmas gift in progress—a pillowcase designed just for him with a partridge as the centerpiece. The partridge was a private matter for her and Brodie alone. Just another way to let him know she cared.

After the quilters and the men left, Rachel hurried to the schoolhouse to retrieve Hannah. Back at the cottage, she was on pins and needles, wondering if Brodie would show for lunch or not. She made an extra sandwich and left it in the refrigerator. When she took the tray into the parlor, Abraham was holding the iPad in front of his face.

"Smile," he said.

Rachel didn't get a chance before she heard a click. He set the iPad in his lap, grinning.

Hannah hopped up and down. "Let me see. Let me see."

"See what?" Rachel asked.

Hannah laughed. "I taught Grandda how to take pictures." She was so proud of herself. She leaned over to look at the image. "But, Mommy, ye're frowning. Do it again, and this time ye better smile."

Rachel raised her eyebrows at her daughter, who was acting like a miniature Deydie. But when she opened her mouth to chastise Hannah, Abraham beat her to it.

He patted her girl's tiny hand, but his words were firm. "Watch how ye speak to yere mum, little one."

Hannah stared up at Rachel. Grandfather and granddaughter had gotten along so well up until now. Rachel wondered how his scold would affect their bond.

Hannah turned back to Abraham, and then dropped her head. "Sorry, Mommy."

Rachel set the tray down and squeezed her daughter's shoulder lovingly. "It's okay, but your grandfather's right. You don't want to get too bossy for your britches. Now, come get a plate for your grandfather and tell us what you have planned for this afternoon."

Hannah bounced around, explaining the game. Rachel had to remind her more than once to attend to her lunch. After they ate, Hannah set up the parlor to play *volcano and hot lava* with washcloths and hand towels laid out on the floor as the only safe places to stand without getting burned.

"I'll be back. I have Christmas presents to work on," she said as she slipped on her coat.

"For me?" Hannah asked.

"No. For Grandma Vivienne and a few others." *One person in particular.* "Now, be good and have fun."

When she returned to Quilting Central, once again, the room was buzzing with the latest gossip.

Pippa, who had recently had twins, filled Rachel and Amy in. "Deydie was griping that her paper scissors aren't where they're supposed to be. She swears they were on her desk when she left yesterday."

Rachel cringed. She'd used the scissors last night, but she felt certain she returned them to their spot.

Pippa continued on, "Mrs. Bruce told me this morning that she made Mr. Menzies two loaves of bread. She left them on the window ledge to cool, and when she returned, one was missing. That's two things that have been taken from her. First the flannel shirt on the line, now the bread."

"Does she think it was Tuck?" Amy asked.

"Yes. Everyone does. But it doesn't make sense," Pippa said.

"I know." Amy nodded. "Moira believes he's getting plenty to eat at their house. But who could it be? We never had a theft problem in Gandiegow before he came."

Rachel thought about the figure she'd seen last night in the shadows. It could've been anyone, but mentioning it would only add to the gossip.

She worked on Brodie's pillowcase, making French seams, wanting his present to be perfect. When she was done, many of the women admired her work, asking questions, but Rachel successfully threw them off the scent. *I like partridges*, she answered, making it sound simple and convincing.

As the dinner hour approached, Quilting Central emptied. Rachel left, too, but stopped by the General Store to pick up the remaining items for her mother's Christmas present.

As luck would have it, Amy was at her post, manning the store. "Ye found us. I was wondering when you might make it in for a few things."

"I was afraid you wouldn't be here and I meant to ask earlier if you could help me." Rachel pulled out her mother's new shopping bag, which she'd quickly sewn together after finishing Brodie's pillowcase. "I want to fill this for my mom, make her a Scotland Survival Kit. Do you have any wellies?"

"Aye," Amy said. "And warm socks, too."

"Good. Let's fill it up. She'll be here tomorrow and I want this under the tree before she arrives."

Amy put in all the essentials and a few indulgences. "My auntie made these Christmas ornaments, if ye'd like to buy one of those also."

The knitted ornament was in the shape of a miniature red and green baubled sweater with tiny bells sewn on.

"Perfect." Rachel thought about the simple patchwork quilt she'd cut out and started for her mother, also.

Amy totaled the survival kit, Rachel paid, and they went their separate ways outside the store. Rachel headed to Abraham's, anxious to see Brodie at dinner, maybe talk to him afterward. But he never showed. When she asked after him, Abraham shrugged.

"I don't know where he is, lass. He comes and goes. But he certainly isn't around much lately."

"I'll make him a plate and put it in the oven. Can you let him know it's there?"

"Aye. Now, Hannah, come here and show me how to play music on the iPad. Ye said this thing will do it, didn't ye?"

"Aye, Grandda," she giggled.

Rachel went into the kitchen and pulled down one of Abraham's stoneware plates. But she didn't fill it right away, instead digging around in the pantry until she located a paper plate and aluminum foil. She filled both plates with the roast, potatoes, carrots, and leeks. She covered them, putting Brodie's plate in the oven, and taking the other with her to round up Hannah.

"Are ye ready to go, sweetie?"

Hannah kissed her grandfather on the cheek. "See ya later, alligator."

Abraham chuckled and this time he didn't end it with a coughing fit.

"Night," she said.

As she and Hannah walked through town, they counted the number of buildings which glowed with holiday lights. *Many more than yesterday.* Everyone was getting into the Christmas spirit. Rachel was, too, but there was only one present she really wanted. And he hadn't bothered to show up for dinner.

At Thistle Glen Lodge, Hannah ran in first. As Rachel stepped in, the smell of pine needles, or something like it, filled her nose. It was sweet and distinctive, and all of Rachel's Christmas memories came flooding back. Her grandparents always had a fresh tree in the lobby of their small hotel. Her mother, too, when she owned Sunnydale. Nice memories. Great Christmases.

"Oh, Mommy!" Hannah exclaimed from the other room.

Rachel dropped her bags, but kept the plate, and rushed in to see. In the corner of the living room was the source of the wonderful smell. Someone had been thoughtful enough to set up a Douglas fir just for them.

"Looky," Hannah squealed, clapping her hands and jumping up and down. "Isn't it grand?"

"Yes. Very." And a great surprise. Rachel moved farther into the room and noticed the two boxes of decorations which sat nearby. Next to them on the couch was a small opened box. Rachel leaned over to see the tree topper nestled in the tissue paper.

She gasped and her heart picked up several beats. It wasn't a star or an angel, but a carved wooden partridge!

"What?" Hannah said. "Let me see."

"Be careful." Rachel handed her the box, keeping her hand underneath so it wouldn't fall.

"Oh, it's *bee-oot-iful*."

Rachel laughed. "Here. Let me put it on the mantel. It's for after we get the rest of the tree decorated. If you hurry with your bath, we'll have time to do it before bed."

Hannah's eyes bugged melodramatically as if she was a child star hamming it up for the director. "I'll be so fast." Then she tore off for the bathroom.

While Hannah was undressing, Rachel found a piece of paper and wrote:

Help yourself.

She set the covered plate on the front porch, along with the note, and turned off the light. She also locked the front door, something she'd started doing when they went to bed at night since she'd seen the man in the shadows.

Hannah had the quickest bath on record. Rachel found some Christmas CDs and loaded the player. They sang along as they decorated the tree, but the whole time, she felt as if the *tree gifter* should be here as well . . . singing along with them.

When they were done, she carefully placed the partridge on top. They turned out the lights, except the tree's multicolored strings, and cuddled on the sofa with "O Christmas Tree" playing in the background. When the song ended, Rachel carried Hannah into their bedroom and tucked her in. They said their prayers and then she kissed her daughter good night. Before leaving the room, Rachel grabbed her thick robe and slipped it on, leaving Hannah to fall asleep.

Back in the living room with the conifer front and center, Rachel felt restless, unable to keep her mind off the man who'd put up the Christmas tree. She peeked out the front window, looking for Brodie, but only noticed the plate was still there. She traveled into the kitchen and put the kettle on, before sitting down to sketch a new quilt in her notebook.

After a couple of minutes, she laid her pencil down. If only she could've seen Brodie tonight and talked to him, she would feel more settled. She touched the locket, wishing it was a summoning device.

But he'd been here. The wooden partridge was evidence. *It has to mean something. Doesn't it?*

The kettle whistled. She left the new quilt design on the table, filled her mug, but the kitchen felt too confined for her thoughts. She wrapped her robe around her tighter and padded outside to the back porch to cool her tea.

The snow-dusted bluff loomed only ten feet away. The sloshing of the waves against the embankment walkway could be heard, even though the quilting dorms sat farthest away from the North Sea. The surety of God's creations—the bluff and the ocean—calmed her. She began humming "Comfort and Joy." Being outside, like this, pulled her from her own head. She leaned over and gazed at the empty lot next to the cottage, and as she did, her mind began to lay the stone, wood, and windows as if constructing the bed and breakfast she'd thought of earlier. If the front porch was positioned just right, the North Sea could be viewed between the buildings. Even better, Rachel would put a balcony on the second floor, so her guests would have an unencumbered panorama of the ocean.

She inhaled sharply. *What am I doing? Am I really considering this?*

Her life was back in Chicago at the Winderly Towers. She had to admit she was being fanciful, and truthfully, she was kind of a mess. Everything she believed to be true was in a massive upheaval. From the moment she saw Brodie again and wanted them to be together, she'd been certain it would all work itself out. She hadn't given any real thought what that life would look like, though . . . where they would live, and how they would carry on. But apparently her subconscious had been mulling over the problem and making plans. Like the B and B.

She shivered and turned around, ready to go back inside. But she wasn't alone. Her breath caught and her hand flew to her throat. She had the odd thought that her only constant was her reaction to the man on the other side of the porch. Brodie looked both masculine and ridiculous with her red polka dot purse dangling at his side.

He frowned at her. "Ye'll catch yere death." He reached for the door and held it open. The look he was giving her was a clear command.

"You scared me."

"Sorry." Though he didn't seem contrite, not one bit. "I saw ye from a distance. What are ye doing out here?"

Without answering, she did as he wanted, returning inside. He wouldn't understand that she felt safe here in Gandiegow, even with someone lurking about, and that she needed open spaces to think. He marched in after her.

The kitchen's interior shined brightly, but everything looked different now. A while ago, she'd been restless for something to happen. Now Brodie was here. His presence changed the context of the room from boring to brooding. Not exactly what she'd hoped for. But at least now they could talk.

He glanced down at his load and sighed heavily as if her purse didn't match his black wellies. "Ye forgot something." He held it out like a bucket of spoiled bait. "Here."

She took it and laid it in a chair.

Brodie's eyes scanned down her robe. He didn't seem to approve of what she was wearing either. "When I came home, I heard yere phone ringing. I brought yere purse over straightaway."

"Did you look to see who was calling?"

He raised an eyebrow. "Real men don't rummage through a woman's handbag. For any reason."

"Not even for a piece of gum," she teased.

The smile she'd hoped for didn't appear.

"Sit down," she said. "I'll pour you a cup of tea."

He moved her purse to another spot and surprisingly took the seat next to where she'd set her mug.

"What's this?" He was examining her notebook.

"I'm designing a new quilt."

"Is it Gandiegow by the sea?"

"That's what I was intending." The extra scraps from the villagers had been crying out for their own quilt. She could see the tartans as the houses of Gandiegow. Then she could use blue prints for the ocean and sky and maybe some different shades of white for the snow-covered bluff. And she liked the name he'd given it: Gandiegow by the Sea.

He gazed at her. "'Tis nice."

He was talking about her design, but the way he was gazing at her led her to imagine he meant more. She faced the cabinet, chewing her lip.

She gave herself a moment to gather courage, then she got on with it. "Thank you for the tree." She closed her eyes and waited, her stomach roiling with anticipation. "Thank you for the other gift, too." When he didn't say anything, she turned back around.

Brodie stared her square in the eye—as if he'd practiced it—and had the blankest look on his face. His expression was laughable. "I don't know what ye're speaking of."

She grabbed his hand and yanked him up, ignoring his look of shock. She dragged him into the living room, doing her utmost to ignore the electrical pulses which passed from his hand into hers. The lamp and overhead light were still turned off so the tree shone bright like a billboard—inviting, the crowning glory of the room. Norman Rockwell couldn't have painted a more perfect Christmas scene.

"There." She didn't let go of his hand. If it was up to her, she'd never let go.

"Nice bird," he drawled.

She'd fashioned the lights around the top like a glowing nest so her partridge could be seen even with the living room lights turned off.

"You did this," she said. "Admit it."

"It must've been the quilting ladies. They probably thought ye needed a tree with yere mum about to arrive. Also, for the girl, of course."

"Really. And the partridge? Which one of the quilting ladies thought to give us such a unique gift?"

He shrugged. "Deydie?"

"Yeah. Sure she did." Rachel deliberated on whether he bought it or if he'd carved it himself.

He let go of her hand. "I better be going."

"Not so fast." She wanted another one of his searing kisses. If only she had some mistletoe.

"'Tis late."

"But I want to talk," she said. "There's so much to say."

"Right now, the only thing we have to talk about is the message I'm to give ye from my grandda. He'd like Hannah to spend Christmas Eve night at the cottage, so she'll be there on Christmas morn." Brodie cocked his head. She speculated if there was more to the message, or if there was something he wanted to add, but couldn't spit it out.

"Yes, she can stay." Rachel wondered how this would work. Only one of them—either her mother or herself—could stay at Abraham's cottage with Hannah. It would be Vivienne. Her mother would insist.

Brodie nodded, looking as if he was reading her thoughts and steeling himself against something unpleasant. He stalked out of the room, heading for the front, his determined gait making it clear he didn't want Rachel running after him.

She did anyway, catching up to him as he was opening the front door. From behind, she wrapped her arms around him, knowing this was a huge risk she was taking by hugging him.

He stilled.

"Stay," she said. "Talk to me." She weaseled her way to the front of him, her arms still encapsulating him, and gazed up into his face. "There's so much I need to say." Six years' worth.

"I can't." He was impenetrable as stone. But she only heard vulnerability in his voice.

She snaked her arms around his neck and pulled him down for a kiss, hoping to crumble his hard exterior and to strengthen herself so she could speak the truth.

The kiss wasn't fervent as their last one had been, but an exploration of unchartered territory. Something new. He wrapped his arms around her, holding her close, delving in, and finding all the places she'd reserved only for him. The kiss seemed to go on and on.

When they pulled away, she laid her head on his chest, smiling. But immediately, she could feel him loosening his hold and slipping away.

This was now or never. She could talk to him for hours, but really everything boiled down to one statement.

Too afraid to look up and face him, she kept her head plastered to his chest, listening to his heart as she asked him the one thing she needed to know. "Can you ever forgive me?" Bravely, she lifted her head and gazed into his face.

He didn't meet her eyes, but shook his head *no*. His exhale deflated him.

She dropped her arms—completely devastated—and let him go.

As he opened the door, her heart was breaking, but then she remembered. *The plate on the front porch!*

She grabbed his arm. "Wait!"

He stopped—half inside, half out—and turned to her with a dampened expression. "What?" It was pretty clear what he really wanted to say. *I already gave you my final answer.*

Her eyes searched for the plate, but it was gone. "Um, nothing. My mistake." She turned to go back inside.

He took her arm, stopping her. "What's going on?"

Rachel looked around for the man in the shadows. She only saw the backs of the houses of Gandiegow.

"Nothing's going on," she finally answered.

Brodie looked down and saw the piece of paper folded into a miniature hat. He reached down and opened it, the words *Help yourself* as plain as day under the streetlamp. "This isn't nothing." He'd said the words quietly.

She looked around one more time. "Not out here. Come back inside."

Chapter Ten

In Brodie's gut, he knew something was wrong. The way Rachel was acting was so strange. He was still reeling from the kiss and her request for forgiveness, but the paper hat on the porch took priority. Besides, he couldn't talk about how she unbalanced him. Later he'd contemplate how he'd lied to her. He could barely admit to himself he was starting to forgive her—*just a little*—though he had no mind to absolve her altogether. What reasonable man would ever forgive Rachel for what she had done?

He ushered her back into the house and followed her into the living room. He switched on every lamp because the room was too damn cozy with just the Christmas tree lights twinkling. It'd taken everything in him not to kiss her when she'd shown him the tree. The tree he couldn't help putting there. The partridge . . . it was an accident. While on the boat today, he'd passed the time whittling a chunk of wood. He'd been one surprised bastard when he'd seen what he'd carved.

She sat on the sofa. He stood at the mantle. He'd done so well staying away from her earlier this evening, hiding out on the boat until he saw her walking across town to Thistle Glen Lodge.

Rachel was silent, looking guilty.

"Tell me," he ordered.

"Everyone is saying that things are missing. They believe it's Tuck."

"I don't listen to gossip."

"But I know you've heard."

He nodded.

She chewed the inside of her cheek, not looking at him. "It's not Tuck. The mystery person isn't tall enough to be him, and his shoulders aren't as broad."

Jealousy pierced Brodie as if his chest was gashed by an oversized treble hook. He detested that Rachel was in Gandiegow and the things she made him feel. He especially detested her describing Tuck. And he detested Tuck, because all the women commented on how well the Almighty had put him together. *Gads!*

Brodie brought his focus back to the issue at hand. "How do you know this person isn't as tall as Tuck?" *Or as broad.*

She shook her head.

Brodie was getting a sinking feeling and stalked toward her. "Explain."

"I saw him," she confessed.

"Who was it?" Brodie asked. "Where were you? When was this?"

She didn't look happy that he was bombarding her with questions, but he couldn't help it. He had to know. So he could keep her safe.

"Out with it."

"Fine," she said, sounding exasperated. "Last night when I was leaving Quilting Central. It was late."

"How late?"

"After eleven."

"Were you by yereself?"

When she nodded, his stomach felt sick. Something terrible could've happened to her. He was steaming mad.

How could she be so reckless? "Tell me everything. Everything that ye saw."

"There's not much to tell. It was just a man. When he saw me, he stepped into the shadows . . . as if he didn't want to be seen." She hesitated. "For a second, I thought it might be you." She turned her head away. "Watching out for me."

God, he wished he'd been that smart.

She exhaled and faced him again. "But the man in the shadows couldn't have been you. Too thin. Not big enough. Not nearly." She skimmed Brodie's exterior, seeming embarrassed, but also not stopping until her eyes had thoroughly looked him over from top to bottom.

Brodie puffed up, although he didn't care that she was assessing him, or that she seemed to approve of what she saw. But he had to admit he felt appeased, but only slightly. But then the impact of it all had air escaping his lungs. "Ye didn't think to tell me about it sooner?"

She straightened up and looked him square in the eye. "You've been AWOL. Remember?"

"Hell." His plan to stay away from her could've gotten her hurt. He was royally ticked off. He crumpled the origami note in his hand. "What was this all about? I assume ye wrote it?"

"I think he's hungry so I fixed him a plate after dinner. I fixed one for you, too. Did you get it? I left it in the oven at the cottage."

It had been nice to get a warm meal when he'd returned home from freezing his arse off on the boat. It was thoughtful of her, but he wasn't going to say it now. He was livid.

"God, woman! How did ye know this stranger isn't out to harm you? Yere kindness to the thief could very well be deadly. Leave milk out for stray cats, but for God's sake, stop inviting danger! What ye've done is to only ask him to come back for more." Brodie glanced down the hall to where Hannah—young, small, and vulnerable—slept behind the door. He wanted to bellow at Rachel that she and her daughter had no choice but to come back to Abraham's now. Brodie could keep them safe there. But he stopped himself from roaring. He wouldn't scare the little one awake. He tamped down his fury and hurled the paper into the empty hearth instead. "Why don't you have a fire going? It's freezing in here."

She wrapped her white robe around her, tightening it. "I—I don't know how."

He stared at her in disbelief. *Holy effing hell*. He'd let them come back over here and she didn't have one ounce of survival skills to stay in a cottage on the northeast coast of Scotland? What had he been thinking?

"Don't look at me that way! I grew up in a hotel. My grandfather switched the wood-burning fireplace with a gas insert when I was a girl. We just had to flip a switch."

This was another glaring difference between them. She was a *flip a switch* type of woman and he was a grunt and muscle man—cutting down the trees, chopping logs, carrying them in, and building a damned fire. Just another reason why he couldn't wait until she was gone. God, he still cared for her, though. But the gulf was too wide. *Too deep*. He'd drown trying to get to her. He would *effing* drown.

But he couldn't think about that now. He walked straight to the hearth, squatted down, and grabbed the paper from the bin. He began crunching them into balls.

"Don't start a fire now," she hissed. "I'm going to bed soon. It wouldn't be safe."

"It'll be fine." His words came out more of a curse than as a comfort. "I'll be here to make sure."

"What?" Her pitch had risen.

He looked back at her. "I've no choice in the matter.

You and *wee bit* need to be watched after. I'll sleep on the sofa."

She sighed exasperatedly, sounding so much like one of Hannah's melodramatic snits. "Seriously, Brodie, the food snatcher is harmless."

He stood, going to her, putting his hands on her shoulders. He gazed into her brown eyes, willing her to see the truth. "Ye don't know that for sure. I couldn't . . ." He faltered. "We couldn't—*Abraham and the rest of the village*—we couldn't have anythin' happen to you." Brodie's eyes bore into her, making sure she knew it all. If something happened to her, it would kill him. It would crush his soul. He would be totally lost. "I mean it." His voice sounded hoarse, like Grandda's after one of his coughing fits.

She nodded and started to reach up with her hand.

Brodie let go and stepped back. "Stand over here so I can teach ye what every Scottish lass is taught before she's three years old." Hannah's lesson would begin tomorrow. "Grab a handful of tinder from the box and spread it over the paper.

It was hell to have Rachel shoulder-to-shoulder with him, but at least she was nearby where he could keep her safe.

He guided her through the rest of the steps on how to build a fire, having her do each part on her own. Finally he stood when the fire was blazing, bringing warmth and comfort into the room.

"You can't stay," Rachel said, going to the sofa, sitting down, and pulling her legs up to her chin.

He disagreed. "Why?"

"Hannah."

"I'll be gone before she wakes. I have to do the morning run on the boat."

"I know Gandiegow," Rachel said. "The gossip will

be thick if they find out you're here." She looked at him as though it saddened her that he couldn't stay.

His chest warmed, as if the idiotic partridge had been swaddled in a quilt.

"Let me take care of Gandiegow," he murmured. "As I said, they wouldn't want anything to happen to ye."

She stood and stared at him, as if it was a dare. "And you? Do you care, too?"

He held on to the mantle to keep from crossing the room and pulling her into his arms. "I care for the girl." That was the only thing he would admit. But he cursed himself that his declaration took all the air from her sails.

He looked at the clock on the wall. "I have to rest before I get up in a few hours."

She put her hands on her hips. "Why did you come here tonight?"

He didn't point out that her red handbag sat in the kitchen as testament as to why he'd come. She didn't know the rationale he'd used to bring it to Thistle Glen Lodge either. *What if she has an emergency and needs her purse in the middle of the night?* He couldn't have her traipsing across the village in that robe of hers to get it. By the way she was acting, did she think he'd stopped by for some other reason? But she was wrong, completely wrong. He wasn't so weak that he needed to make excuses to see a woman.

Her robe and tousled brown hair didn't go with the fierce glare she was firing at him. He wanted to pull her into his arms and kiss her anger away. But the answer to her question as to why he'd come here tonight flickered across his mind as a lighthouse beam passes over the rocks, illuminating them, leading the way to safety. He cocked an eyebrow at her, making sure he got in the last word.

"The Almighty sent me here. Ye're in need of a watchdog tonight."

*   *   *

Rachel stood transfixed as Brodie pulled the quilt out of the tall corner basket. She wanted more from him than to be some kind of guard dog for her. She wanted a *true love*. She wanted to kiss him once more. Maybe twice. If she took the initiative again, she'd do nothing but make herself look foolish. *Or desperate.* He'd been clear. He was never going to forgive her.

She didn't say good night, or thank him for staying over, but left him to stretch out on the couch. She grabbed her notebook before she walked down the hallway. She didn't want to think about what had just passed between them. While she washed her face and brushed her hair, she forced herself to think of something pleasant, like the empty lot next door.

First she imagined the interior of the B and B . . . a warm beachy atmosphere, but it had to feel like a Scottish cottage, too. As she picked out everything in her mind from the window coverings to the sheets on the bed, the obvious question popped up. *The cost.*

She took her notebook to the bedroom next to hers so as not to wake Hannah. As she flipped to a clean page, past all the quilts she'd designed since arriving in Gandiegow, Rachel did her best to pretend Brodie slept at the Arctic Circle instead of only a few steps down the hall. She sat cross-legged on the bed, writing out everything it would take to run a B and B here. Then she made a list of questions which needed to be answered . . . such as who owned the land? Was it for sale? Finally, but most important, did Gandiegow have the traffic to make this whole venture possible?

When Rachel's yawns were making her eyes water, she shut her notebook and headed to her room. She quietly put her nightgown on in the dark and crawled into bed. The idea of her own bed and breakfast had done the trick to keep her brain occupied. But now her mind wandered. Down the hall to the man stretched out on the sofa.

It was nearly unbearable to have him so close, but not be able to crawl into his arms and be with him, and convince him that her feelings were true. But she'd asked him, and his words still haunted her . . . *I care for the girl.* The message couldn't have been any clearer. Loving him was hopeless. She needed to start accepting that he would never come around.

She sighed. Late at night was no time to make rash decisions, though. In the morning, things had to look brighter.

But then she remembered her mother was coming to town.

Sixteen-year-old Harry Stanton watched Thistle Glen Lodge until the lights went out. All of Gandiegow was asleep so it was safe for him to go to bed. He shouldn't have waited here so long. He should've stayed outside Quilting Central, to make sure no one had returned.

He'd thought again about sleeping on a boat, but it was a cold and tricky thing. He'd tried to stow aboard a few times, but the fishermen had a tendency to return to their boats unexpectedly in the evenings, checking God-knows-what. Also, the fishermen were always up early. After sleeping several nights in an old woodshed with a quilt he'd nicked, Harry had found that Quilting Central's door was always open, was warm inside, and had a lovely sofa to lie on. Having a proper restroom for which to clean up was a treat and more than he could've hoped for . . . though the room was meant for lasses and not men. The danged flowers on the wallpaper could be seen in the moonlight.

He felt for the scissors in his pocket, the ones he'd

borrowed from Quilting Central. Christmas was only two days away and he needed to finish the rest of his presents before the day arrived.

As he slipped through the shadows back to the hostel—as he'd taken to thinking of Quilting Central at night—he looked at each of the houses he'd categorized. The preacher's, the doctor's, the tinker's. Like every night, he wondered which cottage held his father.

As he passed the kirk, he caught a reflection of himself in the stained-glass window. Since his mother's death, he never passed a mirror when he didn't wonder if he might look like his da.

Harry didn't have much to go on. For his whole life, his mother told him absolutely nothing about his da . . . until she lay dying in her hospital bed in Edinburgh. In the end, his mother only told him a few things. His dad was tall with dark hair. She cared for his father very much. *He never knew about you,* she'd said. When Harry asked more, she'd only given him one clue . . . *yere da's from Gandiegow.* She'd drifted off to sleep then. If he had known, he would've tried to wake her. Instead he hurried off to a café to do an Internet search to find out where Gandiegow was. An hour later, Mum was gone.

He looked around carefully, scanning for movement about the village, and when he was sure all was safe, he ran for Quilting Central and slipped inside.

He never turned on the lights, and most nights he sat on the floor under the window, using the streetlamp to read one of the books on the shelf. He wished they would stock something other than books that women would like, for Harry loved to read. It helped him to get away from his own world. But tonight he couldn't flip through the pages. He had work to do.

He went to the desk, pulled out the middle drawer, and found more sheets of thick paper. Last night, he'd made a bird for the pie he'd taken. Tonight, he had to make the rest. He took them over to his place by the window and got busy. He needed something special for the owner of the General Store. He'd been desperate. His trainers weren't keeping him warm. It was cold this far north, colder than he'd expected. He only borrowed the items. He would pay back the store owner one day. He'd get a job after he found his father. He'd pay back the lady who'd hung the flannel shirt out on the line at the cottage with the blue door. He'd give back the scissors when he was finished with the presents, too. Of course, he needed to do more for the lady with the kid who left him the only real meal he'd had since coming to find his da.

They'd talked to him at the hospital. It was the law. He would have to go into foster care as he had no relatives. *That they knew about anyway.* This was the reason Harry ran away to Gandiegow. Maybe he should've strolled into the village and asked about his father straightaway, but he was afraid they would call the authorities. No, Harry had done the right thing—stayed out of sight, hiding in various sheds, learning as much as he could about the people who lived here. He had to find his father first so he wouldn't be stuck in some home until he turned eighteen.

But in the meantime, he needed to thank those who'd helped him get by.

He'd read about origami in a book once, but it all seemed too rigid for him. He'd put the book aside and did as he liked. He liked making things with his hands, shapes out of paper, but used scissors to make it become more of what he wanted.

He worked on the presents, fashioning a bear for the lady at Thistle Glen Lodge, thinking her kid could play with it. When he was done, he hid his new creations, with the others, in a plastic container under one of the tables, making sure to put it back exactly where it was. Tomorrow night, like Father Christmas, he would go from house to house and drop off his gifts to thank the people of Gandiegow.

Rachel drifted in and out of sleep, dreaming of Brodie. In her dreams she was even braver than she was in real life. In her dreams, she boldly went to the couch, climbed into his arms, and convinced him they were meant to be together. She woke up when he said, *I do.* The bedroom was dark with moonlight shining through the window. She'd been so happy to finally hear Brodie say the words that would bind them together forever. But it was only a dream.

Maybe she could make it a reality. She could get out of this bed, slink down the hall, and take advantage of him. She'd show him just how much she cared about him with her body, because dropping hints and leaving him clues hadn't worked so far.

She rolled over and spied Hannah across the room, lying in her twin bed surrounded by her dolls. *No. I can't do as I please.* Not anymore. She was a mother. Her job was to remain in her own bed and set an example for her child.

Soon after, she heard Brodie in the kitchen. But when she snuck out of bed to at least tell him *good morning*, she only caught a glimpse of his backside as he walked out the door. From across the room, she could see the lock had been set.

She padded back into her room and crawled into bed. When she awoke, Hannah was lying in her bed talking to Dolly.

"Grandma Vivienne is coming today. She's really nice. I bet she'll bring us a present for Christmas."

Rachel reached for her phone, but there was still no text message from her mother and she was beginning to worry. She slipped out of bed, deciding if she didn't hear from her mom by ten, she'd send the police, the fire department, and perhaps all of Gandiegow to find her mother.

While Hannah readied for the day, Rachel made breakfast and planned how to finish her Christmas projects in time. She was still groggy from her dream-filled night and wanted nothing more than to grab her daughter's guzzy and slip back in bed. Instead, she hurried across town to Abraham's to drop off Hannah.

When Rachel finally made it to Quilting Central, everyone was talking. At first she worried it might be about Brodie sleeping over at the quilting dorm, but then she realized the news was more substantial than a bit of gossip.

She went to Bethia, knowing the elderly woman would tell her what was going on . . . and be kind about it. Deydie, on the other hand, might say it was none of her damned business.

"Our trust is broken," Bethia said sadly. "We haven't had a robbery in fifty years."

"What robbery?" Was another pie stolen?

"The General Store."

"What? No. What did they take?" Rachel couldn't help thinking about the store's unlocked door and how tempting it might be for someone in need. From what she'd seen, several Gandiegowan families needed a lot.

"Amy is at the store, checking the entire inventory. When she got in first thing this morning, she noticed a pair of wellies were gone from the shelf. Also, a hat, gloves, and socks. She came to tell us the news, but then rushed to get Coll to watch baby Wills while she went over the store with a fine-toothed comb."

Rachel's stomach plummeted. The pie thief had stepped it up a notch. "Who would do such a thing?" But she already knew. The thin man in the shadows.

"None of us," Bethia said, with an emphasis on *us*.

"You and the others can't surely think Tuck had anything to do with this. He can't be the wellies snatcher." If only she had a way of telling Bethia to get off Tuck's scent without telling her about what she'd seen. But then Rachel had an idea. "What size boots are missing?"

"I dunno. But that's a very good question." Although Bethia had always been nice to her, she stared at Rachel with somewhat new eyes. "Will ye excuse me? I need to speak with Deydie about this."

Rachel saw what was coming next . . . a version of Cinderella and the glass slipper, except this involved a bunch of fired-up Scots and a pair of stolen wellies.

Rachel checked her phone again. No message from her mother that she'd left the hotel and was heading for Gandiegow. For now, Rachel put her mother out of her mind; she had plenty to do. She took her place behind her sewing machine, needing to work on her mother's patchwork lap quilt. She only had a bit more to go.

While stitching-in-the-ditch, Rachel kept her eye on Bethia and Deydie, who'd put their heads together. Two more joined them, Amy and Moira. Rachel sewed faster—*almost done*. Simultaneously, all four of the quilters looked in her direction. *What the hell?* Moira was even worrying her lip.

Deydie led the group toward Rachel. Amy looked as if she was dragging Moira with her arm looped through hers. The look on Moira's face said she'd rather be disemboweling a fish than part of whatever was going on here.

Rachel snipped the last thread and pulled the nearly completed quilt from the machine. The only thing left was the binding, but making a getaway right now seemed more urgent than finishing a gift for her mother. As Rachel pushed back her chair, Deydie hollered.

"Rachel! Lass! We've something to tell ye." She said it so loud that Rachel couldn't pretend she hadn't heard her over the sewing machines. Besides, the rest of the room had gone quiet to see what the commotion was about.

She held the simple patchwork quilt close, not much protection as the ladies gathered around. She stood. "Yes? What is it?" She tried to sound friendly, but her concierge's voice came rolling out of her mouth, the one she used when the proverbial poo was about to hit the fan.

"It's about yere idea," Bethia said gently.

Deydie moved closer, putting her hands on her hips. "Hell's bells. There's no time to beat around the bush. I'll tell her."

"Tell me what?" Rachel was trying to remain cool and calm.

"We've decided, since ye came up with the idea, that ye'll be the one to make the announcement at the kirk tonight after the Christmas Eve service."

Rachel elected to play dumb. "I don't know what you're talking about."

Deydie huffed, the raging bull in the ring, and about to run Rachel through with her horns. "At the end of the service when Father Andrew calls for the announcements, ye'll git up and ask which one of us wears a size forty-four."

"Forty-four?" Rachel asked, feeling more than a little dumbfounded.

"Aye," Amy answered. "The size of the missing wellies."

Deydie continued on as if Rachel was going along with this crazy plan. "I'll make sure beforehand that the good Father knows ye have something to say."

Rachel shook her head. "I'm not going to church. My mother's coming into town today."

Deydie turned red as if Rachel admitted to being best buds with Lucifer.

Bethia touched Rachel's hand. "Everyone attends service here."

"Everyone," Amy chimed in.

Moira gave her a sad smile as if she wouldn't go to church either, if she had to stand up and accuse one of their own that they were a thief. And Moira was married to the pastor!

"Ye understand why it would be best if it came from you, don't ye?" Bethia said.

"Because it would be easier coming from someone outside of the community?" Rachel's question was rhetorical. She knew the answer. *So much for planning a B and B in Gandiegow.* Her fledgling dream went up in flames before the blueprints could've been drawn. Her public accusation would taint everything Rachel did from here on out . . . especially becoming one of them.

"Just be firm," Deydie said. "Tell them ye volunteered to get to the bottom of things."

Rachel shook her head, not wanting to know the answer, but she asked it anyway. "What happens if no one says they wear the same size wellies?"

"Then tell the whole damned congregation—*men and women*—that they won't be allowed to leave the building until ye make them try on a size forty-four."

Rachel looked down at Deydie's army boots. Though the woman had a personality the size of Paul Bunyan, her feet were small. The way Deydie was glaring at her, there was no sense arguing. No sense in telling them what she saw the other night. Someone was guilty.

She gazed at all four women and chose Bethia, figuring she might answer her truthfully without the pain of getting hit with a broom. "So having me do this is really about some cockeyed retribution?" For stealing Joe and *making* him live in the States with her and then bringing him home in an urn?

Bethia avoided her gaze.

Deydie pounded Rachel on the back. "Damned straight ye are. As sharp as a needle, too."

Sitting at the dock in the wheelhouse of his boat, Brodie gazed out at the sea. He glanced down, his pencil hovering over the logbook; he forgot what he was supposed to write . . . again! He was *effing* useless this morning, as tired as he was, and not because he was distracted. Tuck had just left. *Good riddance.*

The fish didn't cooperate today. Tuck's help had been appreciated, but his incessant blather wasn't. All in all, it had been a rotten morning on the sea. Brodie wished to reboot the day. But he wouldn't regret last night, though he was wiped out now. He'd stayed awake, watching over Rachel and Hannah at the cottage. A stranger in Gandiegow was keeping an eye on Rachel. Well, Brodie was keeping an eye on her, too. He was determined to catch the bastard and find out what game he was playing at. Brodie must've been squeezing too hard because the pencil snapped in two.

With the lead half, he scribbled in the low numbers for the morning and then stalked off the boat. He'd kept his eye out earlier this morning for the man who was lurking around town, and he was going to keep scanning for him nonstop. But if Brodie didn't get home and get a little shut-eye, he'd be driving the boat in his sleep this afternoon.

As he got to the walkway, he spied a woman with two very large roller bags coming from the parking lot.

"What in the world?"

It was a woman dressed in a long coat made of the MacFarlane tartan of red, white, and blue. She wore a matching tammie on her head. She was the same height as Rachel but a little thicker around the middle . . . *and the last person I want to see*. It was too late to pretend he'd forgotten something on the boat, because she'd already seen him, too.

Her look of shock was priceless and he felt satisfied, though it wasn't exactly the Christian thing to think. Of course, her expression caught up with how she felt about him, transforming from stunned to general disapproval, which inhabited every nook and cranny on her face. The last time he'd seen that look of disgust was during Joe and Rachel's wedding, leaving him no doubt Rachel had filled her mother in on the details of what they'd been doing at the ruins of Monadail Castle. What Brodie didn't understand . . . was why.

But he knew why Vivienne Granger was wearing the MacFarlane tartan. The Clachers were part of the Mac-Farlane clan. Rachel's mother was making a statement to one and all. She stood with Joe Clacher. But Joe was dead.

She marched toward Brodie with an eyebrow raised, the type of woman to lead the charge into battle. He could see that trait in Rachel, too. Vivienne lifted her nose a little. "I didn't know you were going to be here."

"Aye." What else could he say? He wasn't happy to see her either, but he could be courteous. "I'll show ye where to get settled. May I?" He held out his hands to take her bags, happy he'd cleaned up on the boat. Fish guts and her *bluidy* luggage wouldn't go well together.

"I wasn't expecting a bellboy, but you'll do." She stood back while he grabbed her bags. "Where will I be staying? At Rhona's like I did before?"

"Nay. Rhona has moved to Dundee to help care for

her grandbairns." Brodie nodded his head in the right direction. "Gandiegow has two converted cottages which serve as the quilting dorms for the Kilts and Quilts retreat."

"The what?"

Gads, he didn't want to explain, but it would be rude to grunt instead of reply. While they walked, he told her about Cait's venture and how the whole town had gotten involved. "Even yere daughter," he said. "She's been teaching her Gandiegow Christmas Tree quilt."

For a second, Vivienne looked puzzled, but then nodded, putting the pieces together about which quilt he meant.

At Thistle Glen Lodge, he opened the door, remembering again the man who had been lurking in the dark. He would have to talk to Cait about making Rachel lock the doors during the night and the day. He held the door wide to let Vivienne go first.

He pointed down the hallway. "The bedrooms are beyond the living room. Unless, of course, ye'd like to sleep in one of the bedrooms upstairs."

"Down here will be fine." She frowned at him as if she didn't know whether to give him a tip or not.

He dipped his head at her. "I'll wait outside to take you to yere daughter." He wasn't happy about accommodating her either. Rachel was one Granger too many, as far as he was concerned. But he thought about his duty to keep her and Hannah safe, and he wondered how Vivienne would view him sleeping on the couch tonight, watching over her, too.

As the loyal dog that he was, he waited for Rachel's mother. He could've left her to find her daughter on her own, but that didn't seem right. He'd take her there, dump her off, and be done with the mess of them. Until tonight at Abraham's.

Vivienne returned outside a few minutes later in her ridiculous coat. "How is your grandfather?" It seemed to pain her to be nice.

"He's managing." Brodie pointed the way for them to go. "Seeing his great-granddaughter has raised his spirits considerably. The lass appears to make Grandda spry indeed."

She slowed down. "I hope my visit doesn't cut into your grandfather's time with Hannah." Which was a very sensible and thoughtful concern.

Brodie couldn't help himself. "There's enough Hannah to go around. The lass is a handful."

She nodded and picked back up the pace. "Yes, she is."

A minute later they were at the entrance of Quilting Central. He wondered if he should give Vivienne a heads-up that she may not receive the warmest of receptions, but he decided to keep quiet. *She'll figure it out.* He opened the door.

He had no intentions of going in. He wanted to walk the perimeter of the village and then get a fortifying nap. He thought about how Hannah's naps made her a new person. That was exactly the kind of outcome he needed to get through Christmas with Rachel and her mother here. But he found himself walking in behind Vivienne, as if he wanted Rachel to see who'd brought her. On a subconscious level, was he trying to ingratiate himself to his dead cousin's widow?

Rachel looked up and saw him first. Their eyes locked. For a second, he let himself gaze upon her, take her in. Seeing her safe calmed him. *No.* It was more than that. Seeing her made him feel powerful, like he could take on the world. Her gaze became intense and he saw the extra message in her eyes. She might be safe, but she was pleading with him to rescue her from the women of Gandiegow. Deydie and Bethia stood near her. Amy and

Moira, too. He started to be her hero, but it wasn't his job to save her from them. Right now, his only job was to deliver her mother. He nodded his head almost imperceptibly toward Vivienne.

Rachel's attention shifted. "Mom!" She shoved a quilt behind her sewing machine and ran toward her mother, hugging her. *So Vivienne gets to be the hero.* But Rachel glanced at Brodie over her mother's shoulder while they embraced . . . with gratitude? Nay. The look Rachel gave him was clear: *Life just got more complicated.* He didn't like that he could read Rachel so easily. When she pulled away, she was fully focused on her mum again.

He turned and left. But he didn't get out the door quick enough.

"Brodie?" Vivienne slightly lifted her nose in the air. "Thank you."

He nodded and stalked out, feeling uncomfortable. It was almost easier sometimes to think people never changed. It wasn't as if Vivienne had altered her position on how she felt about him, but he never expected her to be halfway civil. Not after what he tried to do . . . *steal Rachel from Joe.*

He started his patrol down the walkway, keeping his eyes on the places between the buildings, but in his tired state an old wound surfaced.

For the past six years, Brodie hadn't been able to forgive himself for trying to do what Vivienne had thought . . . steal Rachel from her fiancé. Brodie felt tortured from all directions when it came to Rachel and what they'd done. It was the same old argument in his head . . . he had tried to claim Rachel for himself. Not because Joe had stolen away every lass Brodie had wooed when they were lads, but because Brodie had loved her, *heart and soul.* But it still wasn't much of an excuse. He was an honorable man, and loving Rachel had been an unforgivable sin when it came to someone like himself.

He passed Deydie's house and moved to the rear of the town, seeing no one or anything out of place. Stealthily, he made his way along the back edge of the village, working his way, circling the town, hoping to make it back home for that nap.

As he walked, he came up with a way to catch the thief. Of course, he wouldn't do it alone. Brodie counted on *Rachel being Rachel*—which was something he couldn't stop, even if he tried. Or even if he wanted to.

Chapter Eleven

B onnie Coburn watched through the pub's window as Brodie passed. He seemed to be looking for something. Or someone. Maybe it was her. *Probably not*. Brodie was a tough one to pin down, but she'd tried. She'd flirted with him while wearing her sexiest of sweaters, and she caught him alone whenever she could. She'd even danced with him a time or two. The man was unshakable. She'd dubbed him Gandiegow's most eligible bachelor, but she hoped not for long.

From her pocket, she lifted out her little notebook, the one she'd been writing in for months. She enjoyed playing the field, but looked forward to the coming year. Every four years she seriously thought about landing a man for good. Not just someone to keep her bed warm, but someone to take care of her for the rest of her life. Her looks were holding on, but they wouldn't last forever.

February twenty-ninth was only two short months away. Not only was it Leap Year Day, but it was her birthday as well. The day belonged to her, the day she could do whatever the hell she wanted. She never paid any attention to those who said Leap Year Day was a bad day to be born . . . *my own mum included*. Bonnie cringed at the thought of Mum, smoking her cigarettes in their shabby flat in the bad part of Glasgow. Mum never worked, but depended on her boyfriends for cash and always waiting for her next date. Oh, how Mum thought it was a riot to only celebrate Bonnie's birthday during a Leap Year, refusing to give her presents and a bit of cake on the other years to acknowledge her daughter getting older.

Bonnie knew she was pretty from the start. Mum's lecher boyfriends noticed, always commenting on what a *bonny lass* she was. Being pretty when she was little was fine. She got an extra stick of gum or some chocolate for it. But as she began filling out, Mum's boyfriends began giving her more attention than she wanted— chatting her up and pawing at her whenever they could.

A shiver ran through her. Bonnie had to remind herself she was grown now and safe here in Gandiegow. But the memories kept coming. Her mum saw, but didn't step in and protect her from her *bluidy* boyfriends. Instead Mum blamed her for leading them on with her *perky tits*. On the day the *worst of them* threw Bonnie on her bed, she kicked and screamed her way from underneath his alcohol breath and groping hands, only to find her mum smoking a cigarette on the couch in the next room. Bonnie ran off then, leaving the gray of Glasgow behind, heading north.

She was barely thirteen when she stumbled her way into Gandiegow, ending up at Mrs. Coburn's door. The old dear woman took Bonnie in, never telling her she was *too pretty for her own good*. From the start, Mrs. Coburn kept her safe. When Gandiegow came knocking, wanting to know exactly who the chit was, Mrs. Coburn backed up Bonnie when she'd told everyone her last name was *Coburn*, too, just like the woman who'd taken her in.

Mostly Bonnie kept the past where it belonged. But lately, questions of her mother had been bothering her.

Aye, Mum didn't deserve any kind of consideration. But the questions kept coming. Did her mum ever try to find her? Or had she been happy to be rid of the girl she'd seen as a burden *and competition*. But mostly, she wondered if her mum was still alive.

Without really meaning to, Bonnie left the view at the pub's big window and went to the laptop propped open on the bar. Before she lost her nerve, she googled their old address. Maybe seeing a picture of the dump would remind her how horrible it had been and she'd give up these old, unproductive thoughts. But the rundown building had been gentrified, according to the first article to pop up. The bad side of Glasgow was becoming the hip place for the growing art community to live.

Next, she typed in her mother's name to see where she lived now. As the page loaded, Bonnie expected to see a police report. Instead, it was the one thing she feared most. *An obituary*. With her hand shaking, she clicked the link.

WIGHTMAN, Anne, Suddenly at Glasgow Royal Infirmary . . .

Bonnie stopped when she read the date. Fifteen years ago. Her mother had been gone fifteen years. The few words about her mum said nothing about flowers or a service.

Bonnie choked on a sob. Her eyes fell on the small notebook which lay next to the laptop. The page was too blurry to read.

"Well, that's that." She wiped away the tears. Now she knew, but that didn't change anything. Since she was a teen, she'd put miles between herself and the woman who birthed her . . . both in distance and in her heart.

"I've made something of myself," Bonnie declared

to the empty pub. She held two jobs—barmaid at The Fisherman and receptionist at the North Sea Valve Company. Her mother should've been so lucky. Gandiegow accepted Bonnie for who she was. They didn't always think well of her, but they knew she was a hard worker. Lately, though, things had been changing, evolving, to where she was feeling more like a part of the community. The quilting ladies had even taught her how to sew. She was working on her third quilt and getting better with each one. But she had no mum to give a quilt to since Mrs. Coburn had died eight years ago. She'd been kind to Bonnie until the end, leaving her the small cottage, because Bonnie was the only *family* the old woman had.

But it would be nice to have someone special to share her quilts with now.

Bonnie closed the lid on the laptop and took her list back to the table by the window. She'd written down the name of every bachelor in Gandiegow from eighteen years old to eighty. Any one of them could potentially be her future. But on Leap Year Day, Brodie would be the first one she would propose to—the best looking, the best provider. She'd even bought a new dress for the occasion. If he said *no,* she'd take his coin—as was Gandiegow's tradition—and go on to the next one on the list. Tuck was second, though he wasn't as steady as Brodie. But she'd ask anyway, as he was sure to tell her *no,* too.

She sighed. A girl could make a lot of money on Leap Year Day, a fiver for every rejection. But Bonnie wanted more than a little extra cash. She wanted a man to call her own.

She looked up to see three boats coming into the harbor and suddenly she felt hopeful. The hope spread all the way into her bones that this coming year . . . *will be my year to land a husband.*

*   *   *

Rachel watched Brodie leave, wanting to run after him and tell him the job Deydie had wrangled her into after the Christmas Eve service—accuse someone in Gandiegow of being a thief. Rachel had a belligerent thought. *What if I decide not to go through with it?*

Vivienne brought her back to the here-and-now by motioning to the room of quilters who were working furiously on last-minute presents. "This place wasn't here six years ago."

Deydie and the others had relocated a distance away, but kept watch as if her mother were a rare bird. It was probably her mother's tartan outfit which had them staring so intently.

As Rachel guided her mother over to the tea and scone tray, she explained how she met Cait on the plane and how the Kilts and Quilts retreat was her brainchild. But she left off the bit about Graham.

Vivienne's eyes lit up. "Cait? Graham Buchanan's wife?" Rachel should've known her mother would be up on the latest in *People* magazine. "Will I get to meet him while I'm here?"

"I doubt it." From what Rachel heard from the quilters, even though the biography had come out, they still fiercely protected him and his privacy. Deydie called him a son of Gandiegow.

Vivienne looked around. "Where's my granddaughter?"

"At Abraham's. Shall we go? We can take our scones with us."

Her mother wrapped hers in a napkin. "They are delicious."

"The best. From what I hear, Claire has a scone recipe for every day of the year." Rachel grabbed her coat from the hook, but glanced anxiously at her sewing machine, where her mother's patchwork quilt still needed a binding. She'd have to sneak back and finish it later. The two of them left, leaving the quilting ladies to watch them go.

Once outside, Rachel had to know. "What are you wearing?"

Vivienne looked down, admiring herself. "It's Joe's tartan."

"I know it's Joe's tartan." She'd made Abraham's picture frame out of the same plaid.

Her mother continued on. "I ordered it a while back, and now I have an occasion to wear it."

Rachel wanted to argue with her on that point, but she dropped the subject. "You didn't call and say you were on your way. I was worried."

"You always worry," her mother scolded. "I'm fine. I wanted to surprise you."

Yes, Rachel had been surprised . . . surprised to see Brodie and her mother together.

Vivienne sniffed and adjusted her gloves. "Brodie carried my things to Thistle Glen Lodge." She frowned as if she wanted to complain about the service he'd provided, but apparently she'd decided to take the high road. "The quilting dorm is absolutely charming. It reminds a little of Sunnydale, don't you think?"

"Yes. It does to me as well." Rachel stepped up to Abraham's cottage and opened the door. "We're here."

Vivienne raised a disapproving eyebrow.

That eyebrow always put Rachel on the defensive. "Abraham said for us to make ourselves at home." Besides, he was too ill to get up and down to answer the door all day. She put it aside and hollered down the hall. "Hannah, guess who's here?"

Her daughter came tearing out of the parlor with a wild and uncontained expression of joy on her face. "Grandma Vivienne!"

Hannah slammed into her grandmother and the two of them hugged.

This was why Rachel worked hard at not letting her mother get to her. Hannah loved her grandmother, and Vivienne was so good to Hannah that Rachel couldn't stay upset with her mom for too long. Anyone who loved her daughter was special in Rachel's book. *Like Brodie,* the voice at the back of her mind whispered.

"Come meet Grandda," Hannah said, pulling Vivienne's hand.

Vivienne glanced back at Rachel. "When did she start speaking with a Scottish accent?"

"The moment she stepped foot in Gandiegow," Rachel replied.

"Well, she is Joe's daughter," Vivienne added, always on Joe's side, always defending him.

Rachel took the comment as another jab, though. Every now and then, her mother would hint that Joe might still be alive if Rachel had been a better wife and worked harder on their marriage. But Vivienne didn't know everything about Joe.

"Grandda, this is my grandma Vivienne."

Abraham looked up and laughed. "I know yere gran. Vivienne, come closer and let me see what ye're wearing. The MacFarlane tartan?"

"In honor of Joe," Vivienne said. "Do you like it?"

Abraham nodded. "It pleases me. Some might say ye shouldn't wear it because ye're not a Clacher, like me and Joe, and this little one here, but I say it's grand. Perfectly grand."

Hannah tugged on her grandmother's hand to get her attention. "I'm spending the night at Grandda's tonight. He says Father Christmas is stopping here with presents for me!" She beamed up at Vivienne. "Gran, ye'll be staying here with us."

"Gran?" her mother said to Rachel. "Since when am I *Gran*?"

Rachel shrugged. "I guess starting right now."

Vivienne slipped off her coat and sat on the sofa with Hannah hopping between her two grandparents, putting on quite the show. Rachel spied the near empty plate of Christmas cookies, which explained part of her daughter's hyperactivity.

The front door opened and closed. Rachel held her breath.

Brodie peeked in, looking uncomfortable. "I'm back, Grandda."

"Come greet Rachel's mother," Abraham said.

Vivienne put her hand up. "It's okay. We've already spoken. Brodie helped me get my bags to the quilting dorm."

"If ye'll excuse me." Brodie left the room and hastened up the stairs.

Rachel understood . . . there were way too many Granger women in one room for him. *Maybe too many in Scotland.* "I'll fix us some tea. Mom, are you hungry? That scone couldn't have filled you up."

Hannah picked up the nearly empty cookie plate and held it out to Vivienne precariously. "Here are the biscuits, Gran. They're yummy."

Rachel reached over and rescued the stoneware from sheer disaster. "I'll bring a tray in a minute. Abraham, is there anything besides tea that I can get you?"

The old man beamed at Hannah and the room in general. "I've got all I need."

Forty-five minutes later over Hannah's commotion in the parlor, Rachel heard Brodie come down the stairs. He headed straight out the front door without saying *boo* to anyone. Was this an omen of things to come? *But it's Christmas Eve.* Shouldn't at least some of her dreams come true on this night of all nights?

But the dreaded task of accusing one of the congregation after church floated back into her head and landed with a thump in the pit of her stomach. "We better get to Thistle Glen Lodge to clean up and get changed."

Abraham shifted toward her. "But ye'll be back here after the service. We'll have a light supper. Brodie arranged it with Dominic ages ago. Then tomorrow is the big feast." He winked at Hannah. "I had Brodie increase our order because the little one can sure pack it away."

"Oh, Grandda," Hannah said, smiling. "I don't eat that much."

As the three of them walked back to Thistle Glen Lodge, Rachel's nerves were getting the best of her. She glanced over at the boats tied up at the dock, wondering if she could stow away in one of them until Christmas was over. She really didn't want to make that damned announcement.

As if she'd summoned him, Brodie stepped from the wheelhouse onto the deck of his boat. Their eyes locked, and once again, she didn't understand how he could disregard their connection.

Vivienne followed where she gazed, then back to Rachel, raising that eyebrow. Apparently, Rachel and Brodie's connection was obvious to her mother.

Hannah skipped ahead to the path leading between the buildings.

Vivienne watched and waited until her little ears were out of range. "So you've taken up with *him* again."

If only that were true. "I don't want to talk about it, Mother."

"I must've hit the nail on the head if I'm *Mother* now."

Brodie walked off in the opposite direction, toward home.

For a moment, Rachel considered confiding in her

mom—she did want a relationship with Brodie . . . but he wasn't interested. But what good would the admission do? It had only caused friction between her and her mom six years ago.

Vivienne raised her nose in the air. "The truth is, darling, I don't believe Brodie is good enough for you. He never has been."

Rachel tamped down the truth to keep it from bubbling up. Now wasn't the time to bring up Joe's shortcomings—his wandering eye and philandering body parts. Sure, Rachel had stood up to a few people here in Gandiegow, but confronting her mother seemed impossible. Mom was a force of nature, and if Rachel was being completely honest, she didn't want to disappoint her. Vivienne loved Joe. But if her mother knew the truth, she'd be just as upset with Rachel for putting up with a man who stepped out on her. It was best to let it go. Water under the bridge. Joe was dead.

"Can we talk about something else?"

Her mother told her about all the gifts in her suitcase that she'd bought for Hannah in Edinburgh. "I'm having a coat and hat made in her father's tartan, too. I need to get her measurements while I'm here. Can we do that at Quilting Central? I want her to have it for when she gets home to Chicago."

But the thought of going home wasn't appealing to Rachel. In fact, it made her a little sick to her stomach. Sure, she had challenges here—Brodie not forgiving her and Deydie giving her a hard time every other second. But the village was once again feeling like home. The way it had six years ago when she'd been here before.

But then Rachel remembered what lay ahead for her in an hour from now. The community was going to hate her for sure after this.

*　　*　　*

Back at the cottage, Brodie cleaned up for the Christmas Eve service as quickly as he could so he could see to his grandfather before heading out. Though Grandda was a little better today, Doc insisted he needed to stay out of the cold and rest at home. While Brodie was cutting slices of cheese for his grandfather, Dominic knocked on the back door and stepped in.

Brodie had to do a double take. He had a tray of sandwiches in his hands, but strapped to his chest was baby Nessa. "Ye have a helper, I see."

"Claire needed an extra minute so Nessa decided to come along on the delivery. Here, let's get the sandwiches put away."

Brodie took the tray and slid it into the refrigerator while Nessa laughed at the silly face he made at her.

"Basil soup is in the wagon. Do you mind getting it? Just plug in the Crock-Pot and it'll be hot for later."

"I appreciate this. Especially making extra at the last minute."

"No problem. So how are you holding up with having so much family in town?"

Brodie skipped over the question. "We both better hurry so we aren't late for the service."

Dominic and Nessa left. Brodie finished slicing cheese and set the tray next to Abraham. "I'll be back soon."

Grandda nodded and Brodie left, too.

If he timed this just right, Rachel and her family would already be seated at the kirk before he arrived. If Grandda were there, he'd insist the Granger females join him in the family pew. But as it was, Rachel didn't know where his family had sat for generations.

When the service was about to start, he slipped inside. But when he looked into the sanctuary, he didn't see

Rachel, her mother, or Hannah. Father Andrew nodded as if he better take his seat. But before Brodie stepped in, the door to the kirk flew open and Hannah came tripping in, unzipping her coat. She wore a red velvet dress, black tights, and black patent leather shoes. When she saw Brodie, she broke into a huge grin.

"I ran so I wouldn't be late," she said too loudly for church, but the starting music drowned out her last words. She rushed to Brodie and hugged him. He couldn't help himself; he scooped her into his arms. *The lass has gotten under my skin.*

"Are ye ready to sit?" he said quietly.

"Aye."

The door opened and the two well-put-together Granger women came in gracefully. Abraham was right; Vivienne Granger was handsome. And her daughter was lethal. Was Rachel trying to kill him with how good she looked in black velvet?

Vivienne set her overnight case at the entrance, but not before giving Brodie a disapproving nod. Brodie walked down the aisle, figuring the women would follow him since he was carrying the girl. It wasn't until all eyes were on him before he realized he should've had Hannah walk on her own. The way the villagers were watching him, they were certainly placing bets on when he and Rachel would wed.

But that wasn't his only issue. By carrying Hannah in, he'd ordained where all four of them were to sit. He put the little lass down at his family pew. He started to tell her to *slide in* but that would leave him sitting next to one of the Granger women. He took his seat first, then Hannah, Vivienne, and Rachel. With them lined up all cozy like this, speculation would run rampant.

They rose immediately as the processional started.

Brodie sang "Oh Come, All Ye Faithful" from memory, using the familiar song to calm the tension caused by his pew mates.

Vivienne tugged on Rachel's arm. "There's Graham Buchanan."

Graham and Mattie scooted in next to Cait directly in front of them.

"I know, Mom," Rachel whispered back. "Don't make a big deal."

Brodie had to admire Rachel that she took the town's commitment to Graham seriously. Vivienne would not win any points by trying to get Graham's autograph during the Christmas Eve service.

Brodie put the two women to his left out of his mind. When the service was nearly over, Father Andrew nodded. At first Brodie thought it was to him, but then Graham leaned over and kissed a surprised Cait, before he and Mattie rose and walked to the front.

"We have a special treat this evening," Andrew said, beaming as if handing out Christmas presents to one and all. "Two of our parishioners have asked if they may do a duet."

The congregation was as shocked as Cait, and whispering broke out throughout the kirk.

Andrew held up his hand and the room went quiet as the music began.

Mattie solemnly looked up at his grandfather Graham, and Graham nodded back to him.

"*Silent night*," Mattie sang, his voice soft and his pitch true. "*Holy night. All is calm. All is bright.*"

Graham joined in, smiling at them all, but tears had come to everyone's eyes. Even Brodie's.

Hannah pulled his arm. "Why is everyone crying?"

Brodie kissed the top of her head. "Because we're happy." Mattie had come a long way after enduring so much. To hear him sing, and to know he was healing, was the best Christmas present Gandiegow could ever receive.

When they got to the last verse of the song, Mattie sang by himself again for a few lines, but then he and Graham raised their arms to have everyone join in. The town sang, but amid the joy of the Christmas miracle, noses were being blown throughout the sanctuary.

When they were done, Cait stepped out of the pew and Mattie flew into her arms. "Merry Christmas," he said quietly.

Graham laid a hand on Cait's shoulder as the three of them sat back down.

Andrew tucked his handkerchief in his pocket. "All rise for the final prayer."

When he finished, Brodie expected the music for the recessional to begin, but instead, Andrew called for announcements, not something that was usually done on Christmas Eve.

Brodie was even more surprised when Rachel's hand timidly rose.

"Here."

Andrew motioned her to come to the front.

Rachel glanced around nervously while standing. As she scooted out, his locket swung from side to side. God, what was she up to?

She made it to the lectern, but then froze. "I, ah—"

"Louder," Deydie hollered from her row with the quilting ladies.

Rachel glared at the older woman as if she was undaunted by her or anyone else. Finally, she looked at the rest of them with fierce determination. "As you all know, several things have gone missing around Gandiegow. I've been appointed to get to the bottom of one piece of the puzzle."

The pews lit up with chatter.

Rachel held up her hand. "Does anyone in this room wear a size forty-four boot?"

Brodie wore a forty-six.

Rachel looked around and seemed relieved that no one wore that size.

But a deep voice said, "I wear a forty-four." Tuck rose from his seat and the room gasped.

"Dumb luck," Rachel muttered with a frown on her face, but then brightened as if an idea struck her. "Anyone else? Surely, Tuck isn't the only one in Gandiegow who wears a forty-four."

The crowd glanced from one to the other, silently, but then accusing chatter began to buzz around the room like a swarm of killer hornets.

Rachel looked in Brodie's direction as if she was hoping for his support. She shook her head to convey the news was bad.

Brodie didn't believe for a second Tuck would steal anything, even the wellies, though the bloke's boots had seen better days.

Rachel put her hand up to silence the room, but then she looked to Tuck. "Do you mind staying after for a minute?" She nodded toward the Narthex.

"Sure." Tuck sat. He was frowning, too. He had to know what this was about with all the gossip which had been going around . . . unless the man was deaf.

"Thank you." Rachel ducked her head and made her way back to her seat. Father Andrew called out for the last hymn to begin. Brodie didn't sing, but kept glancing at Rachel to make sure she was all right.

And because he didn't trust Tuck for other reasons besides a damned pair of missing wellies, Brodie was going to stay afterward, too.

When the song was over, Brodie filed out with the rest

of them where a group—Deydie, Bethia, Amy, Father Andrew, and Moira—had gathered in the Narthex. The head quilter was sending the gawkers along their way by glaring at whoever wanted to hang around to see what would happen to Tuck.

As Rachel left the sanctuary, she turned to Vivienne. "Can you take Hannah to Abraham's and tell him we'll be along shortly? I'll bring your overnight bag." She glanced to where it sat by the door.

Vivienne nodded, but she wasn't really paying much attention as she was watching Graham come up the aisle.

"Leave him alone, Mom," Rachel said. "I mean it."

"I just want an introduction," Vivienne whined, sounding an awful lot like Hannah.

"No. It's Christmas. You'll let him be. Abraham is waiting for Hannah."

But apparently there were more sights for Vivienne to appreciate. Behind Graham were Gabriel and his father.

"Oh, my." Vivienne fanned herself. "Now, who's that fine specimen? The older one, of course."

Rachel rolled her eyes. "Leave him alone, too."

Hannah put her hand on her grandmother. "We better go, Gran." Clearly, she was the adult between the two of them.

"Very well." Vivienne turned away and they walked out.

"I'm going to have to put a leash on her," Rachel muttered.

Brodie stood close. "How come ye made the announcement?"

"The quilters made me their talking head. I'm expendable, you see?"

No, he didn't see at all. Brodie laid his hand on her back—for only a moment—to get her moving toward the lynch mob. When Tuck came into the lobby area, he frowned at the assembly. The bloke made his way over, shaking his head.

Deydie harrumphed at the sight of him. "Ye may resemble yere brother, the good Father, but ye're nothing like him. He wouldn't be stealing from the townsfolk, and he would've been here for *yere wedding*."

Tuck put his hand up, courtroom style. "I didn't do anything. I swear."

Andrew appeared pained that his brother had said *swear* within the walls of the kirk.

"I promise," Tuck amended. "I didn't take the wellies or anything else ye want to accuse me of doing."

Hesitating, Moira moved slightly forward, keeping her eyes on the ground. "Tuck is eating plenty at home. I'm certain he hasn't been taking the food."

Brodie knew why Rachel didn't say anything about the plate she'd left out. She had nothing to report definitively. He planned to fix that problem later tonight, though.

"Well, I think ye did the thieving," Deydie said as the resident Scrooge. "But let's take a vote on it. Who thinks Tuck is the thief?" She raised her old hand in the air.

Everyone else looked embarrassed, leaving their arms at their sides.

"He didn't do it," Andrew said. He gripped Tuck's shoulder in a show of solidarity. "I know my brother."

Deydie wrapped her coat around her tighter then pointed a finger at the accused. "I'll be watching ye." She spun around and waddled out the door.

The rest of the group disbanded with a few attempts at *Happy Christmas* but the sentiment fell flat. Amy and Moira retrieved a bag and brought it over.

Amy presented the shopping bag to Rachel. "For you. We thought ye would need it."

Rachel looked a little hesitant to take the sack. He couldn't blame her. He still couldn't believe the quilting ladies had forced Rachel into making that blasted announcement. She finally took the bag. "Thank you."

"Look inside. Moira and I finished it."

Rachel's gaze questioned her, but then she opened the bag and pulled out the patchwork quilt he'd seen earlier.

Moira gave her a weak smile. "We knew ye wouldn't have time to complete it for yere mum before tomorrow morn."

"Thank you both. So much." Rachel looked as if she meant it. "This was so thoughtful."

Amy beamed brightly. "It was the least we could do. Happy Christmas." The two of them left together.

Brodie took the quilt from Rachel and put it back in the bag. He nodded that they should go, too. At the door, he grabbed Vivienne's overnight case. When they were away from the kirk, he spoke. "Ye shouldn't have been the one to get up there." He didn't need to explain what he was talking about.

Rachel shrugged. "Deydie implied she'd ease up on me if I did. What a crazy ordeal. Tuck did not do it."

"I noticed you didn't say anything."

"My vote didn't count. I was just the messenger, not the judge and jury. Besides, I don't know anything for sure."

Exactly what he thought.

She stopped. "But as soon as I catch the little thief, I'm going to drag him to Deydie and then make the old quilter apologize to Tuck."

He laughed, imagining Rachel pulling the man by his ear all the way to Deydie's doorstep, but his merriment died when he thought about Rachel standing up for Tuck. "Do ye care for the man?" Brodie hadn't been with Rachel every second of the day. Had she formed a relationship with Tuck when he wasn't around? But the locket still hung around her neck and the sight of it slightly eased his growing panic.

She was giving him a weird frown as if she wanted to burrow into his head and figure out what he was thinking. "I don't even know Tuck," was her answer.

"But ye'd like to." Brodie was seething a tad more than he wanted to admit.

"I guess," Rachel said. "I want to get to know everyone in Gandiegow. I like it here. I always have."

But Brodie felt stuck on the fact that she wanted to get to know Tuck. Was it his fault, because he'd built a wall of unforgiveness between him and her?

"We're here." Rachel didn't go in, but grabbed his arm. "Thank you for staying behind with me at church. I wasn't sure what was expected of me at the inquisition, but I was relieved you were there with me." She leaned up and kissed his cheek.

He soaked it up, her hand resting on his arm, and her lips on his face. When she pulled away, he felt cheated. The only explanation he could give himself for what happened next was because it was Christmas Eve. He pulled her into his arms and kissed her as if a bushel of mistletoe hung above their heads. Being the one to initiate the kiss was a heady feeling of power, and he understood why Rachel was forever stepping in and making the first move. But when she tried to deepen the kiss, he came to his senses, breaking away. He was breathless and feeling confused. His resentment toward Rachel was all he had, and he clung to it the way Hannah clung to her guzzy. Unfortunately, Rachel's goodness was seeping into him and chipping away at the hard feelings he held for her.

I'm not supposed to care about ye.

"They're waiting." His voice sounded as if he'd swallowed half the rocks on the beach. He opened the door and let her go in first. He seriously considered not entering at all, but he couldn't leave Grandda on Christmas Eve.

They hung up their coats in silence. There was nothing for him to say. He should apologize for kissing her, because he had no plans of rekindling what had started six years ago. He'd kissed her because it felt good to do so. End of story. *It wasn't a damned proposal.* He handed her the bag containing the patchwork quilt.

"I'll get it wrapped." She ran up the stairs.

Vivienne and Hannah had transformed the parlor into a party place by having the food laid out on the side table. Soft Christmas music played in the background. Brodie couldn't help marveling how the all-male fisherman's cottage had turned into a warm home, making Brodie homesick for his boyhood, his mother, and the time before his da had died.

Rachel came into the parlor as Vivienne was stepping out. "I was just headed to the kitchen to get the plates."

"I'll get them," Rachel said, and she was gone.

Vivienne accused him with her eyes. "What's wrong with her?"

He shrugged and took his place beside his grandfather. "Are ye ready for Christmas, Hannah? Have ye been a good girl this year?" He thought about the presents he'd bought. Aye, he'd overdone it, but he might not get another chance to spoil the little lass who'd stolen his heart.

Rachel carried in a stack of plates and set them next to the food. It was more plates than they would use, and for a moment, Brodie wondered if she'd invited guests. But the second she started filling her plate, he knew. He made his way to her as she was slipping from the room with a heaping helping of sandwiches and vegetables.

"Who's that for?" he asked her backside as she walked down the hall.

She spun around. "For me. A snack for later. I thought I'd put it in the refrigerator."

He followed her into the kitchen and found her pulling out the plastic wrap to cover the plate. "Are ye planning to be hungry in the middle of the night then?"

She squeezed the plate in the frig before turning on him. "Are you offering to build up my appetite?"

Now there's an idea. But he ignored her proposition, or at least he tried. Once a thought like that took hold, well, even Lou Ferrigno would have a mighty hard time shaking it off.

Without answering her, he went back to the parlor, wishing he hadn't followed her. He made himself a plate and sat in the corner to eat. But if he thought he would be left alone to brood, he was wrong. Hannah pulled him over to sit next to her. On the other side, she'd put up Joe's picture, as if they were having another blasted tea party.

But the lass was so funny and entertaining that after a while he settled down and enjoyed the evening. He and Hannah made hats for all of them to wear for their Christmas Day meal as Vivienne told them of her travels. Hannah didn't seem to be winding down, but Rachel started preparing the lass for bed.

"Did you see what I brought?" Rachel pulled out *'Twas the Night Before Christmas*. "I'll read this to you before I leave."

"Nay." Hannah grabbed the book from her mother. Before he knew what had happened, she'd dropped it into his lap. "Brodie's going to read to me."

For the first time since the kiss on the porch, Rachel looked directly at him. "Do you mind?"

"Not at all." He sat on the couch and Hannah climbed up beside him, laying her head on his arm. He couldn't help comparing this moment to Christmases in the past.

This Christmas Eve had turned into something more than having a dram of whisky by the fire. He glanced over at Grandda, who appeared to be having the time of his life.

Suddenly, Brodie was surprised at how he felt. He was glad the Granger women had come for the holiday.

Chapter Twelve

Rachel watched Brodie read to her daughter, feeling as if she was falling in love with him all over again. She knew it was one-sided, but her heart had a one-track mind and there was no convincing it otherwise.

But he kissed you, the voice in her head whispered. The voice used to be loud and confident, proclaiming how they were going to be a couple and how the three of them would be a family. Day by day, the voice had become less vocal and less sure. But he had kissed her, and it was wonderful. Pure joy. To feel wanted by Brodie Wallace was bliss personified.

He finished the book and shut it.

"Again! Again!" Hannah said.

"It's bedtime," Rachel announced. "The sooner you go to sleep, the sooner Santa will come."

"Father Christmas," Hannah corrected in her Scots accent.

"Fine. Father Christmas." Rachel reached for her daughter. "Up with you."

But Vivienne was there. "I want to put her to bed. I'm tired, too."

"It's too early for you to go to bed," Rachel said, knowing her mother was a night owl.

"I downloaded a couple of Christmas novels. I thought I would read for a while."

Rachel hugged her mom and whispered into her hair, "Are you going to be okay here without me?"

"Are you trying to mother me again?" Vivienne laughed. "Don't worry. I'll see you in the morning." Her mom picked up the complaining Hannah. "Tell everyone *good night*."

"Night!"

As the two went to the stairs, her mother began singing a made-up song. Hannah laughed at the silly words and sang along with her, "*Merry, happy Christmas from Hannah in Scotland.*"

Rachel went to the hallway and pulled out the box which held her mother's patchwork quilt. She returned to the parlor and laid the box under the tree.

"Have ye been out shopping?" Abraham asked.

She smiled at him. "Something like that. I'm going to head to Thistle Glen Lodge. I'll be back early, as I expect my daughter will be up before the roosters."

"Sleep well, lass," he said.

She headed to the kitchen to get the plate for the man who stayed in the shadows. She wondered if he was warm enough tonight. But then she remembered Aileen's missing quilt, which he'd probably taken. She retrieved the plate and turned around. Brodie was there with his coat already on and with her parka over his arm.

"You don't have to go with me. I know the way and I'll be perfectly safe."

He walked toward her, holding out her coat.

She slipped her first arm in. "Really, Brodie, I'll be fine." She transferred the plate to her other hand and put in her second arm.

But talking to him was like trying to convince a grizzly bear to stay put in his cave when he was hell-bent on doing as he pleases.

"Fine. Do whatever you want." She flounced from the kitchen.

He was being stubborn. Sure, she wanted him at the quilting dorm, but preferred he was there because he'd decided to forgive her. She dreamed what it would be like to be Brodie's wife, and all the *extracurriculars* which went along with marriage. The only thing she was going to get this evening, though, was another sleepless, restless night with him camped out on the couch.

She slung open the front door and marched out. Brodie was right behind her, carrying a small duffel.

"I'll take the other bedroom on the main level."

"So the grizzly bear speaks," she said sarcastically, but that was only because she was crazy about him with no hope of fulfilling her dreams.

"What?" He looked side to side. Of course, he was on the lookout for the shadow stalker.

"But the bear doesn't speak much," she huffed to herself.

When they reached the dorm, she opened the door and started in, but he took her arm.

"Aren't ye going to leave the plate out here?"

"Fine."

"Make sure to set the lock when ye're done."

She laid the plate down then shut the door with them inside.

When she turned around, Brodie was down the hallway, almost to the living room.

"So this is how it's going to be," she said to the floral and plaid window coverings. "I'm going to have a lonely *Blue Christmas*." But that wasn't fair. She had Hannah, her mother, and Abraham.

When she got to the living room, he wasn't there. She

collapsed on the sofa, feeling utterly rejected. But in the next second, when Brodie appeared, wearing flannel pajama bottoms and a T-shirt, her pulse kicked up. He didn't seem to notice she was about to hyperventilate, as he walked to the kitchen without giving her a second glance. She heard the tap go on. He came back with a glass of water and stopped at the edge of the living room.

"Good night, lass." No gazing at her as if he couldn't live without her. Hell, the way he stalked to his bedroom— the one next to hers—and closed the door behind him, she felt as enticing as a snow cone in the dead of winter.

Rachel spoke to the hearth this time. "He has some nerve." She sat there for a long minute, staring down the dark hallway at the light escaping from under the door. She was certain her irrational thoughts were brought on by sexual frustration. She hoped in vain he would sling the door open, march back down the hall, pull her into his arms, and kiss her until she had a *very merry Christmas*. But then the light went out in his room.

She laid her head on the sofa, closing her eyes. "Damn."

Finally she pushed herself up, plodded to her bedroom, and readied for sleep. As she was brushing out her hair, a series of not so innocent thoughts bombarded her mind, which would put her on the naughty list for sure. But she always did the *right thing*, and look what it had gotten her. *Nothing*.

Hesitating only a millisecond, she turned out her light, but didn't climb into bed. Instead, she snuck to the room next to hers and cracked open the door. The moonlight stretched across the room. She was surprised to see his large frame sitting on the side of the bed, staring out the partially frosted over window.

"Did ye get lost?" he rumbled without turning around.

"Yes." It was the truth. She got lost six years ago and she'd been trying to find her way back ever since. She hadn't realized how adrift she'd been until she'd returned to Gandiegow and laid eyes on him. But this truth was too heavy for Brodie. She padded toward him and sat down, bravely leaning against him.

He drew back a little, but didn't scoot away. "What do ye want?" His voice was strained.

It was on the tip of her tongue to say *you*. But she didn't say it; instead she slipped her arm around his waist and laid her head on his shoulder.

His body stiffened as if he was bearing up against rising flood waters. "How do you imagine this is going to play out?"

She liked that he was direct. She would return the favor. "You'll make love to me."

"And then?"

"I don't know. I don't care." That wasn't exactly true. "I want you." That was the truth. But she couldn't tell him all of it . . . she wanted him for *always*. But she would settle for tonight.

He turned to her and touched the locket. "I want ye, too."

Her chest warmed. She was light-headed and giddy. She felt like she could fly.

He tilted his head to the side, maintaining eye contact. "I'm going to be straight with you beforehand. We'll do what ye want, but ye'll have to agree first that you under-stand that making"—he cut himself off and changed his tack—"that going to bed together won't change a thing between us."

Her heart fell. Plummeted. Barely pulsed, as it curled into a ball at the bottom of her soul.

She dropped her arm from his waist.

Since she'd gotten to Gandiegow, she'd been making

one deal after another. So far, she'd been able to keep her end of the bargain. But now? Could she really be with him and not want to change his mind?

"Okay," she heard herself saying. The little voice in her head was agreeing and whispering little encouragements, *Do this, then he'll love you.* But she wasn't fool enough to believe it.

She laid a hand on his back. "Before we go any further, there's something I have to say." She took a deep breath, steeling herself. "I tried to call it off." She didn't explain what *it* was. Brodie was sharp; he had to know what she was talking about. "I even told my mother I couldn't go through with it." Rachel hung her head, remembering. "My mother gave me reason after reason why I had to marry Joe."

Brodie didn't say anything. At this point, he probably didn't even care anymore, but he deserved to hear her confession.

"I'm not blaming my mother. It's my fault. I was weak back then. I only wanted to please her. Please everyone."

Still he said nothing.

Rachel rubbed his back as if that might counteract her words. "I should've been stronger. I can't go back and change things." She paused for a second and told him the whole truth. "And if I could, I wouldn't. I wouldn't have missed Hannah for anything in the world." That might hurt him, but it was true.

He nodded—the only acknowledgment that he'd heard her. He didn't take her into his arms, but went back to staring out the window. She understood; he needed time to process what she'd said. A minute passed. She was very aware of her own breathing. As the second minute was stretching on, anticipation turned into realization that her confession had only made things worse. Brodie didn't want her any longer.

She popped up. "I'll just go to bed." She turned to walk away, but he grabbed her hand.

"Come here." He yanked her to him.

One second she was chilled from the night air, and in the next she was crushed up against him, his mouth on hers, greedy for her attention. Oh, she was easy when it came to him, because she kissed him back as if they'd never kiss again. She didn't even recognize herself. Six years of pent-up hormones were unleashing themselves faster than water rushing from the floodgates. Maybe she should've savored every morsel of his touch, but she was half afraid he was going to change his mind and bolt from the room.

Night clothes were a wonderful thing when she needed to get to bare skin quickly . . . not much on under there. She tugged at his shirt and pulled it over his head. He started on the buttons of her gown, but she returned the favor and pulled it off for him. Pajama bottoms and panties were no match for their impatience. They were naked and on the bed in two seconds flat, mouths on each other's, as if they collectively held the air for each other's lungs.

He broke away. "Condom." He hurried across the room and lifted his discarded pants, digging around in its pockets. She saw a wallet, him fumble, and a "*dammit*" resounded when it hit the floor. A moment later, he was back, ripping open the package.

She was as anxious as he was.

He quickly positioned himself above her as if this was the chance of a lifetime, but then he stopped and stared at her.

"Did you forget something else?" She saw serious determination in his eyes.

"I heard every word ye said. On a rational level, I understand why you did what you did . . . marrying my cousin. But you have to know that I mean it, Rachel. Nothing changes between us."

"I know." She was going into this with no illusions.

With him looming over her and the moonlight flooding in the window, she had a chance to soak him in. Suddenly, she was aware of what was tattooed on his chest.

A partridge! Did he get the tattoo as a souvenir of what they'd shared?

It was on the tip of her tongue to ask. Her eyes went to his, but he was staring at the locket around her neck. There was so much more they needed to discuss. *The locket. The partridge.* But for now, they'd talked enough.

She laid a hand on the tattoo so he would know she'd seen the partridge. He placed a hand over hers as if both of them were holding his heart. The world fell away, replaced with a magical cocoon surrounding them, as his eyes drifted back up and he stared into her face. He eased himself in, never breaking eye contact. His look of tender longing nearly broke her heart, making her love him even more. She shifted, opening up to him, giving him more access as he filled her. She quieted her own thoughts to better hear what his body was saying. No words fit the emotion in his eyes or the way his body consumed her, and he'd done nothing more than cross the threshold.

"Kiss me," she said, afraid she might cry if he gazed at her any longer.

"Aye." He leaned in but didn't devour her as she'd expected. He started at the corner of her mouth, caressing her lips as if she wasn't an emotional mess underneath him.

His approach to their coupling felt like he was composing a love song. He seemed to be looking for the perfect note, the right tone, strumming her, executing each part in perfect time, all meant to produce the most pleasure for her. She felt helpless to give him as much as he was giving her. His lovemaking was excruciating, overwhelming her, and positively breathtaking. Before she could stop them, teardrops tumbled out and annoyingly rolled into her ears.

"Enough," she said, pushing him off. "I want to be on top."

As he moved away, she discreetly wiped her tears on the corner of the pillowcase, thankful for the shadows. As she sat, she nudged him to the mattress, and climbed on top. Before she could do more, he pulled her down for another heart-melting kiss, making her stretch out beside him, both of them lying on their sides.

"*Mo ghràidh*," he whispered into her ear.

Could a woman die from an endearment? For surely, that's what it was.

"Brodie?" She cupped his face and made him look at her. She wanted to pour out her heart and confess how much she still loved him, but she didn't. She couldn't stand it if he pushed her away now. "I can't take much more."

He smiled and then kissed her nose, not seeming to be in a rush at all. She was afraid she might truly start bawling if he didn't hurry his fisherman self along.

"Come here." He lifted her leg, scooted in closer, and joined them together once again.

"That's better," she exhaled, feeling complete. But she had to use all her focus to keep her mouth from revealing her true emotions.

He had been in control up to this point, but his cool manner slipped away. Taking her by surprise, he rolled her on her back and once again he was on top. Whoever said the missionary position wasn't exciting was nuts. Brodie making love to her from above was the most heart-pounding experience she'd ever had, and she was nearing the place of no return. She was so wrapped up in the moment that her heart cried out, "Love me, Brodie."

He came with a shudder and she followed him into the bliss.

As the waves of their coupling rippled away, she realized that he'd stilled. She gazed up to find him staring at her warily.

"I didn't mean it," she said. But she had and he knew it.

He didn't say a word, but pulled out and stood, turning away, looking out the frosted window again.

She scooted off the bed and reached for her twisted nightgown.

"I got carried away," she tried to explain. She didn't understand how they could be so connected one second, and in the next, for him to become as distant and as cold as Antarctica. She longed to wrap an arm around his waist and ride out the storm which was making his back rigid in the moonlight.

She waited, in vain, for him to tell her to come back to bed. Or that he would at least say her name once more. But he'd erected an impenetrable wall between them.

It would do no good to ask him for his forgiveness again. She already knew the answer.

I love you, she wanted to cry out into the darkened room as a cloud came over the moon. But she kept her regard for him to herself—at least this time. As she walked into the hallway, she felt as if she'd given herself away, once again, to the wrong cousin.

Don't lose heart, the little voice said. *He called you mo ghràidh.* But she was certain he was regretting it now, because she'd pleaded with him to love her.

"Lass?" Brodie stared out into the night, unable to calm his pounding heart. "Good night." His blasted voice sounded emotional. He'd told her sex wouldn't mean anything, but somehow it had.

She said nothing but quietly shut his door.

He shouldn't have let it happen. He'd been minding his own business, looking into the night for the person lurking about. Why had he been so weak? He knew the answer. *For a lot of reasons, some even rational.*

He scoffed. "Yeah. Right, rational." What a line of bullshit he'd been feeding himself . . . *closure.* There was no closure in having sex. He'd only opened Pandora's box and totally screwed himself and the resolve he'd built up since she'd married Joe.

Love me, Brodie still hung in the air like perfume. Any man would've been honored for a woman like Rachel to ask him for his love. Aye, her words sounded sweet and sincere, but if he did as she asked, he'd be pulling the rope for the death knell of his weak heart.

If only the damned partridge tattoo didn't want to bust out of his chest, run to her, beg her to come back, tell her that they should make love until they were old and gray.

"Effing hell." He should find Doc right now and have himself committed. A real man should be stronger than this.

Like a gavel, he pounded the bed. He would not run to her. He would stick to his guns. Tomorrow, he would act like nothing had happened. He wouldn't ruin Christmas for Grandda. He would pretend it had all been a dream. He'd get through the holidays and wave goodbye to Rachel when she left, showing her the same amount of emotion as if she were one of the damned retreat-goers. He'd be fine. Abraham had made it all these years without a woman by his side. Brodie could do the same.

He yanked on his pajama bottoms and lay back on the bed. He refused to think about Rachel on the other side of the wall, though her scent was everywhere. He got out of bed, taking the quilt with him, and marched down the hallway to the sofa.

But as the clock ticked on the wall, he was unable to sleep. *Hell.* That's what he got for not being able to control his urges. When he finally dozed off, he was tortured with dreams of Rachel. They were on his boat in midsummer. She was laughing into the wind and smiling at him. He'd never been happier.

At six thirty, he woke to the smell of coffee and Rachel padding around in the kitchen. Without stopping to wish her a Happy Christmas, he readied for the day—externally and internally. When he had composed himself to being as emotional as the retaining wall to the village, he appeared in the kitchen.

Rachel was a vision of contradiction. She wore a long-sleeved red party dress and dark tights, but on her feet were her purple fuzzy slippers. Nothing had changed between them—she knew the score—yet she still wore his locket around her slender neck. This time, instead of the locket making him angry or confused, he was relieved it still hung there. He shouldn't feel that way and cursed his inconsistency. *Damn his gullible heart!*

He took in her face and found her gaze was filled with expectation, *earnestness*, and an I-want-to-talk-about-last-night-before-we-go expression. "I made you a cup of coffee."

He nodded and approached the mug, but not before he remembered his resolve and fortified himself.

As she opened her mouth, he raised his hand to shield against her onslaught.

"Nothing's changed," he said gruffly. But in the background, he could still hear her plea, *Love me, Brodie.* He needed that coffee to clear his throat . . . and his mind.

"But—but . . ." The pain in her voice was killing him.

He changed the subject. "What about the thief? Have ye set out his breakfast?"

"I thought I'd leave him the scones." She pointed to the paper bag lying on the counter. "Maybe something more from the refrigerator, too."

"Fill it up. It's Christmas." If Brodie had any say about it, it was also Reckoning Day. Something had to be done. He couldn't continue to stay at the quilting dorm to watch out for Rachel or he'd lose his mind. *And my heart.* He hated himself for thinking like a sappy schoolgirl.

"I'll get last night's plate." He stomped from the room toward the front of the cottage, not feeling the joy of Christmas in the least. One thing was for certain, he'd better straighten out his mood before going home to Grandda.

When he yanked open the door, not only was the empty plate sitting on the stoop, but another paper statue. This time, though, it was a bear. *A damn bear.* The thief had given the American lass a bear. Was he sweet on her?

Brodie needed to catch this bastard.

He bent down, retrieved both items, and took them back to the kitchen. "Ye have an admirer." The taste was bitter in his mouth. If this was Tuck playing some kind of prank, Brodie was going to straighten him out with a boot up his arse.

She took the things Brodie offered and smiled at the bear. "He's talented."

"And a criminal."

She shrugged. "Do you think this will hold him off

until dinner?" She had stacked three scones and four leftover bangers on the plate, covering it all with plastic wrap.

"Aye. Go put that out front and let's get home. Hannah will probably be up."

Rachel smiled at him, the smile that was always on her face when she was thinking of her daughter. "For my mother's sake, I hope she hasn't been awake too long." Rachel left with the plate.

Brodie retrieved his coat and met her at the front. He pulled the door closed, locked it, and stepped over the plate of food. They walked in silence to the cottage, but he could tell Rachel still wanted to talk. He wouldn't allow her to draw him in. He wouldn't ask how she fared today. He was a rock. Immovable, inaccessible. But the waves breaking on the walkway sang out, *Love me, Brodie.*

At his grandfather's cottage, Brodie barred the door with his hand as Rachel reached for the knob. "I have an errand to run."

"On Christmas?" She sounded circumspect.

"Don't open the presents without me." He waited until she was safe inside, before heading into the shadows at the back of the houses. Winter didn't provide a lot of camouflage, but at least it was still dark, due to the short days. He circled around to the quilting dorms, ready to catch the thief in action. God, he hoped the bastard hadn't picked up his meal while Brodie was getting Rachel to Grandda's in one piece.

Brodie took up his position behind the lounge chair at Duncan's Den, waiting and watching the full plate Rachel had left.

It was damned cold this morning, and only minutes into his stakeout, Brodie was wishing for long underwear and a stack of quilts to burrow under. He considered slipping into the quilting dorm to get one when there was movement in the shadows across from Thistle Glen Lodge.

Rachel was right; the bandit wasn't big enough to be Tuck. But the body shape and the way he moved confirmed the stalker was a *he*. He lurked in the shadows for several seconds, probably to make sure it was safe to come out. Finally, he slunk forward, shadow to shadow, until the last place to go was the porch. Brodie readied himself. The moment the thief bent down to get the plate, he rushed from his hiding spot and grabbed the man by the scruff of his coat collar.

"Uh!" came the thief's surprise. "Leave off." He swung wildly.

Suddenly, Brodie realized he wasn't a man at all, but a tall kid. A teen. Skinny. Hannah had enough strength to hold him off. "Who are ye?" Brodie let go, certain he could stop the kid if he decided to run.

The teen straightened himself up indignantly. "I'm Harry."

Brodie didn't recognize him from Gandiegow or one of the surrounding villages. "Harry who?"

"Harry Stanton."

"What are ye doing here?" Brodie asked.

"Looking for me father."

"Who's yere father?"

The kid's eyes dropped to his feet. "I dunno."

"Ah, hell." Brodie shook his head, feeling kind of stupid for trying to be a badass. He'd caught him, but now what was he going to do with the lad? "Pick up yere plate. We're going to my grandfather's." He couldn't believe he was doing this, taking home a delinquent for Christmas. "Watch what ye do and say at my house. My family's there." The thought struck him strangely how it wasn't just Abraham he was thinking about. Rachel, Hannah, and even Vivienne were his family, too.

The kid stood there, looking at him closely.

"Stop staring at me," Brodie said. "I'm not *yere da.* Now, let's get going."

The kid grabbed the plate, but couldn't keep his eyes off the food as they trudged down the walkway.

"Go ahead and eat something. There'll be more when we get to the cottage." Brodie had never known real hunger, but he recognized the teen's.

When they arrived at Abraham's, Brodie let the kid in and showed him where to put his snow-dusted wellies— *size forty-four.* Next he pointed where to hang his coat, then showed him to the parlor, where Hannah was chatting nonstop with the rest of the family laughing at her antics.

"Ye're here," Abraham said as Brodie stepped into the entryway.

Hannah rushed him. "Brodie!" Instead of letting her hug him, he shifted her to the side, putting a protective arm around her.

With his other hand, he grabbed Harry's sleeve and pulled him into the room. "We have a guest." The kid still held the plate, and Rachel's eyes fell to the breakfast she'd made him. She lifted her eyebrows at Brodie as if waiting for an explanation. "He'll be spending Christmas with us." He didn't know any other way to keep an eye on the kid.

"Welcome," Grandda said. "Come get warm by the fire. We were just getting ready to open presents."

Hannah hopped up and down. "Yeah!"

Harry walked over to the fireplace, looking miserable, and sat down on the stone hearth with his plate.

"Hold off on the presents for a moment. I need to grab something to eat." The smell of sausage from the kitchen was powerful. Brodie would make another plate for Harry, too.

Hannah ran after him into the hallway and grabbed his hand. "Hurry, Brodie. Hurry."

He couldn't help himself; he squatted down to hug the lass. "Happy Christmas, wee princess."

She kissed him on the cheek. "Happy Christmas to ye, Sir Knight!" She raced back to the parlor.

A few minutes later, he returned with two plates, hearing the last of the introductions to the newcomer in the room. Harry mentioned nothing about looking for his father, only saying that he was passing through. Brodie handed him the new plate of food, nodding to him that he'd done the right thing. Today wasn't the day to be accusing the men of Gandiegow of fathering a child and abandoning him.

For a moment, Joe passed through Brodie's mind. Could he be Harry's father? Nay. It was too far-fetched and too much of a coincidence to have Harry land in this house looking for his kin.

Hannah was so hyperactive at this point that both Rachel and her mother seemed to have given up trying to contain her enthusiasm.

"Do I get the first present?" the girl chirped.

Brodie swallowed his bite of scone. "Aye." He went to the tree and rolled out a crudely wrapped present. He didn't know a lot about little girls, but when he'd seen it in the store at Inverness, he thought it would be perfect for dolly. "Here."

Hannah shredded the wrapping paper as if a pot of gold were hidden inside. "A stroller!" she squealed. She snatched her doll off Abraham's lap and shoved her in there as if she were stuffing a pillow into its case.

"I hope ye like it," Brodie said awkwardly.

"Tell Brodie *thank you*," Rachel prodded.

"Thank ye," Hannah said. She looked over at Grandda. "I *fancy* it a lot."

Abraham winked at her as if she'd used the word correctly.

Harry snickered, reminding Brodie that he was in the room.

"What?" Harry said a little belligerently. "The lass is cute."

Hannah, never shy, beamed at Harry.

"Who's next?" Rachel said. "How about one for Abraham?" She reached under the tree and pulled out a flat box. "Hannah, give this to your grandfather."

The lass dropped the handles of her buggy and skipped over to Rachel. She took the gift, ran to Grandda, and shoved the present at him. "Here."

With arthritic hands that had seen better days while fishing, Grandda unwrapped the gift with much more restraint than Hannah until tartan fabric appeared. Quickly, he ripped off the rest of the paper. "It's the MacFarlane tartan."

"Turn it over," Rachel said.

Grandda flipped the frame and on the other side was *them* . . . Rachel, Hannah, Abraham, and Brodie. "A family portrait." Grandda seemed choked up when he looked at Rachel. "Ye're a thoughtful lass." He put his hand out to her.

Rachel came to him and squeezed his hand, then kissed his cheek. "Merry Christmas."

Once again Brodie was touched by how kind she was to his grandfather.

Abraham patted the gift. "Did ye make this, Rachel?"

"Aye," Hannah said, butting in. "She made it all by herself, except I helped to put the picture in the frame."

Grandda beamed at the girl. "Ye're a thoughtful one, too."

Rachel reached under the tree and discreetly tore the tag off the next gift as she lifted it out. "If I'm not mistaken, I think Santa left a present here for Harry."

The teen's head popped up. "What?"

"Father Christmas," Hannah said, correcting her mother.

"Yes, right, Father Christmas. Here, Harry." Rachel held out the medium-size box to the boy.

"For me?" He looked around at them as if they were a group of forest animals who had suddenly learned to talk. Finally, he took the gift and tore into it as if he'd taken lessons from Hannah. It was the simple patchwork quilt, meant for Vivienne, nothing elaborate, but Harry gazed upon it as if it were that pot of gold.

All of a sudden, the kid looked embarrassed. "Thanks," he mumbled. He crumpled the quilt to his chest and held it tight.

"Who's next?" Hannah cried. "Me?"

Brodie stepped forward and pulled a present from under the tree. "How about another one for Grandda?" Normally, he got his grandfather a good bottle of whisky, but this year, Brodie had gone all out. He handed the present over. "Here."

Abraham opened the rectangular box and looked up at Brodie more than a little shocked. "'Tis too expensive."

"Nay. I thought ye and Hannah could FaceTime when she goes back to the States." But the thought of them leaving Scotland made the scone in Brodie's stomach turn to stone.

"FaceTime?" Abraham said.

"I'll show ye, Grandda." Hannah took the iPad box and flipped it over. "It's easy."

More presents were handed out. Brodie gave Hannah the child's rocking chair, which had been his as a boy. Rachel gave Vivienne what she called a *Scotland Survival Kit* with warm boots and goodies from the store. Then more presents for Hannah were ripped into, while Harry sat with his quilt and watched as he ate the two plates of food.

The one present Brodie didn't bring out was left upstairs, tucked in the back of his closet. The leather-bound notebook of hand-pressed paper was for Rachel. He remembered how she liked to sketch when she'd been here six years ago. The gift didn't mean anything, and he had no intention of giving it to her in front of everyone. They might read too much into it.

Grandda was beaming at them with wrapping paper scattered at his feet. "How about another family picture?"

"I'll do it," Rachel said.

Vivienne took her phone from her. "You get in the picture. I'll take it."

Harry stood. "Nay. I'll do it."

Vivienne gave him a generous smile and handed over the mobile.

Brodie took his place behind his grandfather. Instead of Rachel keeping her distance, the minx sidled up next to him and his nose picked up her familiar scent. It wafted over him the same way the waves caressed the beach. *Love me, Brodie* filled his senses and he had a hard time keeping it together.

Harry held the phone up, but then dropped it to his chest. "Ye'll have to squeeze in."

Rachel leaned into Brodie, tormenting him further. Automatically, his arm rose to pull her in closer, but he stopped himself in time. He stared straight ahead, enduring the close contact as if she had a contagious ailment that he could catch.

"On the count of three," Harry said. The kid stretched the photo session out longer than necessary by snapping several pictures.

When he went to give the cell phone back, Hannah insisted they do a selfie with the whole family, Harry included. It made Harry happy, but Brodie just wanted this *picture perfect moment* to be over.

Afterward, the kid and Hannah cleaned up the wrapping paper from the floor. Rachel and Vivienne went off to the kitchen and Brodie had time to think about what to do about their Christmas guest.

"Harry?" Abraham said. "Grab the checkerboard and set it up. I think ye and I should play a game since the wee lass is busy with her dolls." Yes, dolls. Rachel had bought her one. Vivienne, too. Abraham must've commissioned Deydie to bring one from the General Store. Hannah's dolls took up so much room on the couch that none of them had a place to sit.

Harry got the checkerboard and Brodie slipped from the room to check if the other two needed help in the kitchen. But before he reached the doorway, he stopped as he heard his name.

"Did you sleep with Brodie last night? I noticed he wasn't here this morning." Vivienne spoke with disapproval dripping from each word.

"No," Rachel said.

Brodie nodded; Rachel spoke the truth. They hadn't *slept* together.

"Where did he sleep last night?"

"On the couch at the quilting dorm," Rachel answered. Honest once again. "He was worried about the person taking things around town. Mostly food. As it turns out, it was Harry."

"Oh." Vivienne seemed to have run out of accusations. But Brodie was too generous with his conclusions. "I mean it, Rachel. You need someone more like you. Brodie is too rough around the edges."

"I know, Mom. I promise you, there's nothing going on." Rachel's voice was sad.

Nothing's going on? Irrationally, he wanted to burst into the room and set her straight. They'd made love last night and, *dammit,* it had meant something. She'd said, *Love me, Brodie.* But apparently Rachel hadn't meant it and what they'd shared really had been *nothing.*

Immediately, he reined himself in, because he was losing his *effing* mind! He was the one who'd told her nothing had changed!

Rachel came around the corner suddenly. He put his hand out to stop her from spilling the tray.

"Sorry," he mumbled. "I was just coming in to get Abraham's medicine."

"He's already had it," Rachel said. She was searching his face like she'd done a thousand times since arriving in Gandiegow.

Brodie walked away before she found something that hadn't been there before . . . like his renewing affection for her.

"I'm going to check on the boat," he said as he passed by the parlor. "I'll be back before the meal."

Outside the wind had kicked up and with it a rush of sensibility hit him. He couldn't go to the boat. He'd left a stranger—*a thief,* no less—at home with the people Brodie cared most about in the world. That realization was even more uncomfortable, because it wasn't just Abraham he held in his heart.

Ah, hell. Brodie turned around and opened the door, going back in. He'd give them all today. He would screw a smile on his face and be pleasant. He'd do it for his grandda's sake and make this the best damn Christmas the old man ever had.

But tomorrow, Brodie was stepping back into his real life, one where he remembered the past—*Rachel's betrayal*—and remembered his place. According to Vivienne, he was a fisherman who wasn't nearly good enough for her daughter.

Chapter Thirteen

Grace Armstrong loved spending time with her grand-children, especially being here with them on Christmas morning. Dand was learning how to use his new fishing rod, and baby Irene was playing with a discarded box. Maggie, Grace's daughter-in-law, was in the kitchen with John, her grown son, the two of them having a cuddle, sipping their tea, and watching their children. Grace should be content, but she felt restless.

She went to her room, sat on the bed, and pulled her mobile from her purse. She hadn't wanted a smart phone, thinking it was an extravagance. But her three sons had gone together and given her the phone on the last Mothering Sunday. She was grateful, especially now. She texted a note to Casper.

Meet me at the car?

Casper had brought his own vehicle to Gandiegow when he'd moved here, though he'd made it available to the whole village by adding it to the list of cars that could be checked out at the General Store. The car had been one of their secret meeting places. It was cold, but they'd found a way to warm it up without turning on the key.

She sat looking at the blank screen, waiting. It was

Christmas and Casper was with his son, Gabriel, and his family—Emma and little Angus.

Her phone dinged back.

15 minutes

Giddy, she went to her top drawer and retrieved the small gift she'd wrapped for Casper in golden tissue paper. John and Maggie wouldn't think anything of her going for a walk. Grace had taken a lot of them since coming to Gandiegow. Besides meeting with Casper, she understood that even though she was home in her cottage, it wasn't really hers anymore. Maggie was the woman of the house now. She and John had built a life here just as Grace and Alistair had done when they were young.

Guilt flooded her, making her drop the gift back into the drawer. She looked at the door and then at the room she'd once shared with her husband. Ross had made this room his own when she'd moved to Glasgow to care for her sister—a new wall color, a new bed, flea market fishing paintings, and an old dinghy that he'd converted into a bookcase. The shelves were empty as she hadn't filled them yet. This wasn't home to her anymore and she truly felt like a fish out of water . . . floundering between guilt and what lay ahead.

She should break it off with Casper, but not today. Not Christmas. She picked up his gift again, ignoring the guilt, and grabbed her phone. She slipped his present into the pocket of her lined pants and walked into the living room.

"Going for a walk, Mum?" John said as he lifted his mug to his mouth.

"Aye. I shan't be long." Grace grabbed her coat, hoping the heat which flooded her cheeks wasn't obvious. She was sneaking off as if she were once again the young woman who'd snuck from her parents' home to be with her first love, Alistair.

But it wasn't Alistair she was going to meet. This would be her last rendezvous with Casper. She meant it this time.

Outside, she hurried across the small expanse of the village to the parking lot on the far side of town, next to the pub. She could see Casper getting in his car and she walked faster, glancing around to see if anyone might be peering out of their windows.

At the car, she got in quickly.

"Hallo," she said, feeling shy. He always made her feel this way. Excited, breathless, the anticipation making her heart pound.

"Hallo, lass." He leaned over and she leaned in automatically.

Grace never felt old with Casper. At fifty-eight, she still felt the same as she did when she was eighteen. But she and Casper weren't young kids. At their age, a hug or a kiss on the cheek should've been the norm, but it wasn't. Their kisses had enough heat behind them to set Gandiegow on fire and make her insides flutter as if a flock of gulls had launched into the sky. She and Casper always kissed as if they were in the prime of their life.

When they pulled away, she took the box from her pocket. "I brought you a gift."

"And I, as well." He held out a small flat box, too. "You first."

"I'm surprised. I know yere views on Christmas."

"I wanted ye to have something special."

She beamed at him as she took the lid off to reveal a three-cornered Celtic brooch with different colored agate stones in each tip and one in the center. "Oh, Casper, it's lovely." She'd never seen one like it before. She knew enough about Casper that he probably selected this one not only for its uniqueness, but because it symbolized something more . . . the Trinity. She gazed up at him and was washed with emotion. "Oh, Casper," she said again.

He kissed her fingertips. "I'm glad ye like it. I would rather have done it by the fire at either yere house or my son's, not in a car, as if we're ashamed to be together."

"But we've discussed this." Her sons would never understand that she was seeing another man and with their father gone only four years.

Casper took her hand. "I'm not one to hide. God sees me no matter where I am." He paused as if he was letting that sink in for her. "If I am to be God's vessel, I have to be transparent. I want to court ye openly and hide no more."

She looked down at his hand, holding hers, fighting how right he felt. She shook her head. "I can't." Her sons were everything to her. She dropped Casper's hand. "I have yere present, too." There was no excitement in her voice as she pulled out his gift. This was the end. She handed it to him.

He took it, but he seemed sad and disappointed in her. He undid the tissue, revealing the bagpipe tie clip that she'd found for him in Glasgow and had waited months to give to him. Casper told her he'd played the pipes as a young man in the Royal Edinburgh Military Tattoo.

He smiled sadly at the clasp. "Thank ye."

But she'd ruined Christmas and what they had between them.

"Won't you reconsider?" he asked, hopeful. "Can't ye find a way to be at peace with us?"

"Happy Christmas, Casper." Grace slipped from the car, and with her head held high, she trudged home.

Rachel heard the front door slam and Brodie reappeared not long after announcing he was going to the boat. She continued talking with Harry, careful not to make the young man defensive. "But where is your mother now?"

Harry looked down at his hands and was quiet for a long moment. "She died in hospital."

So this sweet teenage boy was without any family.

Abraham glanced up as Brodie stood in the doorway. "The boat? Is she all right?"

"Brodie! Brodie!" Hannah ran to him, flying into his arms.

Her daughter hugged him as Brodie lifted her up, the movement as natural, fluid, and flawless as if they'd performed this dance a million times.

Hannah thrust a paper swan in his face. "Look what Harry made me."

He examined the gift then turned his scrutiny on the boy. "How old are ye, Harry?"

The kid looked up at him, surprised. "Um, eighteen."

Rachel was pretty sure he was younger, but it was hard to gauge what age exactly—seventeen, sixteen?

"Where do ye hail from, Harry?" Brodie asked.

Harry's mouth formed a hard line and he glared at Brodie as if he'd rather walk on needles than be interrogated.

"Harry's from the city," Hannah piped in, patting Brodie's chest as if to calm him down. "Grandda wanted to know if the boat is all right."

Good ole Hannah. Her daughter liked Harry and had decided to protect him.

Brodie seemed to force cheerfulness to his face. "The boat's fine, Grandda."

Hannah bounced the swan on Brodie's shoulder. "Do ye like it?"

"Harry did a fine job on the swan," Brodie agreed. He walked farther into the room and set Hannah down next to Abraham. "Is it time to roast some chestnuts?"

Hannah jumped up. "Aye. Can I do it?"

She'd asked Brodie, but Abraham answered. "Ye can, but Brodie'll have to supervise."

Rachel heard the kitchen door open.

"Food's here," came a male voice.

"It's Dominic," Brodie said, heading out the door. "Chestnuts will have to wait until after our meal."

Rachel followed him into the kitchen and watched as a box of delicious-smelling food was being transferred from one man to the other.

"I'll get the turkey." Dominic headed for the back door.

"I really appreciate it," Brodie said, acting as if Rachel wasn't in the room. "Ye know Grandda and I could never have made such a meal."

"Cooking lessons." Dominic handed him a pan which contained a foil-wrapped turkey. "I told ye, I could teach you." He glanced up to see Rachel. "Ye agree, don't you? Men need to know how to cook."

"Absolutely. Especially if the man is a confirmed bachelor."

Brodie made a low guttural noise—probably something Gaelic and not a word her daughter, the mimic, should repeat.

Dominic laughed, smiling at both of them. "I better get home to the family. Gabe, Emma, and Casper are coming over for our Christmas feast. Happy Christmas to ye all." He waved good-bye and left.

Brodie guffawed and grumbled, "Happy Christmas, my arse." He turned around and frowned in Rachel's direction as if they'd never shared anything more intimate than planet Earth.

She wanted to yell at him to wake up. To really look at her. For him to forgive her for the stupid things she'd done. But he'd never take a second chance on them. That ship had sailed and gotten lost at sea.

She looked behind her to make sure they were alone. When she saw they were, she leaned toward him and hissed, "Why won't you talk to me?" Those were brave words from a woman whose heart was breaking off, piece by piece. She already knew the answer. He didn't love her and he probably had a clue how much she loved him. Unfortunately, love could be the most powerful repellent in the world.

"*Nothing* is the matter," he said, accentuating the word.

She moved closer and touched his arm.

He flinched, but she was determined.

"Did I do something wrong?" *Besides ask you for the impossible when we were in the throes of passion.* "You were less testy earlier this morning."

His jaw clenched.

"What happened that I don't know about? You're being a big Scrooge to me now."

Brodie lifted an eyebrow. "I promise . . . *there's nothing going on.* I'm a bit *rough around the edges* today."

Realization dawned. "You overheard my conversation with my mother."

He turned away and began unloading the box.

She laid a hand on his back. "What did you expect me to tell her?" Rachel leaned in and whispered, "That we had incredible sex last night?"

His back stiffened as if his whole body was listening, and not just his ears. He grumbled something unintelligible.

"What was that?" She rubbed his back, hoping to soothe his hurt pride.

He turned around and faced her. "'Twas incredible." He gazed into her eyes for a couple of seconds, as if he was searching them, but then he opened his mouth. "It—"

She cut him off, sure he was going to ruin the admission. "Don't say it. You've been clear. Incredible or not, last night *doesn't change a thing*." Another piece of her heart chipped away, leaving her feeling raw.

As if he couldn't stand to see her so, he spun back to the food box. "Aye. *Doesna* change a thing." His voice was gruff, but determined.

She longed to crawl into his arms, flatten herself against him, and wish him a proper Merry Christmas with a kiss. But she'd gotten what she longed for—to make love to Brodie. For six years, he'd haunted her dreams while she slept. Now that she knew firsthand what she'd been missing, he would haunt her waking hours, too.

"I have a present for you," she said to his back.

When she spun around, Hannah was standing there, her eyes beaming. "What did ye get Brodie? I want to see."

Brodie jerked around, too, and gawked at her daughter, but recovered quickly. "Lass, if it's the last thing I do, I'm going to put bells on yere shoelaces."

Hannah hopped up and down, smiling. "Really? I could be like the horses on Mommy's Christmas movie."

Brodie looked at Rachel, clearly puzzled.

"*Holiday Inn*," she answered.

"Where's Brodie's present?" Hannah asked.

Rachel was backed into a corner. "It's in my purse."

Brodie tensed, asking Rachel with his eyes if this was *a good idea*. The way he acted, did he think she was going to present him with a box of condoms?

Rachel shook her head in reply.

"Come on, Hannah," she said. "I'll let you give it to him."

Brodie followed them into the parlor.

Rachel pulled the wrapped present from her purse and announced to the room, "I forgot I had this tucked away."

"It's a present for Brodie." Hannah's squeal of excitement made it seem as if the gift were for herself and not her cousin.

Rachel held out the package to her daughter. "Here."

Hannah grabbed it and raced for Brodie. "Can I open it for ye?"

"No," Rachel said before he could answer.

All eyes were on Brodie as he took the gift. He looked torn as to whether he should open it or go stomping from the house.

She needed to prepare him. "Remember the partridge you told me about?" she said nonchalantly.

His head snapped up. "What?" He acted as if he might look down at his chest, but stopped midway and brought his head back up. "Aye. The partridge, by the ruins of Monadail Castle."

Now it was Rachel's turn to be waylaid. How could he announce to the room the place where they'd shared their first kiss? She'd never told anyone about the ruins, not even her mother when Rachel had tried to call off the wedding. Monadail Castle was *theirs*. Hers and Brodie's. The man didn't play fair. Not fair at all. "Yes, that partridge."

He ripped open the package.

She went on with her explanation. "I was so intrigued that I wanted to make you your own partridge. So you would have it for always." That last bit was a little payback, but it was also the truth. Of course, that was before she'd known he'd had one inked on his chest for all time.

He held the pillowcase up in front of his face as if he was examining it. She suspected he was screwing his emotions on straight before looking at them all. He was probably mad as hell at her for sewing it for him.

"I wanna see." Hannah jumped up, grabbing for it.

"Stop that," Rachel said.

Brodie turned it around for all of them to appreciate. For a second, he locked eyes with her. He didn't look mad. He looked confused.

Heck, he should join the club.

"I'm hungry," Hannah announced, Brodie's present now forgotten.

"Come help me set the table," Vivienne said. Before she left the parlor, she shot Rachel a black look which delivered her message: *I didn't miss the interplay between you and that fisherman.*

Great. Mom would be riding her again. Maybe Vivienne could decipher where things stood between her and Brodie, because Rachel sure as hell couldn't. Even more important, someone needed to clue her in on what she should do next.

Chapter Fourteen

Brodie carefully draped the pillowcase over the banister, admiring the partridge fashioned with different printed fabrics. Rachel had captured the essence of the bird perfectly. But what he didn't get was why she'd done it. What was her motive? Was she trying to torture him? Giving him such an intimate present in front of everyone was inconsiderate. Embarrassing. *Heartwarming.* He was still reeling from it. But to be fair, Hannah had given her no choice. He glanced one more time at the pillowcase and then hiked into the kitchen.

Vivienne was pulling food from the box. The turkey sat on the stove. The food seemed to take up the whole room. Brodie calculated the space around the small kitchen table. He should've given some thought as to where everyone should sit before he'd brought another guest home for Christmas.

Abraham shuffled into the room and set his teacup on the counter. "Dinner smells great." He scrutinized the room, too. "Let's make plates and sit in the parlor."

Solution found. "I'll lay a quilt on the floor in case Hannah wants to have a picnic."

Abraham touched Brodie's arm and spoke quietly. "Ye did right by bringing the lad here."

Brodie nodded. There was nothing else he could do.

"If he needs a bed," Abraham said, "offer him one of ours."

Aye. Harry would have to bed down here until his father could be located. Brodie would help with the search tomorrow.

He went to the parlor and found Harry making a boat out of a leftover piece of wrapping paper. "Come in the kitchen and make a plate."

Harry set the finished boat on the side table next to Abraham's spot. Brodie was impressed with the kid's artistic skills.

"Listen, Harry, ye'll sleep here tonight. We have an extra bedroom upstairs."

Harry stared at him. "Why are ye doing this? Feeding me. Giving me a place to stay." He twisted, looking at his quilt, but he didn't mention the present Rachel had given him.

Brodie was straight with the kid. "Ye'll be staying here until ye can locate yere father so I can keep an eye on ye."

Harry nodded as if the explanation seemed fair.

Truthfully, the kid didn't give off bad vibes. It was clear Hannah liked him.

Abraham was fine with the kid being here, too. Grandda, though, had a history of taking in strays . . . such as Joe and himself, and a few vagrants who had passed through over the years. They'd have room in the cottage, as Hannah and Vivienne would be back at the quilting dorm tonight. From nowhere, a flash of disappointment hit Brodie. Tonight he wouldn't be under the same roof as Rachel, *or the same bed.*

But he corrected his thinking quickly. Rachel was his past. Today was an exception for Abraham's sake, but come tomorrow, Brodie was going to keep his distance from the woman who had obliterated his heart. *Love me,*

Brodie. He hoped she would go home soon so he could get back to his quiet life and stop hearing her in his head.

Brodie pointed the way to the kitchen. "This way." He followed Harry down the hall.

As it turned out, Harry, Hannah, and all her dolls had a grand picnic on the floor, which entertained Grandda. Harry quickly made himself a paper hat to wear, as was the tradition in all of Scotland for the Christmas dinner. Brodie stuck his paper hat on his head and pulled a chair over in the corner to watch as Vivienne had a serious conversation with Rachel. Every once in a while, the two would glance in his direction. Vivienne wore a superior my-daughter's-too-good-for-the-likes-of-you expression while Rachel's hand gripped the locket around her neck.

"Brodie?" Hannah said, drawing his attention away. "Where's yere mum? Where's Auntie?"

"Uh, home I guess." The lass sure had a way of taking him off guard.

"Auntie?" Vivienne seemed to be taken off guard, too.

"My daughter, Robena," Grandda explained. "Brodie's mum."

"But it's Christmas," Hannah said. "Why *isna* she here? Mommy says we're supposed to be with family at Christmas."

Rachel glanced at Vivienne as if she were *Exhibit A.* She then turned her gaze on him as if Hannah had a point. He couldn't believe she had no intention of bailing him out. After all, this was her daughter that was vexing him.

"Well, lass, it's complicated," Brodie admitted.

Harry shifted uncomfortably and Brodie felt like an arse. The lad's mother had recently passed and Harry would probably give anything for another Christmas with her, and here Brodie was saying it was complicated. He expected, to Harry, no complication would've kept him from his mother today.

"I'll call her later," Brodie said, trying to appease the child and take the focus off himself.

"I want her to come see us today. I like Auntie." The lass was relentless. "I bet she has a Christmas present for ye."

He doubted it. Brodie wasn't a *verra* good son. But it wasn't necessarily his fault. He just couldn't get over his unforgiveness. "We'll see."

Hannah rose and came to him, cupping his shoulder and laying her head on his arm. She was an expert when it came to persuasion, and if it had been anyone else but the lass who asked . . .

"I'll go call her now."

"Yippee!" Hannah returned to her place on the quilt, dropping back into her cross-legged position on the floor.

Brodie set his half-eaten plate on his chair and went into the kitchen to ring his mother, not exactly sure what he was going to say.

"Mum?" he said when she picked up.

"Brodie?" She seemed as puzzled as he was by the call. "Is everything all right? Is Da okay?"

"Aye. Everything's fine. I was wondering, well, Hannah actually, if ye were free to stop by later. For a cup of Christmas punch?" He felt awkward and lame as if this were the first time he'd ever used a phone.

There was silence on the other end.

Brodie knew why she hesitated. "Ask Keith if he'd like to come, too." Brodie never thought he'd utter those words. Keith had taken his mother away from him, and that was something a son could never forget.

They discussed and set a time. Brodie hung up and realized—*with the disgust of a lad trying to be a man*—that his hand was shaking. He was amazed at the lengths he would go to please that little girl in the other room. First a barrette in his hair and now this.

He took a deep breath and walked back to the parlor, surprisingly feeling lighter. Before he could even sit down, Hannah was hounding him.

"Well? Is she coming?"

"Aye. Seven o'clock. To have some Christmas punch." Brodie took his plate in his hands and sat down.

"Good." Hannah gathered up her dolls and stood.

Brodie figured Rachel had told her she was to take a nap. But he should've known better. When it came to Hannah, he could never guess what she was up to next.

"I'm ready now, Mommy. I want to see Daddy's grave."

Rachel sighed. Ever since she'd mentioned to her daughter that they'd visit the cemetery, Hannah had been chatting about it, but hadn't shown any real interest. Rachel wanted to tell her *not today*, but all the experts said when it came to children and a dead parent, it was important to let the child take the lead.

Hannah gave one of her digging-my-heels-in stares. "It's Christmas Day and Daddy's lonely. He needs to see all my new dolls so he'll feel better."

Brodie mumbled under his breath. "The lass is quite the negotiator." He seemed to be enjoying Rachel's discomfort. Perhaps because now the tables were turned on her.

Vivienne went to the window and pulled back the curtain. "The weather seems calm. Taking her now might be a good idea." Her mother wasn't just remembering the gale force wind on the day of her and Joe's wedding. Rachel had discussed what she'd learned from books and speaking with professionals about how to raise her child without her father. "If you went now, you could be back before Brodie's parents arrived."

Brodie recoiled. He opened his mouth and then shut it.

"Keith isn't Brodie's father," Rachel interjected. "He's his stepfather."

Brodie's glower said *stepfather* wasn't much better.

"Here. Give me your dolls and go get your boots on." Rachel set her plate on the side table. She gathered the dolls from Hannah for the trip up the bluff. She couldn't help remembering and feeling a little sick about what Brodie had revealed about Joe's past when they last visited the cemetery. "I'll put these in your backpack, okay?"

"Brodie has to go with us," Hannah announced. "Otherwise, my dolls might be sad that Daddy's dead."

That makes no sense, Rachel thought. Brodie's dumbfounded stare at her daughter and then at her held the exact same sentiment.

Vivienne's frown said she'd changed her mind about the weather being congenial. But in the next second, her mom plastered a smile on her face. "You go. Harry and I will clean up the dishes."

Rachel was proud of her mom for putting Hannah first and relieved her mother wasn't going to make a big deal about Brodie going along. Vivienne really was good to them. But those warm feelings were easily tripped up. As her mother leaned over to pick up Abraham's dishes, she shot Rachel a sideways glance. She might as well have shaken her finger and said what was on her mind . . . *you better watch yourself with him.*

Rachel turned away, but only to find Harry staring at Hannah with sad compassion. Those two had more in common than sharing a picnic on the parlor floor . . . they both had lost a parent.

Finally, Rachel glanced at Brodie to see how he felt about going with them. He didn't look happy, but he stood as if he had no choice in the matter. She felt sorry for how miserable she'd made him. He'd be ecstatic when they left town as he'd gotten stuck with so much more than he'd bargained for when they'd pulled into Gandiegow.

In the foyer, Rachel loaded Hannah's dolls into her backpack. Brodie took the pack from her while she slipped into her coat. Instead of returning it, he hiked the strap up on his shoulder.

Rachel stifled a laugh. "You look ridiculous." But he was the most attractive man she'd ever met . . . both inside and out.

"What?" he asked, looking down as if he'd spilled food down his front.

"The backpack. I never imagined you as a pink backpack kind of guy."

He shrugged good-naturedly and then squatted down to make sure Hannah's boots were on correctly, her coat was buttoned up to her collar, and her hat was securely on her head. When he seemed satisfied, they left.

What a strange procession they made. As they walked up the bluff, she and Brodie were silent, each holding one of Hannah's hands, while her daughter sang a tune to herself between them. The song was about dollies and graves, and Daddy being happy. Where the path narrowed in places, Hannah let go of Rachel, keeping ahold of Brodie. It was another little poke to Rachel's heart that her daughter was growing a little beyond her and at times preferred someone else.

At the edge of the cemetery, Rachel could glimpse something on Joe's grave. As they approached, a wreath came into view, one with a bright tartan ribbon. She glanced over at Brodie but he wouldn't meet her eyes.

"Is that Daddy's tombstone?"

"Yes. The one with the pretty wreath on it," Rachel

said, preparing herself for anything. Tears, anger, complacency—she didn't know what to expect from her daughter.

Hannah gazed up to Brodie, her eyes bright. "Do ye think Father Christmas left the wreath for my da?"

Brodie nodded. "I expect he did."

Hannah reached for the backpack and he handed it over. She slipped it on her shoulders and ran the last few feet to the grave. Immediately, she dropped the bag to the ground, unzipped it, and pulled out a doll.

"Hi, Daddy. I mean Da. This is Dolly. I got her from my new friend, Glenna. Her da is the church's pastor." She looked back to Brodie, a frown between her brows.

"Kirk," he corrected.

Hannah nodded solemnly as she was committing the Scottish word to heart. "Aye. The kirk's pastor." She told Joe all about going to school and playing with Mattie and Dand afterward at Grandda's cottage.

Hannah pulled out another doll while shoving Dolly back in. Brodie took the backpack, wiped snow from the bottom, and stood back. Hannah introduced all her dolls, telling a story with each one. She was so animated that Rachel was beginning to believe Joe was sitting atop his tombstone, listening while he sipped a pop.

When each of Hannah's dolls had a chance to meet Joe, she turned back to her. "Mommy, do you have anythin' ye want to say to Da?"

Not really; she'd said all she wanted to say before, but Rachel stepped forward anyway. "I hope you're having a great time in heaven."

Hannah took her hand and squeezed. But then she dropped it and went to Brodie. "Up."

He reached down and lifted her into his arms. "I'm gonna have to teach ye a new Scottish word, lass. It's a *verra* important one."

She laid her head on his shoulder. "What is it?" She yawned.

"The word is *please*. We use it often here."

"Okay."

He chuckled and held her close.

Hannah's eyes were closed before they were out of the cemetery. Rachel's heart was warmed by how wonderful this rugged fisherman was to her daughter. Which would be fine if he wanted Rachel as much as she wanted him. Another chip fell off her heart. If he didn't stop being so great, she knew she would never recover from loving him. Forever was a long time to go for a woman with a broken heart.

As Brodie laid Hannah in the room upstairs, he wondered that the lass didn't rouse, not even a little. Christmas had been overly exciting for her. Being around her had been quite the education, and had given him a glimpse into having a family of his own.

Back downstairs, Abraham was dozing in his chair, while Rachel, Vivienne, and Harry were set up in the kitchen. All a bit too cozy for Brodie right now. He grabbed his coat and headed to the boat.

He needed fresh air and open spaces before the next ordeal. Brodie was dreading his mother and Keith coming over, but this was how it was with Rachel and Hannah in town, being dragged into one exploit or another. He would give them today, but tomorrow the agony would stop. He would no longer need to spend time with Rachel. Soon, when she was gone, he could resume his old life.

A pang hit his chest. He was going to miss the little princess. Hannah was something special, but he'd have to give her up. Spending time with Hannah meant sharing the same air as Hannah's mother. He couldn't take another day of being near Rachel and not want to really *be with her*.

He walked to the dock and back to kill time. When he saw his mother and her husband on the walkway, moving toward Abraham's side of town, Brodie returned home and hung his coat. He touched Grandda's shoulder to wake him. "Mum'll be here in a moment."

As if Hannah had an internal alarm set to *guests o'clock*, she padded downstairs and into the parlor, crawling up beside Abraham. "Did I miss Auntie?"

"Nay."

There was a light tap at the door. A second later, they'd let themselves in.

Rachel and Vivienne met his mother and Keith in the hallway. He should've been the one to introduce Vivienne to his mother, and Keith to everyone else, but Brodie stayed put in the parlor, feeling as stubborn as ever.

Keith stepped into the room first. "Brodie."

"Keith." Brodie was done making conversation with his mother's husband.

Robena came in behind him, glancing around carefully as if the furniture might bite. She wasn't ready for the little body that slammed into her. Brodie had to reach out a hand to steady his mother.

"Auntie!" Hannah cried. "Ye came."

"Aye," his mother said, laughing. "That I did."

Brodie couldn't ever remember his mother laughing in Abraham's house.

Keith strode to Abraham confidently and stuck out his hand. "Happy Christmas."

Abraham shook it heartily. "And to ye." Grandda had always seemed more comfortable around Keith than his own daughter. "How's farm life treating ye?"

Keith chuckled. "Cold as fishing, but not nearly as wet."

Abraham returned the joviality by smiling happily.

Brodie's unease was worth whatever happiness Grandda got out of the day.

Hannah dragged Robena over to Abraham.

"Wish him a Merry Christmas," Hannah insisted.

Rachel intervened. "Miss bossy britches, mind your manners."

Hannah looked up at Robena. "Sorry."

"It's okay, sweets." She smiled at Hannah fondly before turning to Abraham. "Happy Christmas, Da. Thanks for having us."

"'Twas the lass's idea," Grandda said.

His mother winced, but Keith jumped in to the rescue.

"It was a grand idea." He squatted down in front of Hannah and extended his hand. "We haven't met. I'm Keith."

Curiously, Hannah glanced from Keith to Robena, and then back to Keith. "Are ye my grandda?"

Keith chuckled and rubbed her head as he stood. "I'm Robena's husband," he said proudly.

"If she's my auntie," Hannah said, "then ye must be my uncle."

"That would be fine." Rachel seemed to physically guide Hannah in a different direction by turning her body toward her stack of toys. "Why don't you get your stroller and your dolls and show them to your auntie."

His mother's smile toward Rachel seemed grateful. But Brodie knew Rachel had done it *for him*. He was sure of it.

Vivienne and Robena hit it off as if they both were acting like doting grandmothers, each one commenting on how cute Hannah was. Harry wandered into the room. Brodie started to introduce Harry to his mother and Keith, planning to keep it short, but the little princess took Harry by the hand and laid out his story to both

Robena and Keith . . . twice. Thankfully, Harry hadn't shared the bit about looking for his da with the wee lass.

Harry appeared highly uncomfortable with the attention, but he didn't remove his hand from Hannah's. The princess had won over more than one frog in the room.

"Ye've got to see the pillowcase," Hannah said to Robena, dropping Harry's hand and tearing out of the room.

"What pillowcase?" his mother asked.

Before he or Rachel could say anything, Harry piped in. "Rachel made Brodie a pillowcase with a partridge on it."

"Oh?" His mother's eyebrows lifted into the air. Her eagle gaze went from him to Rachel to the locket, and then back to him again.

Damn Harry. Here Brodie was just praising the kid's good sense that he knew how to keep his mouth shut.

Hannah was back and thrust it at his mother. "Isn't it *bee-oot-iful*?"

"Very." His mother looked as if she had the wrong idea about what was going on between him and Rachel. She neatly folded the pillowcase so the partridge showed on top, laid it on her leg, and patted it gently as if it were a babe's bottom.

Brodie couldn't stand it. He popped up and snatched the pillowcase. "I'll put this away." He didn't look at any of their faces as he went straight upstairs to his room and shoved the damned partridge under his pillow.

When he returned to the parlor, something had happened. The air was filled with awkward tension.

Robena stood, looking sheepish. "Da, should I go make the Christmas punch?"

Once again, Brodie got a glimpse of what it must've been like for his mother growing up. In this cottage, she never acted like the strong woman that Brodie knew her to be.

"Christmas punch, Christmas punch," Hannah sang.

Abraham nodded. "Aye. Thank ye, daughter."

Robena beamed before hurrying from the room.

Brodie followed her into the kitchen. He stood in the doorway as she pulled the cranberries from the refrigerator.

"Ye'll have to make the *bairn version* of yere punch." He remembered her making it when he was a lad.

"Aye." Robena stopped and smiled at him. "She's a sweet child. 'Tis a shame Joe isn't here; a shame she's growing up without a father."

Brodie stepped farther into the room. "I thank ye for coming." He should've extended the invitation to her weeks ago—no—*years ago*.

Her smile held love for him. "It's my pleasure." She looked hopeful that the tension between them was gone.

But Brodie had an old streak of hurt that lashed out as if he were a kid again, ready to douse her hope. "Hannah wanted ye here." He walked from the kitchen and stood in the hallway, hating himself. Why couldn't he get over something small, like his mother being disloyal to his father's memory?

A scripture from Sunday service came back to him. *When I became a man, I put aside childish things.* He hadn't completely. Brodie held on to his resentment like a lifeline. But it was Christmas, the New Year only days away. He wanted to be a better man moving forward. He marched back into the kitchen.

"Mum?"

She turned and faced him, her cheeks red, and her eyes wary as if preparing herself for another jab.

"I'm sorry. For hurtin' ye just now. I really am glad ye

came." Because he'd been a total jerk, he went the extra mile. "I'm glad Keith came, too." Though Brodie didn't fully mean it.

But Keith had been perfectly nice to everyone, including himself. Hannah had taken quite a shine to him, which only spoke well of Keith. Abraham seemed to enjoy having his company, too.

His mother didn't say anything, almost as if she was waiting for more.

"I hope ye'll forgive me." Brodie didn't stay to see if she accepted it. He couldn't. *What if she's like me and isn't the forgiving type, too?*

After the punch was carried into the room and everyone had had a glass, his mother claimed they needed to head home—*animals to tend to.* Brodie knew the truth. He'd caused her to leave early.

"We better get to the quilting dorm, also," Rachel said, nodding to Hannah, who was rocking in the chair he'd given her, looking ready to nose-dive because she was so tired.

"Vivienne, I'll get yere bag from upstairs," Brodie said. "Harry?"

The teen looked up.

"Follow me and I'll show ye to yere room."

Upstairs, Brodie pointed out the bedroom, the loo, and where the towels were kept in the linen closet. From his own room, he pulled out a clean T-shirt and sweatpants for Harry. Before he left, he took Rachel's present from his drawer, hoping to have a moment to hand it off to her. He shoved the wrapped notebook under his arm and met the kid out in the hallway with the clean clothes. "These'll swim on ye while yere things are being washed. But ye need to take a shower. When ye're done, check on Abraham to see if he needs anything."

He waited for the kid to nod.

"I'll be back."

When Brodie returned downstairs, he shoved Rachel's present into the inside pocket of his jacket. The day was nearly through, his duty nearly over. He would carry Vivienne's luggage back to the dorm this one last time.

But the gift weighed heavy on the inside of his coat. He had to give it to Rachel tonight, because this was it. He wouldn't see her again. He'd do everything in his power to steer clear of her as if she were the dangerous line of rocks half a nautical mile from Gandiegow.

The females each told Abraham good night, the little one making outrageous promises to be back early in the morning. She looked as if she might sleep until the New Year.

As Brodie walked them through the village and then to the foot of the bluff, he thought how he'd developed a habit of escorting Rachel around town. Well, that was ending, too.

He planned to leave Vivienne's roller bag just inside the doorway, but Hannah had other plans.

"Mommy, I want Brodie to put me to bed."

Rachel did a pretty good job when it came to reading him. "Honey, he can't. He has to get home so he can get to bed, too." But the word *bed* seemed to get caught on her teeth on its way out.

Vivienne—halfway down the hall already—stopped at the word *bed,* too, her back stiffening as straight as the planks on his boat. She hesitated, but then she continued on to the bedroom.

Brodie couldn't help going to the same place he assumed Rachel had. Their time together had been all-consuming, but he put the image out of his mind. However, he couldn't prevent hearing *Love me, Brodie* every other second. *Gads!* He'd needed a new playlist to get rid of this particular love song that was stuck in his head.

Hannah wrapped an arm around his leg as if she was anchoring him to the spot. "Please, cousin Brodie. I want ye to tell me a story."

He sighed. Good thing he wasn't her father; he had a hard time telling the lass *no*. "Okay. But only one."

"She'll be ready in a minute." Rachel took her by the hand and led her down the hallway.

Brodie was left with his own thoughts. They were crazy thoughts. Thoughts about him and Rachel . . . together. What that might look like. How he might feel if he *was* Hannah's father. But he waved them away with his hand. "*Childish things*," he said to himself. He'd had these visions before . . . six years ago. But they weren't real.

"She's ready," Rachel said.

Brodie plodded down the hallway, noticing Vivienne was in *his room* with the door shut. He went to the room Hannah shared with her mother. Rachel pulled Hannah's covers up, going to stand in the doorway, but going no farther as if she were attached to him by an invisible fishing line. A stack of picture books was beside Hannah's bed. He picked up the one from the top and flipped through the pages. "Do you have a particular story you want to hear?"

"Aye," Hannah said. "Tell me a story about my daddy."

Chapter Fifteen

Rachel stepped outside the room and leaned against the wall, feeling as shocked as Brodie must be with her daughter's request. She listened while he shared the antics of two wild and free boys who had the world at their fingertips. There was a vast difference between how Brodie and Joe were raised and the life Hannah led.

Her daughter was growing up in a world of locked doors, predators, and dangers around every Chicago street corner. Rachel dreaded the day, not too long from now, when Hannah would begin kindergarten and have to walk to the school four blocks from the Winderly Towers.

But as soon as Rachel thought it, a comforting image appeared in her mind's eye—her own bed and breakfast, sitting next door to Thistle Glen Lodge. But it was only a deluded fantasy. There would be no future with Brodie; he'd made that clear.

Wait a minute, the little voice in her head said. Not the same voice which had been cheerleading for a lifetime with Brodie. This was a different voice, one that had only recently been vying for Rachel's attention.

What does owning a bed and breakfast have to do with Brodie? Can't you build a B and B anywhere you damn well please? Can't you raise your child here if you want?

But these empowering thoughts only presented more complications, more questions, and more decisions to make.

Rachel hadn't touched Joe's life insurance money, not a dime. She didn't feel as if she should. They had been separated when he'd died and were planning to get a divorce.

"Good night, princess," Brodie said.

Rachel peeked back into the room. Hannah wrapped her arms around his neck. "I love ye, Brodie."

He stilled, but then he whispered to her daughter, "I love ye, too."

The words nearly crushed Rachel. She was so conflicted. She wanted those words for herself. She wiped away the mist that had sprung to her eyes. But if she couldn't get his love, at least her daughter could. She stepped away from the door before he found her spying.

She waited for him in the living room. When he appeared, she handed him his coat. "Thank you for doing that. You made her day."

Brodie smiled, but it wasn't really at Rachel. "She made everyone's day. Grandda couldn't have been happier. I hope ye'll bring her back for more Christmases . . . for Grandda's sake."

Rachel gave a noncommittal shrug. Not because she didn't want Hannah to spend her Christmases with Abraham, but because the future, a new version of it, was only now coming into focus.

"Come outside with me for a second," he said.

She couldn't help it—her old rampant imagination went into overdrive, hoping he meant to give her a good night kiss. She slipped on her coat and followed him out.

"I wanted to get ye alone."

She waited for him to make the move. But instead, he reached inside his coat and pulled out a small wrapped package. He handed it over.

"Yere Christmas gift."

She motioned to the cottage and the tree inside. "But you already gave me a lovely gift. Our tree and the partridge on the top."

He looked as if he was struggling with something. He turned away. "Thank you for the pillowcase."

"I hoped it was all right that you had to open it in front of everyone," she said honestly. "I never meant for that to happen."

"It was no big deal." But he seemed to work at keeping his emotions under control.

"Sorry," she said.

"It's okay." He motioned to the package in her hand. "Open it."

She pulled back the paper to reveal a dark brown leather cover with a Celtic knot stamped into the top. "It's beautiful." She opened the notebook to reveal thick parchment paper.

"I saw it and thought you would like it. I know how ye like to sketch." Then he looked injured. "At least ye did . . . before."

Before I backed out on our future together. She really couldn't blame him that he wanted nothing to do with her now.

He said something very quietly.

"What?" She heard the word *leaving.* Was he asking her to stay?

"I said . . ." His voice was thick with emotion. "When are ye leaving?"

She stared at him, once again kicking herself that she had gotten it all wrong. "I don't know." She looked down at the Celtic notebook in her hand.

He tipped her chin up. He dropped his hand and stood tall. "Good-bye, Rachel." His eyes lingered on her, as if taking a mental photograph, and then he walked away.

As he did, the fog lifted and she realized what had just happened. He hadn't said *good night*, he'd said *good-bye*.

She wanted to run after him, but he was already through the buildings and on the walkway toward home. It wouldn't do any good anyway. The magic of Christmas was over. Brodie had stayed true and right from the beginning: *Nothing will change between us*. Her second chance with Brodie was truly gone.

Cait waited on the sofa as her husband, Graham, turned off the lamp in the parlor. The Christmas tree lights and the glow of the fire, plus the soft music in the background, provided the perfect ambience. Deydie had gone home for the evening and Mattie was in bed. Cait felt jittery inside for what she needed to tell Graham.

But they'd been down this path before and it had ended in sorrow, disappointment, and shame. A million times she'd asked herself what was wrong with her that she couldn't carry a baby for very long. But today marked the first day of her second trimester. She wasn't feeling wholly safe she would carry this baby full-term, but she would keep the secret no longer from the love of her life.

Graham gazed at her from across the room. "Finally. Alone at last. Two months is a long time to be away from ye, lass. I'm so glad to be home." His brogue was especially heavy when he had love on his mind, as he did now.

"Come, husband. Sit." She patted the seat beside her on the sofa.

He strode across the room, giving her the smile a million women had swooned over, but this smile was only for her. He draped his arm around her shoulders as he nestled up beside her. "Happy Christmas." He kissed her thoroughly and deeply.

God, how she loved this man. She laid a hand on his

chest when he was done. "Enough with that until after we talk." She reached over and opened the drawer of the side table, pulling out the wrapped baby stocking. "I have one more Christmas gift for you."

He didn't take it right away, but gazed into her eyes. "But ye're the only present I need, my love. Don't ye know that?"

"Open it," she said.

He removed his arm from around her shoulder and tore open the package. The baby stocking fell into his lap. He lifted it up. "What's this?"

She chewed her lip and waited. "What do you think it is?" She gave him her best ye're-a-smart-man-figure-it-out look.

"Is it for Dingus?"

The Sheltie's head popped up from the pillow by the fireplace.

"Not for the dog," she said, giving him mock frustration.

Realization grew across his face, along with pure joy, but just as quickly, he turned guarded. She understood.

"Does this mean ye're nesting?" The excitement wasn't there as when she'd missed her period the first time . . . then miscarried. He'd been in New Zealand and she had been here. The loss of the baby and the separation from him had been nearly unbearable.

"Aye. I'm nesting."

"When?" he asked cautiously.

She took his hand and squeezed it. "I'm four months today."

A hurt expression crossed his face, but he pulled her to him, hugging her anyway. "I'm happy. Really I am. But ye have to know, ye're all I need. If this doesn't pan out . . ."

Anger shot through her. "No negative thoughts. We're

not going to talk that way! We're only going to think positive." Cait clutched her abdomen. "I want this baby!"

There was a gasp in the doorway. Both she and Graham cranked around to see Deydie standing there gob smacked.

"What baby?" her grandmother growled. "Ye're pregnant and didn't have the decency to tell yere own relation? Well, that's a fine kettle of fish."

"Gran," Cait pleaded while unfolding herself from the couch. "I didn't want to get yere hopes up again."

"She only just told me," Graham complained, "and I'm her husband." He definitely wasn't happy that she'd waited to tell him, too.

Cait looked from one to the other. This wasn't how she'd planned it. "I'm going to bed." She stomped from the room and fled up the stairs, knowing her hormones were making her more emotional than usual.

Five minutes later, Graham walked into their bedroom. "Can I turn on the light?"

"No." She was being irrational, but he deserved it.

He came to her in the dark and climbed in beside her. "Come here." He pulled her to him and she instantly felt better.

She'd missed him. She'd missed making love to him these last several months. She kissed him, and as she did, her hands weaseled their way to his pants and she began unbuttoning his fly.

He stilled her hand. "No."

She pulled away. "Why? I've been waiting impatiently for ye to return home."

"We can't," he said gruffly.

He was being ridiculous. She ran her hand down the plane of his stomach. "Ye're contractually obligated to satisfy me. I'm yere wife, remember?"

He clutched her hand before she got to the goods. "No. No sex. Not until after the baby."

Brodie woke up in his own bed the next morning, not rested, but the harrowing deed was done. Now he could put all his energy into avoiding Rachel until she went home to America. Aye, he was a realist. Gandiegow was a village, smaller than most, with only sixty-three houses. Not seeing or running into Rachel was impossible, but now he didn't have to sit across the table from her at meals, and he certainly didn't have to worry she might wander into his bedroom at night. Their one chance together was history. Every other moment, though, he couldn't help thinking of them and how they'd been together.

But thinking and doing were two different things, and there wouldn't be a repeat.

Brodie climbed out of the rack and went across the hall. He tapped on the door. "Harry, time to wake up."

He talked to the teen after he returned home last night. The kid would help him and Tuck on the boat, keeping Harry occupied until Brodie could find a way to help him figure out which man in Gandiegow was his da. *If any.*

They hurried to the boat, but thirty minutes and several mishaps later, Brodie was regretting his decision to have the kid aboard. The teen knew as much about fishing as Brodie knew about cosmetology. The kid had never been on a boat, didn't know how to swim, and was clumsy as hell. Even worse, Tuck wouldn't leave off with his sunny disposition and his nonstop talking.

How had Brodie gotten himself into another tangled mess?

Tuck hollered up to him. "Rough holiday? Ye look as if ye might run the boat up on the rocks to end it all."

Brodie glared at him, then put his sights on the water ahead.

"Don't worry," Tuck said. "I've got this."

Brodie didn't know what he meant. An hour later, he did. Tuck stepped up and took Harry under his wing. With patience no man should have, Tuck showed the kid the ropes, and every time he screwed up, Tuck corrected him with kindness.

Maybe Tuck and Father Andrew really were related.

When they arrived in Gandiegow, back from the morning run, Brodie was on the lookout for pitfalls . . . those concerning Rachel. What he hadn't expected was Deydie.

She waved her broom at him. "Git over here, Brodie. Bring that boy, too."

Oh, God. "Come on, Harry." He glanced over at the kid. "Yeah, ye should look worried."

"Inside," Deydie ordered, waddling through the doorway.

Brodie motioned for Harry to go in, which gave him the opportunity to scan the room first before entering. His eyes immediately landed on Rachel. Quickly, he looked away. "What can we do for ye, Deydie?"

She thrust a paper dragon in Harry's face. "Rachel says ye're the one responsible for these."

"These?" Brodie asked.

Harry dropped his head. "I made one for each of the folks who lent me something."

"Lent?" Deydie bayed. "Is that what ye call it? *Reiving* is more like it."

"Sorry," Harry said. "I was hungry and cold." He shuffled his feet. "I can give back the quilt I borrowed." He glanced over at Rachel as if to acknowledge that she'd given him his own quilt on Christmas Day. "I left it in the container over there. I took good care of it."

Deydie nodded with a frown. "Aileen will be glad to have it back." She eyed him with a stare of withering accusation. "Why are ye here, boy? We don't take well to strangers. Especially those who steal when we aren't looking." The old woman gestured to her desk as if pointing something out.

Brodie did a double take. A pair of scissors had been secured with a padlock.

One look at Harry and Brodie wished he'd warned the kid to keep quiet. Talking about his da could be a touchy subject. Especially if his Gandiegowan father was a married man.

But Harry was a kid and had no better sense than a baby seal being preyed upon by a shark. He lifted his chin. "I'm looking for my da."

That shut Deydie up. The room went still, the women frozen in place . . . all except for one, and she was making her way over to them like an ambulance to an accident.

Rachel sidled up next to Harry, wrapping her arm around him protectively. "Are you okay?"

He looked over and nodded.

"Well? Who's yere da?" Deydie asked.

Harry's eyes dropped to the floor. "I dunno."

Deydie grabbed him by the scruff of his neck and dragged him in front of a window.

"Don't," Rachel protested, following. "What are you doing? He's just a boy."

Deydie gripped Harry's chin and turned his head this way and that. "I don't see that ye look like anyone of us, but me eyes aren't what they used to be." She turned to the other women in the room, who had stood and were inching their way to them as if being pulled in by a slow-moving net. "Git over here and take a look. All of yees."

They needed no more permission than that. They

scuttled over and peered closely at Harry as if he was a complicated quilt.

Brodie was suddenly propelled into action and stepped in front of the kid, but bumped into Rachel, who was doing the same thing.

"Leave off," Brodie said to the gawping women. "Harry, head on back to the cottage. Put the tea on for Abraham."

Harry gave Brodie a glance of gratitude before he tore out of there as if a rocket was strapped to his back. When the door slammed behind him, Brodie addressed the room.

"Leave the lad alone. I'm going to help him get to the bottom of this." He sucked in a deep breath, thoroughly disgusted that somehow he'd appointed himself the chief investigator. No one in Gandiegow would thank him for the sacrifice either. Hell, just the opposite.

For the next several days, Brodie kept a low profile—from Rachel and the townsfolk. But the gossip mill was in full swing and speculation was running rampart, like a contagious fever. He never paid attention to the chin-wagging about others, but this was hard to ignore as everyone was up in his face asking questions about the lad. Brodie had to even withstand several complaining husbands who had been accused, banished from their beds, and forced to sleep on their cold boats. Hell, even Brodie was having trouble going home and relaxing in his own cottage; Rachel, Vivienne, and Hannah had taken to mothering poor Harry to the point even Abraham was peevish about the attention the kid was taking away from him.

But Brodie didn't have any real beef with the kid, except he was no fisherman. Harry was excellent with Grandda, a companion for him when Brodie couldn't be. Harry made sure Abraham had his tea and was taking his medicine on time. Brodie would have to talk to Kirsty about getting the kid into school. Maybe he'd catch her before the festivities tonight, the Hogmanay *céilidh*, their New Year's Eve dance.

He put the boat's log books away and left the wheel-house, staring out at the dark evening sky. Gandie-gow's Hogmanay was known far and wide for its rowdy celebration of ringing in the New Year. Brodie's only problem was that Rachel hadn't left yet. Even more disconcerting . . . she seemed to be settling in.

Brodie hurried home and was relieved when it was only Harry and Grandda who were there.

He headed into the parlor. "Hey."

Harry was putting another log on the fire. "I was get-ting ready to bring in a sandwich for yere grandda. Do ye want one, too?"

"Sure." Brodie needed the space to speak with his grandfather in private.

When Harry left the room, Brodie sat in the chair next to Abraham. "What does Rachel say about returning to the States?"

Grandda scratched his chin as if trying to remember. "I don't know. I don't recall any talk of it lately. Only Vivienne speaks of leaving and visiting the south of France. Why do you ask?"

Because I want my life to get back to normal.

I'm tired of hiding out.

Having Rachel here is too hard on my heart.

"No reason. I was just wondering."

Abraham's eyes turned unusually sharp, reminding Brodie of his younger days when he'd been caught steal-ing a turnip from Mr. Menzies's garden. Grandda's scru-tiny made Brodie extremely uncomfortable. He went across the room and stood.

"Ye've been avoiding Rachel," Abraham said. "Why?"

"I haven't been avoiding anyone," he lied, turning his head toward the logs burning in the fireplace.

When he glanced over his shoulder, Abraham was assessing him with the shake of his head.

Brodie wanted to remind his grandfather that he was the one who'd told him, *Women can't be trusted.* Drilled it into his head his whole life. Brodie was only protecting himself from Rachel. Keeping his distance and staying away seemed the only sensible thing to do. But arguing with Grandda about what he'd taught him was disrespectful, especially for all the kindness his grandfather had shown him.

Abraham glanced at the doorway. "I wish I was going to the *céilidh* tonight. It's been a while since I've danced a jig."

"Ye must be on the mend," Brodie commented aloud. He was eternally grateful Grandda had dropped the subject of Rachel.

Abraham inhaled deeply. "I'm breathing easier."

Brodie, too, just hearing him say that.

Grandda gave him a knowing gaze, the one which reminded him that he could look into his soul. "I think it's because the lasses have come to visit. They've been good for me. *Good for ye, too.* I think Rachel and Hannah should stay."

Brodie didn't think so.

Abraham nodded determinedly. "I believe I'll speak with Rachel in the morn about remaining in Gandiegow permanently."

"Don't!" Brodie boomed, immediately regretting the force with which he'd said it.

Abraham slapped his knee, clearly pleased. "Ye fancy the lass." Then he took to watching Brodie more closely than if he were baiting a hook.

"Och, do what ye want." Brodie turned to walk out,

but Harry stood in the doorway, transfixed, with the tray in his hands.

Great. An audience. Brodie had just wanted to get some information from his grandfather, but he definitely got more than he'd bargained for. Abraham now seemed determined—*since I went and opened my effing mouth*—to have Rachel stay forever.

Plus, Brodie had given the gossip mill more than a wee bite to chew on for the foreseeable future. Maybe he should find some duct tape and gag Harry's mouth. The kid had shown, on more than one occasion, that he couldn't keep anything to himself.

Harry watched as Brodie stomped out of the cottage. Until now, Harry had spent little time around men. He never realized they could be so moody.

"Harry?" Abraham said.

He'd forgotten he had the tray in his hand with the old man's tea on it. "Here." He set the tray beside him.

Abraham gestured toward the doorway. "Deydie asked if she could borrow *our* Crock-Pot for the gathering tonight. Do you mind taking it to her? At this hour, she'll be at the grand dining room above the restaurant."

Harry really liked the old man. Abraham told him straight out he could stay here for as long as he wanted. But it was how the old man did and said things afterward that let Harry know he really meant it. Harry felt like part of the family. "Sure. I'll get it." *Our* Crock-Pot. It was little things like that.

But Harry wasn't thrilled about meeting up with Deydie again. The hag was hard to avoid as she kept stopping by the cottage to wait on Abraham. She made Harry help put up the new curtains in the front windows, barking at him the whole time, and about bit his head off when he'd said to himself the curtains were *too girly*. He guessed they made the entryway cheery like Abraham said. The old man asked Deydie to sit with him a while afterward, too.

A funny thought hit Harry. Brodie might fancy Rachel, but he wondered if Abraham fancied Deydie. A shiver went up his spine. "Ooo." He opened the cabinet door. Abraham was sharp, but he'd lost his mind to think so highly of that bossy old woman. She was mean. She'd embarrassed Harry by pulling his face this way and that every chance she got, trying to see if he looked like anyone in town.

Harry retrieved the Crock-Pot and returned to the parlor. "I'll be back." He left out the front door and walked across town, warm and toasty in his new clothes. Brodie had dropped a bundle on his bed a few days ago, grumbling, *The women of Gandiegow sent these over for ye*.

Brodie might be moody, but he'd taken Harry in, too, and given him a job on the boat. He wondered if Brodie might be in a better mood every now and then if he and Rachel got together.

Harry stopped in front of the restaurant, Pastas & Pastries, a white three-story stone building. The bottom level was the restaurant, the second floor the grand dining room, and the top floor was where Dominic and Claire lived with their baby.

Man, Dominic was one hell of a cook, and Claire's scones were the best. It was great not to be hungry anymore.

Harry opened the door, went in, and headed straight up the side stairs. There were tons of people roaming about, setting up for tonight. The town was celebrating Hogmanay with a *céilidh*. Harry knew nothing about dancing. When he'd said as much around Hannah, the little girl said she'd teach him. He smiled. *I really like her.* She was the little cousin he'd never had.

He didn't have to look for Deydie as she zeroed in on him the second he stepped into the grand dining room. She barreled in his direction. His first instinct was to make a run for it because she had her broom in her hand. He held the Crock-Pot out in front of him as protection.

"How's Abraham today?" Deydie barked.

"Uh . . ." Harry wasn't used to her asking questions. Whenever she saw him, she was usually bossing someone around—*including him*—or frowning because she couldn't figure out whom he belonged to.

"Spit it out, boy. Abraham, is he well? I thought he looked a might peaked yesterday."

"He's okay. He was reading the news on his iPad when I left." Because he thought he should say it, he added, "I made him some tea before I brought this over."

Deydie bobbed her head once and took the Crock-Pot from his hands, frowning. "We've had no luck in figuring out who yere da is."

He'd heard the whispers that short of DNA testing all the men in town, his father remained a mystery.

Harry looked up as Bethia joined them. He liked her. She was nice, the opposite of Deydie.

"I heard you two talking." Bethia gave him a sad smile. "Harry, did ye ever think maybe yere father had moved away long ago?"

He had, many times. But now that he was feeling settled in, the thought of his da no longer living here didn't make him feel sick as when he first arrived in the village.

Bethia patted his arm. "We can put our heads together and make ye a list who has left over the past eighteen years."

He might as well be honest. "Sixteen."

"Aye, sixteen years," Bethia said. "But ye may consider just staying in Gandiegow." She smiled at him as if he were a cherished grandson.

"Aye," Deydie agreed, which surprised him. "Abraham needs watching after. Besides, ye're a child of Gandiegow. We take care of our own."

A blanket of warmth covered Harry as if he were seven again and being tucked into bed. He hadn't felt like this—safe, secure—since before Mum got sick.

Bethia wrapped an arm around him. "Let's go get some cocoa."

"I could use another scone," Deydie said.

Harry could feel the stupid grin on his face, but he couldn't help it, as the two old women led him away.

Chapter Sixteen

Rachel scanned the grand dining room. The room was abuzz as the people of Gandiegow decorated for the big shindig tonight to celebrate their New Year's Eve. But there was no Brodie in sight.

Since Christmas, she'd had a constant ache in her heart; she missed him. But every day there were signs—having nothing to do with Brodie—that something new might be coming together for her—a Gandiegowan here and there being nice to her or including her in their activities. Rachel was working hard to assure herself that her Brodie-in-shining-armor vision was a thing of the past. She was coming to realize that it was entirely up to her to fix her own broken heart. She couldn't mope forever.

Kirsty waved to her from across the room and then made her way over. "I was wondering if Hannah would be attending school after the holidays."

Rachel had been pondering the same thing. "Yes. I think Hannah would enjoy that." Last night, she'd read online the requirements of enrolling Hannah into school full-time. She'd need her birth certificate, which could be sent. Thanks to Joe, Hannah held dual citizenship in both the US and the UK. Joe had been adamant about his daughter having her passports ready to visit Abraham when she was big enough. The passports had arrived, but only after Joe had died.

Kirsty touched her arm. "Good. I'm glad we'll have Hannah in the classroom. She's such a delight." She grinned at her fiancé, Oliver, who was hanging streamers. "I better go help him before Deydie thinks I'm slacking off." She rushed back to her beau.

Kirsty was right. Deydie had been extra grouchy for several days, barking at everyone more than usual. Surprisingly, though, the old woman was walking congenially with Harry across the room right now, instead of whacking him with her broom. What was weird was now that the news about Cait's pregnancy was out, Deydie had been grumbling more and glaring at her granddaughter every other second.

Rachel wandered over to Cait. "Hi."

Cait was frowning at her grandmother.

Rachel nodded toward Deydie. "Do you want to talk about it?"

Cait turned to her and focused, her frown disappearing. "My gran is angry."

"I can see that." *The whole town could.*

"She thinks I should've told her right away I was pregnant."

"Did you explain that you didn't even tell your husband?" Rachel asked.

"She won't listen. She won't let me help with anything either. She's treating me as if I'm an invalid." Cait glanced at Deydie with an unkind smile on her face. "I wish she would get over being mad."

Rachel touched her arm. "She probably felt left out. Deydie seems to enjoy being in the thick of things, good or bad."

Cait paused, as if mulling it over. "Maybe ye're right. But I'm not ready to apologize. I didn't do anything wrong." She put her hand on her abdomen as if protecting the baby from what she was thinking.

Rachel chewed her lip. Cait was the only person she trusted to ask, and this was as good a time as any. "While I have you, can you tell me what something means?" She'd repeated the words over and over in her mind since Christmas Eve so she wouldn't forget how Brodie had said it. "*Mo ghràidh?*" she whispered.

Cait's hand dropped and she grinned at Rachel as if she'd learned a new bit of gossip. "Where did ye hear it?"

"Around," Rachel hedged. There was no way she was going to confess the circumstances under which the words were said. *While I was naked and lying next to Brodie.*

Cait was the one who took her arm this time, giving it a squeeze. "It means *my dear.*" Her knowing smile embarrassed Rachel.

"Thanks."

"Cait!" Deydie grabbed her broom. "I told ye to put yere feet up."

Cait rolled her eyes. "I'll talk to you later. I'm going home."

Rachel was left alone, feeling both elated and downcast. Brodie had called her *my dear,* but afterward she ruined it by speaking from her heart and telling him what she needed. *Love me, Brodie.*

She laid a hand on the locket around her neck, feeling a sinking depression coming on. She should make an appointment with Emma, the town's therapist, to help her wade through her crushed dreams and get beyond them.

Rachel had been doing a lot of soul-searching over the last week since she had time on her hands. Here in Gandiegow, Hannah didn't need her as much, as her little girl had made the village her own. Hannah raced through town with the other children, taking turns to play at each other's houses. Her daughter had really settled in and enjoyed a freedom here she'd never have back in Chicago.

That thought churned with all the other discombobulated feelings which were bombarding Rachel. Hannah might be happy, but *Hannah's mother* was a bit conflicted—half miserable *and half contented*. What a strange state to be in. Since Christmas night, she hadn't been near enough to Brodie to speak with him. When he'd said *good-bye,* he wasn't kidding. But he'd found ways to see Hannah when Rachel wasn't around—at least that was the report from her daughter. He'd taken Hannah to show her *their* boat. He'd given Hannah a small pail of shells for the two of them to sort. He'd gifted her with a tiny fishing rod, teaching her how to cast her line in Abraham's parlor. She had to hand it to Brodie . . . he was an expert at avoiding *Hannah's mother*.

She missed him terribly, and at the same time, she'd never felt more at peace with herself because of this community. As if gazing at a new outfit through the storefront window, Rachel visualized what it would be like to make Gandiegow her home . . . permanently. All looked well, except she had one huge complication to overcome. Could she live so close to the man she loved and accept he would never love her back?

That strong empowering voice harrumphed in her head. *Hell yes! You are the mistress of your destiny. Live life and be happy no matter the circumstances.*

Deydie glowered at her from the doorway and began trudging toward her. Rachel was pretty sure the old woman didn't want to compare nail polish. Yes, she'd been dawdling, but the head quilter didn't understand she had a lot on her mind.

It was best to head her off at the pass, so Rachel met

her halfway. "I have a question for you." She liked throwing the dour-faced woman off guard.

"What?" Deydie asked.

"Where do out-of-town guests stay if the quilting dorms are full from a quilt retreat?"

"What?"

Rachel had spoken clearly. "Let's say, that when Hannah and I arrived, the quilting dorms had been full. Where would we have stayed?"

Deydie stared her down. "There's the room over the pub, but it only has the one bed." The old woman frowned. "I guess ye would've had to stay with one of us, if ye didn't have Abraham as family."

"I heard Kit Armstrong brings in her American clients for her matchmaking service. Where do they stay?"

"We have to plan it so that no quilt retreat is going on."

"Has that been a problem?"

"Nay! The Kilts and Quilts retreat comes before her *Real Men of Scotland* business. I've made that perfectly clear. Though sometimes Kit gets her britches twisted up over it."

"And tourism?" Rachel went on bravely, now that she had Deydie's attention. "Do you ever have people come here for the beautiful ocean and the fresh air?"

Deydie stepped closer, peering up at her. "What are you getting at?"

Rachel took a step backward. "Nothing. I was only wondering."

Deydie huffed. "Git back to work." She hustled away.

Rachel stared at the door, having one of her weak moments, wishing a certain fisherman would walk through. But he didn't. She longed to go back in time to Christmas night and kiss him once more. She would plant such a kiss on him that the memory would last her for a lifetime.

She wandered over to the stack of tablecloths and took one from the top. Again, she wondered if she should run her B and B idea past Brodie before she went any further.

Hell no! The strong inner voice guffawed. *He doesn't get a vote. It's your decision.*

True. He'd said good-bye. Maybe it was time for Rachel to step confidently into the next phase of her life. One that made sense. No more past-their-expiration-date second chances. No more crazy fantasies of a family that would never be. Hannah was her family. Her mother, too. A bed and breakfast in Gandiegow would make a great adventure for her and Hannah.

A bit of anger bubbled up. *If Brodie doesn't like it, then he can walk the plank.*

"Why the maniacal grin?" Vivienne said.

Rachel jumped. "Where did you come from?"

"I was sent on an errand." Her mother's face was glowing as if illuminated by the sun.

Rachel knew that look. "What's going on?"

"I saw that gorgeous man, again," Vivienne purred.

"The village is full of them."

"Ah, but this one is for me. I asked around. He's single."

Rachel felt embarrassed, not for her mother, but for herself. She couldn't have her mom hitting on the men of Gandiegow if she was to have a B and B here. "Dare I ask who it is?"

"The one I saw after church. The doctor's father, Casper MacGregor. I hear he hasn't lived here very long."

"But you're headed off to France tomorrow." Rachel should've encouraged her to go right after Christmas.

"France can wait." Vivienne looked like Hannah right now, as if she were about to unwrap a new present. "Even better, maybe I can convince Casper to go with me. Travel is much more fun with a companion."

Normally, Rachel would tell her mother to *knock herself out*, because her trysts never reflected on her. But this was different.

Vivienne frowned. "Stop looking at me like that. We're of age."

"True. But—"

As if it was a sign from heaven, the door opened and Casper came walking in, carrying his grandson Angus. His daughter-in-law Emma was beside him.

"No time like the present." Vivienne winked at Rachel and then sauntered over to him.

Rachel started to go after her, but something caught her eye: Grace Armstrong straightened as if she'd been pierced by a harpoon. She followed to where Grace was looking. First Casper, then to Vivienne's killer hips sashaying over to the retired reverend.

Rachel wasn't the only one who noticed. Emma was watching the whole thing unfold, too. Rachel took a step toward her mother to stop her, but the expression on Emma's face said she wasn't going to intervene.

Rachel mulled that over. If she got in the middle of this, she'd be as bad as Vivienne, who always wanted to control whom she dated. *Whom I married.* The sobering truth settled in. She had no right to get involved with her mother's affairs. Rachel could only observe and hope for the best.

Vivienne sidled up to Casper and began chatting him up.

Deydie harrumphed loudly. Rachel glanced around and found the old woman glaring not ten feet away with her broom at her side.

Rachel put her hand up to keep the woman from coming closer. "Fine. I'll get back to work." She shook out the cloth and smoothed it over the table.

Next she joined Coll and Amy, who were setting up

chairs around the perimeter of the room. The job was mindless, giving Rachel more time to think about her bed and breakfast. When she got a moment, she was going to start sketching out her dream.

"Need help?" Emma asked.

"Yes." *With more than just the chairs.* "Can I ask you a question?"

Emma took the chair from her and placed it against the wall. "Certainly."

Rachel wasn't sure where to begin. "I never touched my husband's life insurance money." She told her how she'd moved to the hotel, how their marriage ceased to exist, how when he died—though she was the beneficiary— Rachel didn't feel as if she had a right to use the insurance.

Emma listened while they worked, nodding her head with each new piece of information. Finally, she sat in one of the chairs. "There's only one thing for you to consider."

"That is?"

"Are you raising Joe's daughter?"

"Yes."

Emma laid a hand on Rachel's arm. "In there lies your answer. He must've had confidence you would use the money wisely if something happened to him."

True. Joe had trusted her when it came to money. He'd even said once he knew she was the one to marry when he saw how frugal she was. Also, he was the type of person who would've changed his policy if he thought she would squander the insurance.

A weight lifted. It had been heavy on her mind for so long that without it there, Rachel felt a little uncomfortable.

"Don't worry," Emma said. "You'll get used to the idea."

"I guess it'll take some time."

"Mommy!" Hannah ran at her. "Did ye know there's a dance tonight? Dand says so. Glenna said I can wear a pretty dress." She twirled around as if she had the dress on now. "I love to dance."

"I know you do." Rachel picked her up and hugged her close while doing a mini waltz. Feeling lighter made it easier to dance. She looked at Emma over her shoulder. "What do I owe you for your help?"

Emma shook her head. "What do the Americans say? It's *on the house*?"

"Thank you."

Hannah laid a hand on her cheek. "What did Emma do for ye, Mummy?"

Rachel liked being called *mommy*, but her girl was determined to be a Scottish lass. "Emma helped me with a problem."

"I'm glad." Hannah hugged her again. "I like it when ye're happy."

It occurred to Rachel, that since Christmas, she'd been seriously down in the dumps.

But no more. Hannah needed her *mum* happy.

Rachel twirled and Hannah squealed. Tonight at the dance was the perfect time to embrace something new. It would be a good life.

"There's Glenna." Hannah slid out of her arms and ran off.

Rachel smiled. Gandiegow was the right place to raise her daughter and the right place for her to be. Rachel would help out with the retreat-goers while they were at the quilting dorm. She'd teach a class here and there. She'd build her B and B and stay busy running it. She was making a new start. Second chances were for dreamers, and Rachel was a grown woman with a daughter to care for. She should've realized from the start that it takes two to make a relationship. It was time to silence the little voice forever and embrace the voice which told her to be strong.

She couldn't afford to waste another second on what would never be. Without giving herself a moment to reconsider, she reached up and unclasped the necklace from around her neck. The locket fell into her hand and she shoved it into her jeans pocket.

Her neck felt naked. But she would get used to that, too. Emptiness was expected when change was taking place. *Time for me to grow up and move on.*

"Brodie!" Hannah yelled from across the room. "Mummy, it's Brodie!"

Slowly, Rachel turned around to see him carrying a table through the doorway. He set it down and caught Hannah as she launched herself into his arms. His eyes came up and met Rachel's. His features were guarded and his wariness conveyed his message clearly—*give me space*—as if he were five inches away instead of thirty feet.

"Stop worrying. I'm all done," she whispered to him, assuring him, assuring herself, tired from the imaginary world she'd built where she could have him for always. She reached in her pocket and touched the locket again. "I never should've assumed anything."

Hannah came running back to her. "Brodie's going to be at the dance tonight. Are ye going to dance with him?"

"No, sweetie. I'm not going to dance with him."

Hannah cocked her head to the side. "Don't ye like him anymore?" The room's chatter ceased, going unusually quiet. "Ye said ye liked Brodie a lot when ye kissed him." Her little voice rang out as if she were on the loud speaker.

Rachel cringed. More than a few heads whipped around, actually all of them. Her chest and face felt on fire, and she refused to look in Brodie's direction again.

She took Hannah's hand and began walking, almost dragging her daughter along. "I like Brodie fine. Now, let's go." Rachel didn't want to stop at the quilting dorm to change. She wanted to keep on walking, out the door, out of Gandiegow, but wouldn't leave the village now that she'd decided to stay. But she could hide out for an hour or so and try to forget all the humiliating mistakes she'd ever made.

Chapter Seventeen

Brodie planted his feet and stared down the damned decorating committee, one by one. Rachel might run away, but he wasn't one to stick his head in the sand and hide. Not anymore.

"Back to work," Deydie hollered.

He flipped the table over, pulled down the legs, and set it up. Hell, worrying over what might tumble out of Harry's mouth had been wasted energy. Brodie should've been guarding himself against the forty-inch-tall five-year-old who was known for saying the most outrageous things.

But I heard Rachel with my own ears; she said she liked me.

That didn't mean a thing. He liked broccoli.

But he knew she liked him from the one night they'd been together. *Love me, Brodie.*

He finished his task with only a few glances from the folks about the room. But as he left, Deydie shot him a quizzical look, which was weird. She normally had a scowl on her face while she was running shotgun over the village.

At home, he spent time with his grandfather, getting him settled in for the evening. Hannah had been by earlier and helped Grandda choose and download some new apps for his iPad.

Brodie caught sight of the screen as he moved the tablet to the side table. "Seriously, ye're playing that. *Little Girl Magic*?"

Abraham chuckled. "The lass insisted."

"Of course she did, and ye couldn't deny her."

"Not our Hannah."

"Are ye sure you don't want me to stay home with ye?" Brodie sailing his boat into a storm seemed preferable to going to the dance tonight.

Abraham peered over at him. "Ye've been out of sorts of late. Does yere dark mood have anything to do with a certain American lass?"

Brodie shifted his gaze to the window. "Nay. I don't feel much like celebrating the New Year, is all." He took the bowl of beef stew from the tray and handed it to his grandfather. "I could use the time to catch up on the books. Or play checkers with you."

"Gandiegow is expecting ye to sing tonight. Ye can't let them down."

But the partridge on Brodie's chest wasn't in the mood to sing. Brooding was more like it. He needed time to think. He'd done so well avoiding Rachel this past week and he didn't want to ruin his good streak. Being near her might set him back, might make him like her more, or might convince his bruised heart to develop a permanent case of amnesia where Rachel was concerned. He especially didn't want to go to the dance tonight after what happened in the grand dining room earlier. The news that they'd kissed would've spread by now to the far reaches of the village, the best piece of gossip in a while.

After he finished getting Abraham settled, Brodie dressed for the evening in a black button-down shirt and black jeans, and then he trekked across town. The music sounded from one end of the village to the other, infinitesimally lifting his dark spirits.

He walked into the restaurant and climbed the stairs to the second floor. He stood in the doorway of the grand dining room watching the townsfolk cutting loose in the low-lighted room, the disco ball twirling like it was 1980. The anticipation was thick that anything could happen tonight.

Bonnie popped up beside him and grabbed his hand. "Come on, sailor. The song's half over and I've been waiting to dance." She pulled him out on the floor before his eyes had really adjusted to the dark.

It was a fast song, but Bonnie clutched him and swayed to the music like it was a slow ballad. He felt trapped with her body crushed up against his. He looked at the punch table. He glanced at the band. When he peered past Bonnie's shoulder, everyone was dancing, except the one person who stood in the middle of the floor, staring at him. *Rachel.*

Hannah danced around her, flapping her arms like an eaglet trying to get her mum's attention. Rachel plastered on a smile for her daughter, took her hand, and danced along.

The scene was all wrong. *Damn Joe.* Rachel shouldn't have to raise her daughter all alone.

The song ended. Brodie half wanted to go to Rachel and Hannah—and dance with them both. It's what Andrew, Moira, and Glenna were doing. But while he was mulling over the idea, a tall figure blocked his view of Rachel. Brodie didn't have to see Tuck's face to know what he was about. He'd done nothing but ask about Rachel since day one.

"Brodie," Lochie said over the loud speaker. "Come up and sing."

Brodie couldn't. He had an arse to kick. Why the devil was Tuck sniffing about a single mother? He wasn't the kind of man to take on *real* responsibility.

"Brodie," Lochie said again into the microphone. "We're waiting on ye."

Brodie tramped over to where the band had set up. He took the mike and nodded to Lochie. But instead of striking up a rousing reel, Lochie cued up "I Once Loved a Lass." Brodie shook it off, but Lochie kept playing, shrugging his shoulders like it was a done deal.

Brodie amended his list . . . first kick Lochie's arse when this was over then Tuck, who had taken Rachel into his arms. He glared one more time at Lochie and then began singing . . .

"I once loved a lass and I loved her so well
And I hated all others who spoke of her ill.
And now she's rewarded me well for my love,
For she's gone and she's wed another."

The words hit so close to home, Brodie wondered if Lochie hadn't planned it. But the bloke looked oblivious while he strummed his guitar as if he had a certain someone in mind. Each *effing* chorus ended the same: *For she's gone and she's wed another.* The song clawed at Brodie's chest as Rachel danced with Tuck. Once again, he had the sinking feeling he had missed the boat. Rachel wasn't mooning over him anymore; she was laughing, because apparently, Tuck was the most charming dance partner on the planet. Didn't she know he wasn't right for her?

Tuck led them closer and closer to the band. Rachel kept her eyes on Tuck, never looking up. If she had, she would've seen Brodie staring at her.

Something was off. Way off about her. Then Brodie noticed: She no longer wore his locket.

Rachel feigned happiness. *Fake it before you make it,* her first boss at the Winderly used to say when dealing with exasperating customers. But she could apply this to her current situation. Happiness would surely follow if she pretended as if *all was well*. She was only dancing with Tuck because she was moving on. She wasn't trying to make Brodie jealous; Tuck was just the first person to approach her. She hoped there would be others. More people to distract her and help her listen to that empowered inner voice of hers. *Brodie is not singing to me.*

She glanced around for Hannah and found her at the cake table talking to Dand and Mattie. Rachel would get through this heartache if she kept focused on her daughter.

But something else caught her attention . . . Cait and Deydie. Cait seemed to be pleading with Deydie, but the old woman had the determined look of one who had been wronged. Others in the room appeared to be unhappy. Sinnie looked to be arguing with her beau, Colin, a local well-to-do farmer. Grace Armstrong appeared to be as miserable as Rachel as she sat in the corner with her granddaughter Irene. Rachel followed to where she stared . . . Vivienne dancing with Casper MacGregor.

The song ended. Rachel stared up at Tuck's good-looking face. "Thank you."

"Dance another with me," he said as Brodie broke into an up-tempo tune.

"I need to check on my mother." Rachel spoke the truth. She stepped out of Tuck's arms, going back on her decision to let her mother lead her own life. Her mother should back off from Casper. But as she made her way to Vivienne, who was laughing and hanging on to his arm, Kit stepped into Rachel's path.

"Hold up. She's my mother-in-law, and I see it, too." Kit tilted her head toward Grace first, then Vivienne, who was shamelessly throwing herself at Casper. "I think we should let it play out, don't you?"

Rachel glanced at Vivienne. "I don't know. You may be a matchmaker, but my mother can be tenacious when it comes to men. She seems determined to get Casper in her clutches."

Kit nodded knowingly. "I believe your mother might just be what Grace needs to propel her into action."

Rachel looked over at Grace. "She looks more defeated than propelled."

Kit touched her arm reassuringly. "This is just the calm before the storm. She'll wake up soon to what she's missing out on."

"Do I need to be worried for my mother?"

"I think she can take care of herself, don't you?"

"Yes. You're right."

Kit gestured at the band. "Can I help with your situation? I would be happy to set something up with Brodie for you."

"No," Rachel squeaked, utterly embarrassed. "Please, don't. What you heard through the grapevine was nothing but a misunderstanding." Sure, Rachel had kissed Brodie. But that was before she'd seen the truth . . . he would never be hers.

"Okay." Kit might have gone along with her, but her expression said she didn't believe a word Rachel said.

Hannah tugged her hand. "Mummy, I don't feel so good." Her cheeks were bright red.

Rachel touched her forehead. "You're burning up." She picked her up. "Let's get you to the quilting dorm."

Kit looked worried. "Do you need Doc MacGregor?"

"No. It's probably just a bug." It wasn't the first time Hannah had gone from being fine to suddenly ill. The pediatrician said it was normal for kids to be okay one second and sick in the next. "Can you let my mother know I'm taking Hannah back?"

"Yes. No problem."

Rachel gathered their coats and set Hannah to her feet to slip hers on.

"But I didn't even get to dance with my friends," Hannah whined.

"I know, sweetie. There will be other parties." Rachel thought about the children's Tylenol she had brought with her from Chicago. She tried to remember what was in the refrigerator at the dorm to keep Hannah hydrated. She could always send her mother to the General Store for supplies as the door was once again open twenty-four hours a day. Amy had put Harry to work to pay for the things he'd *borrowed*.

Back at the dorm, Rachel gave Hannah a dose of medicine and settled her into bed. Guzzy was requested and retrieved. Then Rachel had to kiss each one of Hannah's dolls before positioning them on the bed beside her.

"Mummy, I'm going to shut my eyes, but I'm not going to sleep. Can you read to me?"

"Yes, but how about I make myself a cup of herbal tea first?"

Hannah's eyes were already closed when she nodded.

Rachel went into the kitchen. She really did need a cup of tea, but before she could put the kettle on, there was a quiet knock at the front door. She padded down the hall to answer it.

Doc MacGregor, with his medical bag in hand, stood next to Brodie.

"I hear yere daughter's ill?" Gabriel said.

Rachel held the door wider for them to walk in while glancing at Brodie, who looked worried. "Hannah must've gotten a touch of something. She's probably asleep by now."

Gabriel nodded. "Then we'll let her be."

"Go check on her, Doc," Brodie urged. "Ye're already here." It was sweet of Brodie to be concerned.

"Sure." Gabriel seemed to want to appease Brodie.

"She's in the back bedroom."

When the three adults quietly entered the room, Hannah's eyes were closed. But she opened them, as if sensing their presence. Her little girl was fighting sleep as she always wanted to be part of the action.

"Brodie," Hannah said. "You came to read to me."

"That's right, princess."

Rachel told her heart not to go all gooey. *Brodie loves Hannah. That's it, nothing more.*

"I'll read to you, but first, Doc wants to take yere temperature."

Hannah looked up at Gabriel matter-of-factly. "Mummy says I'm burning up."

Doc chuckled, stepping forward. "Mothers are usually right about these things." He took her temperature, pulse, and listened to her heart. When he was done, he patted her hand. "I prescribe lots of fluids and rest."

Brodie picked up a book and sat on Rachel's bed across from her. "I'll read while Doc talks to yere mum, okay?"

Hannah nodded.

Gabriel walked Rachel out. "It looks like the same virus the oldest Bruce child had. The fever should be gone in a couple of days. If she gets worse, call me." He handed her his card.

"Thank you so much for coming."

Gabriel glanced back down the hall, grinning. "Brodie didn't give me much choice."

Rachel felt her cheeks heat up, which was ridiculous. Hannah was Brodie's cousin and he cared for her. There was no reason for her to be embarrassed at his insistence. "I was just putting on some tea. Would you like some?"

"Thanks, no. I'll return to the celebration. But call if you need anything."

She shook his hand and he left.

Brodie came into the kitchen as she was pouring herself a cup.

"She's asleep," he announced. He went to the cabinet, pulled down a mug, and poured himself a cup, also. "I shut the door so she wouldn't be disturbed."

She wondered at him making himself at home when he'd made it clear he didn't want to be near her anymore.

"Listen, Rachel," he started, but he didn't get to finish.

The front door slammed, footsteps hurried through the house, and Vivienne appeared in the doorway of the kitchen. She stared at Brodie, gave him a sideways frown as if he wasn't worth her time, and turned on Rachel. "Why didn't you tell me my granddaughter was sick?"

"She's okay. It's just a fever. Doc looked at her and said it was the same virus that had been going around."

"Yes. I hurried as soon as I got word the doctor had been sent for."

Somebody overreacted, Rachel wanted to say. But Vivienne, now that she'd dismissed Brodie with her behavior, wouldn't have been pleased to know Brodie had spearheaded the house call.

Rachel went to her and put her arm around her mother. "It's okay. Hannah is going to be fine."

Brodie stood. "I better go." He looked one more second at Rachel, then left, without taking a sip of his tea.

She wondered what he had started to say before her mother came in. But she could guess. He would reiterate what he'd said all along . . . nothing had changed between them.

Vivienne picked up Brodie's cup, poured it in the sink, and rinsed it out. "Why was he here?"

"He was concerned about Hannah, too." Rachel was

tired of the same conversation with her mother and felt it was time to end it. "Mom, he wasn't here to see me. I promise."

"Are you sure? Because that man is not good enough for you."

The dam cracked in Rachel's façade and the truth poured forth. "But Joe cheating on me from nearly the beginning is the kind of man I deserve?" She made sure to say it quietly, conscious of her little girl sleeping down the hall.

Vivienne halted. "What?"

"Yes, Mom. I looked the other way for some time, but when I ended up with an STD at my six-week checkup after Hannah, I drew the line and called it quits." Rachel's voice caught. She'd worked so hard to make her marriage work, though from the beginning, she'd known she'd married the wrong man.

"Oh, honey! Why didn't you tell me?"

"How could I? I was so embarrassed at my situation. I knew months before the wedding that things were wrong. I stayed in denial, because I wanted to believe he was the perfect man."

"And because I insisted that you go through with it." Vivienne pulled her in for a hug. "You should've said something."

"But I couldn't. You loved Joe so much. I thought it was better if I kept it all to myself."

Vivienne gazed at her with sadness. "I want you to feel like you can tell me anything."

"I promise I will in the future." Rachel felt the healing take place—the loose seam between her and her mother was finally being pulled together and stitched properly in place.

"Joe certainly was charismatic," Vivienne sighed.

"So was Don Juan. But he wouldn't make the best kind of husband either."

They both laughed, relieving some of the tension that had been present between them.

"About Brodie—" Vivienne started.

Rachel put her hand up. "It's okay. I'm not with him. But you have to know . . . he's a good man. Loyal. True. And he loves Hannah very much. For that alone, he deserves your respect."

Her mother nodded. "Okay. I'll try."

"Thank you." Her mother was finally going to give Brodie a chance and Rachel wanted to laugh. Not because it was funny, but because it was only six years too late.

Grace just about had enough of Rachel's mother pawing Casper when Kit said something to the *Jezebel* and she rushed out. Before any other women in Gandiegow laid claim to him, Grace found her son John and handed off his daughter to him. "There's something I need to do."

As she crossed the floor, she suddenly felt fine with her decision to openly date Casper. She loved her sons, but they had their own lives to live and they couldn't be upset with her for living hers. She wanted to be with Casper. He made her laugh. He made her feel like an attractive woman again, instead of past her prime. But most of all, being around him made her feel whole. She was in love with him, and she was tired of telling herself that she wasn't.

But before she had time to walk across the floor, Bonnie sauntered over and was chatting Casper up. Grace was not deterred. She marched the rest of way.

"Excuse me, Bonnie," Grace said sweetly. "The reverend promised me the next dance." And the one after that, and the one after that, if she had her way.

Bonnie glared at her as if it wasn't true. "He's a free man."

Grace turned to him to make the next move and he didn't disappoint.

Casper gave Bonnie an emphatic shake of his head. "Sorry, lass. I'm not free anymore."

He took Grace's hand and twirled her onto the dance floor.

Brodie finished with the boat's log and headed home. For the last week, he'd stayed away from the quilting dorm while the tyke recovered. It had been one of the hardest things he'd ever done, but he'd listened to reason.

"I'll take my broom after ye," Deydie had threatened, "if ye spread Hannah's illness to Abraham. Yere grandda is finally on the mend." The old quilter was right; Grandda had turned a corner in the right direction, setting his sails to healing completely. Deydie also promised she and her ladies would see to the Americans' comfort, being clear, *Ye're not needed in that quarter.*

Aye, that may be true. But every day, Brodie passed a gift to Moira to take to *Princess Hannah*—his favorite fishing bobber, a stuffed animal from the General Store, or a handwritten note. He wanted the little one to know she hadn't been forgotten.

Though he tried not to, his thoughts were on Rachel nonstop. If Vivienne hadn't shown up in the kitchen on the night Hannah got sick, he might have said something which could've been misconstrued. Now that several days had passed, he felt he could say it perfectly. He needed to explain to Rachel that she shouldn't be raising Hannah on her own. The lass needed a father.

But am I volunteering?

No. *Hell, no.* He couldn't take Joe's place. Guilt filled his gut as if he'd killed his cousin to take his wife. He shook it off. He didn't kill anyone.

But the lass needs a father. Aye, she did. Brodie didn't

have all the kinks worked out yet to get her one. Also, he thought, feeling chagrined . . . with Vivienne off to France, she wouldn't be around to bail him out again if he needed it.

The cottage came into sight. Today was the first day Hannah was cleared by Doc to come see Grandda. Brodie was free to see her, too, as Rachel had headed to Inverness. He wanted to spend as much time with his little cousin before she left Scotland for the States. Strange rumors of them staying had been floating around town, but he didn't believe them. He expected any day now for Rachel to pack their bags for Chicago. The vision of her leaving felt real. He ignored the pain of Rachel wheeling her luggage to the shuttle waiting in the parking lot to whisk her and Hannah out of his life. He played the scene over and over, trying to get used to the horrible inevitable future.

He opened the door to the cottage, heard a squeal, and then little footsteps.

"Brodie!" Hannah ran to him with her arms wide.

He swung her into the air. "Are ye all better then?"

"Aye. Doc says I'm *fit as a fiddle*." Hannah hugged him.

Harry came into the hall and waved before heading to the kitchen.

Hannah leaned back and gave Brodie her most disgruntled face. "Why didn't ye come to see me? I missed ye."

"I couldn't. Ye know that, princess. Moira said she explained it to you."

"Did ye know Doc says I can go back to school tomorrow?"

"School? I thought ye might be leaving for Chicago."

Was the speculation true then? Had Rachel really been asking after the land next to Thistle Glen Lodge? Did she really mean to build a B and B?

"Mummy says we're staying here." Hannah laid a hand on his cheek. "Ye're glad, aren't ye, Brodie?"

"So glad." The partridge on his chest came alive and Brodie took his first full breath in a week. "I'll get to see ye whenever I want." He wanted to break into a sea chanty. "How about a tea party?" He couldn't believe he was suggesting it. "We'll make Grandda and Harry attend. What do ye think?"

Her eyes lit up with mischief. "Will they let me fix their hair?"

"Of course." How he loved this little girl. "They have to do what the Chieftain says."

Hannah's eyes grew as wide as a captain's wheel. "I get to be the Chieftain?"

Brodie laughed. "Aye. Ye'll be the Chieftain. Just like yere da used to be."

Hannah's excitement shifted and her brows pulled together in serious thought. "Brodie, now that we're staying, will ye be my da?"

He stopped breathing and a war began inside him that knew no victor. For a long second he stared into her earnest face, but had to tell her the truth. "I can't." She was Joe's kid. Brodie couldn't come in and claim her as his own.

She squinted and clutched at his T-shirt. "But ye have to. I say so. I'm the Chieftain. Ye said everyone has to obey the Chieftain."

He sat on the bench in the foyer with her in his lap and held her close. "Hannah, this is a serious matter and playing the Chieftain is a game. What ye're asking me to do is a grown-up decision, not one for a child."

She slipped off his lap and crossed her arms. "Glenna has two daddies. I want two daddies, too." Her bottom lip stuck out as a warning. She stomped her foot. "Ye have to be my da! I'm the Chieftain!"

Brodie was feeling uncomfortable. He glanced around, hoping Rachel would appear. "It's more complicated than me being yere da." Rachel would be part of the deal. But how could he explain that?

Hannah turned red in the face and stomped her foot again and again. "I hate you, Brodie." She burst into tears and ran upstairs, slamming the bathroom door behind her.

He was stunned, but one thing became clear: He was an idiot. The one Granger woman who loved him now hated his guts. He'd made a real mess of things.

Harry stood in the kitchen doorway, staring at him.

"Leave off," Brodie said. He didn't want to discuss this with another child.

Brodie left out the front door and went back to the cold boat. He sat in the wheelhouse and brooded over his situation. At least on his boat, he didn't have to deal with irrational females. The females weren't only irrational but unpredictable as well. He never knew what was going to happen from one minute to the next. He could never live like that. He stared out at the calm ocean, but instead of feeling settled, his insides churned as the tide began to change within him.

He wasn't being truthful with himself. He'd enjoyed the life and noise Hannah and Rachel had infused into the household. Maybe a little unpredictability wasn't such a bad thing. He thought about the vision he'd had when Rachel and Hannah had been on the dance floor, how he'd seen a man in the picture, too. Could he be that man? Could he take Joe's family and make them his own? Could he get past his guilt? Of course, Brodie could never forgive Rachel completely for what she'd done to him, but he had positioned himself someplace in the middle . . . a place where he could still hold on to his unforgiveness, and at the same time, he could have the one thing that was missing in his life. He couldn't name the one thing, but the partridge on his chest being content was a good place to start.

He went back out onto the deck and inhaled deeply the salt of the sea and the cold of winter. Tonight, when Rachel returned, he'd seek her out and explain what had happened today. Surely they could come to some understanding for Hannah's sake.

Brodie smiled at the arrangement. He could have Hannah for his daughter and at night he'd have Rachel to keep him warm in his bed. It seemed like the perfect solution. They would get married and live like some crazy fairytale . . . happily ever after.

Chapter Eighteen

Rachel decided today officially marked the beginning of her new life. As she pulled into Gandiegow's parking lot, she glanced over at the folder next to her. Inside was the deed to the property next to Thistle Glen Lodge, future home of Partridge House, her own B and B. She wasn't trying to punish herself by naming her establishment after a moment she and Brodie had shared. The name was her way of filing away the past and giving it new meaning.

The list was long of things to do and Rachel had been systematically checking them off. After many years at the Winderly Towers, it wasn't easy to tender her resignation. As hard as it had been, Rachel had been putting off telling the one person who wouldn't take well her decision to stay here. *The one person besides Brodie.* Before she went any further, she pulled out her phone, but then looked out at the ocean, watching as the waves rolled in. She sighed, and then finally placed the call.

"Hi, Mom, do you have a minute?"

"Sure. I'm only getting ready to lie down for a nap. Late night, last night."

"You're having fun then?" Rachel said, procrastinating.

"Loads. Now what's going on?"

"I don't want you to be upset. Okay?"

"Is Hannah all right?" Vivienne's voice was laced with panic and worry.

"She's fine. Actually, she's great. All better and having fun again with her friends."

"Then what's this about?" Vivienne's tone had taken on the lower pitch of impatience.

Rachel bit her lip and then spit it out. "I'm building a B and B."

"A B and B? But you never wanted a small establishment."

"What?" Rachel choked. "How did you know?"

"Rachel, I'm your mother. I pay attention. I had hoped you would take over the Sunnydale Hotel, but I knew you wouldn't. You loved working at the Winderly Towers."

She was flabbergasted. Her mom had known all along? She paused for a second to let it sink in. All those years, Rachel had fretted for nothing. What wasted time and energy. She should've spoken up sooner and told her mom how she was feeling.

"Why a B and B now?" Vivienne asked.

"I've changed. A bed and breakfast is perfect for us."

"I can see that."

Now came the hard part. Rachel was still getting used to the idea of her mom not being a short drive away. She was just going to come out with it, because the deed was done, *literally*, lying next to her in the car. "I bought the property next to Thistle Glen Lodge." She went quiet, waiting for the explosion on the other end.

Her mother only sighed. "My granddaughter certainly loves that village."

"Then you're okay with it?"

"Rachel." Her mother sounded exasperated. "You don't need my approval. You're a grown woman."

Rachel didn't feel like a grown-up right now. Her voice dropped to nearly a whisper. "But I'm still your daughter and I'd like to have your blessing."

"Oh, sweetie." Vivienne's laugh felt light and comforting. "Of course you have my blessing. I love you. Though I haven't done the best job of saying it, I believe in you, too."

The unspoken lay in the ether between them. If only Rachel had been assertive with her mom six years ago—*she knew now that's all it would've taken*—she would've had the confidence to walk away from the wedding that had been planned.

"Mom, I love you, too."

"I know, darling. Give Hannah a *skwunch* from me, okay?"

"I will. See you in March?"

"Yes. But Rachel?"

"Hm?"

"Make sure my granddaughter hasn't immersed herself too much and is only speaking Gaelic when I return."

Rachel laughed, they said their good-byes, and she hung up. She opened the car door and breathed in the fresh sea air. Today really did feel like a new beginning.

Tonight marked a new beginning, too. Since New Year's Eve, Tuck had been hounding her to go out with him. She finally agreed, but only on one condition: She wasn't interested in a relationship. Apparently, neither was he. They were going out as friends, or she wasn't going at all.

When Rachel arrived at Abraham's, Hannah didn't come running out. She found her daughter in the parlor with her grandfather and Harry. She was subdued while Harry and Abraham played checkers.

"What's going on, peapod?" Rachel asked.

Hannah looked up at her, but it was Harry who answered.

"She and Brodie had a fight."

Rachel's *mother bear* instincts went into high alert. "About what?" Brodie better not have hurt Hannah's feelings.

Hannah huffed. "He said he won't be *my da*."

Rachel was stunned. "He what?" And though it shouldn't have, the thought hurt.

Harry once again spoke for her daughter. "She asked Brodie if he would be her da and he said he couldn't."

Rachel got that part, and she was sure Hannah was taking it hard, but not as hard as the pit which grew in Rachel's stomach. It was just another final word from the man she'd loved for so long. She'd buried the second chance she'd wanted with Brodie. She expunged that kind of wishful thinking from her heart. Then why did Brodie's rejection hurt so much?

Abraham seemed to watch her closely.

Rachel donned a veneer exterior for her daughter's sake, and hopefully hid how she was dying inside. "Did you hear or see what happened?" she asked the old man.

"I was dozing. Didn't hear a thing."

That's convenient, she thought.

"Brodie left right after, slamming the door," Harry supplied. "We haven't seen him since."

Rachel wanted to give Brodie an earful. It was one thing to reject her, but it was quite another to *not* let her daughter down gently.

"Hannah, we have to go," Rachel said. She hated she had to leave her again tonight after being gone today, but this was the life of a single mother. "You're going to play with Glenna this evening."

Hannah popped up. "Really?"

"Yup." Rachel loved that her daughter could snap out of a bad mood quickly. She hoped she was this lucky when Hannah was a teenager. "Abraham? Harry? Do you need anything before we go?"

"Deydie will be by this evening to play canasta." The old man seemed to brighten just mentioning the bossy quilter's name.

"I'm going to make myself scarce," Harry said.

Abraham laughed. "Her bark is worse than her bite."

Harry grinned. "I know. But still."

"We'll see you tomorrow after church," Rachel supplied.

"See ye later, alligator," Hannah said.

"After a while, crocodile," said Abraham and Harry in unison. Abraham seemed happy to oblige Hannah on her ritual; Harry, not so much. But it said loads about him that he would do it for Hannah anyway.

Outside, Hannah skipped while Rachel held her hand. "Where are ye going tonight, Mummy?"

"Out with a friend," Rachel said truthfully.

"Who?"

Rachel tried to divert her. "What are you going to take to Glenna's? Your dolls and your stroller?"

"Aye. But just the doll Glenna gave me. I want to show her how happy Dolly is to live with me. Who are ye going out with tonight?"

It wasn't a big deal. "Tuck."

"How come ye don't go out with Brodie?"

Because he never asked me. "Because I'm going out with Tuck. We're just friends." It was best to make that clear with Hannah upfront. Rachel suddenly remembered why she had to be careful with whom she saw. Brodie was living proof that Hannah could get attached easily and get her heart broken when things didn't work out.

Hannah gazed up at her. "Why doesn't Brodie love us anymore, Mummy?"

Rachel leaned over and picked up her daughter, holding her close. "Make no mistake, sweetie, Brodie still loves you." Rachel would make sure he fixed whatever had happened between them today. Though it sounded like Hannah had backed him into a corner.

At the quilting dorm, both of them readied for their evenings. Hannah filled her backpack with her guzzy and some doll clothes. Rachel threw on a loose sweater and blue jeans. It was good enough for having dinner at the restaurant.

A knock came at the door.

Rachel needed to put her earrings on. "Can you let Tuck in and tell him I'll be out in a minute?"

"Sure." Hannah hopped away as if she were Peter Rabbit, which took twice as long to get to the door as if she'd walked.

Rachel opened the slotted container she used for her jewelry. The first thing that caught her eye was Brodie's locket. She needed to return it, and she would. Her head said it was past time, but her heart wanted to hang on to it a little while longer.

Hannah yelled from the living room, "Ye're right, Mummy. It's Tuck."

Good. No surprises. Rachel had to keep telling herself that going out this evening was the right thing to do; it was good for her. She walked out of the bedroom and down the hall. Tuck looked handsome and the man knew it. By the amount of products in his hair and the perfect turn of his cuffs, he was one of those guys who put time into his appearance.

Rachel picked up her purse. "I hope you don't mind, but I need to drop Hannah at your brother's."

"I'm playing with Glenna," Hannah piped in. "Mummy has a date."

Tuck's eyebrow went up. "That's good to know." He looked as if Hannah's words were a green light on more interesting activities than friendship tonight.

"Yes, a date *between friends*," Rachel added firmly.

She helped Hannah with her coat, Tuck grabbed the pink backpack, and Hannah manned the buggy with Dolly inside. To an outsider, they probably looked like a cozy family heading out for a stroll. But on the other side of the door, Rachel stopped dead in her tracks at who stood there.

Brodie!

He seemed to take in the scene as if witnessing a crime, cataloging every detail, his shock playing out on his face.

Hannah glanced at Rachel. "Ye were right, Mummy. Brodie does still love us."

That was not love in his eyes. For Rachel or for Tuck.

Hannah tugged on Brodie's arm. "I'm on my way to Glenna's while Mummy goes on a date with Tuck."

"Hannah!" Rachel said. "I told you—"

Brodie put his hand up, blocking, as if Rachel's image burned his eyes. "I was just stopping by, um, to see if Hannah was all right. We had a tiff."

"She's fine," Rachel tried.

But Brodie was already moving off, and was speaking over his shoulder. "Good. Hannah, I'll see ye later. I have to get home to Grandda."

Oh, crap. Rachel wanted to run after him, but he wasn't part of her *new beginning*. She watched as his large frame got smaller and smaller the farther he got away. She finally turned back to Tuck and Hannah. "I—I . . ."

Tuck looked down at her strangely. "Are ye sure you want to do this tonight?"

She plastered a smile on her face. She had promised herself she would be happy for Hannah's sake, no matter what. *Practice makes perfect.* But what she really felt was loss. Grief. That she would never truly be happy again.

*   *   *

For the rest of January and most of February, Brodie kept his head down and threw himself into work—fishing no matter the weather—morning, noon, and night. In the evenings, he trudged to the pub, making sure to never return home if he might have a chance meeting with Rachel. He prided himself that he saw Hannah every couple of days as the lass was the only ray of sunshine in his bleak existence. He'd missed out on being with Rachel; she and Tuck were an item now.

Tonight, as Brodie walked to The Fisherman, he wondered at Tuck. The longer the bloke dated Rachel, the quieter the man became on the boat, which was excellent on Brodie's ears. In fact, he said nearly nothing to Brodie's grunted orders while fishing. Harry complained how working with them was as much fun as gutting a fish. Brodie didn't care what the lad thought . . . though Harry was becoming right useful on the boat, handling the bait.

On the way to the pub, he saw Moira, Amy, and Sadie—arms loaded—heading to the restaurant. He sighed heavily. The Gandiegow women were planning another dance.

The Valentine's *céilidh* had been canceled because of a major winter storm. The single men of the village were hoping for more than a storm to stop the Leap Year Day dance tomorrow night; they were praying for a hurricane to nix it.

Every four years when the men tried to hide, Deydie would threaten them with her broom and remind them to be available when the women came-to-calling. It was also a warning to start building up reserve cash to pay for each rejected proposal that Leap Year Day brought. Many of the women looked to Leap Year Day as a profitable windfall, as five pounds a rejection could really add up. Especially since the women from the surrounding farms came to town looking for a husband, too.

Brodie might have seen the humor in it at one time, but he didn't now as he climbed the stairs to the pub and opened the door. In fact, he hadn't seen the humor in anything since Tuck had become a fixture in Rachel's life. Brodie had seen them all over town together—Tuck, Rachel, Hannah, and Glenna. Tuck had even taken to sitting next to the American lasses at church. Rumors were flying of an early spring wedding, which settled into Brodie's stomach like spoiled haggis. But what could he do? He'd tried, but missed the boat, out of his own damned pride.

He dreaded the upcoming *céilidh*, having no desire to watch as Tuck wooed Rachel further, holding her in his arms and flaunting how Brodie had failed.

Remembering New Year's Eve made Brodie's blood boil. "Whisky," he growled at Bonnie, who manned the bar.

The last *céilidh* had been a disaster. Brodie's misadventure hadn't been the only one on Hogmanay. There must've been something caustic in the wind blowing off the ocean that night—several of the men claimed to have slept on the sofa because their wives had been teed off for one reason or another. The only one who seemed truly happy with the outcome of Hogmanay was Lochie. Rumor had it he'd abandoned the other musicians to dance with Bonnie. Brodie thought the man had been mooning over her ever since. Night after night, Lochie hung out at the pub—like tonight—strumming his acoustic guitar while sitting at the bar, and stealing glances at Bonnie whenever he thought no one was looking.

Brodie sat down next to Ross, taking his drink as Bonnie slid it to him.

"Have ye been wondering about this?" Ross asked, motioning to Lochie.

Brodie nodded while sipping his dram.

Ross tapped Lochie on the shoulder. "Whatever happened to that American lass? Morgan was her name, right? The one ye were seen kissing . . . the first time Kit brought her American clients to town?"

Lochie stopped playing and leaned on his guitar. "Ah, well, it seems my eyes wandered one time too many." He glanced over at Bonnie. "Kit set Morgan up with a bloke from Aviemore. I hear they married last month. I wish her my best." He went back to strumming.

The background music didn't soothe Brodie's soul. He finished his drink and walked out with Ross. They were quiet until they reached the walkway up to Ross and Sadie's cottage.

Ross grinned over at him. "Are ye concerned about who might ask for yere hand on Leap Year Day?"

"Nay. It's only a headache to endure," Brodie said. "Ye no longer have to worry over it."

Ross glanced at his house as Sadie's silhouette crossed the curtained picture window. "I'm a lucky man." He clamped a hand on Brodie's shoulder. "I wish ye the same luck."

"Nay," Brodie said again. "I'm satisfied with the life I have." But the truth was he was miserable.

When he arrived home, Abraham was coming down the stairs in his Sunday suit.

"Where are ye headed off to?" Brodie asked.

"I'm going to take a walk," Abraham said.

"Where are ye going? Did Doc give you his stamp of approval?"

Abraham hitched his eyebrow, which had lesser men running for the hills. "I don't need another man to tell me what I can and *cannae* do."

This was a good sign that Grandda was better. Much better.

Abraham sauntered the rest of the way down. "So ye

don't worry like a mother hen, I mean to walk to Deydie's."

"What? Deydie? You fancy that"—*Crone?* Brodie
amended himself before letting it slip—"I mean, bossy
quilter?"

"Watch what ye think there, lad. Deydie is a good soul."

Certainly they were speaking of two different people.

Abraham looked at the curtains as if he could see
beyond them. "Deydie is braw." But then he turned his
razor-sharp gaze on Brodie. "What about ye? Are you
ready to tell Rachel how ye feel about her?"

Brodie walked away, down the hall. He should keep
going—straight out the back door.

The old man chuckled in his wake, following him into
the kitchen.

"Too close for comfort?" Grandda chided. "Rachel's
a good lass. Always been good to me. Deydie and Rachel
got me to think that maybe I haven't had the right of it
about women . . . all these years. Maybe some of them
are the trustworthy kind."

Brodie wanted to argue. His grandfather didn't have
firsthand experience with the pain Rachel could inflict.
Brodie did. Not to mention that she'd taken up with Tuck
and had shredded what was left of his heart.

"Ye know, I even respect the lass for honoring her
commitments." Abraham paused. "I never said anything
when she was here before, but that must've taken some
gumption to marry Joe—*because she'd promised him she
would*—when she clearly didn't love him. Like—"

"Nay." *Don't say another word.* Brodie had stopped
halfway to the stove with the filled tea kettle in his hand.
Surely Grandda hadn't known how Brodie had once
loved Rachel. The thought caught in his mind, but he
wouldn't admit anything about his feeling for her now.

Abraham laid a hand on his shoulder. "Sit. There's something I need to tell ye."

"I'm not in the mood to talk," Brodie said truthfully.

"Good. Because ye won't have to. Ye'll listen." Grandda really must be better, because he was back to being the captain. "I done ye wrong all these years."

"Not true. Ye've done everything for me," Brodie countered.

Abraham held up his hand. "Not just ye, but Joe . . . and Richard."

Brodie couldn't ever remember Grandda mentioning Uncle Richard's name since that horrible night.

Abraham looked Brodie square in the eye. "I filled my son with bitterness for women. I did the same with Joe . . . and with ye. I couldn't see past what Margaret had done to me." He seemed to struggle with her name, the grandmother Brodie had never met. "Being ill gave me a lot of time to think. I should've forgiven her a long time ago. Things might have been different." He shifted, looking out the window as if it were the past. "I could've found love again. Had more children. Had someone by my side in my old age."

"I'm here," Brodie said. "I won't leave ye." But he had left him. For six years, while Brodie was licking his own wounds from his broken heart.

Abraham smiled at him. "It's not the same, lad. A woman can brighten a life in a way us men can't imagine . . . until she's gone. Rachel and her bairn have made me remember that."

Brodie wasn't going to agree with him out loud on that count.

"If I had forgiven yere grandmother, maybe Richard's heart wouldn't have turned black. It's my fault Joe suffered at Richard's hand." Abraham's words caught. "I wish I could take it all back. If only I'd figured it out sooner."

The room was filled with the silent message of what the long arms of unforgiveness could do. Even reaching the innocent.

Brodie couldn't imagine having something terrible happen to Hannah, as fate had dealt to Joe. Brodie felt like a father to the lass. He felt Abraham's pain for what had been done in this house to Joe and what it must be like for Grandda to know his own child had turned out bad.

"It's been a heavy anchor strapped to my heart," Abraham said, bringing Brodie back. "I never meant to pass my burdens to anyone. I thought I was just warning ye lads so ye wouldn't get hurt. But my unforgiveness only magnified the damage, spreading it on to the ones I loved." His gnarled hand reached out and gripped Brodie's, the strength behind it becoming part of the message. "Don't do what I did. I missed out all these years. Don't turn into the person my son became, and I suspect Joe was becoming, too. Ye have a better heart than most men, Brodie. Don't throw it away because of me and what I've said and how I've lived my life. I'm beggin' ye, lad."

Brodie's hand was going numb, but the pain was driving home the point.

Water swam in Grandda's rheumy eyes. "Promise me ye'll do better and not be like yere foolish old grandda."

Brodie nodded, but he wanted to cry out like a little boy, *But I don't know where to start.*

Grandda released him. "Ye're a good boy, laddie. A good boy. It's time to take a chance and put yere heart out there."

Cait hung up the phone and went to find Graham. As she stomped up the stairs, her anger increased. Why did

Graham have to be this way? Everything was going so well. Mattie had been speaking more and more since singing at the Christmas Eve service. The babe inside Cait was growing. The only problem she had was her husband, and last night had been the last straw. He'd slept in the den, refusing to be in the same bed with her, so she did something drastic. She wasn't proud of herself either.

For two months she did everything she could to get Graham to ravish her. She tried every trick, every caress, and every naughty whisper. She'd ordered lingerie and dressed up like a five-pound hooker. She scoured the Internet for advice. Nothing worked. He'd wasted their two months together. He had to leave again soon. The idiot was steadfast and it annoyed the hell out of her. *Sex did not cause my previous miscarriages.* She was feeling desperate. Graham was heading out on location in a week, and Cait was in the mood!

"Graham!" she hollered when she reached the top step. *I really don't have time for this today.* Even though Deydie wouldn't let her oversee the decorations for the dance tonight, Cait wanted to be there. But instead of helping, she was forced to make her pigheaded husband go to Inverness.

"In here," Graham said. "Why are you yelling?"

She marched into the office, feeling too much like Deydie to be the sweet loving wife she should be. She took a deep breath, trying to center herself so she didn't come off as a banshee. "I need ye to come with me."

He looked up from his book, wary.

Yeah, she'd used this same phrase before . . . to lure him down to the wine cellar. She'd put the moves on him, but he hadn't caved.

He didn't look happy with her now. "I'm busy."

"Ye're reading. I need you to take me to the physician in Inverness."

He quickly stood, his book hitting the floor. "Is it the baby? Are ye feeling okay? Does Doc need to come along?"

Cait started to say she was fine, but didn't. She didn't want to scare him, but she needed him to go. She needed to fix him. She needed Graham to be normal. At least she'd finally gotten Deydie straightened out and being nice to her. Rachel had been right. Cait just needed to explain that she hadn't meant to exclude her; she just needed time for the babe to grow.

She laid her hand on her belly. "No. I don't want Doc to go along."

Graham looked around wildly. "What about Mattie?"

"He's playing with Dand."

"Let's go." Graham gently took her elbow as if she were a geriatric. Nearly the same way Deydie had been treating her, but her gran wasn't nearly as tender as her husband.

Once outside, he shot her a concerned look. "I should've called a helicopter."

He'd done that when she lost baby number two.

"We don't need the helicopter," she said.

The line between his eyebrows wasn't put there by some Hollywood script. Graham looked as if he was praying. "Stay here and let me get the Range Rover." Ever since he'd found out she was pregnant again, he'd been threatening to have a road built to the big house, whether the ground was thawed or not.

She took his hand and pulled him to a stop. "I'm okay. *We're* okay. I didn't mean to worry ye." In her heart, she knew this baby would go full term. Her previous pregnancies had ended so very early with her having cramps almost from the start. But this baby had made it well into her second trimester. This baby was strong. Cait hadn't sensed whether the baby was a boy or a girl, but she could feel its fighting spirit. "We're going to see the doctor for *a visit.*"

"Are ye sure?" His worry-lined brow started to ease.

"I'm sure." She squeezed his hand. "I love you."

"I love ye, too," he said hoarsely.

She leaned up and brushed her lips against his. He wrapped an arm around her and they walked the rest of the way to the car.

Two hours later, Graham's grimace suggested he wasn't so thrilled with her now, or the ambush she'd orchestrated with her obstetrician. Cait's young physician explained very clinically that having intercourse with his wife hadn't caused her two earlier pregnancies to terminate. Unfortunately, the doctor took it a step further and suggested that if his fears continued, then maybe Graham should seek counseling. The way he stomped from the office made Cait certain her plan had backfired and it would be a long drive back to Gandiegow.

She chased Graham down the hospital hallway. "I'm sorry." She took his hand.

He stopped and scowled at her. "Ye made me out for the fool."

"I didn't mean to. You weren't listening to me. I thought if the doctor explained then, well . . ." Her eyes fell to the floor. She might've gotten this all wrong. Maybe Graham didn't find her attractive now that she was getting so big. She'd heard some men had a hang-up and would no longer have sex with their wives because they were going to be mothers. She chewed her lip. From the beginning of their marriage, she'd wanted to have Graham's baby more than anything. But not at the cost of losing him.

He tipped her chin up with a finger, the anger on his face gone. "What are ye thinking, lass?"

She searched his eyes. She really didn't want to ask,

but she had to know. "Is it because I'm getting as big as the *Titanic*?"

Graham chuckled and soaked her in. "Ah, lass, wanting ye has never been the problem. You know that." His gaze turned serious. "It's true. I was scared. I just didn't want to hurt you or the babe."

She laid his hand on her belly. "Our bairn is fine."

He rubbed her abdomen and then gazed at her as if she were the only woman in the world for him. Which was amazing since he'd been an international heartthrob for his whole adult life. "Then I don't have to worry?" he said.

"Everything is going to be all right."

At that moment, the babe put its two pence in and kicked . . . *hard*. Cait jumped. Graham jumped. Each stared at the other in wonder.

Graham pulled her close, laughing. "I'll take that as a sign. Ye're right, my luv. Everything is going to be all right."

Chapter Nineteen

Robena tapped on Abraham's front door, but then went in. No one but her father would be home at this hour as Brodie and Harry would be on the boat. She hadn't been to the cottage since Christmas as she didn't feel welcome in his house. But tomorrow, March first, was his birthday and she'd made him a shepherd's pie. She didn't expect an invitation to his birthday dinner, but as always, she wanted to do something special for him just the same.

She went straight to the kitchen to slip the dish into the refrigerator. She left the paper with the cooking instructions on the counter for the men to find. Though the kitchen was nearly spotless, she grabbed the dishrag from the sink and wiped a smudge from the stove.

On her way back to the front door, she stuck her head into the parlor, knowing this would be the hardest and most uncomfortable thing she did today . . . speak to her father.

Abraham was in his wingback chair, staring across the room as if he were looking upon the North Sea.

"Da?"

He looked up. "What are ye doing here?"

Aye, uncomfortable. "Tomorrow's yere birthday. I made you a shepherd's pie so you could start celebrating early."

He nodded, then his eyes drifted back to where he'd been staring.

She stepped into the room to see. On the far wall, in a blast of whimsical color, a mural had been painted. The scene was indeed the ocean with many boats sailing in the distance with a large boat in the center. A laughing girl, resembling Hannah, was at the helm, delighted to have the North Sea as her playground. Robena turned back to her father. "Who?"

"Harry. He's been working on it for the past week, but keeping it covered so I couldn't see. When I came down this morning, there it was. An early birthday present. He's a good lad."

Robena's shepherd's pie seemed like a lark compared to Harry's artistry. She wanted to remove it from the refrigerator and feed it to Dominic's pig.

"What's wrong?" Abraham stared at her as if this was the first time he'd noticed his only daughter.

Everything. She looked down at her hands, feeling as inadequate as she had when she was nine years old. She was ashamed, too. She should be happy her father received such an amazing and thoughtful gift from his young boarder.

"Sit," he said. "I've something to say."

She exhaled and shuffled farther into the room. When she was here in this cottage, she didn't recognize herself. At home with her husband, she was a force to be reckoned with . . . Keith had said it many times with love in his eyes.

She sat on the far end of the sofa, not sure what her da wanted from her.

Abraham stood and walked steadily to sit near her. He really was feeling better and she was glad of it.

"Robena," he started, but then he stopped, looking down at his liver-spotted hands. Hands that had made a living for her and Richard when they were children. "This isn't easy for me."

She didn't have the fortitude to question what he was saying, so she remained quiet.

"I haven't been a good da to ye."

She opened her mouth—not sure what she was going to say—but he held up his hand.

"I never minded what I said around you and I should've. Around both ye and Richard and the boys. I'm sorry for it." Da went quiet.

She didn't know how to respond. "I'm not sure what ye're speaking of."

Da took her hand and squeezed it. The feeling was foreign. She couldn't remember him ever holding her hand or giving her a hug in her life. She always thought they were just one of those families who didn't show their affection. But when she'd had Brodie, she'd smothered him with hugs, kisses, and love. In the end, it hadn't mattered; their relationship was still tattered and torn.

"I spoke ill of yere mother," Abraham said. "It was wrong. A parent should never do that. I'm so sorry."

"But she left us," Robena said, defending the father who had given her and Richard a roof over their head when their mother had abandoned them.

He patted her hand. "Aye, but I clung to my bitterness like a damned barnacle to a ship. I said things about women I never should've uttered."

Robena remembered him once damning all women to hell.

Abraham wiped at his eyes. "I regret every word of it. While I've been sick and unable to do anything, I had lots of time to think. While I was still, I began to recognize all the damage I'd done. Especially to ye."

She looked into her father's withered face. She saw kindness and love. Shock kept her from reacting.

"Forgive me," he said hoarsely.

"Ah, Da." Tears sprang to her eyes and rolled down her face.

Abraham put his arms around her, hugging her. "I was a damned fool. I'm so proud ye're my daughter. The best of us all, ye are."

As he patted her back and Robena cried, she felt the pain of her childhood begin to slip away. "I love ye, Da. I really do." She'd never said that to him before, because she never thought she could.

"I love ye, too, daughter. Ye're loyal and trustworthy. Ye make me proud to be yere da."

Leap Year Day was a big deal in Gandiegow. Rachel was sitting next to her sewing machine, listening to the women around her who were scheming and planning for tonight's dance. Rachel was trying to keep her head down and stay out of the fray.

The last seven weeks had been hard on her as she moved on with her life. *Baby steps,* she kept telling herself. She saw Brodie here and there, but never close enough for them to speak.

She'd kept busy with Hannah, always staying focused on this new phase in their life. She was determined to heal her broken heart, and on good days, she thought she was making progress.

Rachel gazed down at the nearly completed Gandiegow by the Sea quilt, as Brodie had named it. The old Rachel would've been making the quilt for him because he'd shown such interest in the drawing. But *new* Rachel was finishing it for herself. She'd come a long way, learning to focus on the blessings instead of what she'd lost.

She glanced around at the women of Quilting Central and was grateful for every one of them. *Even Deydie.*

The old woman was becoming much easier to get along with since she and Cait had made up. But *poor Cait*; Deydie wasn't letting her lift a finger to do anything.

There were many blessings for Rachel to count, too. Tuck had become a good friend, spending time with her and Hannah a couple times a week, and bringing Glenna along when he did. Tuck didn't have a crush on Rachel; he'd been using her and she didn't mind . . . not at all. Andrew and Moira, being newlyweds, needed alone time. It was easier to claim he had plans with Rachel than to admit he was getting Glenna and himself out of their hair for a couple of hours.

Rachel knew the town was gossiping about her and Tuck, but she didn't care. It was for a good cause. But she did worry about him. Tuck had a long road ahead to win over the villagers as they still didn't accept him. She suspected that teaching at the quilt retreats had greased her way into the community.

Her greatest blessing, though, was her daughter. Hannah was healthy and happy, and her little girl loved being part of Gandiegow. Harry's mural depicted exactly how much her daughter belonged here. Hannah's latest accomplishment was to join Sadie's book club for kids, as she was beginning to read. Hannah adored the Gandiegow Fish quilt when Rachel finished it. Guzzy was given a new home—a decorated shoebox that sat next to Hannah's bed in case she needed a guzzy fix in the middle of the night. Her Gandiegow Fish quilt had taken guzzy's place and was now dragged all over town.

Rachel looked down and smiled as she pulled the needle through the last stitch of the Gandiegow by the Sea quilt. There was no fanfare for it being done, but there should have been for the journey the tartan scraps had traveled.

The fabric had been transformed from a pile of left-overs from the generous quilters into something beautiful and meaningful. Rachel had sewn in her own journey—putting her love and loss into every stitch. In the process, she had been transformed, too. Much wiser than the woman who'd come to Scotland for Christmas. More mature. Much more realistic. There was only one thing left to do to make her transformation complete . . . *return the locket.* Maybe she shouldn't have held on to it for the last two months, but she was feeling stronger . . . and ready. She'd stuck the locket in her pocket this morning, intending to find Brodie today and give it back. This last act would free Rachel from her shattered dreams.

Bethia approached with a huge smile on her face. "Och, lass." She took a corner of the finished quilt and held it up. "'Tis amazing what ye did with a few scraps." She looked Rachel square in the eye. "A million others might have given up on the bits of fabric, but a true quilter believes in *second chances.* For the fabric . . . and the quilter."

The words hit Rachel in the stomach . . . like the swing coming back and walloping her when she wasn't looking. *But I'm done with second chances!* She wanted to tell Bethia that quilters believed in moving past the pain of the pricking of the needle and the cut from the scissors.

Deydie waddled over and took another corner, examining the stitches. "It turned out well. So have ye, Rachel. Ye're quite the quilter." Deydie gazed at her as if she was proud.

Rachel's mouth hung open. Surely she hadn't heard correctly. But Bethia seemed as shocked as she was.

"Stop yere gaping." Deydie bobbed her head. "We better get to the grand dining room. I put Bonnie in charge of the decorations and she might need our help."

Rachel smiled as the old softy propped her broom by the door and left.

Since coming to Gandiegow, Deydie had made Rachel jump through a lot of hoops, but now it felt worth it. The two of them seemed to have reached an understanding, and now Rachel felt like one of Gandiegow's quilting ladies.

"Ready?" Bethia said, pointing at the door.

Sinnie was retrieving her jacket from a hook. She handed over Rachel and Bethia's as well. The three of them headed to the restaurant, too.

The entrance overflowed with people heading inside to help with preparations for tonight's dance. Rachel and her companions took their place in line for their turn to carry items upstairs.

"The New Year's Eve dance wasn't this busy. Is this dance a big deal?" Rachel asked.

"Oh, it is," Sinnie said. "The Leap Year Day *céilidh* is grand fun. It brings all the men together in one spot." Sinnie, normally quiet, acted as if she liked to watch the men squirm.

"Leap Year Day in the States isn't really celebrated," Rachel said to Sinnie and Bethia. "Unless, of course, it's your birthday that only comes around once every four years."

Sinnie gawked at her and laughed good-naturedly. "I can't imagine. As you can tell, in Gandiegow it's a huge affair. Some of the women have been planning for months."

"There'll be lasses coming in from the countryside," Bethia said. "Even some lads who work at Spalding Farm and live in the outlying crofts will head into the village; nice blokes who want to marry."

Rachel nodded. "I've heard talk of the marriage proposals at Quilting Central." The gulf between the sexes, over the last several weeks, had widened, men and women settling into their own separate camps. "Did anyone else notice that the men are scarce today?" Rachel was curious if the guys would boycott the dance and the only ones left would be the disappointed women.

Brodie fluttered through her mind, just like her wishful thinking from the old days, but she pushed his image away.

"Aye. The men are hiding out." Sinnie laughed again. "Staying off the radar."

Rachel had observed as the single women's anticipation had grown, the bachelors had been grumbling more than usual.

Bethia nodded sympathetically. "The *poor dears*. They're trying to avoid the marriage proposals."

"And paying the lasses when they refuse," Sinnie interjected.

Their turn came up and they each grabbed a covered dish and headed for the stairs.

"How much money are we talking about?" Rachel asked.

"Five pounds a refusal," Bethia answered. "It's our tradition, ye see."

"It's a bit of fun," Sinnie exclaimed. "Some of the lasses look at it as a way to pad their pockets."

"But ye have to be careful," Bethia warned.

Sinnie glanced toward the head quilter and nodded. "If the man surprises ye and agrees to marry, tradition says we have to go through with it." Her tone was serious. "Ye can't go asking *willy-nilly*, if ye see what I mean."

"But hiding out won't do the *poor dears* any good. All the single men have to come to the *céilidh* whether they want to or not."

Once again, Brodie crossed Rachel's mind. This time

she let him linger in her thoughts as she imagined returning the locket to him.

Bethia smiled at Rachel. "It's going to be quite a
night."

Yes, it will, but Rachel wasn't feeling the giddy eagerness which hung in the air. Returning the locket would
close the door forever to this chapter in her life.

Rachel turned to Sinnie. "And you? How did you
make out on the last Leap Year Day?"

She shook her head. "I was only eighteen. A bit shy.
I asked no one to marry me."

"What about now? Are you going to pop the question?" Rachel had seen Sinnie dancing with Colin at the
New Year's Eve *céilidh* before Hannah got sick.

Sinnie shook her head. "Heavens no. I'm not ready to
marry. Besides, I'm a bit old-fashioned when it comes to
things like that. My sister Rowena thinks I'm daft, but I
want the man to do *the asking.* Ye know, *claim his woman*
and all."

Bethia smiled at her fondly. "Aye."

Rachel nodded, too. She knew exactly what Sinnie
meant. Rachel wanted the same thing, but it hadn't happened. She kept assuring herself the pain would dull over
time.

She also kept the vision of her new beginning ever
present. There was no rule that said she had to have a
man in the picture for her to be happy. Her family portrait was complete with Hannah and herself . . . and of
course, Abraham and Vivienne. Brodie's connection to
Hannah had nothing to do with Rachel. With a smile
plastered on her face, she would continue to endure Hannah recapping her adventures with Brodie—like walks
to the cemetery, more picnics on the parlor floor, and
Brodie helping her catch her first fish. Brodie was doing

an excellent job of being a good relative to Hannah, and at the same time, he was doing an exceptional job of arranging his days so Rachel's path never crossed his.

What we had is in the past, Rachel told herself. Their time at the ruins of Monadail Castle six years ago, the stolen kisses since she'd arrived, and the one night of them making love were tucked away in the farthest reaches of her mind. Memories like those were not to be pulled out and examined a hundred times a day.

Besides, hadn't she kept very busy over the last eight weeks? The Kilts and Quilts retreats were a godsend—one in January and one last week. Rachel had taught her Gandiegow Fish quilt at each, but her main responsibility was to care for the quilting dorms and their occupants. The work felt familiar and good; also, it made her more a part of the community. But Rachel's other activity was the one which caused her the greatest excitement.

Local contractor Mr. Sinclair would break ground on her B and B in April—the actual day would depend upon the weather. The supplies were ordered and laborers lined up. Gandiegow had really gotten involved. Everywhere Rachel went, this person or that was sharing their opinions on what her place should be and how she should run it. Especially the quilters with whom she spent the majority of her time. Rachel appreciated their input, but in the end, she would have the business she wanted, plus she would have the home she always dreamed of for her and Hannah.

"I'll head back downstairs for another load," Rachel said to Sinnie and Bethia. But when she reached the restaurant, she never expected Brodie to be there, sitting by the window, gazing out at the setting sun.

She paused to take him in, the features she knew so well—the breadth of his body, his hair the color of mahogany curling at his shoulders, and the solemn dark expression encompassing his face. She could get lost staring at him. She could get lost loving him forever. But that time in her life was over. Without giving herself a chance to change her mind, Rachel reached in her pocket, pulled out the locket, and approached the man she had mistakenly believed would be her future.

Chapter Twenty

B rodie never took for granted the beauty of a setting sun. Every fisherman understood the meaning behind a sunset. The Almighty was reassuring them, delivering one last message before putting them into darkness for the night—the sun would indeed rise again tomorrow. This evening's view was extraordinary. Extra bright, full of deep shades of orange and yellow, a spectacular splash of color across the sky. As if for visual interest, a low thunderhead partially covered the sun. Maybe it wasn't for visual effect at all; maybe He was giving them all another message. The clouds and storms were what made life meaningful, for without them, we wouldn't know beauty at all.

Hell, Brodie thought, *I'm being awfully maudlin.*

Truthfully, he'd been in a foul mood for weeks. He'd settled into it the way he'd settled into the other undesirable mind-sets he'd acquired. It was as if all his unforgiveness had stacked up, one upon the other, and was crushing him.

When he came in, he was the only man in the restaurant. All the single blokes didn't think it was safe to be out in the open today. But Brodie didn't give a shit about Leap Year Day, the dance tonight, or the four proposals he'd received already. Bonnie had knocked on Abraham's door first this morning. Brodie had given her a fiver and sent her on her way.

He shut his eyes and ran a hand through his hair. Could a man live like this forever? He honestly didn't care about anything anymore. He could no longer hear Rachel's plea, *Love me, Brodie.* It was almost as if it had never happened.

"I—I . . ." came a most familiar voice a foot away.

He spun around and Rachel was there. For one crazy moment, less than a split second actually, he wondered—*or hoped?*—was she going to take advantage of Leap Year Day and make this proposal number five?

But then he took in her face—every line, every nuance—and saw the pain pour out of her. He wanted to erase the hurt by holding her, but he had no right. She was with Tuck now. He stood, not sure what to do next, but then his eyes fell on the black velvet bag in her hand, the one the locket had been in . . . *is in.* For she hadn't worn the locket in two months.

She held it out. "I need to return this to you. I should've given it back a long time ago." Her wounded eyes and the regret in her voice spoke the unspoken . . . *I never should've taken the locket in the first place.*

For a moment, he was paralyzed, the locket in between them. He couldn't stay like that forever, but he couldn't stretch his hand out to her either . . . *for that would mark the end.*

Finally, with the strength of a hundred fishermen, he unclutched his fist and offered his palm. She didn't drop the locket in, but gently placed it in his hand, as if it was a baby bird.

Stupidly, he left his hand out as if he was offering it back, or giving her a chance to change her mind. He didn't know which. They both stared at it for a long moment.

"Rachel . . ." His whispered plea came too late. She was hurrying out the door.

Bonnie stepped into the grand dining room's restroom, not for a breather, but to check her list. She sat in one of the comfortable chairs and pulled the paper from her cleavage. She marked off Wylie, Mac, and Kolby and added their pounds to the total for the day. Aye, she'd lined her pockets, starting with Brodie first thing this morning, but her list was dwindling . . . and she wasn't getting any younger. A lass wanted a man to take care of her in her old age. She wished Kit the matchmaker had some foresight to bring her bachelors in this year instead of mentioning it would be fun to do it for the next Leap Year Day.

Bonnie tapped the next name on the list and grinned. Though Lochie had been sweet on her since they were teens, she hadn't given him much notice until one of Kit's clients from America chose Lochie to be hers. It was amazing how his positive attributes had become clearer when another lass wanted him. He was pretty good on the guitar and his voice wasn't half bad. He could dance better than most of the fishermen in the village, and he always made Bonnie laugh on even her worst days. Of course, Lochie didn't have Brodie's good looks or Graham's fortune, but he was a decent fellow. Bonnie had thought Lochie and the American lass would get married for sure, but then she'd left and Lochie was back to staring at Bonnie as if she was the prettiest lass in the world. *Aye. The man definitely has some good attributes.*

"Bonnie! Git out here!" Deydie hollered from the other side of the restroom door.

Can't a lass get a moment to herself?

Bonnie secured her list between her breasts and stood. The decorations were nearly done, the room magical, so the old quilter shouldn't have any complaints. More than anyone, Bonnie wanted everything to be perfect tonight to prove she'd done a good job of being in charge. To that end, she had to be perfect as well. She'd make it clear to Deydie that she needed to get home to doll up for the *céilidh* . . . so when she returned, Lochie would be there, setting up with the band.

She held her head high, ready to take on Deydie, and stepped from her temporary sanctuary. But she stopped short at the hushed dining room, and then there was the strum of a guitar.

Her eyes landed on who produced the beginning of the familiar song. Lochie sat ten feet away on a stool, instrument propped on his lap, and his fingers making magic with the melody. His eyes, though, were gazing at her.

He began to sing. "*You . . . are so beautiful . . . to me.*"

Something unfamiliar came over her and she felt shy. She chewed her lip, but couldn't look away as Lochie sang to her.

"*You're everything I hoped for . . .*"

As he sang on, she realized the village had gathered around them, a cocoon. She'd come to Gandiegow as a teenager, an outsider. Slowly over the years, because of the kindness of her protector, Mrs. Coburn, Bonnie had been included more and more. But it was today, when Deydie put her in charge of the decorations, that Bonnie knew she'd finally become a full-fledged member of the community. Maybe it was Lochie singing to her, or maybe it was the village around them, but something changed, making Bonnie melt. She'd never felt softer and safer in her whole life.

The song ended and Lochie handed his guitar to Coll. He walked straight to Bonnie, clearly determined, and more attractive than she'd ever seen him before.

"What do ye say?" Lochie took her hand, intertwining their fingers, and waited.

The room was hushed with quiet anticipation. Bonnie glanced at each one of the quilting ladies standing around her. Some of them nodded; others showed their approval with their smiles and their eyes. It was not that Bonnie needed their permission, but it felt good to know she had it.

She gazed at Lochie and the rest of the room fell away. She saw her future. One of laughter and companionship. Perhaps sitting with Lochie while he strummed his guitar. She wouldn't be alone anymore. It was a future she would like very much. A smile spread across her face . . . and into her whole body.

Bonnie squeezed his hand. "Will ye marry me?"

He laughed. "Aye." The room broke into applause as he picked her up and spun her, as if she were a wee thing and not a tall lass. "I've been waiting forever for ye to ask."

Brodie dropped back into his seat at the restaurant with the locket still in his hand. He'd screwed this up, but he just didn't see how he could've done anything differently. He pulled the locket from the bag and set it on the table in front of him as if it were a million years ago and he was in secondary school biology class . . . readying himself for a dissection.

Before he could analyze anything, the door to the restaurant opened. Automatically, he turned to see if it was Rachel, but as he cranked his head around, he caught sight of his mother.

Robena was as sharp as a hawk, seeing two steps in front of everyone else. As a lad, Brodie never got away with anything. Her eyes flicked down to the table. He saw the locket register on her face and then she laid a hand on Freda's arm. "Go on without me." The crew went to the stairwell and up.

His mother gave him a sad look. *Aye, two steps ahead of even me.* The realization was still sinking in of what he'd lost. No, what he'd given up, if he was being honest.

Mum came to the table, pointing at the other chair. "May I?" The air between them was always too polite for Brodie to feel comfortable, but he didn't know how to change it either.

He reached over and pulled the chair out for her.

His mother stared at the necklace that had once been hers, as if she was watching an egg hatch. "Have I ever told ye the story of the locket?" She shook her head, answering her own question. "No. I never did, did I?" She gazed up at him, giving him the same intense study she'd given the piece of jewelry. "I couldn't tell ye, Brodie, not back then." She reached her hand out to take his, but pulled back as if remembering she could get burned.

Silence settled over the table. His mother seemed to be struggling, and Brodie, the horrible son that he was, he let her.

Robena smiled as if suddenly remembering the happiest of thoughts. "The locket is magical."

He wasn't expecting that. "I don't necessarily agree." It had only caused him grief.

"The locket was the way I knew yere da truly loved me." Her eyes misted. "He was my best friend when we were kids. We played together. We shared our secrets . . . and our grievances. He always had my back. He knew what it was like for me to grow up with yere grandda." She looked away, her cheeks reddening as if she'd said too much.

"I know, Mum."

Her eyes came back to him. "I guess ye do."

Brodie felt the need to defend his grandfather. "But Grandda has changed. Really he has."

"I know." Absently, she reached for the locket and toyed with the chain.

Brodie nodded to her hands. "How did the locket convince you?"

Her eyes were filled with warmth for him. "As I said, yere da and I were friends. When we were barely adults, yere da told me how he planned to marry me. I laughed at the thought. I knew everything about him, all the childish things he'd ever done. He knew all of mine. He was still a lad in my mind. I hadn't realized he'd grown into a man. I hadn't seen the changes." She smiled, holding back happy tears.

Brodie remembered how much his mum and da adored each other. Sometimes, they'd ignore him because they were so consumed with one another. He never minded it, though. With them being so much in love, he felt safe and secure.

Brodie leaned forward, feeling like a kid who had been left with a cliffhanger. "How did Da convince ye?" He needed this piece of the puzzle like he needed air and water and food.

"He told me of the money he'd saved from fishing, of the cottage he was going to rent for us, how he could support and take care of me. All the things a good man should be doing if he was to ask a lass to marry him." Robena opened the locket and gazed at the pictures. "But I was a young woman who had the romantic dreams of love. I didn't care about whether he could support me or not. It never occurred to me that love could come from friendship. I'd never heard of such a thing. But then yere da presented me with the locket. He'd put our pictures inside. He told me he loved me, couldn't imagine a life without me. These were all the things a young woman needed—the romance of a locket, words of love. I'd always loved yere da, but that moment changed who we were together." She shook her head. "No. It only made us into more." She shut the locket and scooted it back to the center.

Brodie was subdued by the story. He pushed the locket back to his mother. "Ye should have it. As a keepsake."

She laid her hand over his, stopping him. "The locket was magical before. It can be again." She squeezed his hand. "I don't need it. Yere da is in my heart. He'll always be there."

"But I thought you forgot all about da," Brodie blurted. Because the polite air between them had been broken and replaced with a raw truthfulness, he barreled on and said the rest. "Da was barely gone when ye married Keith. Mum, how could you?" It was an accusation, not a question. All the anger rushed back into him, fresh as a live fish pulled from the water . . . and gasping for air.

Brodie tried to pull his hand away, but she clamped down harder.

"Oh, Brodie, it's my fault."

He agreed.

"This is way overdue. I should've explained. I should've told ye everything back then. But I was trying to protect you."

"Protect me from what?" He felt hot and needed air. Why wouldn't she let him go?

She squeezed his hand and then surprised him by freeing her grasp. "I had no way of supporting you and me. I had to marry quickly." Her voice dropped and she glanced toward Claire, who was wiping down the counter. "Ye remember, don't you, the women and children who left Gandiegow after the *Rose* went down? I'm so glad Claire found her way back. But ye see, don't ye, so many didn't return to Gandiegow. Gone from their homes. Their community. From the people who knew them and loved them."

Brodie had been surprised to find Claire back in the village when he returned home from his six-year absence.

"So many widows left for the city to find work. But I couldn't bear for ye to lose yere town, yere grandda, and Joe, right after losing yere da. I saw a way to stay. I asked Keith if he would marry me so you wouldn't have to leave."

"*You* asked Keith to marry ye?" Brodie always assumed the man had swooped in and taken advantage of his mother when she was hurting and vulnerable. But he should've known. His mother was always two steps ahead.

"I asked Keith and made him agree to live in town so nothing would change. He did that for ye and more."

"Like what?" Guilt washed over Brodie, ratcheting away at how he'd felt justified in not forgiving his mother.

"Keith is a good man. When ye wouldn't come live with us, it was Keith who sorted through things and considered yere feelings." She paused for a second as if the memory was from yesterday and not two decades old. "Keith was concerned for my da. Abraham lost a son . . . *my brother.* Keith could see how Abraham needed ye and Joe there to be with him to see him through."

Brodie never considered that his mom had grieved for her brother Richard. She'd lost two loved ones in the storm, and a pang of hurt tore through him. "I'm sorry." His words didn't feel like enough.

"Aye," she acknowledged, but then moved on. "Keith knew how much fishermen made. Do ye think ye would've had all you had, or that Joe would've been able to go to university on my da's income alone? Nay. Keith gave yere grandda room and board . . . for both ye and Joe."

Brodie's mouth hung open. He shut it.

She stared at him, waiting patiently until it sank in.

"I never knew," Brodie finally said, feeling so ashamed.

He'd been unkind to Keith in his mind. He'd accused his mother of wretched things in his thoughts. He'd been wrong. So wrong.

"I love Keith," his mother said boldly. "It didn't happen all at once. It wasn't the romantic love of a young woman receiving a locket, a love built on friendship. My love for Keith was built on necessity . . . and the love for my son. It developed over time. But I love Keith with all my heart. Just like I still love yere da."

In that instant, Brodie was deluged with understanding. His idea of love expanded. His perception of the truth shifted. Forgiveness overwhelmed him as tears filled his eyes.

He jumped up, embarrassed by the flood of emotion, but mostly because the weight of unforgiveness had been lifted. He pulled his mother to her feet and hugged her, dying inside for how much he loved this woman. She'd done everything for him. He started to beat himself up—he'd been an ass, a complete ass—but God whispered in his ear, *Forgive yourself, too.*

"I love you, Mum."

"I love ye, too."

"I'm so happy ye have Keith." Brodie pulled away to look into his mother's tearing eyes. "I should've come to live with ye. There's so much I should've done." There wasn't enough time to list all the things he'd gotten wrong over the years. "I'm so ashamed of all the time I've wasted. I regret all the things we could've shared. I ask ye to forgive me."

"It's done. Forgotten." She kissed his cheek.

He gazed at her, stunned with her generosity. "But how can ye forgive me so quickly?"

She gave him that knowing smile, the one she'd used on him from the time he was a wee lad. "I'm a mother. It's what we do."

He hugged her again, and as he did, another revelation hit him. *Forgiving feels so incredibly good that I want to do it again.* Rachel appeared in his mind, and the partridge sang. He'd slowly been forgiving her, but the rest of it fell away now. She'd only been trying to do the right thing, as Grandda had pointed out. Brodie couldn't fault her for that. He couldn't blame her for moving on and giving up on him either. He loved her and only wanted the best for her now. If Tuck could make her happy, then he would learn to be happy with her decision.

His mother snapped him out of his vision. She reached for the locket and placed it in his hand. "Ye'll make good use of this? Ye'll not waste the magic?"

He couldn't make any promises. Brodie latched on to the locket as if it were a life-preserver which had come too late. "Thank you."

"Will ye be all right?" Robena glanced toward the stairs as if only just remembering a broom might be waiting for her backside if she didn't go help the others.

"Aye. I'm better. Much better."

His mother left him, and once again, he sat down with the locket, having a totally different perspective. The locket really was magic; it brought him and his mother back together. He opened it to reveal his parents. *So very young.* Maybe Brodie should replace the pictures with his mother and Keith and give it back to his mum. This would be a tangible way to show them that he supported their union, though the gesture was many years late.

Brodie gently removed the pictures of his da and mum. "What the hell." Two other pictures had been placed behind them.

On the left side was the picture from Rachel's first day back in town, when they'd taken the family picture, but it was only of the two of them. Rachel was facing forward, but Brodie wasn't. He was staring at her and his longing was clear.

He examined the other photo. *Christmas Day.* He remembered how he didn't want to sit for another family picture, but Hannah and Grandda had insisted. This photo had been cropped, also. In this picture, she was staring at him; he'd been oblivious to what was plain for him to see now. She longed for him, too.

His eyes went from one side to the other, another picture becoming clearer . . . the big picture. They looked so right together—he and Rachel. He could see them as a family. He loved Hannah so *verra* much, as if she was his own. But more important, he loved Rachel. It had always been her. *Always.*

"I've only been kidding myself that I could get over ye," he said to her picture.

Suddenly, he didn't care that she was with Tuck. He jumped to his feet. He carefully slipped his parents' picture into the pocket over his heart, over the tattoo of the partridge that guarded everything he knew to be true. Brodie had to take a chance. He had to find Rachel. She'd loved him once. Maybe she could love him again.

Chapter Twenty-one

Rachel sought refuge in Thistle Glen Lodge, sitting in front of the empty fireplace. She'd given the locket back, but hadn't anticipated feeling the loss of Brodie all over again. Suddenly, Ailsa and Aileen came bustling through the door.

"Rachel?" Ailsa said.

"Are ye here?" Aileen echoed.

Rachel closed her eyes. "Yes." She stood as if she'd just finished with an inventory of the clean towels.

"Deydie wants ye back at the grand dining room," Ailsa said.

"Claire said that ye'd left," Aileen added.

Rachel picked up her notebook, the one Brodie had given her. "I have some things I have to do. For the bed and breakfast," she clarified, hoping to sound convincing.

Ailsa turned to her sister. "What should we tell Deydie?"

Aileen looked worried.

Rachel felt sorry for them and reached out, touching both of their arms. "Tell Deydie I won't be long." She held up the notebook to remind them. Then to get them moving toward the door, she walked that way as well and went outside as if she had a meeting set with Mr. Sinclair.

The three of them stood on the stoop, looking at one another.

"I'll be there in a while." Rachel needed some time to pull herself together. She walked toward the businesses as if she was on a mission as Ailsa and Aileen hustled in the direction of the restaurant.

Once on the walkway, Rachel glanced around for another place to hide. She couldn't handle decorating for the dance tonight or listen to any more hopeful chatter about proposing. Returning the locket to Brodie had felt so final. She needed a quiet moment alone to let her fate sink in, without the company of people who were certain true love existed and won out in the end.

She heard voices from behind her. Not wanting any more of Deydie's crew to track her down, or to hear any of the proposals that were happening all over town, Rachel opened the door to the church and stepped inside, grateful this building was kept unlocked, too. The building hummed with calmed stillness, which drew her in. She treaded softly into the sanctuary, nearly to the front, and chose a pew on the far left.

As she sat, peace and understanding bathed her as surely as the sunlight streamed through the stained glass window and shone on the altar. God was sending her a clear sign that she and Hannah were going to be all right. She'd had glimpses of it all along, but now the straight path was revealed.

The community, like the sun, would be a beacon for them, showing them the way. She took a moment to bask in the revelation. She smiled; this was what it was like to be part of a tight-knit community. *Maybe I should get back*. But as she was about to stand, the church door creaked open.

"In here?" a deep voice said, the door slamming shut.

Rachel should've made herself known to them, but instinctively she crouched down so as not to be seen.

"Aye. In here," said a female who sounded like Grace Armstrong. "There's a question I've been waiting to ask ye."

"Oh?"

Rachel leaned out, peered up the aisle, and saw Grace and Casper standing at the entrance to the sanctuary. Since New Year's Eve, the two of them had been inseparable and the talk of the town. Gandiegow had gotten behind the twosome, and Rachel agreed—they made a nice pair. Also, there was something reassuring about a mature couple finding love. It gave her hope that her mother would find someone special one day. Rachel looked again, but before she could stand up and say, *You're not alone,* Casper was planting a kiss on Grace. Rachel squatted down farther, kicking herself for being here. *Maybe they won't stay long.*

Grace laughed. "Okay, Reverend, enough of that."

"What do ye need to ask me?" But he sounded as if he knew.

In that second, Rachel knew, too. She'd come in here to hide from this day, but God had delivered her a front row seat to one of Gandiegow's cherished traditions. She couldn't help peeking out again.

Grace took Casper's hands. "Since the first moment I met you, I knew ye were going to be someone special in my life."

"Aye. Me, too."

"As ye know, I was a wee slow in accepting it, but I'm not backing away from it now." She stepped closer to him. "Casper MacGregor, I love you. Will ye marry me?"

"Oh, Grace, of course I will." He hugged her. "Ye know how much I love you. I've wanted ye to be my wife from nearly the moment I laid eyes on you. But I knew ye needed time."

"Thank you for being patient."

Casper kissed her cheek and hugged her one more time. "Are ye ready to tell our families?"

"Mine first," she said. "I want my sons to know how happy I am."

They hurried from the building. Rachel waited until she was certain they were gone before standing. She should go to the grand dining room this minute before someone else snuck in here for another proposal.

But as she made her way up the aisle, she realized there was one more thing she had to do. Yes, she'd given Brodie the locket, but that hadn't given her complete closure. If her heart was going to say good-bye to Brodie forever, then she had to visit the place where she'd kissed him for the first time.

The place where she'd fallen in love with him.

The place where the dream had begun.

She picked up her notebook and headed to the ruins of Monadail Castle.

Brodie hurried down the walkway feeling desperate. He'd looked everywhere for Rachel. Both quilting dorms. The General Store. His cottage, in case she stopped in to see Abraham. But she wasn't there. When he popped into Quilting Central, he had to hurry out. Rowena rushed toward him with proposing in her eyes, and dammit, he didn't have time. As he slammed the door behind him and sped away, he vowed to give a fiver to Rowena later, because right now he had to find Rachel. Almost as a last straw, he stopped in at the surgery to see if Rachel had fallen and hurt herself. Doc wasn't there, which was best because Brodie wasn't sure how he would've explained his frantic behavior.

He was ready to start going door to door, but as he passed the kirk, the answer came to him. He knew where she must be. *Monadail Castle*. He ran through town to the path that led up to the ruins. As soon as he reached the summit, his eyes searched and found her, sitting under the archway. His heart beat faster. His chest expanded. Life was good. As he drew near, he saw the Celtic notebook he'd given her. Careful not to disturb the family of partridges that nibbled at the snow, he quietly made his way over to where she sat.

As he got closer, he realized she wasn't sketching the birds or designing a quilt, but was instead working on a sign:

PARTRIDGE HOUSE
BED & BREAKFAST

"When does it open?" he asked, thinking he'd caught her by surprise.

But not *his Rachel*. She kept her head down and kept drawing. "This coming summer. I hope."

"Aye. Perfect timing." He came closer.

She glanced up at him warily. "Why *perfect timing*?" She seemed more skittish than the birds. He was afraid if he made one wrong step now, she might fly away.

He sat down on the rock wall and scooted closer to her. "I've been contemplating moving out of Grandda's."

"Harry cramping your style?" she asked.

"Aye." Sure. The kid could be the perfect excuse. "I'll be looking for a place to live, ye know." He nodded toward her notepad. "Maybe there'll be room for me at Partridge House."

She shook her head, not looking up. "Booked solid. You should try the room over the pub."

This wasn't going well. He'd been dismissed. But he needed this one chance to state his case. If she still wanted Tuck after he was done telling her how he felt, then Brodie would back out. Forever. "Look, Rachel, I want to be serious for a minute."

She glanced up at him, but then back at her paper, sketching a large partridge next to the lettering. "Fire away."

He pulled the locket from his pocket. "I know ye're with Tuck now—"

Her head shot up. "What?"

Brodie continued on. "I shouldn't be horning in on another man's woman, but dammit, Rachel, all bets are off when it comes to love."

She gaped at him and then at the locket he held out.

"Take it back." His voice was hoarse, raw with what he felt for her. The partridge on his chest was beating its wings, making his pulse run rapid. He wanted a second chance. If only she would say, *Love me, Brodie.* "I fixed the locket how it should be. Look inside."

He took her hand and laid it in her palm. He watched as she touched a finger to their pictures and waited to see if she saw what he saw.

He inched even closer, wanting to touch her, but he spoke instead. Now was the time for him to tell her everything. "I see it now. We're a family. You, me, and Hannah. I was stupid for letting a tiny mistake happen . . . like ye marrying my cousin." He gave her weak smile.

"You made the mistake? I—"

"Aye. It was my fault." He took a chance and captured her hand. When she didn't pull away, he felt encouraged. The partridge on his chest began to relax. "I should've been clear. I should've told ye I loved you. I should've told ye that you couldn't marry Joe. I should've explained how I had the means to support you. I should've gone with ye to tell Joe, yere mother, and everyone in town that you were meant for me, and I for you." Holding her hand wasn't enough. He gathered her into his arms. "I've never stopped loving ye." He searched her eyes, looking for the truth, and then he found it. Right where it had always been.

She rested a hand on his cheek. "I never stopped loving you either. Tuck and I have been nothing more than friends."

He nodded, feeling elated. He could've broken into a song, but he leaned in and kissed her instead.

The kiss was sweet, heavy with promise, and drove away the years they weren't together. Now and the future were the only things that mattered. Their love uniting them for all time.

When the kiss was over, he didn't let go. He should've been content, but he wanted everything. "Rachel, now that we have that settled, ye need to get on with it."

The confusion in her eyes was sincere.

He brushed her hair back. "Isn't there a question ye need to ask me?"

Rachel was giddy with happiness that Brodie loved her. *High on life.* But still foggy from the kiss. "What do you mean?" But the second she spoke, she knew what he was fishing for. She thought about Sinnie and how she wanted her *man to be a man.*

Rachel wanted the same thing. But she wasn't Sinnie. Rachel was a mother.

"Brodie, we should have a serious talk first. A blended family isn't going to be easy." She'd seen what her employees went through with their stepkids and worried about burdening him with extra responsibility. She would have to learn to compromise, too. She suspected Brodie would have to learn how to give a little, also. "I know you love Hannah, but I'm afraid as time goes on that you might resent taking on such an obligation. As you know, Hannah can be a handful. And me, I'm not used to sharing her." Though she'd learned to share a little since coming to Gandiegow.

He nodded, caressing her arm. "Don't worry. I don't expect it to be smooth sailing, lass. We won't always agree. But I'll never resent being by your side. We'll have each other. It can't have been easy for ye to raise Hannah on yere own. But now, you'll have me to lean on. Let me share the load and be a father to Hannah."

"I just want to make sure you're going into this with your eyes wide open and won't have regrets later."

Brodie gazed at her. "I'm done with regrets."

She entwined her hand with his. "I'm done with regrets, too."

They stared at one another, soaking each other in, their six years apart melting into nothingness.

But then his expression changed into a mock frown. "I'm a patient man, lass, but I'm getting weary waiting for ye to ask me that question."

"What question?" she feigned.

He shook his head as if he was disappointed she wasn't quicker on her feet. "It's Leap Year Day. I'm growing older here by the second." He brushed back her hair.

She felt light and airy, playful. "Leap Year Day? Sorry. Doesn't ring a bell."

His mock impatience was turning into real frustration. "Ye know what I'm talking about. I see it in yere eyes. It's a Gandiegow tradition."

Rachel held firm.

Brodie shrugged. "Well, Bonnie was at the cottage first thing this morning, looking to marry me. Rowena, not fifteen minutes ago, was ready to get down on one knee and ask me a certain question."

Rachel's blood boiled, at least momentarily, but she didn't take the bait. "I can understand why." She patted his chest. "You're quite the catch."

He looked horrified and stepped back, dropping his arms.

She gave him a sweet smile. "I hope you're carrying plenty of five-pound notes. From what I hear, you're in hot demand. I'm certain you'll be busy tonight at the dance."

He ran a hand through his hair. "Ye're not going to make me an honest man before then? Ye'll make me endure an evening of marriage proposals?"

"That depends." She looked at him with her eyebrows raised, as if she was waiting.

"On what?"

"I'm an old-fashioned girl, Brodie. I like my man to make the first move."

He guffawed. "Really? Am I to forget that ye kissed me first? A chap doesn't forget a kiss like that."

They both looked up at the archway, the same thought surely crossing their minds. *This is where it all began.*

But then Brodie took the locket from her hand and worked at undoing the clasp. "Turn around."

She did as he said.

He ran a finger along her neck before looping the chain around her. "Rachel, will ye do me the honor of becoming my wife?" He didn't wait for her to answer, but hooked the clasp, as if the locket around her neck was a binding contract.

"I will." She'd waited forever to say those words.

He gently turned her back to face him. "Tomorrow, we'll get a ring."

She kissed him and they held on to each other as if a ring didn't matter.

He pulled away, taking her hand in his, looping their fingers together. "We need to go back now. There's a wee lass who needs me to ask her a question."

"And that is?" A crazy tea party flashed through her

mind. Then other scenes: Seeing from a distance Hannah trussed up in her life vest on the deck of Brodie's boat. Or the two of them dancing in the parlor with Hannah standing on top of his shoes.

Brodie grinned at her. "I need to ask the wee lass if she'll let me change my answer to her previous question. I want a second chance on the position she wants me to fill. I hope she'll still have me."

Rachel squeezed his hand, loving him so much more because he cared about Hannah as much as she did. "I bet she will."

They walked down the bluff hand in hand, ready to tell the whole world, their world—*Gandiegow*—the big news. They were getting married, and their family was going to live happily ever after.

Don't miss Patience Griffin's

The Trouble With Scotland,

available now!
Continue reading for an excerpt.

At twenty-two, Sadie Middleton didn't like zombie movies, but as she stepped off the bus a mile out of Gandiegow, Scotland, she felt like the lead in her own dreadful film. *Sadie of the Dead.* Not some glamourous zombie either, but a plain zombie who wanted to vanish. The other women around her were excited, giddy about their first evening at the quilt retreat. Sadie only felt waylaid. Shell-shocked. Miserable. If she was still at home in North Carolina, she would be sitting on the porch with Gigi, her grandmother, drinking sweet tea and waiting for the July 4th fireworks to begin.

Except they weren't in the U.S.

And Gigi was dead.

The gravel crunched under Sadie's feet as she made her way, along with the other quilters, to the North Sea Valve Company's factory door. Their bus had died and coasted into the parking lot, and they were to wait here until she and the others could be transported into the small town. She leaned against the building, unfolded the printed email, and read it again:

Dear Sadie and Gigi,

Pack your bags! Your team has won the grand prize in the quilt block challenge. Congratulations!

You are coming to Gandiegow! For complete information regarding your Kilts and Quilts Retreat and all-expense paid trip to Scotland, please email us back.

Sincerely,
Cait Buchanan
Owner, Kilts and Quilts Retreat

Having read the note a hundred times, Sadie shoved it back in her pocket. It seemed a cruel joke from the universe—to receive this letter only hours after Gigi's funeral.

At hearing the news about the retreat, her brother Oliver had gone into hyper drive, using his grief to propel him into action. While insisting Gigi would want Sadie to fulfill their dream of a quilt retreat abroad, Oliver had made all the arrangements for Scotland—packing her bags and having her out the door before Sadie knew what had happened. His bullying made the trip feel more like a kidnapping than a prize.

Sadie's grief had immobilized her, made her want to crawl under a quilt and never come out. She waffled between feeling despondent and angry. But the one constant was her guilt for the part she'd played in her grandmother's death.

Her quilted Mondo bag slipped from her shoulder . . . the bag that matched Gigi's that they'd made at their last quilting retreat together. Memories of that glorious weekend were stitched into Sadie, the moments long and meaningful. She pulled the bag up, held it close, and squeezed her eyes shut.

The last twenty-four hours were wearing on her. Sadie was exhausted, depleted. But she had to keep it hidden at all costs. She glanced over at her ever-helpful brother as he assisted the rest of the women off the bus. *Good*.

He was being kept busy. She was sick to death of Oliver fussing over her and telling her what to do.

At that moment, two vans pulled up. A tall, nice-looking man got out of one and a very pregnant strawberry blond got out of the other. As they spoke to the bus driver, the woman handed over her keys to him.

Oliver, who had only just finished unloading the last quilter from the bus, hurried to the couple who'd brought the vans. "Excuse me?"

"Yes," answered the man. From his accent, he clearly was from the States. Texas, perhaps.

Oliver pointed to Sadie. "My sister needs to be in the first group into town."

Embarrassment radiated from her toes to her scalp. *Dammit, Oliver.* Sadie ducked behind another woman as the two newcomers turned in her direction.

"Sure," the man said. "We can take her into Gandie-gow first. I'm Max, by the way."

Oliver introduced himself, too, and unfortunately felt the need to explain further. "My sister is ill."

The couple's curious eyes transformed into compassion. The women around Sadie spun on her with pity as well, staring at her as if they hadn't just spent the last couple of hours with her on the bus in quasi-normal companionship. To them, Sadie had been another quilter, a fellow-retreat goer. Now, she wasn't. She was to be flooded with sympathy. No longer included. On the outside because of her disease.

Oliver spoke to Sadie but pointed to the vans. "Get in. They'll get you to town." He'd said it as if Sadie's problem was with her ears and not her kidneys.

Without a word and anxious to hide her red face, Sadie walked to the van with a compliant exterior. On the inside, though, she was seething. She climbed in and took a seat in the back. A minute later, others were climbing in as well. No one sat next to her, leaving her alone to frown out the window at her overly responsible brother.

The couple climbed into the front of the van and began chatting with the other quilters. Sadie found out more about them and their connection to Gandiegow— Max and Pippa were engineers at the North Sea Valve Company and newlyweds. They kept up a steady conversation, asking the quilters about themselves, and explaining about the upcoming wedding between their Episcopal priest and a town favorite. Mercifully they left Sadie alone.

A few minutes later, when they reached Gandiegow's parking lot, a group of men and women were waiting for them.

"We're a closed community," Pippa explained. "No cars within the village. Everyone is here to help carry yere things to the quilting dorms." Sure enough, many of the women had wagons beside them, while the men had their muscles. "Deydie will want everyone at Quilting Central as soon as possible. She's the head quilter and town matriarch." Pippa made it sound as if they better do as Deydie bid or there might be trouble.

One by one, they disembarked from the van. When Sadie got out, a young woman in a plain plum-colored dress with a double-hearted silver brooch moved forward. Next to her was a young girl.

"I'm Moira," the woman said, "and this is my cousin Glenna. We'll help ye get settled into the quilting dorm."

Sadie followed them, immediately pleased with both of her handlers; Moira and Glenna seemed blessedly quiet and shy.

Even though it was early evening, the sun was still in the sky, due to how far north Gandiegow was. They walked through the miniscule town along a concrete path which served as a wall against the ocean with no railings for safety. Moira pointed to where Oliver was to stay, Duncan's Den, and then took Sadie next door to the other quilting dorm, Thistle Glen Lodge. It was nothing more than a bungalow set against the green bluffs of summer which rose nearly straight up at the back of the town.

Glenna shot Sadie a shy glance, then turned to Moira. "Should I let Deydie know that she's made it?"

"Aye. We'll be along shortly," Moira said. The girl ran off between the buildings.

Moira led Sadie inside to the way-too-cheery interior and down the hall to a room with three beds. The decorations were plaid and floral—a little French country on the northeast coast of Scotland—and too optimistic and exuberant for Sadie.

Moira motioned for her to go on in. "You can store yere clothes in the armoire. The kitchen is stocked with tea, coffee, and snacks. But all yere meals are provided either at Quilting Central or the restaurant. I can bring ye scones and tea in the morns, if ye like, though."

Sadie set her Mondo bag on one of the beds. Moira was nice, but Sadie only wanted to be left alone to crawl under the quilt and hibernate until life wasn't so crushing. And she was so very tired. People didn't understand that though she looked fine, she was often exhausted and feeling generally cruddy . . . her new norm. Patients with Chronic Kidney Disease, CKD, usually weren't diagnosed until it was too late, already in Stage Four like herself, and in need of a kidney transplant.

She'd only found out last month. Gigi had promised to be with Sadie every step of the way. But Gigi was gone, leaving Sadie to deal with everything alone. Oliver couldn't; he had his own life, his cyber-security consulting business. He didn't have time to sit with her while she had her blood drawn week after week. He couldn't put his life on hold while Sadie waited for the day to come when the doctors would move her to the active transplant list.

Sadie looked up, realizing she'd slipped into herself again, something she'd been doing a lot ever since her diagnosis.

Moira, though, seemed to understand and went to the doorway. "I'll give ye a few minutes to settle in. Then Deydie expects all the quilters at Quilting Central for introductions and the quilting stories." It was another warning that Sadie shouldn't dawdle.

She jumped at the sound of hard knocking at the front door.

Moira put her hand up, either to calm Sadie's frazzled nerves or to stop her from going for the door herself. "I'll see who it is."

Sadie dropped down beside her bag and smoothed her hand over the Pinwheel quilt that covered the bed. A minute later she heard her brother's exasperating voice at the entrance. Heavy footsteps came down the hall. She thought seriously about crawling out the window to escape what was sure to be more nagging.

She didn't turn to greet him. "What do you want, Oliver?"

"I came to walk you to the retreat. We have to hurry though. One of my clients needs me to hop online and check for a bug."

If only Gandiegow didn't have high speed internet then Oliver wouldn't have been hell-bent on coming to Scotland to keep an eye on me! But her brother's IT business was portable.

Moira saved Sadie. "Don't worry. I'll get her to Quilting Central safely."

He remained where he was. Sadie could feel his gaze boring into her back.

"Go on, Oliver. Your customer is waiting."

She still didn't hear him leave. Sadie rolled her eyes heavenward and heaved herself off the bed. She plastered on a fake smile and faced him. "I'm fine. Really."

"Okay. But if you need me, I'll be next door at Duncan's Den." The other quilting dorm, only a few steps from this one.

Sadie nodded.

Oliver held his phone up as if to show her he was only a call away.

"Come," Moira said. "It's time to meet Deydie and the other quilting ladies."

Oliver pinned one more worried glance on Sadie, then left. She grabbed her bag and a sweater.

Outside, Sadie trudged along, wishing to be anywhere but here.

Moira peeked over at her. "Gandiegow only has sixty-three houses."

"It's very quaint." For the first time, Sadie really looked around. The village arced like a smile facing the ocean, the little stone cottages an array of mismatched teeth, but seemed to fit together. The rounded green bluff loomed at the backs of the houses, a town blocked in, but cozy. Yes, the village was *quaint* with its oceanfront views from nearly every house. But sadness swept over Sadie once again. Gigi would've loved it here, as she'd often reminisced fondly about the small town in Montana along the Bitterroot River where she'd grown up.

Moira stopped in front of a building with a sign that read Quilting Central. "This is it."

Without realizing that she should prepare herself, Sadie opened the door and stepped in. A tidal wave of anxiety hit her, the emotion so overwhelming, she wanted to flee.

The smell of starch.

White and gray-headed women.
Fabric stacked and stashed everywhere.

All the things that reminded her of Gigi. If that wasn't enough to have her bolting for the door, a crowd of women scuttled toward her. She backed up.

One tall, thin, elderly woman clasped her arm, stilling her. "We're so glad ye're here. I'm Bethia."

A short battleax of a woman barreled through to get to Sadie, grabbing her other arm. "I'm Deydie. We've been waiting on ye."

Sadie was short of oxygen. She desperately wanted out.

Gray-haired twins, wearing matching plaid dresses of different colors, stepped in her path. The red plaid one spoke first.

"Sister and I were distraught when we lost our gran."

They knew. Sadie looked at the faces around the room. *They all knew.*

The green-plaided one bobbed her head up and down. "That was many years ago. We've all experienced loss." She gestured toward the crowd. "We understand what ye're going through."

The other whispered loudly to her sister. "But not about the kidney disease."

No! How could he! Sadie wasn't the all-out swearing type, but internally she formed a string of obscenities to sling at her brother that made her cringe.

"Back," Deydie said to the twins. "Give the lass room to breathe and to get her bearings. She's not well."

Well enough to scream!

A thirty-something woman, carrying a baby, made her way to Sadie. "I'm Emma. And this is Angus." She had a British accent, not a Scots like the others. She turned to Deydie. "I should take over, don't you think?"

Deydie nodded vigorously. "Right. Right. It should be ye." The old woman cleared the others away.

"Come sit down," Emma said. "The town can be a bit overbearing. But they mean well." She led Sadie to a sofa.

Deydie called everyone's attention to the front and began welcoming all the quilters.

Emma leaned over. "I'm a therapist. Most people when they're grieving should talk to someone. I wanted to let you know that I'm available if you need me."

A moment ago, Sadie thought the woman had her best interest at heart, but she was like the others, trying to suffocate her, trying to tell her how to deal with her grief. Sadie didn't deserve their attention. Her selfishness had killed her grandmother. She opened her mouth to set the well-meaning therapist straight, but the woman's baby fortuitously spewed down his mother's blouse.

"Excuse me." Emma stood with the little one. "We'll talk later."

Or not.

Emma's leaving should've given Sadie's senses a reprieve, but in some respects, all the women smothering her had been a distraction. The room, *this place*, was too much; she couldn't sit here with a huge group of women reminding her of her grandmother. And with Gigi newly buried. The guilt. The grief . . . everything. Sadie had to get out of here . . . escape!

She looked longingly toward the door, only ten feet away. Everyone was listening to Deydie, finally not focused on her. She stood nonchalantly and walked toward the exit, slowly and with purpose, like she'd left her curling iron on back at the dorm.

Two more steps. She eased the door open so carefully that the bell above the door barely jingled.

She slipped out, gulping in the cool evening air like it was water and she'd been stuck in the desert. But it wasn't enough. The town still felt claustrophobic. She'd do anything to get out of here!

The tide was up and the ocean was slapping itself against the walkway with increasing ferocity and passion. The sea was alive, the waves crashing, telling her to run.

And on the breeze, she heard the strangest thing . . . male voices singing. It was surreal. She followed the sound, heading back in the direction of the parking lot where the van had dropped them off. She stopped outside the first building in town, a pub called The Fisherman where the tune was coming from. The song pulled her up the steps and had her opening the door. As she crossed the threshold, the song came to an end.

The room was mostly filled with men, all sizes. The vast majority looked as if they could've done a magazine shoot for *Fishermen Now*. A few looked her way, but being plain, she didn't have to worry about anyone hitting on her or even approaching.

She put her head down, made her way to the bar, and sat at the far end on the only open stool. Next to her was a particular large, rugged, all-muscle—and what she could see of his profile—handsome man, undoubtedly one of the fishermen, too. Another man, short and squat, stepped between them, partially blocking her view of Handsome.

Squat clamped a hand on Handsome's shoulder. "Ye'd like my niece, Euna. She can cook and sew. She'd make ye a good wife. I promise, she will. At least meet her while she's here for the retreat."

The way Handsome was scowling over his drink, Sadie was certain he hadn't been one of the men singing moments ago. He looked as if he'd given up singing permanently.

The bartender waved to Sadie. "What can I get ye?"

"Water," she said automatically. Cola and alcohol were out-of-bounds. She would do everything she could to keep off the active transplant list for as long as possible.

Handsome glanced her way, and damn, he was good-looking. Not that a guy like him would notice someone like her. Sure enough, he went back to his drink without a word.

Squat was fidgeting, beginning to look desperate. "What do ye say? I told Euna ye'd see her. Take her to dinner. Or maybe have a stroll to the top of the bluff." He chewed the inside of his cheek. "The exercise would do her good."

Sadie felt sorry for Handsome. Couldn't Squat see that he didn't want to do it? The bartender set her glass in front of her and left to help a patron at the other end.

"Dammit, Harry," Handsome growled. "Ye're putting me in a hell of a spot."

Sadie made a snap decision. She reached for her glass and clumsily knocked it aside, spilling water all over Harry.

He jumped back. "What'd'ya do that for?"

She reached for the towel at the end of the bar and began blotting at the water on Harry's shirt. "So sorry. I guess I wasn't paying attention."

When Harry wasn't looking, she tilted her head at Handsome for him to make a run for it. This fisherman was no dummy. He was out the door before she could order Harry a drink to make up for the drenching she gave him.

Once Harry was settled and complaining to the barkeep about her clumsiness, Sadie decided to leave before she brought any more attention to herself. She headed for the door, no closer to finding a way out of Gandiegow.

Outside, she paused on the top step and spoke to the

vast ocean in front on her. "I have to get out of here!" That's when she realized she wasn't alone.

Leaning against the edge of the building a few feet away stood Handsome. He walked toward her and stuck out his hand to help her down the last few steps. "I owe you, lass. Tell me where you want to go. I've got a truck."